### Also by Mignon G. Eberhart

Alpine Condo Crossfire     Man Missing
Another Man's Murder     Murder in Waiting
The Bayou Road     Next of Kin
Casa Madrone     The Patient in Cabin C
Danger Money     Postmark Murder
A Fighting Chance     Run Scared
Family Affair     Unidentified Woman
Hasty Wedding     The Unknown Quantity
Hunt With the Hounds     Witness at Large
Wolf in Man's Clothing

### Published by
### WARNER BOOKS

# MIGNON G. EBERHART'S
## BEST MYSTERY STORIES

**WARNER BOOKS**

A Warner Communications Company

WARNER BOOKS EDITION

Copyright © 1934, 1938, 1942, 1952, 1953, 1958 and 1988 by
Mignon G. Eberhart
Copyrights renewed.

Some of these stories have appeared in two previous collections
by the author entitled *The Cases of Susan Dare* and *Deadly Is
The Diamond.*

Cover illustration by Sonja Lamut and Nerad Jakesevic

Warner Books, Inc.
666 Fifth Avenue
New York, N.Y. 10103

Ⓦ A Warner Communications Company

Printed in the United States of America

First Warner Books Printing: August, 1988

10 9 8 7 6 5 4 3 2 1

# Contents

Murder by Night / 1

The Valentine Murder / 15

The Gate at Number Ninety / 27

The Dangerous Widows / 47

The Jade Cup / 59

The Blonde from Sumatra / 87

The Old Man's Diamond / 96

Mr. Wickwire's Gun Moll / 119

The Wagstaff Pearls / 133

Introducing Susan Dare / 145

The Calico Dog / 175

Bermuda Grapevine / 206

The Crimson Paw / 266

Murder in Waltz Time / 322

# Preface

A novel may be almost a biography of its fictional characters; in the words of a distinguished editor, this may present "an entire cake." For lack of space, a short story (or a play) can be only a "slice" of that cake but should suggest the flavor of the entire cake.

So the writer must know not the characters themselves but the *kind* of persons they may be. Most writers rarely use a real-life character, not in the cause of prudence but owing to the plain fact that the real-life person does not fit the story. A character takes life and breath only in the story; he grows as the story grows; his motivations and consequent actions are entirely fictional.

Writers themselves are rather like blotting paper; what they see or know may be almost subconsciously stored up, but if or when that information emerges in a story, the original outlines are blurred to fit the needs of the story. Settings, of course, must be accurate and factual. But mere incidents—a comment heard at dinner, an item in a newspaper— anything may prove to be grist to the writer's mill. This may be the slightest incident, such as an incident with an apple in the Sarah Keate story herewith, which happened to me; but it was not an apple: it was my handbag I dropped, and only a swift clutch at it rescued it from falling into the depths of the cold, gray Atlantic.

Now I don't know any writer who is another Shakespeare or Dostoyevski; we only hope to entertain, and if a little humor develops, we hope it will act as a bit of yeast. But we must entertain what I have found to be a very alert and intelligent readership. I know that because if I make a mistake (such as putting a new moon in the sky after midnight), there are indignant and numerous reproofs.

So, I must add, no writing is really a piece of cake.

*Introducing Mr. Wickwire's dreadful dog,
for whom he has an abandoned affection.
Also introducing Mr. Wickwire, for whom
I have an affection.*

❑

# Murder by Night

One of the three people seated with me around the dinner table had forged a check and, only three days before that, murdered a man. I had the photograph of the murderer and forger in my pocket. Yet I was utterly unable to identify the person who had forged the check with Horace Wells's signature and then shot his nephew Lassiter Wells.

My name is James Wickwire. I am a senior vice president of the bank within whose walls I have spent most of my life. Horace Wells is my longtime friend and client. When Lassiter was shot, Horace, who was in Rome on a government mission, sent me an urgent air mail letter. The letter, as well as the photograph, was in my pocket.

> Dear Jim:
>    You may have seen it in the papers; my nephew Lassiter was found shot last night. In his own room at the farm. Only three other people in the house. Gun from my own gun cabinet in the library. His fingerprints on it—faked, I am sure. It would take only a few seconds. The police called it suicide. It was murder.
>    These are the facts. Lassiter acted as my secretary.

Yesterday he discovered a forged check on my account. The check was drawn to Lassiter for two thousand dollars; it was endorsed with Lassiter's name and signed with a forgery of my name. It was cashed at your bank, where Lassiter is not known. The check came from my farm checkbook.

Lassiter reported this to me by cable. He said that the person cashing the check must have presented some sort of identification and that his wallet, containing club membership cards and that sort of thing, had been missing for a time. The wallet later turned up again, but he thought he knew who had taken it. He said to leave it to him; he didn't want to accuse anybody until he had investigated, but he'd settle the thing. That night he was shot.

Now the three people in the house at the time are the only people who had access to the checkbook; the farm and house help live outside the main house. These three people are John Murdock, my farm manager; Lisa Benly, his assistant; and Chloe Henderson—Mrs. Henderson, young widow, my guest. Jim, will you go to the farm and clear it up for me? I'll cable Murdock and tell you you are going to appraise the farm.

It was signed "Horace Wells."

I replied by cable—and rather too confidently. "Identification simple, as have photograph forger. Sympathy, Wickwire." I then went to the farm.

Since Horace Wells had paved my way, no one questioned my arrival—no one, that is, except an enormous, liver-colored dog that appeared from nowhere as I walked up the lane from the village taxi. He looked, I must say, rather like the Hound of the Baskervilles and uttered a deep growl that stopped me in my tracks. However, I like dogs and can say honestly that they like me; so I put out my hand, palm downward in the etiquette right-thinking dogs expect. He sniffed at my hand, examined my shoes and my bag, apparently decided in my favor, and wagged his tail. I scratched his ears, the tail wagged faster, there was some sound, and the dog loped swiftly away as the house door opened.

A thin, nondescript sort of man came to meet me. "Mr. Wickwire? We were expecting you. I'm John Murdock. You're just in time for dinner."

It was then that my reliance upon the photograph suffered its first shock. And when he led me into the house and introduced me to Mrs. Henderson and Lisa Benly, my heart sank. I realized at once that my confidence had been decidedly premature. The face in the photograph was the face of one of the three, and I couldn't tell which one.

Someone gave me a cocktail, and we went in to dinner, where I munched roast pheasant, listened to the talk around the table (which did not so much as mention Lassiter Wells, dead only three days), and fended off a red setter who snatched at a biscuit in my hand. The talk was mainly of dogs and horses, of which there seemed to be an inordinate supply not only on the farm but in the dining room. Horses, painted in oils, with brass nameplates and moody expressions, stared at me from the walls. Dogs panted, scratched, and thumped around our feet, although my liver-colored friend was not among them. A fat houseman served salad and was the only person present who could not be the murderer, and this was simply because he was fat.

I finished my pheasant. A large Siamese cat appeared in the door of the library and achieved the tabletop, a pheasant bone from my plate, and the library again with what appeared to be one leap. The dogs charged after him. Nobody so much as lifted an eyebrow; baffled yelps came presently from the library suggesting that the cat had eluded his pursuers, and dessert was placed on the table. Chloe Henderson suggested bridge. John Murdock said shortly that it was an excellent game, and we, too, adjourned to the library, where the cat sat on the mantel, polishing off the pheasant bone and ignoring the circle of dogs that stared at it angrily and helplessly from below. A gun cabinet—*the* gun cabinet—was built into the wall across the room. Mrs. Henderson poured coffee and led the way to the bridge table.

"I live next door," she told me during the first rubber. "It's so dear of Horace to invite me to stay here while my house is being redecorated."

John Murdock gave her a glowering look. "You're a spendthrift, Chloe. You'd have done better to put that money in a new roof for your cattle barn."

She shrugged prettily. "I was thankful that I was here when the—the tragedy occurred. Poor Horace! I sent him a cable at once."

John Murdock glowered again. "Your bid, Mr. Wickwire."

"One no trump," I said, too hastily as it developed, and then risked a direct question. "You were referring to Lassiter Wells's suicide? Horace wrote to me about it. Just how did it happen?"

John Murdock said, "Two spades."

Chloe Henderson said, "It was dreadful. None of us had any idea that he was thinking of such a thing. We were asleep, and there was just the sound of the gun. . . . Shocking. By the time we got thoroughly awake and the lights turned on and . . . as Lassiter didn't come into the hall, we went into his room. By that time he was—was dead. He must have died at once; I told Horace that. Three clubs."

I had practically no clubs, a disconcerting fact I suddenly discovered. Lisa Benly said, "Four diamonds."

My partner, Chloe Henderson, paid no attention to my endeavor to convey to her the clubless state of my hand, took the bid in clubs, and we went down. Nor can I say that I distinguished myself in any succeeding hands, for I was still trying and failing to identify one of the three faces around the bridge table as the face in the photograph in my pocket.

The photograph's existence was not due to chance. We had had some petty forgeries at the bank. Now I need not say that there is a certain prejudice in banking circles against forgery. There is also a sound reason for taking action regarding it, for, as may not be generally known, a bank protects its depositors' accounts to the extent of making good any fraudulent checks that have been mistakenly cashed. So the forgeries had to be stopped, and one of the measures we took was the installation of cameras at the tellers' windows, plus a workable plan not only for quietly taking the picture of any face presenting itself at the window but for filing the resultant photograph and the requisite data concerning it. The experiment had been in operation at the time of the Wells forgery; a photograph of the person who had posed as Lassiter Wells and boldly presented the forged check had been consequently available to me.

But the fact was—and by the end of the first rubber I was obliged to accept it—the face in the photograph could have been almost anybody's face. Perhaps the teller had not chosen an auspicious moment for pressing the lever of the camera; the head was bent and the face was shadowed by a hat pulled low over the eyes. But mainly it was one of those faces that seem to fade to complete anonymity before a camera—and I had perceived its anonymity only when the problem of specific identification presented itself. I was not even sure now whether it was the face of a man or a woman. The person pictured wore men's clothing, but women have on occasion successfully assumed men's dress. The face was a slender blob; the hair was cut short. That was all.

And the three people around the table might each have been in a state of disguise so far as any likeness or unlikeness to the photograph was concerned. John Murdock was totally unremarkable; his was the kind of face one might see a hundred times a day and fail to note. Chloe Henderson, slender and attractive, was so heavily made up with eyebrow pencil, lipstick, and such that her face was like a painted mask. And Lisa Benly, slender, too, was masked in another way, for she wore no makeup at all, which left her face a bare and slightly shining oval, as unremarkable as John Murdock's face. Mrs. Henderson's hair was black and curly; Lisa Benly's was straight and brown. But both women wore their hair cut very short. Inwardly I cursed the current feminine fashion, and wished that Horace Wells had called on more expert assistance than mine.

Eventually the houseman waddled in with a tray of ice

water and decanters and departed for the night, and Chloe Henderson yawned and said, "One more rubber"—and everyone and everything in the room froze.

I was aware of that before I knew what had happened, for I chanced to be watching Lisa Benly, who suddenly and for no apparent reason turned perfectly and coldly white. A dog near me did not so much as lift its head, but its hackles rose. John Murdock gripped his cards so hard that they slowly crumpled. The cat stood soundlessly upright, arched its back and tail, and its blue eyes turned ruby red. It was like a horrifying spell put upon the room, yet there wasn't a sound. Then Chloe Henderson looked up from her cards, took in the situation with one swift glance, and said, "Good gracious. It's Happy."

She turned to look over her shoulder; the movement gave me a view of the doorway, and the Hound of the Baskervilles, my liver-colored friend, stood there. It is true that his silent regard did have something rather ominous about it, but as its eyes met mine, its tail gave a tentative wag. Naturally I started to rise, intending to meet any friendly overture halfway, but Murdock seized my arm in a steely grip that clamped me to my seat. And Chloe Henderson sprang up, advanced upon the great creature, grasped its collar, administered a smart slap on its enormous jaw, and led it out of the room and upstairs.

Nobody, not even the cat, moved until a door somewhere above closed. Lisa Benly then dabbed at her white lips with a handkerchief, and John Murdock dropped his cards and laughed shakily. "We've got to do something about that dog. He's a killer. We ought to have let him die. He's not worth the vet's bill. He was Lassiter's dog, with him every instant. Only Lass could manage him. Lass and Chloe."

"That dog is no killer," I said indignantly, upon which Murdock and Lisa Benly both gave me a look of utter scorn, and Chloe Henderson returned. "I put him in Lass's room," she said. "I'll let him out later, when you've all gone to bed." She sat down and picked up her cards. Lisa Benly said she'd had enough of cards for the evening; Murdock agreed with her. And under the pretense of getting out my own handkerchief, I contrived to withdraw, at the same time, the photograph and drop it on the table.

I am not a brave man; neither am I an impulsive one. I daresay I acted merely on the principle of stirring up muddy waters to see what would happen. And the trouble was that, just then, nothing happened. All three, quite naturally, glanced at the photograph; I was sure of that. But Chloe Henderson merely put her cards together. John Murdock said he had to be at the horse barns early in the morning. Lisa Benly said good night and disappeared. I picked up the photograph and restored it to my pocket. The dogs surged up from various spots around the room, and the cat leaped ahead of us and up the stairs.

It was a pleasant guest room to which Mrs. Henderson showed me, although rather full of chintz and photographs of horses and dogs. "I'm sorry Horace isn't here to see you," she said. "Horace and I—well, we're thinking of marriage, you know."

This explained not only her hostesslike manner, but also some of Horace's anxiety. It did not, however, clear her of murder. I could not avoid the swift reflection that the removal of Lassiter Wells removed at the same time a contending heir, so to speak, to Horace's fortune. Also, Murdock had called her a spendthrift, and something, perhaps the banker's curiously developed sense of money and people, suggested to me that it was an accurate statement. So she might have forged a check, finding herself in need of cash; and when Lassiter accused her, she could have taken a desperate way out by killing young Lassiter. And, of course, without its mask of makeup, her face could have been that in the bank's photograph.

But then, Lisa Benly's face or John Murdock's could have been the face in the photograph too. After uttering suitable remarks, I said, "I've never met Murdock before. Has he worked for Horace for a long time?"

"Five years," she replied. "Horace pays him well, you know. Too well, I think. John Murdock is only waiting until he can save enough money to buy a farm of his own. The minute he does that he'll leave Horace like a shot."

"I expect Miss Benly could carry on, in that event."

Mrs. Henderson's eyes snapped. "Lisa," she said, "would do anything for money! I've advised Horace not to count on her. Good night, Mr. Wickwire."

With that she swept away, first ejecting a red setter and a spaniel that had drifted into the room, and remarking that she always shut the dogs in the kitchen before she released Happy, who, I took it, prowled the house at night. I bolted the door only to discover that the Siamese cat had settled down among framed pictures on top of a bookcase. It eyed me with shining blue slits that were eyes and refused to be dislodged.

So each of them, if I accepted unsolicited testimony, had a motive for forgery and murder. Chloe, the spendthrift. Lisa, who would do anything for money. John Murdock, who was only serving time until he could purchase his own place. I got out the photograph again—and as (study it though I might and did) the face remained a pale and anonymous smudge, I returned it impatiently to my pocket. It was the cat that initiated a point of exploration I ought to have undertaken in the beginning, but then I am no expert. Either from innate devilry or because it wished to make itself more comfortable on the crowded bookcase, it put out a sepia-colored paw, gave a silver-framed picture a deliberate push, and then stretched its neck to follow the picture's fall to the floor with a kind of smug interest. Naturally, I went to pick up the picture. It was a group picture, five people in an admiring circle around a horse.

Horace Wells, huge and fleshy, was smiling. A younger man, also big and fleshy, was obviously Lassiter Wells, for he strongly resembled his uncle; clearly, if I had had any doubts, his was not the face of the forger. John Murdock stood nearby; before the camera his thin face took on harsh and predatory lines. Lisa Benly, in blue jeans and white shirt, held the bridle; her face, certainly bare of makeup, was a glistening oval. And Chloe Henderson looked liked a film beauty in smart riding clothes and a graceful pose. The horse looked bored, and I knew who had forged the check and murdered Lassiter.

That is to say, I knew it logically. I knew of no way to prove it.

A creature padded along the hall and sniffed under my door in such a ravening manner that I knew it was Happy. After a time it padded away again, and suddenly I thought: Lassiter's dog, who never left Lassiter, and would have permitted only Chloe Henderson to enter Lassiter's room— where he was killed.

I thought for some time. Eventually a scrap of conversation from the previous evening floated into my mind and, if it meant what I thought it might mean, might lead to something—I didn't know exactly what, but something. I don't believe in hunches, yet perhaps they are in fact the sum total of observation and instinct. In any event, I went downstairs.

I made no attempt to move quietly. I was reasonably sure that somewhere there was a pair of wakeful and listening ears, warned by my possession of the photograph, and I wished them to record my activities. The dog Happy, of course, was on the prowl somewhere, but since I could not really accept the theory that it was a lurking fiend in canine shape, I only hoped that it would not bark and arouse the house. And halfway along the hall a cold nose suddenly thrust itself against my hand. It gave me rather a start, but after a moment it withdrew silently into the darkness, and I found my way into the library. I left the door a little ajar to permit my voice to be overheard and groped my way to a telephone I had observed standing on a table. Here, assisted by the operator, who knew and rang the number I desired, I made a local call. The reply to my question was what I had thought it might be.

I waited for a moment, listening. After a time I was sure I heard a faint sound from the hall. So I had to take some action and, since I could think of nothing else, I put in a call via transatlantic telephone to Horace Wells in his hotel in Rome—except I didn't, but held the switch firmly depressed. And all the time I listened.

When there was the whisper of the door opening, I admit that my flesh crawled. But I shouted into the telephone, as somehow one does shout over transatlantic telephone, no matter how good the connection: "Horace! I'm at the farm." I paused to lend verisimilitude to my pretended conversation; then I replied to a question that hadn't been spoken. "Yes, Lassiter was murdered. No doubt of it. And I know who did it. I've got evidence. . . ." Here I paused again, thinking that Horace would have said something at this point—and thus heard a small but unmistakable click from across the room. It was the door of the gun cabinet, the dangerous proximity to the telephone and to me I had forgotten.

I am not sure what I did just then, but I believe I acted with a degree of alacrity, for all at once I was crouching behind the sofa, the voice of an aroused telephone operator sounding metallically from the table where I had dropped the telephone and thus released the switch. Other than that there was an utter and, I might say, extremely unnerving silence. I don't know how long it was before I sensed that some new element had added itself to the room.

There was still no sound; a sheerly atavistic instinct announced its presence to me. It identified itself, however, by a sudden and terrible growl. A chair went over with a thud. Revolver shots crashed through the darkness.

They stopped; their echoes died away. And in the silence arose a shrill and indescribably eerie scream.

The scream was that of the telephone operator. After a startled moment I realized that. I also realized that six shots had been fired and must have counted them at the time although I did so unconsciously. So I crept toward the table, groped upward, found a lamp, and turned on the light.

Lisa Benly stood with a gun in her hand, backed into a corner. The dog Happy made a dive at her throat just as I reached the dog and got both hands on its collar and pulled back as hard as I could. Lisa screamed, "Hold him," and dropped the gun.

I shouted, "Down, Happy! Down!"

I don't know why I expected Happy to obey, nor indeed why it obeyed, but it did drop down at my feet. Lisa Benly gave me a long look and put her hands over her face as Chloe Henderson and Murdock rushed into the room.

The police arrived within moments, summoned by the terrified telephone operator. There was considerable conversation, in which I found it rather difficult to engage, owing to the dog, who seemed agreeably moved by the rapport between us and made strenuous gestures of friendship. I fended off its enormous paws as best I could and told the police that I believed that Lisa Benly had forged the check; that Lassiter Wells had had reason, probably we would never know exactly what reason, to suspect that she had used cards belonging to him for purposes of identification; that he had accused her and that she had shot him. "I don't know what she has done with the money, but I suggest you'll find it, possibly in the checking account under another name. Also," I got the bank's photograph from my pocket, "I suggest that you give this photograph and a framed picture in the guest room to experts for comparison."

Both policemen looked as blank as the face in the photograph, so I was obliged to explain. "A camera does odd things to faces. Some faces seem to blank out and obscure; others leap into a great clarity of feature in a photograph—those of movie stars, for instance. Mrs. Henderson's face, in the picture upstairs, is what is called photogenic in the extreme; her picture, indeed, is far more beautiful than she is in fact."

Mrs. Henderson gave a pained sort of murmur. I continued. "John Murdock's face is photogenic, too—although in a different way, as his features in a picture become decidedly ugly—I should say, rugged." John Murdock hitched up insecurely anchored trousers and, surprisingly, seemed pleased. "On the other hand," I said, "there are faces that are remarkably unphotogenic. They seem to blank out almost unrecognizably before a camera. You have doubtless heard people say that no two pictures of them are alike and that none of their pictures resemble them. Miss Benly is one of those people; she is, in short, nonphotogenic. As is the face in this photograph. Since it is the photograph of one of these three people, and Murdock and Mrs. Henderson are eliminated, it is obviously the photograph of Lisa Benly.''

It was not, however, so obvious to the policemen, even after I explained the photograph. They eyed me skeptically. However, one of them said dubiously, ''She did have a gun.''

''She may have intended me as a target, for she overheard what she took to be a conversation that was very dangerous to her. But in fact she shot at the dog. He is supposed to be a killer.'' Here, to my intense annoyance, Happy turned over on his back and rolled his eyes fondly at me. The policemen's looks of skepticism deepened. Clearly, a more concrete piece of evidence was required, so I gave it to them. ''John Murdock is afraid of the dog. But Lisa Benly is terrified. The dog was devoted to Lassiter. She would not have dared enter Lassiter's room at night, had the dog been present. This evening Murdock said something about the dog's vet bill; I telephoned the vet a short time ago. He said that the dog was in his care the night Lassiter was shot; he said the dog had been poisoned. I suggest that she poisoned Happy to get the dog out of the way—and I rather think that you'll find that she procured poison at some drugstore in the vicinity and gave a farm-related need as her reason for buying it.''

Here John Murdock made his only, but pertinent, remark. ''Arsenic. Said she got it for rats. Bought it the afternoon before Lass was shot.''

''Now *that*,'' said one of the policemen, ''is more like *evidence*.'' But he stretched out his hand for the photograph. The gesture affected Happy adversely. I was obliged to drag the dog upstairs with me in order to procure the framed group picture for the police. And here I had rather a shock.

I had turned on the bright overhead light. I happened to merely glance in the mirror. The face in the mirror, my own face, was blanked out and nullified by the glaring light. It was in fact completely anonymous.

It explains my passport photographs, which I have attributed to downright malice on the part of the passport photographer. But while I have always known that mine is an undistinguished sort of face, still I cannot say that it was gratifying to discover that it, too, in a picture could be anybody's face.

I had another shock a few days after Horace Wells's return; this was an enormous crate, delivered at the bank, with a card attached to the outside and hair-raising howls from the inside. Before I could stop him, the expressman opened the crate, gave a wild shout, and made for the door, pursued hotly by a large, familiar, liver-colored form. Guards came running; patrons took to countertops. The note was from Horace Wells and began, "Dear Jim. Happy is pining; Chloe says for you. Well, dogs are like that. He requires only about ten miles a day exercise and prefers steak, say five pounds to a meal—" I read no further but returned Happy to the crate.

I should say, I attempted to return Happy to the crate. However, the dog is not incapable of compromise and has settled for a run around the reservoir and, since I am only a banker, no steaks—although its diet is supplemented by such rugs, table legs, and shoes as it fancies.

*Mr. Wickwire is not really taken from life;*
*fictional characters are rarely taken, boldly,*
*from real people. But he is very like some of*
*my longtime friends who, after many years,*
*are still my friends—although I can't see any*
*one of them undertaking Mr. Wickwire's*
*chores.*

❑

# The Valentine Murder

I looked at the lacy object on my desk. *"What is this?"*

The young assistant cashier replied, "It's a handkerchief. Possibly intended for the valentine trade," he hazarded thoughtfully. "It's shaped like a heart."

"I can see that!"

The handkerchief was undoubtedly heart shaped and outlined with lace. Written on it in bright red were words and numerals. I touched the writing cautiously.

The assistant cashier said, "It's not blood. It's lipstick."

"I'm not so old I don't know lipstick when I see it."

"Yes, sir," he said hurriedly. "I mean, no, sir. Shall I tell them to cash it?"

I debated, seething with exasperation. For the thing was, incredibly, a check—and a check for twenty thousand dollars. It was made out to one Ronald Murch and it was signed by Clarissa Hartridge, and Clarissa was one of my widows.

I hasten to say that I am, and—*Deo favente*—intend to remain, a bachelor. My name is James Wickwire. I am a senior vice president at the bank within whose sedate walls I have spent most of my life.

Clarissa was one of my widows only in the sense that her

estate, along with that of sundry other widows, was in my care.

One way or another, my widows have caused me considerable mental anguish, due in the main to their recurrent impulses to invest money in nonexistent oil wells or to finance expeditions for the discovery of buried pirate treasure.

Up to that day, however, Clarissa had given me very little anxiety. She had kept well within her income, had never made mistakes in subtraction, and was an extremely charming and pretty woman.

Consequently, I had felt deeply grateful to her and enjoyed dining with her and a Miss Gray, who shared her house, once or twice a year in the comfortable certainty that Clarissa would not ask me to balance her checkbook.

But this fantastic check was not merely an illusion shattered for me. It represented a large share of Clarissa's capital. The walls of the bank did not in fact rock, but I myself was shaken to the core. It was all too clear that something had happened to Clarissa, and it was quite as clear what that something was. For my widows do not invariably remain widows. Sometimes they follow the same remarkable quality of impulse in choosing second husbands that they do in choosing investments.

"You say this Ronald Murch is out there now?" I asked the assistant cashier.

"Yes, sir. Young. Dark. Handsome. Presented the check as cool as you please. They brought it to me, and I thought you'd better see it."

"Of course." I tapped the lacy edge of the handkerchief. Young, dark, and handsome! Clarissa was fifty if she was a day, and if I'd had my fingers on her plump little neck just then, I really think I'd have twisted it. Instead I told my secretary to get Mrs. Hartridge on the telephone, and then, perceiving the inquisitive gleam in the assistant cashier's pale blue eyes, I told him he could go and I'd see to it. He looked frustrated but went away.

Clarissa came on the phone and began at once to speak. "James, I know why you're calling me," she said airily. "It's all right about the check. Cash it."

I daresay I uttered a rather strangled sound. She said coolly, "Have you got a cold, James?"

"No! What is the meaning—"

"I'm buying a formula for face cream."

"*Face*—Clarissa, this is capital!"

She laughed lightly. "Of course. I sold those Turnpike bonds."

A choking sensation gripped me. She said, "Oh, by the way, James, can you return that check to me yourself? After you've cashed it, I mean. I don't want it to go through all that routine in the bank."

"I can understand that!" I said acidly, but she had hung up.

When I had got control of myself, I sent for Mr. Ronald Murch, who was still waiting. He was, indeed, dark, young, and handsome, with a charm that raked my elderly, lacerated nerves. And to my intense surprise, a young lady with a great many golden curls and a sallow but heavily made-up face was hanging fondly on his arm. He introduced her.

"This is Miss April Moon."

The young lady gave me a coquettish smile. "Soon to be Mrs. Ronald Murch," she said, and hugged his arm. "We just got the license."

I was rather taken aback, since I had believed Clarissa destined for this dubious honor. Ronald Murch nodded at the heart-shaped handkerchief with its red writing. "That does look rather silly, doesn't it?" he said.

"May I ask why it is written in this remarkable way?"

For an instant something puzzling flashed in his dark eyes. "It was a whim of Clarissa's—I mean, Mrs. Hartridge's. Just an impulse. She said it was suitable—lipstick, cosmetics. You see?"

"I can't say that I do," I replied shortly.

Miss April Moon giggled. "What does it matter how the old girl wanted to write it! It's legal. He gets the cash. She gets her formula. We get married."

He drew a folded paper from an inner pocket and waved it at me. "This is my formula for face cream."

I reached automatically for the paper, but he returned it quickly to his pocket. "Sorry," he said, "but it's a secret. I developed it myself. Believe me, it's an oil well."

The words struck a sensitive nerve within me. I said icily, "Does Mrs. Hartridge know of your approaching marriage?"

Miss Moon giggled. Mr. Murch assumed a businesslike air. "That has nothing to do with you, Mr. Wickwire. If you have any doubt about this check, kindly phone Mrs. Hartridge."

So I was obliged to give directions to the effect that the absurd check was to be cashed. I also saw to it that the handkerchief itself was given to me. I placed it in my desk, and there was nothing further that I could do. Clarissa's instructions had been definite. I had already exceeded such small authority as I had. And Clarissa was in love. I know little about women, but I know when I'm licked.

However, scarcely an hour later Clarissa telephoned to me. "James," she said, "he's dead! Ronald Murch. He's been shot. Right in my library. The police are here. They say he's been murdered. Please come!"

Her neat if unpretentious little house in the East Nineties was surrounded by policemen. Once inside the living room, a police lieutenant fell upon me and questioned me exhaustively and, I must say, rather suspiciously (for they were somewhat short of suspects), until I convinced him that I had a firm alibi and, besides, no possible interest in murdering young Ronald Murch. I had, it is true, taken a strong dislike to him, but I am not an impulsive man.

The lieutenant then told me the circumstances of the murder. "He's in there," he said, nodding toward the tiny library that adjoined the living room. The door was open; a cluster of men, some in uniform and some in plainclothes, moved apart a little, and I could see feet in highly polished black oxfords at an odd angle on the rug. I could not see the rest of the body.

"Shot twice," the lieutenant said. "One bullet got him through the heart. Mrs. Hartridge claims she heard the shots and thought it was a backfire from the street. After a time she came downstairs. Saw the guy in there, on the rug.

Dead as a duck. Says she phoned to the police right away. She was alone in the house.''

There were no servants in the household, but there was Miss Gray. I said, ''There's a Miss Gray who lived with Mrs. Hartridge—''

The lieutenant interrupted. ''She's gone shopping. She hasn't come back yet.''

''Did you find the murder gun?'' I asked.

He nodded solemnly. ''That's the clincher. The gun belonged to Mrs. Hartridge. She says it was her husband's. Kept it in a drawer of the table in the hall. Says she hasn't touched it, knows nothing of it. There were no fingerprints. She probably wore gloves.''

''Do you mean to say you suspect Mrs. Hartridge?''

''Who else?'' he said, and rose as if to end the interview.

''Wait,'' I said hurriedly. ''She had no motive, no reason—''

He gave me a cold and skeptical look. ''Listen. The guy had twenty thousand dollars in his pocket. Mrs. Hartridge admits that she gave him a check for the cash this morning. He had a key to this house in his pocket—a key to *this* house. She's an elderly widow with money. *And* he had another girl!'' He eyed me triumphantly. ''There was a marriage license in his pocket. What does it look like to you?''

It looked extremely serious, as a matter of fact. I swallowed hard. ''What about the girl?''

''*She* didn't kill him. We traced her right away. She's at a beauty shop getting her hair curled, and she's been there for an hour. I've sent a squad car for her.''

I could not comprehend Miss Moon's unbridled desire for still more curls, but I did comprehend the solid nature of her alibi. I said, ''Didn't Mrs. Hartridge tell you that she gave him the twenty thousand dollars for the purchase of a face-cream formula?''

He laughed shortly. ''Oh, sure. She also admitted that she'd picked him up on the street! Didn't know anything about his background. Claims she didn't know he was going to be married! Probably that's not the first money she's given him. By the way—you say you're her banker—we'll have to take a look through her canceled checks."

And I'd be obliged to give them a check written, fatally, in lipstick on a heart-shaped handkerchief. It seemed wiser to tell him of it at once, give him Murch's own explanation for it and—if possible—thus minimize its disastrous effect. So, very carefully, I related the whole incident.

But the lieutenant was again triumphant. He smacked Clarissa's little Pembroke table with a fist that nearly broke it. "That proves it! She was in love with the guy. You're a banker. Did you ever get a check written like that before?"

I was obliged to confess I hadn't. "It was an impulse," I told him again. "Lipstick—cosmetic business—there's a connection. He said he had a face-cream formula. It was in his pocket."

He shook his head. "He was lying to you. So was she, because she knew you'd question that check. She wouldn't have wanted you to know her real reason for giving him that money. There's no forumla. I went through his pockets myself." He looked at the door as another policeman entered. "What is it, Jake?"

It was Clarissa's friend and housemate, Miss Gray, returned from her shopping trip and horrified. They ushered her into the room and let me remain while they questioned her.

Naturally I listened with some interest. I knew Miss Gray, of course. She was a pleasant, rather plain young woman, although she looked handsomer than usual that morning, for the light from the window fell directly upon her, revealing a really dazzling complexion that seemed to make her dark eyes glow. She wore a neat gray suit and hat and clutched a black handbag.

She knew Mr. Murch, of course, she said to the lieutenant; he had been a frequent guest of Clarissa's. She had gone shopping that morning. When asked if she had talked to anyone who could identify her, she grasped the intent of the question at once, with a flash of her dark eyes. But she said that she doubted it very much. She had made only one purchase, stockings, and that was not a charge; she had paid cash. The box of stockings was in the hall. Most of the morning she had simply strolled, window shopping.

The lieutenant pounced:

"Mrs. Hartridge was very fond of Ronald Murch, wasn't she? In fact, there was quite a romance going on there. Tell us the truth, Miss Gray."

She rose angrily, her eyes blazing. "That is outrageous! How dare you suggest such a thing!"

"Suppose I say that we have proof of it. Suppose I say that Mrs. Hartridge quarreled with him over a girl and shot him."

"Then I'd say you don't know what you're talking about! There was nothing like that between them, nothing! I'll swear to it in court if it comes to that."

I interposed. "A formula for face cream seems to have disappeared, Miss Gray. Do you mind if the lieutenant—er—searches your handbag?"

She lifted her eyebrows but gave her handbag to the lieutenant, who searched it rapidly, returned it to her, and said to me, "I tell you there's no such formula, Mr. Wickwire. See here, you go and talk to Mrs. Hartridge. Get her to confess. It'll save trouble all the way around. Jake—" The policeman stepped forward. "Take him to her."

I followed Jake's broad blue back up the little stairway to Clarissa's room. Another policeman, at a word from Jake, permitted me to enter, and Clarissa came quickly to me. "James! I believe they think I shot him!"

She was very pretty, with blue eyes, brown hair, and an astonishing complexion—so lovely indeed, and so much more youthful than I remembered, that this alone sharpened my anxiety.

It has always been said that love beautifies a woman, and certainly she looked glowing and younger than her years. On the other hand, she certainly showed no signs of grief, or indeed any sort of emotion. But, of course, murderers are said to be remarkably callous and cold-blooded.

I said gloomily, "You'd better tell me all about it."

She did. Her story differed in no detail from what she had told the police. When I asked her how young Murch had got a key to the front door, her blue eyes widened. "I don't know! I didn't give him a key."

I didn't, I couldn't, believe her. "Clarissa, when and where did you meet this young man?"

This, too, squared with the lieutenant's account. She said, with deplorable candor, that it was in a taxi. "That is, I was waiting for a taxi, and so was he. It was raining. A taxi came, and he offered it to me and, of course, I had to ask him to share it. We were going the same way. By the way, James, the formula for the face cream is mine. I paid for it, remember, and he had come to deliver it to me. So be sure you claim it for me."

"Clarissa, are you telling the truth about this formula?"

"Certainly!" Her eyes snapped, and she swished past me into a dressing room and back again. She had a white jar with a black top, unlabeled, in her hand. She held it under my nose. "This is the cream!"

I thrust it away with some force. After a moment I said, "Clarissa, *why* did you write that check in lipstick?"

She sniffed the cream, absently. "I'd never have thought of it myself. But then I realized it was an excellent idea."

I caught her by the shoulders. "*Who* thought of it? *Who* suggested it? Young Murch?"

She told me.

I went downstairs at once, and as I got to the foot of the stairs, the door opened and April Moon, sobbing wildly between two policemen, surged into the hall. The lieutenant and Miss Gray emerged from the library. And there was only one course for me to pursue.

A flat parcel, wrapped and tied, lay on the hall table. I snatched it up. Miss Gray hurled herself upon me like a tiger defending its young. Miss Moon screamed. I thrust the flat parcel at the lieutenant and dived behind him, evading Miss Gray's fingers. Miss Gray whirled around and made for the door, where the two policemen seized her.

The formula for the face cream was neatly tucked into the folds of a pair of stockings.

I explained it, although, of course, it was perfectly clear. "It's an excellent face cream. They've both been using it.

Mrs. Hartridge and—'' I nodded at Miss Gray, whose flawless complexion was now a blazing white, as her eyes were blazing black. "Both of them realized the value of the formula; both of them wanted it. Miss April Moon only wanted the money from its purchase."

"I've never used it!" Miss Moon cried. "It's no good. Ronald told me so. He said it was only a mixture of junk! He said it was a trick to get money from—" She clapped both hands over her mouth.

I said to the lieutenant, "The formula is in fact excellent. Obviously, Murch didn't know that; he hit on it by chance. He meant merely to use the formula as an excuse to get money from Mrs. Hartridge. But both Miss Gray and Mrs. Hartridge have developed beautiful complexions by using the cream.

"Mrs. Hartridge made a deal with Murch for its purchase. He was to deliver it to her this morning. Miss Gray knew that it was her last chance to get the formula for herself. So she determined upon a subtle but rather neat plan."

"Huh?" the lieutenant remarked.

"It occurred to her to suggest a romance between Mrs. Hartridge and young Murch. It was a perfect setup. Elderly widow with money; charming and poor young man. When Mrs. Hartridge was actually about to write a check to Murch for the formula, Miss Gray suggested that she write it in lipstick, on a heart-shaped handkerchief, as a good omen to the cosmetic business. Mrs. Hartridge, er, did so."

Here was something for which I had no possible explanation. I went on hurriedly, "Murch himself was puzzled by it. However, Miss Gray meant the check to suggest exactly what it did suggest to me. And to you.

"Miss Gray knew you'd see the check, which was sufficiently out-of-the-ordinary to attract attention. She denied the romance, indignantly, knowing that her defense of Mrs. Hartridge would incline you to exonerate Miss Gray— for if she had shot him, she reasoned, you would expect her to leap at the suggestion of Mrs. Hartridge's guilt." I paused, struck with the oddity of human reflexes.

"But—" the lieutenant said, "how did she find out—"

I replied, "I suggest that Miss Gray knew that Murch was to come to the house. I suggest that she returned quietly, waited for him, let him in, took him to the library—and cold-bloodedly shot him.

"Then she had to hurry. She put her house key in his pocket—to add to the theory of a romance—snatched the formula, and escaped, probably by the kitchen door. She hid the formula in the parcel with the stockings merely, I think, because it struck her as a hiding place that was very likely to be overlooked.

"So when that occurred to me, I snatched the stockings, because—well, you see, if there had been nothing of importance in the parcel, she would have done nothing.

"Instead of that—" Something tingled on my cheek; I dabbed at it with my handkerchief, which came away with streaks of red on it from the scratches left by Miss Gray's fingernails—and I then perceived that her hands were opening and closing in so restless and eager a way that I told the lieutenant I had to return to the bank and did so at once.

Not long ago I dined with Clarissa in her new and magnificent penthouse. As possibly everyone knows, she has made an enormous amount of money from her astute marketing of a face cream called, simply but suitably, Clarissa's Cream. Perhaps much of the success she has had in its merchandising is due to its trademark—which is a gay, red-and-white photograph of a heart-shaped handkerchief with a check written on it. It proved to be one of those extraordinary flukes of genius in advertising.

"So that," I said, "is why you wanted the check in good condition."

She smiled at me. "James," she said, "I have so much money. You must tell me all about investments."

I looked at her elegant gown, her matchless pearls, the sapphires and diamonds on her hands. "No, my dear," I said. "You tell me."

*Sometimes one may have to employ a quotation, and here it is:*
*"Black Tragedy lets slip her grim disguise."*

*It is sincerely hoped that this does not rob the story of a setting that is a very New York—or Chicago, or San Francisco—or any other city's fashionable if occasional nucleus of a woman's life.*

❏

# The Gate at Number Ninety

Nancy looked at Mrs. Blyker in the mirror, and Mrs. Blyker looked at Mrs. Blyker. It was a great, three-fold mirror that took on and imparted a flattering tint from the pink walls of the luxurious fitting room, but with or without rosy lights young Mrs. Blyker was something to look at, even in the dress she was then trying on. From the tip of her soft, golden hair to the pointed toes of her brown suede pumps, Estelle Blyker was a dream of perfection. She was, however, a dream that had apparently no style sense. Nancy wondered how some saleswoman (at Mentonne's Fashions a saleswoman was called a vendeuse) had induced Mrs. Blyker to purchase exactly the right smart suit that now lay over a chair, while Mrs. Blyker was selecting, with unerring accuracy, exactly the wrong dresses. Nancy took a long breath and hinted, "Wouldn't you like to try a color? There's a beautiful green—"

Estelle Blyker turned pansy-soft brown eyes toward Nancy. "Oh, I think this dress will do nicely."

Nancy glanced at the rack that held the two dresses her customer had already chosen, both black, simple it was true, but as dowdy as Mentonne Fashions ever permitted itself. *Be frank with a customer,* she reminded herself and said, "Honestly, Mrs. Blyker, I'd like to see you try on something with a little more—color, chic—" Mrs. Blyker's eyes widened. Nancy said hastily, "More becoming."

There was utter blankness of comprehension in the lovely little face. How could Nancy tell her that the black dress cast a sallow shade upon that perfect ivory skin? Mrs. Blyker said gently, "I'll take this dress, too."

The purchase brought the entire bill up to a few hundred dollars. *Be frank with a customer but don't quarrel with her,* Nancy thought, and gave up. "I'll call the fitter."

"But they seem to fit perfectly. They are all size ten, aren't they?"

"I was thinking of the length. You'll want them shorter."

Mrs. Blyker glanced again into the mirror. "I think they'll do just as they are. Will you put a rush delivery on them so I'll get them today? I'm going on a trip."

Nancy swallowed hard. A few inches off the hemlines of the skirts would have been at least a small improvement.

"Yes, Mrs. Blyker," she said as she wrote out the charge and computed the sales tax. Mrs. Blyker slid out of the dowdy dress, revealing a breathtaking figure clad in a delicate silk slip. Again Nancy wondered who had talked her into buying the slip. *If left to herself, she'd probably have bought flannelette,* Nancy thought crisply, and said, "Oh, let me help you—"

"Thanks." Estelle Blyker picked up the exquisite, smart brown suit she had worn intó the store. "You've been so very helpful and kind." Her smile had such a beautiful and candid appeal that it was like a child's. Nancy's heart, never very hard, melted.

"You can go anywhere in the store, can't you?" Mrs. Blyker said. "I need some other things—gloves, stockings, a hat perhaps. I wonder if you—"

"Of course, I'd like to."

An hour later Nancy returned to her own department with a high opinion of young Mrs. Blyker's gentle charm and (if she were honest with herself, and Nancy usually was) no great opinion of Mrs. Blyker's intelligence. She was as unresponsive as a wax model, and scarcely more animated.

*But a beautiful wax model,* Nancy thought with a kind of exasperation, because such beauty could prove itself so thoroughly dull. She turned to her next customer with half-ashamed relief.

By five o'clock and closing time, Nancy's arms and feet ached, but nevertheless, as she got off the bus and walked through the fine spring rain to her apartment, she began to feel as if she had wings. The softness of the spring night sent its age-old promise through her pulses, and she was going to have dinner tonight with Steve Marshal.

She ran up the stairs, let herself into her own apartment, made herself tea, and then lay stretched on the big sofa with cushions high under her feet, blissfully relaxed. It was a pleasant room, furnished in inexpensive but charming light woods of modern design and charmingly blended colors of primrose yellow, jade green, and, for accent, the deep-red sofa. If Steve did ask her to marry him, she thought dreamily, there would be very little in the way of household furnishings they would have to buy. How could she induce him to broach the subject of marriage?

He had said that he believed a man should be able to support a wife before he married. He had said it only once and swiftly steered away from the topic, but he had said it firmly.

A nice girl didn't inveigle a man into marriage—*ho, didn't she?* Nancy thought. Indeed she did, and always had done. Nancy smiled as she thought of Steve's face; thoughtful, rather reticent, with only a deep twinkle in his gray eyes that revealed his dry, New England humor. How it would change if she said, point-blank, "Let's get married."

He'd be appalled and embarrassed—although he wasn't easily embarrassed. But there was, she was sure there had been now and then, a certain unmistakable look in those deep-set, observant gray eyes. She was counting on that— and just possibly her new dress and the spring night. Anything can happen on a spring night, anything unexpected, anything lovely, anything magical. She looked at the clock and sprang up when she saw that it was already after six.

Seven o'clock came, but Steve did not. Seven-thirty chimed musically and Nancy brushed her shining, neat brown hair again, looked at herself in the mirror again, removed some lipstick and put it back on again. At eight she began to listen for the telephone. At nine o'clock she went purposefully to the mirror again and looked more earnestly at the girl's face it reflected. It was a nice face, she was frankly sure of that; it had fine bones and dark blue eyes shaded with long, black lashes and arched over with firm, dark eyebrows. A nice mouth, too, full enough and curved normally rather gaily. Drooping just a bit at the moment, but definitely not the kind of mouth (or the kind of face, or the kind of figure if it came to that) to be stood up by a date. If he couldn't come, he could have telephoned. *There are always telephones!*

He might have been in some street accident—oh, but he hadn't been, not Steve, who always knew exactly where he was going and got there.

At nine-thirty she took off her new dress, a smart and seductive dark blue chiffon with short, swirling skirts (a Mentonne dress, as a matter of fact, on sale and purchased at her saleswoman's discount), got into a worn, red dressing gown and went to the kitchen. *No sense in starving because your date doesn't arrive,* she thought, and the doorbell rang. She ran to open the door, and it was Steve.

"Nancy—" He came in, put his arms around her hard, and kissed her. As always when Steve kissed her, her heart took a great and glorious leap. He said, "I'm sorry."

She nestled her face against his shoulder. "It's all right. It won't take me a minute to get back into my dress."

"Well—" He sounded troubled. "That's it, Nancy. I can't make it tonight."

She pressed her face against his shoulder for a still instant or two and then said, "Oh?"

"Nancy—look at me." He lifted her face. His eyes were dark and intent. "Something came up at the office. I've got to work."

Disappointment made her inexplicably irritable. "You could have phoned."

"No, I couldn't. The old man got me in his office and kept me there going over the main points of a brief. He's taking it to court tomorrow. He's just left, and I've got to find precedents, cases, decisions—go through practically our whole law library. I'll be lucky if I get home by dawn."

*So there go my hopes for what an enchanting new dress and an enchanting spring night might do,* Nancy thought dismally. Contrarily, her voice came out with poisoned sweetness. "Then you'd better hurry back to the office. And something that's important to you."

Steve's face tightened; there was a deep flash in his eyes. "*You* are important to me."

"Oh, I'm sure of it! You could have phoned—"

"But this is my job, Nancy. And it *is* important to me, and one of the reasons—" The telephone rang.

She left him standing near the door and went to answer the telephone. A man's voice said, "Doll, I'm taking you dancing."

It was Danny Gibbs, a little two handsome, a little too boyishly exuberant in a way that somehow wasn't really boyish. She said automatically, "Oh, no. I'm sorry, Danny, but I can't—"

"Don't say no to me, doll. Get on your dancing dress. I'll be there in fifteen minutes."

"But really, Danny—" She stopped. Steve was listening; he couldn't help listening. A feminine demon took possession of her and argued swiftly that it was better to go dancing, even with Danny Gibbs, than to sit at home moping for Steve. She put an exaggerated warmth into her voice that would not have been there if Steve had not been listening. "Thanks, Danny, I'd love to."

"Don't keep me waiting, doll," Danny said, and hung up.

She turned to face Steve, who was looking rather white although there were steely sparks in his eyes. "It's perfectly all right about dinner, Steve," she said with false gaiety. "I'm going dancing with Danny Gibbs."

It was curious that she had never before noticed how hard

Steve's jaw could become. "All right," he said, "if that's the way you feel about it."

Without another word he went out and closed the door behind him, not hard but with a kind of finality that suddenly struck straight to her heart.

Appalled, ashamed compunction caught her. Steve was tired; there were shadows around his weary eyes. He did have to work that night. Steve had never lied to her about the smallest thing.

He had gone and he'd never come back. She was miserably sure of that. And she richly deserved it. *So there go my hopes for everything,* she thought. No man wants a wife who rails at him because he has to work.

And just as the telephone rang—what had Steve been saying? His job was important to him, and "one of the reasons—"

One of the reasons! Had he been about to say that she was one of the reasons for working so hard? Had he been about to say he wanted her sometime to marry him?

So the telephone rang and another man had asked her to go dancing, and she had leaped at the invitation like a fool fish. And Steve now knew just exactly the kind of woman she was—irritable, nagging, ready to jump at a chance to go out with a man she didn't even like. *Oh,* why *did I do that,* she thought. Why *didn't I show at least some good manners, some sort of understanding!* That's what a really loyal and nice woman would have done. That's what a man wants in a wife.

The point was, Steve wouldn't come back.

There was no use crying about it. She swept the sleeve of her dressing gown across her eyes. Such a stupid, unexpected flare of temper, her own fault—and in a moment all her dreams were swept away.

Well, anyway, she wasn't going out with Danny. She started for the telephone and then remembered that she didn't know Danny's telephone number and wasn't sure even where he lived. She had some vague notion that he had sublet a small apartment somewhere. There was no way to reach him and tell him that she'd got a headache, broken her ankle, died—anything.

In utter cold misery, she got back into the lovely dress she had hoped would help break through Steve's reserve. She had a suspicion that the reason Danny occasionally asked her out—rarely, though, since Steve had come into her life—was simply because he liked a decorative date, and thanks to Mentonne Fashions as much as to Mother Nature she was decorative. He arrived as she pulled on her emerald green taffeta coat, and his first words confirmed her suspicions. "Doll," he said admiringly, his pale blue eyes slightly protuberant. "Have you got class! Come on, the taxi's waiting."

Sometimes Danny was, as he called it, in the chips, and sometimes he was not; but this was one of the times when nothing but the best would do—the best dinner, the best champagne, the best orchestra—and it was wasted on Nancy. *This,* she thought, *is what they mean by eating the bitter bread of repentance.*

She put her hand over her champagne glass when the waiter started to pour another drink. *I'll swallow my pride,* she decided; *I'll telephone Steve, I'll tell him I'm sorry. But I'll never to able to erase what I've done to him tonight. He knows now that I'm not the girl for him. Oh, what a fool I am!*

"Dance, doll," Danny said and rose.

"No," Nancy said. "It's late. I've got to go home."

He didn't like it, but she was firm, and he took her home in bored silence. At a corner he stopped the taxi, while he picked up the latest edition of a newspaper. When they arrived at her apartment, Danny, always glossily polite, told the taxi to wait while he escorted her up the stairs and to her door. As she was digging into her handbag for her key, Danny glanced at the black headlines of the newspaper and whistled. "Look at this! Suicide! Blyker—the big financier."

Nancy's jaws clicked so hard it hurt.

"Suicide—no, they're not sure. May have been a thief. Found dead in his study. . . wife found him about four this afternoon . . . shot with his own gun . . . windows open . . . room apparently ransacked . . . wife called the police. . . . H'mm.'' Danny pursed his mouth. "Good-looking dame. Here's her picture."

Nancy looked with shocked dismay at the lovely little face in the press photograph. "Oh, how dreadful! That poor girl! Why, she's wearing one of the dresses I sold her this morning."

"*You* sold her—"

"M'm," Nancy nodded absently as she read. "Three black dresses, gloves, stockings to match—a horrible dowdy hat. . . . I'm so sorry for her."

Danny took her key from her hand, unlocked and opened the door, and stood aside for her to enter. It was clearly his intention to enter, too.

"Oh, Danny—it's late. I'm a working girl, you know."

"I'll only stay a minute." He took the newspaper over to the nearest lamp and read again, more slowly, his big blond head with its thick curls bent over the paper. Something about his stillness sent a faint uneasiness over Nancy. "Danny," she said. "Really—you've got to get out of here. I'm tired—"

"What kind of a dame is she?" he asked.

"Mrs. Blyker? She's lovely. Like a little girl. Not a bit smart but—"

He laughed. "Dumb like a fox. She married millions."

"I didn't mean dumb. I meant she's not—oh, chic, style-smart."

Danny's eyes fixed on her brightly. "Have you got the sales slips or whatever you call them for the things she bought?"

"Why, they're filed for the bills, of course. What on earth—"

"And you say everything she got was black?"

"Well, yes. I tried to talk her into a color but—" Danny's eyes were so bright and so fixed that the wave of uneasiness became a sharp tingle. "Why do you want to know?"

He stuffed the newspaper into his pocket and went to the

door. "Doll," he said. "We're in business. Don't worry. I'll see that you get your cut."

He went out and closed the door behind him.

She stood frozen, staring at the door, puzzled, uneasy, troubled, groping into a strange world—which all at once then revealed itself in horror. "Danny!" she screamed and flung open the door.

He was gone, had gone while she searched for the ugly thing that suddenly and terribly revealed itself.

Blackmail. Danny couldn't have meant blackmail. But he did mean it.

She closed and bolted the door as if she could keep out a ruthless, dreadful shape; but it was there, in the room, hovering around her.

There had been no suggestion that Estelle Blyker was under suspicion for the murder of her husband, not a word of it in the paper.

But she had bought black clothes—unbecoming, dowdy black clothes, the morning *before* her husband was murdered. If the police knew of those purchases, wouldn't it suggest to them that she had in fact bought mourning clothes—in anticipation of her husband's murder?

Nancy's shocked, frightened thoughts leaped on. Wouldn't it suggest, even, that Mrs. Blyker had deliberately planned, in effect, to change her appearance and personality from that of a chic, money-spending beauty who just might have had some motive (money—or another man) for murdering her husband, to that of a pathetic, dowdy, and simple young woman who could not conceivably have touched a gun or thought of murder?

Again, all that in anticipation of murder. That was the key word, *anticipation,* that certainly could be construed to imply guilt.

And then she saw that the thing that mattered was what Danny intended to do, and that was to threaten lovely little Estelle Blyker. So that because of her innocence—*well, stupidity,* Nancy thought tersely—she would pay Danny to keep his mouth shut.

"You'll get your cut," Danny had said to her, incredibly. Her skin crawled.

She knew instinctively but without question that there was no use in appealing to Danny, even if she had known how and where to find him. She also knew that out of decency she must protect Estelle Blyker.

If Nancy went to the police and told them that she herself had been the unintentional cause of setting a blackmail plot going, she would only arouse their suspicion; they would believe her story but they would also automatically suspect Estelle Blyker—suspect, question, perhaps even arrest her and charge her with murder. With horror, Nancy's mind raced on to a trial, even the conviction of an innocent woman.

She must do something, take some action to prevent the dreadful thing she herself had started. All right, then, what?

It was curious, she thought, how instantaneously Danny had revealed himself to be utterly ruthless, utterly unscrupulous about money. His view was so completely myopic that he had even included her in the simple and, to Danny, obvious creed that anybody who needed money would do anything, without question, to get money.

But then he knew, too, that he didn't really need Nancy in his horrible and simple scheme; all he had to do was threaten Mrs. Blyker, terrify her, get money out of her—and disappear.

And little Estelle Blyker—with her sweet, childlike mouth and her soft brown eyes—*would* be terrified and *would* pay. But wouldn't any woman pay rather than be suspected of murder?

She wasn't sure about that. And she must do something. Steve! Steve would know what to do, and Steve was a lawyer.

Her hands were cold and shaking. She dialed his office number; the telephone buzzed and buzzed before Steve answered, sounding surprised. "Hello—"

"Steve! I thought you'd never answer!"

"Oh, it's you." His voice became a little chilly. "Well—did you have a good time?"

"A horrible time. Steve—listen—"

He listened, without saying a word. When she had finished, he still didn't speak for so long that she cried desperately, "Don't you see? I—we've got to do something about it."

"What?" Steve said.

"Why, I don't know but—something. Don't you *understand*? Danny Gibbs—"

He cut in. "Are you sure you're not letting your imagination run away with you, Nancy? Blackmail is a serious offense. I can't believe that Danny Gibbs means anything of the kind—and even if he did mean it, how can you accuse him of it? It's your word against his; he'd deny it."

"But that poor woman—"

"If you go to the police with this story, you'll only make trouble for her. Don't stir up a hornet's nest. Leave things to the police. They know what they're doing. You stay out of this."

"Steve, you don't understand—"

"I understand you, Nancy, better than you know. Don't jump to conclusions and do something impulsive and—oh, I do know you and how you feel, but just wait—"

"You don't know at all," she cried, half-sobbing. "You don't even care!" She whacked down the telephone and hoped that the clatter hurt his ears.

A small inner voice said that Steve was sensible and he might even be right, but a stronger sense of urgency rejected it. Besides, she was right, too; if Steve really understood her need for him, he'd do something besides talk. He *didn't* care, and time was important—she was deeply, strangely sure of it. It was as if every tick of the clock said, *hurry.*

A sudden thought struck her. She flung off her green taffeta coat, snatched up her brown tweed coat and a handbag, and let herself out of her apartment. As she ran down the stairs, she thought she heard her telephone ringing but wouldn't go back; it was Steve, and she'd just let him ring. She knew—she *knew* Danny's purpose and the danger to Mrs. Blyker.

Her intention was to go to an all-night newsstand around

the corner and get the very latest edition of the papers; it was perfectly possible that the police had already found the thief, the real murderer, and that Estelle Blyker was already cleared and need fear nothing that Danny Gibbs might do. That would settle Danny. But as she passed the drugstore, she saw the big clock in the lighted window, and it now read one o'clock. The edition of the paper that Danny had taken away with him was certainly the latest one.

But it was *only* one o'clock. Danny might even now be attempting to get in touch with Estelle Blyker.

A telephone booth stood below the clock, and Nancy ducked into the drugstore.

Luckily the Blyker number was listed; she dialed it and waited. And, luckily, she thought again, a soft voice answered. "Yes . . ."

"Mrs. Blyker? This is Nancy Wilkes. You wouldn't know my name, but I work at Mentonne's. I sold you some clothes today."

There was a long pause. Then Mrs. Blyker said, "Oh, I remember."

Nancy plunged on. "It's dreadful to call you at this hour and—and just now, but I've got to tell you. There's something you should know. It's important. I wouldn't bother you but—"

"Wait a minute," Mrs. Blyker said. She seemed to think. Then she said gently, "Do you mean you'd like to see me?"

See her? Of course. It would be far better to talk to her face to face, explain it, insist that Mrs. Blyker understand and call her lawyer. "Yes, I would like to see you," Nancy said. "I know it's late, but—"

"I wasn't asleep," Mrs. Blyker said. "Can you come to my house? Don't come to the front door. There's a gate off the side street, just around the corner. It has the house number, ninety, on it. I'll unlock it and you'll see the light. Is that convenient?"

"Oh, yes, Mrs. Blyker," Nancy cried thankfully. "I'll be there as soon as I can get a cab."

"Thank you," Mrs. Blyker said and hung up.

Even in tragedy, Mrs. Blyker was gentle, kind, and

understanding, Nancy thought admiringly. There had been no question, no chilly reproof. Nancy ran from the drugstore and caught a lonely cab wandering along.

Fifth Avenue was almost deserted at that hour. The vast stretch of Central Park lay dark and mysterious, its lights haloed in mist. On the other side, the dark towers of apartment buildings reared skyward and were dotted only occasionally with lights. The headlights of a lone cab traveling a block or so behind her own cab flashed in the driver's mirror. He turned at her direction into the side street. Nancy got out and paid him. Sure enough, there was a tall, grilled iron gate with bronze numerals, ninety, dimly visible in the half-light. She put her hand on the cold latch, and it was unlocked as she had been told it would be.

A path led through shrubbery beyond which a light gleamed faintly as if from behind drawn curtains. She rounded a thick clump of laurels, found a door, and knocked lightly.

Mrs. Blyker opened it. "Come in."

Her fair hair was neat and shining; she wore a long pink silk dressing gown. The room was a kind of lounge, with rattan furniture and brilliant green curtains, which were drawn. Enormous gilded bird cages dotted the room, and a cockatoo fixed beady black eyes on Nancy.

The room was very warm, like a hothouse. Mrs. Blyker closed the door behind Nancy.

"Don't scream," she said. "Don't move." She drew her right hand from behind her flowing pink silks and pointed a revolver straight at Nancy.

It *was* a revolver. Nancy could not believe her eyes, but there it was, shining and remarkably efficient-looking. The room rocked; Nancy felt as if she were on shipboard, for even the floor seemed to quaver and move. Somewhere on the periphery of a swirling chaos centered about the lovely little figure in its pink silk, the cockatoo uttered a hoarse croak. Nancy's lips moved, but they were so dry that no word, no sound emerged. Mrs. Blyker said, "I know exactly why you came here. There's nothing doing in that line."

Again Nancy struggled to speak and achieved a blurred croak—rather like the cockatoo's. Mrs. Blyker's lovely little face was white and set as stone. "He—my husband—always said I wasn't very smart. So I made a mistake. So I got all that black junk before I needed it—except I did need it. How could I look like a grief-stricken widow in clothes like—" She glanced down at the extravagantly styled dressing gown that made her look like a medieval princess dressed for court, "like this! Police—reporters! And I had to look as unattractive and dowdy as I could! If I didn't, they'd think right away that maybe there was another man or—or I wanted my husband's money or something." Her soft brown eyes were as fixed as the gun in her hand.

*And you do want another man,* Nancy thought with certainty—*another man and your husband's money, too. . . .*

Nancy was literally dizzy. The room was too hot, she thought vaguely. She said in a queer, blank voice, "Why, you—you killed him! And I *liked* you. I came to help you."

"I know why you came. But I'm going to stop you."

"Don't point that gun at me—"

"Be quiet! There is a policeman in the front of the house."

Nancy made an instinctive move, and the gun jerked. "Stop that! He can't hear us—there are doors between. That's why I had you come to the side entrance. There's only one policeman, and he's here to protect me from curious sightseers. You should have seen the crowd on the street when they saw the police and all that. The police are sorry for me. They believe every word I've told them."

"But you—why, you *can't* get away with murder!"

"I have so far. The only problem now is you."

"You can't do a thing to me! The policeman would hear the gun. I'm going to walk out that door—"

"And accuse me! You'll do no such thing." Mrs. Blyker moved swiftly to stand between Nancy and the door. The gun didn't so much as waver.

*This is a nightmare,* Nancy thought. *Something will happen. I'll wake up. This cannot be happening.* But it was happening. She said, as reasonably as she could, "What can you do with me? You can't hide me in the house—"

"I can't let you go either," Mrs. Blyker said and debated with dreadful practicality. "The servants are on the third floor. They'll never know. There is a closet for fur coats—I could lose the key. Or there's the wine closet—" She bit a perfect, pink lip worriedly. "But it would really be better outside—" There was a slight sound at the door, and Estelle Blyker jerked around but held the gun pointed at Nancy.

The door was open the barest fraction of an inch. It was the policeman, it had to be the policeman, Nancy thught, and perhaps he had been listening. She took a quick breath; she would scream. Then the door opened, and Danny Gibbs came in.

He wore a raincoat and a hat pulled low over his face and a broad smile. "So," he said to Nancy. "You thought you'd pull a fast one on me. You thought you'd get here first. I was afraid you'd do that, you little double-crosser. I waited across the street from your apartment and followed you." He turned to Estelle Blyker. "I'm the one you're to pay."

Estelle Blyker had moved as swiftly as a cat; the gun now covered both Nancy and Danny Gibbs. "So you're in this, too," she said to Danny.

Danny's white teeth flashed. His eyes, though, were as bright and hard as the cockatoo's. "You can call me the mastermind. Now, then—how about cash?"

"You'll keep on asking for money. You'll keep on and on—"

"What are you going to do about it?" Danny asked with a fantastic air of reason. "You're sunk. A word from me and, I gather from what I heard at the door, that one word will put the police on the right track. You're guilty as hell, and I can have you sent up for murder."

"All right," Estelle Blyker said, "I'll pay. But I'll pay only you and on one condition. Get rid of that girl for me."

Danny drew back abruptly. "But that—" Danny's face glistened with sudden moisture. He licked his lips. "You can't mean—"

"Danny!" Nancy cried. "We can get the gun away from her! There are two of us! Quick—"

Danny's eyes were fixed on Estelle. "Why do you want me to—get rid of her?"

"I can't pay two of you. I'll pay you and make it worth your while. But not both of you. This way—" Something shrewd and cunning glittered in Estelle's eyes. "This way," she said gently to Danny, "you'll get it all. You'll not have to divide with her."

Danny was shaken. He shoved back his hat and wiped his hand across his forehead. "What can I do with her?"

Estelle was ashy white but sure of herself, too. "There's the river. There's—oh, that's up to you. Just get her out of here quietly, right now. Tomorrow I'll see that you get some money."

He was going to agree. *This is not possible,* Nancy thought. *We were dancing together, only an hour or two ago. And now he's really trying to think of some way to murder me!*

"Danny, this is a scheme!" Nancy cried wildly. "Don't listen to her! She thinks once you—you murder me—" She forced out the bizarre, the utterly unbelievable word and went on. "Once you murder me, she'll think of some way to stop you. She—why, she'll have the police investigate you, she'll—"

"Is it a deal?" Estelle asked Danny.

There was a curious moment of silence. Danny wiped his forehead again. Estelle simply watched with those soft brown eyes—and a steady white hand holding the gun. "All right," Danny said at last and took a queer, shaking breath.

Estelle gave a kind of sigh. "Be quick about it," she said. "Phone me in the morning. Be careful what you say."

"It won't be easy," Danny said. "You've got millions, now you've killed your husband. Murder—" An uneasy yet frightening grin twisted his mouth. "Murder comes high."

"We'll settle that. Now get out—"

Without any warning the garden door flung open, a policeman in blue uniform plunged into the room, knocked the gun from Estelle's hand with one sweep of his fist, and then as the gun thudded to the floor said in a businesslike way, "I wouldn't do that if I were you."

He had an equally businesslike revolver in his other hand. Estelle Blyker screamed and the cockatoo screamed and Danny Gibbs shrank back and yelled, "Don't touch me, Steve. I didn't do anything—don't—"

Only then Nancy saw Steve. He wore an overcoat and his dark head was bare and he was starting for Danny, his fists doubled up.

"Now, now!" the policeman said sharply. "None of that. We'll see to him."

"Steve!" Nancy cried on a great breath. "Oh, Steve!"

It deflected him from Danny. He looked at her; his eyes were blazing. "This was a fool thing for you to do!"

She had been on the verge of flinging herself into his arms; she wasn't prepared for anger. She flared back at him. "I had to! *You* didn't care! *You* wouldn't do anything—"

The policeman gave her a flashing look. He seemed not only to understand but to approve of Steve's anger. "He did just the right thing," he snapped. "And you'd better thank him for it, young lady. He came to the house, saw me in the vestibule, knocked on the window, told me he was afraid you were here somewhere, and insisted on taking a look around the house. And there was the door and we heard voices and—You need a guardian, young woman," he said sternly and turned to Steve. "There's a call box on the corner. Just take the phone off the hook and the precinct desk will answer."

Estelle lifted her face to the policeman. "I don't know what that man has told you—but the truth is, this girl threatened me with blackmail, and I was terrified and—"

"Tell that to the Marines," Steve said, still blazing with anger—and, Nancy then realized, with fright for her. "Okay, officer," he said. "I'll go to the call box."

Two hours later Nancy got into the front seat of Steve's car, parked on the side street, and as he took his place beside her, she nestled against his arm. He drove in steady silence, though. After a long time she said, "I'm sorry, Steve. You *did* believe me."

"No, I didn't," he said stubbornly. "I was wrong, but I didn't believe it really could be blackmail—or murder. But you didn't answer your phone, so I drove to your apartment and you didn't answer the bell and I knew perfectly well where you'd gone. So I—had to see to you."

"Oh," she said flatly. "Well—thanks, just the same."

He drove on again in steady silence. Finally she said in a small voice, "The policeman was right. I do need a guardian."

After a long time again, the arm she leaned against moved and then went around her. He said, "Guardian is not the right word."

He did understand her and her need for him, she thought with sudden certainty—and as certainly and clearly she understood him. The rest of it, she knew, with a quiet, deep trust, would come later, as and when it might. Just now there was no need for words. She moved closer against him, and when he stopped for the next light, he looked at her for a moment and then kissed her.

*In my own experience I have found trust officers in a bank to be most helpful; they have indeed saved many widows from making foolish, even dangerous, investments. But none whom I know have had anything like the experience in this story, and indeed would avoid it at all costs!*

❑

# The Dangerous Widows

One of my widows telephoned to me at one o'clock, Friday, and the other telephoned me at three o'clock, Friday, and both of them invited me urgently to spend the weekend at their country place.

Neither invitation, however, was social; each widow said frankly that she was in need of my advice. In fact, it was an invitation to murder.

In literal fact, neither woman was my widow in the accepted sense. They were Henry Briggs's widows. Both, however, were very likely to fall within my scope of duty, for I am a banker, elderly enough to be entrusted with the somewhat difficult chore of advising, coaxing, cajoling, and generally acting as nursemaid to widows who seem strangely determined to invest in nonexistent uranium ore deposits and dry oil wells.

The two Mrs. Briggs were Henry's wives; one was his first wife, Frances Briggs, divorced and never remarried; the other, Eloise Briggs, was his second and the official Mrs. Briggs. Henry Briggs had been one of my old clients. And the country house each referred to was the same country house, for it had been left to them, jointly, in his will.

Consequently, a rather delicate situation was in the making. I took the five-thirty train to Stamford.

Henry Briggs had been a client of the bank for a long time, and, especially during his long illness, I had had much to do with his affairs. I had never met either Mrs. Briggs.

I cannot say that I faced the prospect with any pleasure. I do not like strife or emotional outbursts, and both were far too likely to develop. As I got off the train and looked down the long platform, I wondered which one would meet me and thus possibly endeavor to get in her claims first.

Neither did. A thickset, red-faced man, done to a turn in flagrantly countrified clothes, approached me and said with a hearty, jolly manner, "Mr. Wickwire?"

I nodded. He put out a large red hand. His face was jovial and friendly; he had shrewd, cold blue eyes. "I'm Al Muller—friend of Henry's. The station wagon is this way."

I said, "Quite so," and followed him.

He put my bag in the station wagon and wedged himself, puffing, behind the wheel. "I'm staying at the house. Thought I might be of some service to them." He negotiated to turn amid traffic.

I said, "Indeed."

His blue eyes shot me a rather narrow glance. "Yes; Frances—that's the first wife—arrived Thursday night by train. Henry was buried that afternoon, you'll remember. Eloise—that's the second wife—was here, of course."

I said, perhaps rather dryly, "And when did you arrive, Mr. Muller?"

He paused to examine a road sign rather deliberately. "Oh, I came up later Thursday night. Seemed to me I owed it to Henry. It's an odd situation, leaving the property like that. Do you know either of the Mrs. Briggs?"

Something about his manner went against my grain. I said stiffly that I hadn't had that pleasure.

He chuckled. "They're as alike as two peas in a pod. You'll see. And there's a fight brewing there, mark my words. Neither is the sort to give up easily. I don't envy you, Mr Wickwire."

"I am in no sense an arbiter. I'll leave that to the

lawyers." I spoke coldly enough to penetrate even Mr. Al Muller's hide. We concluded our ride along the winding country roads in silence.

The house and grounds, when we reached them, proved to be on a rather lavish scale, with velvety lawns, swimming pool, tennis court, gardens. It represented, I knew, the whole of Henry Briggs's property; he had had a fairly large income but had lived up to it. I had arrived at an approximate sum that I thought the property might fetch and was deducting, in my mind, such things as possible capital gains and taxes when we drew up to the white-columned entrance.

Here two women stood waiting; both advanced to greet me as I got out of the car. And at least in one instance Muller was right; allowing for possibly fifteen years' difference in age, they were very much alike. Both slender, fine featured, blond, and extremely attractive.

The younger, the official Mrs. Briggs, spoke to me first, putting out a jeweled hand toward mine; she introduced me to the first Mrs. Briggs, while Al Muller stood watching with a rather stupid grin on his red face and a very watchful look in those shrewd eyes. We went at once into the house.

A maid took my bag upstairs. Cocktails were set out on a tray in the spacious living room. It was an imposing room, full of what might be called objects of art and dominated by a huge portrait of Henry Briggs, done apparently when he was a rather young man, at least twenty years before his death.

Eloise, the young Mrs. Briggs, in her proper role of hostess, saw to it that I was comfortably seated and asked me my preference as to cocktails. In the soft light from the table lamps, the likeness between the two women diminished. They were the same general type, that was all.

The first Mrs. Briggs, Frances, was thinner and finer drawn than the second, with darker hair but penetrating blue eyes. She wore a simple and certainly inexpensive white cotton dress and no jewelry beyond her wedding ring.

Eloise was almost beautiful, with creamy, magnolia-smooth skin, soft red mouth, and a rather luxuriant figure. Her dress was simple, too, but even my bachelor eyes perceived that it was an expensive simplicity; a diamond bracelet sparkled on her wrist.

It was Eloise who, again assuming her unquestionably correct position of authority, said that, if I agreed, both she and the other Mrs. Briggs preferred to postpose our discussion of business until morning. I agreed, most sincerely. Al Muller helped himself to another drink, at which both Mrs. Briggs looked at him coldly. The maid who had taken my bag announced dinner.

Aside from the fact that Al Muller became talkative in a jovial, rallying way, it was a quiet and merely social dinner. Not a word that was said, not a gesture, suggested potential strife between the two Mrs. Briggs. They were, in short, perfect ladies.

The evening ended early, and Eloise showed me to my room. "I hope you'll not mind coming down to breakfast," she said. "The maid lives in the village and goes home at night."

I assured her that it didn't matter. "By the way, Mrs. Briggs, exactly why did you ask me to come here?"

She hesitated for a second. Then she came close to me; her lovely mouth smiled invitingly. She put both hands appealingly on my arm. "Because I need your help."

Perfume wafted toward me; there was a deep glow in her eyes. I recoiled slightly. "I'm afraid the only help I can give you is to advise you to put the settlement of the estate in the hands of your lawyer."

Her hands, of necessity, dropped. She eyed me for a moment. Then she said, "Of course. Good night, Mr. Wickwire."

It was all very calm, all very polite. But there was something very wrong in the house. I was obliged to wait, however, until the house was quiet before I went quietly downstairs again and out the door. I took the road to the village. It was a dark night, with scudding clouds.

The village was still lighted, and the drugstore had a pay telephone.

There are certain shortcuts a banker knows that will lead him to certain kinds of information. Nevertheless, since it was by then rather late, it took some time to accomplish my purpose.

Fortunately, in a way, I was under the interested observation of the young man behind the soda fountain the whole time, and I bought several magazines and an ice-cream soda from him. He had, however, told me that he'd have to shut up shop in another ten minutes when my New York call came through.

He turned off the lights as I left the drugstore and took my way back to the Briggs house. It seemed a rather short walk, for I was thinking deeply, and it was with a sense of surprise that I turned in at the gates.

I stopped there, struck with another kind of surprise. The house was ablaze with lights. And then I heard the thud of automobiles. Indeed, I ducked out of the driveway barely in time as the first one took the curve and shot up to the entrance.

Other cars and motorcycles followed it. By the time I had run across the grass and reached the house, the entire village constabulary as well as state troopers were swarming into the house, where Al Muller lay, dead of a revolver shot, on the rug below Henry's portrait.

I pushed my way there, passing Eloise and Frances, white and frightened, in the hall.

Al Muller's thick body lay apparently as it had fallen. His too-fancy country oxfords were sprawled wide apart. His brightly checked jacket was crumpled. A gun lay near his hand.

It was dawn when the police at last went away. Both Mrs. Briggs exhausted and tense with strain, went upstairs as the last police car disappeared down the drive. I watched them go. And I wondered which one had murdered him.

Not that the police called it murder. The inquiry had been a long one, their questions had been many; they had taken our fingerprints; they had determined the ownership of the gun, which had belonged to Henry. But they had been guarded and reticent. They had not—as yet—called it murder.

They had listened to my own story, which luckily the young man in the drugstore could substantiate. They had listened to the stories of the two Mrs. Briggs, which were identical. Each had been awakened, she said, by the sound of the shot; each had waited a few moments, questioning it; each had come into the hall at almost the same time as the other. They had gone downstairs together to find Al Muller—dead.

They had telephoned for the police. They had tried to arouse me and discovered my absence. They had been afraid that I, too, had been a victim of some robber who might still be about the grounds. When asked if either of them believed that Al Muller had been depressed by Henry's death to the point of suicide, each appeared doubtful.

It was not suicide. It was murder.

But I didn't know which one had murdered him. I listened as their light footsteps, the whisper of their movements, died away above. Then I went back to the living room. Al Muller's body had been removed, but the room still seemed to hold his presence, and it was not a pleasant one.

The room was in considerable disorder—chairs pushed around, the rug upon which Al Muller had died rolled up into a corner, small tables and lamps shoved around carelessly. The portrait of Henry Briggs was slightly askew on the wall.

I preferred not to touch the rug, or indeed approach it, but being a banker and a bachelor and possibly somewhat finicky in habits of tidiness, I straightened chairs and tables. No clues, of course; I hadn't really expected that there would be. I went to Henry's huge portrait with its heavy frame and straightened that, too. It seemed rather oddly out of place. Someone's shoulder must have brushed against it.

I measured, absently really, my own shoulder height below the portrait. I am not a tall man, but the lower corner of the gilded frame was at least a foot above my own shoulder. So someone's hand had pushed it aside. I stood looking at Henry for a moment. Then I got a chair and climbed on it and looked behind the portrait.

Some time later I straightened the portrait carefully, got down from the chair, restored it to its place, and sat down in it. Something was going to happen, and it would have to happen rather soon.

I cannot say it was a pleasant wait. I hoped there was not another gun in the house. Somewhere a clock was ticking with an ominous warning note, as if to remind me of the fleeting quality of time.

It had run out swiftly for Al Muller. I am not a brave man; when I heard the faint rustle of a woman's garment on the stairway, the very soft whisper of footsteps, I had to force myself to remain . . . waiting.

She must have seen the light in the room; still, she thought it was empty, for when she appeared as quietly as a ghost in the doorway and saw me she caught her breath and flung both hands to her throat. It was Frances, the first Mrs. Briggs.

After a moment she came toward me, her negligee gathered around her. Her fine eyes were very bright. "I didn't know you were here. I came to—to look. I had to see if there was something, anything, the police didn't see. Mr. Wickwire—Eloise killed him."

It was, of course, in the cards. One of them would accuse the other; indeed, each might accuse the other, the murderess because she must shield herself with a lie, the other because she must shield herself with the truth. I said, "Why?"

Her hands moved toward each other. "I don't know. But I think it had something to do with money. Al Muller was simply not the kind of man to come here and stay out of sympathy. He wanted something."

"Mrs. Briggs, why did you send for me?"

Her bright eyes didn't waver. "Because Muller was here. I didn't trust him. I was going to ask you to get rid of him. But I know Eloise killed him, because I didn't. And there was no one else."

"I didn't kill him," Eloise said clearly from the doorway. "So it must have been you!" She was wearing a long, floating negligee, and she had a gun in her hand.

Violence has never been, so to speak, my dish. I felt a kind of creeping chill up my backbone. But I had to get both women and myself out of the room, and of course I'd have to get that gun.

I said, "We are all very tired. I suggest that you two ladies—er—dress while I prepare some sort of breakfast for us." I went to Eloise. "Whose gun is that?"

"Mine. Henry got it for me."

"What were you going to do with it?"

She looked at me. "I don't know," she said blankly and I think truthfully.

"You'd better give it to me."

She did so at once, which both surprised and pleased me. I then said briskly, "Now I'll see to coffee," and went out of the room and through the dining room to the kitchen, where I made a great clatter about cupboard doors and pots and pans. I made a mistake, however, when for safety's sake, I dropped the gun into the flour bin.

I gave them barely time to dress and accomplish what one of them had to accomplish in the living room, and consequently burned the toast while I was watching the clock. But as I took it and coffee into the dining room, Frances Briggs came in, charming and fresh in blue linen. After a moment Eloise, lovely and fresh in pink, entered also.

Both seized upon coffee, neither spoke, and I was rather uneasily aware of stored-up dynamite. A very slight jar was all too likely to induce an explosion, and I was not ready for that. So when I spoke I did so cautiously.

"In view of the circumstances, I'd like to suggest that we postpone our business talk. But I have a request to make. I was an old friend of Henry's. If neither of you wish to keep the portrait of him, I wonder if you would be so kind as to give it to me."

Eloise's eyes leaped to me above the rim of her coffee cup. She put the cup down and put her handkerchief to her eyes. She said from behind it, "Of course. I didn't realize that you felt that way about Henry. I have other pictures of Henry. He—he would want you to have it." She dabbed at her eyes with her handkercheif.

"Thank you," I said and turned to Frances, who had risen.

She said, "I'm sorry. I'll not pretend that I was in love with Henry when he met you, Eloise. I was not heartbroken when he asked me for a divorce; I agreed to it. But once, when Henry and I were young, when that portrait was made, I loved him. I'm sorry, Mr. Wickwire; I want the portrait."

So I knew what I had to know. I said something about understanding it, made an excuse, and left the room.

I let myself out, cautiously, through the back door. A grape arbor ran along there, toward the garage, and I took shelter behind it. I reached the garage and was opening the door of the station wagon when Eloise ran into the garage.

"Mr. Wickwire—where are you going?"

"To the state police—will you drive? I'm not accustomed to this car. Besides, it might be safer."

"Safer! Do you mean she—" She gave a kind of quick gasp and then slid behind the wheel. "Take the back way down to the road," I said. "The trees and the shrubbery may shield us from the house."

The sun was up, streaking across shrubbery and lawns and making a bright path of the country road. Eloise knew the way to the state police headquarters. She went in with me, and the young lieutenant who had directed the night's inquiry was at his desk, using the telephone, when we were shown into his office. He looked pleased and relaxed; his revolver lay on the desk.

"Oh, there you are. I was about to phone you. The fingerprints on the gun are Al Muller's. So it was probably suicide."

Fingerprints, of course, can be placed on guns after death, but I didn't care to argue with him about that. I gave one longing thought toward the gun in the flour bin and said, "I'm afraid I have evidence to the contrary. If you'll search the Briggs house, you'll find a package of notes, given for loans advanced by Al Muller and signed by Henry Briggs. The signatures are forgeries. And in the meantime—" I cleared my throat. "Kindly arrest this Mrs. Briggs at once and charge her—"

I couldn't finish because Eloise was too quick; she snatched the officer's revolver. Two shots went wild, a third crashed through the window, and then the young lieutenant had her tight in his arms, but it was not a loverlike embrace.

He released her when other troopers rushed in. I crawled out from under the desk with such dignity as I could summon. The young lieutenant was also very quick. "The notes," he said, panting and blushing deeply, "are probably on her. Get the matron from the village, Sergeant."

He was right. The notes, a rather bulky package, were concealed in a feminine garment that I believe is called a bra. I must say I was relieved to see them; she had had neither time nor the opportunity to destroy them, but I had run it rather fine.

Back at the house, after certain formalities had been concluded, I had a conversation with the lieutenant and with Frances Briggs. "So Muller lent her all that money," the lieutenant said, "and I take it he thought he was lending it to Henry during his illness, but she forged Henry's signatures."

I nodded. "He probably discovered, or knew from the beginning, that it was forgery. After Henry's death, he, er...er..."

"Put the screws on," the lieutenant said. "He wouldn't give up; he must have demanded quite a price. So she shot him. But then—"

"Then she had to get out of the room and up the back stairs in a hurry. She got the notes out of his pocket, shoved them behind the portrait, put his fingerprints on the gun, and ran up the back way. Frances Briggs came into the hall at about that time."

"But how did you know?"

"I found the notes. I didn't know which woman had shot him or which one had forged the notes and thus had to get possession of them again. I gave both women time, I was afraid too much time, but—at any rate, then I asked for Henry's portrait. I knew that the woman who had shot Muller would not want the portrait; she wouldn't want any association with so strong a reminder of guilt. So a rejection of the portrait would be a indication of guilt—and an indication that the notes had been successfully removed.

Eloise leaped at the chance to get rid of the portrait. Frances,'' I said as I bowed toward the other Mrs. Briggs, ''wished to keep it.''

The lieutenant eyed me. So did Frances.

I added, ''I must tell you that I had had occasion to make some inquiries by telephone regarding Eloise. She was wearing jewelry; she was dressed expensively. In short, I found that she had staggering charge accounts and spent far more money than Henry could have given her. Remember, I am in a position to know. So where was she getting the money? Why was Al Muller there at the house?''

''Oh,'' Frances said.

But the lieutenant said astutely, ''You must have more solid—well, evidence. Some definite basis for suspicion!''

I sighed. There is a sad truth in a banker's life that he must recognize early and arm himself against. I told the lieutenant, ''When anybody urgently wishes to see any banker, he—she—wants to borrow money. Frances Briggs had a different reason that was sound and sensible. But Eloise—''

''She wanted to borrow enough money on the property to pay off Muller!'' the lieutenant cried. ''Did she ask you for a loan?''

''Not,'' I said, ''precisely.''

Suddenly the lieutenant grinned. ''Oh, I see. But you weren't having any—I mean to say that you were not—that is, her charm—that is . . .'' He blushed, looked apologetic, and tried to stop grinning.

''Oh, Mr. Wickwire!'' Frances Briggs leaned toward me with a lovely smile, her magnificent eyes warm. ''You *are* a detective! And a very courageous man.''

There are more ways than one in which an attractive widow may be dangerous. I rose rather quickly and said I had to return to town. Indeed, when another widow invited me to her house on Long Island the next weekend, I sent a subordinate in my place.

"The Jade Cup" was written as a result of a visit to the fabulous Jade Room in Gumps, San Francisco. I searched out all I could about jade, and it still has a great fascination for me. Also, I was presented an extra dividend: my husband gave me a simple and lovely jade necklace.

But nothing in this story really happened, I am pleased to say.

□

# The Jade Cup

The unexpected and extremely public death of Ben Dojoue was, like Gaul, divided in three parts for young Mr. Constant. And there were really three causes for your Mr. Constant's initial and reluctant plunge into murder circles. There was, first, the matter of his broken arm, which had refused to heal properly so that he was obliged to take a leave of absence from Holy Gate (a small college where he held, due again to causes beyond his own control, a chair in the English department). There was, second, the matter of the chauffeur he'd been obliged to engage while his arm was healing. And third and most important was Miss Cecile Dojoue's remarkable and extraordinary prettiness.

She was putting a sign in the window when he first saw her. Otto (his chauffeur; born on Chicago's West Side, an erstwhile top sergeant, prizefighter, and graduate of certain informal and impulsive groups) had permitted himself to engage in persiflage about a parking space with two taxi drivers and a traffic policeman, and so was late in arriving at the corner where he was to meet young Mr. Constant. Thus, Mr. Constant, strolling idly down the street, passed the old brownstone house where Ben Dojoue, Importer, was housed and saw Cecile Dojoue leaning over to put the sign in the window.

He stopped at once. Mr. Constant was markedly susceptible to feminine beauty, but even a sternly unsusceptible man might have lingered to look at Cecile Dojoue. She was young and dark. Her demure silk dress outlined the most softly and delicately curved little figure. Her lace collar was as white as the curved chin above it. Her hair was black and fitted her head smoothly, like a soft black velvet cap. There was a sweep of silken black lashes along her creamy cheeks, a spread of shining slender eyebrows that were like wings, and a very faint black shadow above her red mouth, which on a Frenchwoman spells beauty—and Cecile was French in every line and motion. Mr. Constant held his breath, waiting for her to lift her eyes.

But she did not. She set the sign upright, adjusting it with lovely, soft hands that were small, too, and delicate; one of them wore an extremely fine jade cabochon set simply in a ring. But young Mr. Constant had only the barest speaking acquaintance with jade and was very much more interested in the hand that wore it.

The position of the sign met her approval, and she turned from the window without even glancing at Mr. Constant and vanished in the dusky interior of the store.

He sighed. He looked then, at the sign, which read Auction Tomorrow, Tuesday, 4:00 P.M. He bent his head back to look at the name above the door: Ben Dojoue, Importer. It was at that point that Otto stopped the car smoothly at the curb, got out, took off his cap, and opened the back door of the car invitingly. It was, by the way, a very handsome and impressive machine; Mr. Constant was not—again luckily, and due to the foresight of a distant Constant—dependent upon his salary from Holy Gate. He had also a secret and rather diffident admiration and fondness for the beautiful synchronization and great power of expensive motor cars.

Now, however, he looked dreamily at Otto, although he did approach the car. But at the very door he changed his mind.

"I've an errand in here, Otto," he said briskly. "Come back in half an hour."

"Yes, sir," said Otto respectfully; but with secret joy he closed the door, got into the car, and headed back for the disputed parking space. With luck the two taxi drivers, but not the policeman, would still be there.

And Mr. Constant touched his tie—he had a rather nice taste in ties—pulled his smart black fedora jauntily over his eyes, and advanced upon Ben Dojoue, Importer.

Even at the moment of entering, however, there was something unpleasant about the place, so definitely unpleasant that Mr. Constant faltered involuntarily just inside the door. It was dingy, and it was crowded with objects of art, which ranged from the crudest and ugliest of modern Chinese art to—though Mr. Constant did not recognize it—the finest and oldest. There were counters and shelves, all laden; screens and practically life-size Buddhas; cases full of rose quartz and inferior jade.

Then as his eyes became better adjusted to the dim interior light, Mr. Constant was aware of Miss Cecile Dojoue's advancing with the self-possessed grace of a sleek young cat and looking into his eyes from across the counter. Her eyes, he found, were very dark: a liquid, changing darkness—cool, perhaps, and businesslike, but very, very beautiful indeed.

Probably she made some inquiry as to his wants. Certainly Mr. Constant heard himself asking to look at jade, which he had no desire at all to look at, being preoccupied with the girl's eyes.

"One moment," she said gently, turned, and disappeared along the dim aisle leading toward rooms at the rear of the showroom.

Instantly a man took her place. It was Ben Dojoue, dark, swarthy, with very large white teeth below a trim black mustache. His sister, he explained after introducing himself suavely to a startled Mr. Constant, knew little of jade. And was there anything in particular the gentleman wished to see?

Mr. Constant blinked behind horn-rimmed spectacles and

drew on the slightest encyclopedic knowledge. "Have you," he said, wishing he had resisted the impulse that had led him into the store, "have you any particularly fine pieces of jade? Gem jade, I mean."

Ben Dojoue's eyes, dark like his sister's, took on a livelier sparkle. He looked Mr. Constant up and down in one swift appraisal: young, well-bred, a good manner; extremely good tailoring; no jewels on his hands but often they didn't wear jewels, though Mr. Dojoue himself always wore a ring or two. There was nothing about the young man that spoke of money, and he certainly looked a bit vague and absentminded behind those horn-rimmed eyeglasses. Still—

Mr. Dojoue spread his hands with a Gallic gesture and bowed. But, yes, they had gem jade. One or two remarkably fine pieces. Would the gentleman—

"My name is Constant."

Ben Dojoue didn't recognize the name as that of a collector or a wealthy patron, but he covered his disappointment. If Mr. Constant would come to the back of the shop—naturally they didn't keep their fine pieces out on the shelves.

Mr. Constant would follow him.

Thinking of it afterward, as he was destined frequently to do, it seemed to Mr. Constant that it was that short walk from the front of the store, back along the dim aisle bordered with teakwood and mother-of-pearl screens and squatting, secretly smiling Buddhas, and into deeper shadow at the rear, that actually entangled him irrevocably with the Dojoue affair. Up until then he could and ought to have withdrawn. It was the barest impulse that had taken him into Ben Dojoue's store in the beginning. If Cecile Dojoue had not been so confoundedly pretty; if he had not had time to waste; if it had not been spring—

"In here, Mr. Constant," said Ben Dojoue. They went through an office, extremely businesslike and lined with steel files, and into a little dark passage. "In here," said Ben Dojoue, opening a door and pressing an electric switch in the room beyond.

Again and instinctively, Mr. Constant hesitated. It was a

smallish room lined with dark wood panels, and it smelled of incense and old Chinese robes and mingled dusty fragrances of a thousand years. There was a long table of carved teakwood in the middle of the room; there were Chinese rugs, heavy and silent, on the floor; there were chairs, also teakwood but upholstered in tarnished brocades. On the table were a few oddments: a reading glass with an ornate handle of inferior jade, though Mr. Constant didn't know it was inferior; and an enormous book at least three feet long, which he did recognize at once as being privately and expensively printed.

Overcoming the feeling of strangeness and reluctance, he crossed the threshold and went to the book. And by that act he entered, all unaware, the dark, wholly ruthless affair.

"A history of jade?" observed Mr. Constant, opening the book and glancing through the first pages.

"Yes, written by one of our greatest collectors, an authority on jade. The books came to me—" Mr. Dojoue stopped abruptly. "Won't you sit down?" he said, indicating one of the chairs. "Now then, what would you like to see? I have a very fine necklace; several beautiful pieces for a chain . . ."

Mr. Constant sat down. The author of the book on jade was one Carter Muir. It was dedicated to his wife and appeared to be written with the certainty of authority. Mr. Constant noted it all briefly because he dealt in books and couldn't help noting such things. As he wondered uneasily if he was going to be obliged to buy a piece of jade. While the income derived from the distant Constant's foresight in leaving a trust fund behind him was ample and sufficient for Mr. Constant's needs, he was not at all sure that it would run to casual shopping in jade.

The panels, he perceived, were actually doors of cupboards lining the room from floor to ceiling. There were no keyholes visible; probably they were hidden somewhere in the carving. Mr. Dojoue followed his look.

"My treasures," he said suddenly, smiling, and became all at once expansive. "I have here some of the finest jade in the world. Really—the finest."

He said it quietly, yet with a complacency and pride that

was convincing. Mr. Constant, for no good reason, felt an urgent desire to remove himself rapidly and completely and forever from Ben Dojoue, Importer.

"In that case..." he began, intending to add, "I'm afraid your pieces are far too expensive for me." But Mr. Dojoue, leaping to a conclusion, interpreted it in a different way.

"At once," he cried, interrupting, and showing all his very white teeth. He went to the door and called: "My key, Cecile."

Cecile, thought Mr. Constant. So that was her name. And she was this Ben Dojoue's sister, so probably her name was Cecile Dojoue. At least, he hadn't observed a wedding ring on her hands. He sighed and looked at his watch, put his hat and stick on the table, and felt himself an impostor as the girl entered, gave her brother the key, and remained.

She watched while Mr. Constant, who couldn't help himself, was initiated into the strange and secret world of jade.

This was actually an exceptionally fine collection, Mr. Constant began to realize. And he was in the hands of a man who knew jade as probably very few people knew it. Mr. Dojoue spoke of this and that piece affectionately and yet with a kind of awe. He inserted the little key into the hidden keyholes and opened panel after panel to reveal the treasures behind.

"This vase," he was saying, "is three thousand years old. Observe the carving. Over here is probably the finest statuette known—soft as a baby's cheek, is it not, Mr. Constant? Touch it with your fingers. In money value it is worth sixteen thousand dollars; I would sell it for that. In real value it is priceless. I have collected these myself over a period of years. Do you know much of the tradition and superstition of jade, Mr. Constant?"

It was then for the first time that the girl, Cecile, interrupted. "Perhaps he is not interested in all this, brother," she said softly.

By this time the zeal of the evangelist had overtaken the importer. Mr. Constant's protest that he was most interested was quite submerged by Mr. Dojoue's forceful assertion to the same effect.

"Bring me the cup, Cecile," he continued. "One of the reasons, Mr. Constant, for the high value the ancient Chinese set upon jade was owing to it curious chemical properties. The exact nature of these qualities has been disputed and even superficially and speciously disproved. But nevertheless—ah, thank you, Cecile." There was a subtle change in the importer's voice as a kind of tenseness crept into it.

Mr. Constant looked with increased interest at the cup the girl held. It was a small, elaborately carved dish of apple-green jade, a cup without a handle. The importer took it reverently into his hands, looked at the girl, and said sharply as if deflected: "Cecile! You are wearing the cabochon!"

The girl drew her hand away. The cabochon, thought Mr. Constant vaguely, and then saw the shining green stone on the girl's hand. Jade, of course, gem jade of a translucent green that looked as if all the greens of the world had been brought together and fused into that one living, breathing green oval.

Cecile's long lashes went down over her cheek. "Why, yes," she said quietly. "It needed wearing."

Her brother's face flushed a dark red. "I told you—" he began, checked himself suddenly, as if biting words back, then continued smoothly: "See that you return it to the safe. It is not prudent to wear it about when the store is open to chance visitors." He turned, smiling again, to Mr. Constant. His smile was very broad and very toothy and reminded Mr. Constant momentarily but irresistibly of the tiger who came back from the ride with the lady inside.

"This cup," he said, "belonged to a Chinese emperor. It actually detects any foreign substance in water or tea. Nobody knows why—many people indeed say it is impossible, but they are wrong. I will show you."

Mr. Constant, bemused, his imagination caught and held by glimpses of faraway and ancient times and long-dead emperors, watched absently while Cecile brought water in a small silver pitcher.

"Observe," said Mr. Dojoue. "Plain water that I pour into the cup remains clear and untroubled. Likewise—though you must take my word for it—tea. But pour into it any foreign matter—" He held out the cup to Cecile, who from some mysterious recess had produced a box labeled Soda and who, at her brother's gesture, shook a small portion of the white powder into the cup. "Pour into it any foreign matter and—look, Mr. Constant." He held the green cup toward Mr. Constant. The liquid in the cup immediately bubbled and frothed effervescently.

"Not very unusual," said Mr. Constant unimpressed. "Soda in water always effervesces."

"Not in cold water, Mr. Constant," said the importer suavely. "Test the temperature. Put your finger on the cup—there."

It was cold. Mr. Constant lifted one eyebrow a bit skeptically but acknowledged it. The importer's smile widened. He nodded mysteriously and, to Mr. Constant's astonishment, lifted the cup and drank the soda-charged water at a gulp and chuckled.

"Showmanship," he said in a confidential manner. "I do it at auctions—it impresses the audience. I tell them of the marvelous properties of jade, how it detects foreign substances; then I show them—as I have shown you—except they do not know it is merely soda. And when I drink the stuff (after telling them at length of the ancient value of jade as poison detector), it gives them what you call in America a kick." He chuckled again as if congratulating himself on the cleverness of the trick.

"Well," said Mr. Constant dubiously, "so long as it isn't poison—"

The girl was frowning. "I think it is very childish," she said. "My brother likes these tricks. I do not."

"You are not a psychologist, my good Cecile," said her brother. "Tell me, am I not a good salesman? Do not what you call childish tricks bring very good returns?"

She shrugged her beautiful shoulders a little, took the cup

from his hand, and turned away. "Oh, yes," she said over her shoulder, "You, you would sell—anything."

Again the importer's swarthy face went a deep red, and his smile became a little fixed. "And why not?" he demanded of the girl's back, with what seemed to Mr. Constant undue violence. "Why not? I am a businessman. I cannot afford to possess these things myself. I must sell and buy, and buy and sell."

Cecile put the cup and silver pitcher on a shelf, while Mr. Constant admired her in a rather detached way; detached because he was mainly thinking of the jade and of the—well, Cecile's word described it, childish little gesture of the cup. But then, doubtless Ben Dojoue was a good salesman; certainly the money invested in his business proclaimed it. Mr. Constant rose.

"Thank you very much," he said. I've taken a great deal of your time and bought nothing—"

"It's been a pleasure, Mr. Constant," said the importer, rubbing his hands together and bowing. "People seldom buy the first time they look at jade. Love for jade is a slow growth. But a stubborn one, Mr. Constant. A tenacious one. It becomes," he said, letting his fingers touch an apple-green bowl, "a passion."

That was the first part of the affair of the royal cabochon and murder.

Cecile turned and bowed distantly as Mr. Constant went away. The importer accompanied him to the door. Otto and the impressive car were waiting at the curb. Mr. Dojoue glanced at the car shrewdly and immediately asked Mr. Constant to come again.

"There is an auction tomorrow," he said. "At four. Some very interesting pieces are to be sold. Including the cabochon. You will come, Mr. Constant?"

"The cabochon?"

"Ah, yes, the royal cabochon. You saw it on my sister's hand. One of the finest pieces of gem jade in existence. It has an interesting history, too; it was taken a year or so ago from the looted tomb of the Dowager Empress. You will come? That's good. Good day, Mr. Constant. Good day. Good day."

Mr. Constant got into the car. It was nice to be in the sunshine and fresh air again, but it had also been, he decided idly, a pleasant excursion into another and older world—a world of infinite beauty, infinite patience. Wasn't it Chinese, that saying about time being a stream into which we dip but lightly? They'd had time, then, to spend years carving one locket—carving it so finely that you needed a magnifying glass to perceive the real perfection of the design.

Well, it had been a silly impulse, but it had led to an interesting, idle hour. He thought a bit regretfully of Cecile's beautiful eyes, realized he was late to his appointment, and told Otto to step on it. Otto did so with the greatest pleasure.

Mr. Constant had no intention whatever of attending the auction the next day, had indeed no thought of ever visiting Ben Dojoue, Importer, again. He did wonder vaguely, however, about the story of the royal cabochon and wished he had looked at the jewel more closely. That was the same night, at the opera, during the last act of *Don Giovanni*.

It was probably because of a curious but trivial incident that took place during the entr'acte and that was curious only because it presented an odd little link with the business of the morning. That was when his hostess, strolling with Mr. Constant outside the boxes, whispered: "Look, there's Mrs. Carter Muir—over there in white satin."

Mr. Constant looked in the direction indicated; he saw a tall, gray-haired woman whose white satin gown trailed luxuriously on the floor and whose wrinkled neck, arms, and hands were ablaze with jewels. Diamonds for the most part, he thought, though there were emeralds, too. A chinchilla evening wrap hung over one arm, and she was talking vivaciously to a youngish man with her, who looked bored and replied but briefly.

"You mean the woman with all those diamonds?" Mr. Constant asked his hostess.

She nodded. "The story is," she said cautiously, "that all

her jewels are paste. Copies, you know, of the original stones. Her husband, who died last year, was once enormously rich. They say that he left her without a cent—with indeed the heaviest obligations. Of course," said his hostess with engaging frankness, "I don't know Mrs. Carter Muir—that is, I've only a speaking acquaintance with her. She's very old family and all that; seldom goes out except to opera. But they do say her love for jewels was one of the things that ruined Carter Muir."

"Who's the man?" inquired Mr. Constant.

A speculative glint came in his hostess's eye. "His name is Jimmy Walsh. She is seen with him a lot. There's a shocking difference in age, and he has no money or expectations. But nobody knows what her intentions are. At least, that's the story. There's the bell."

*Carter Muir,* thought Mr. Constant absently; he'd heard the name somewhere, recently. Through subconscious association of ideas, probably, he fell to thinking of the royal cabochon. And as the flames of hell shot theatrically out to seize Don Giovanni, he remembered.

"Wasn't he an authority on jade?" he whispered to his hostess.

"Who? What jade?"

"Carter Muir."

She looked startled. "Good heavens! I always thought the absentminded professor was a myth."

Carter Muir—jade—Cecile Dojoue. He put them all out of his mind and felt cautiously before the lights went up to be sure his white tie was straight. Mr. Constant had an unashamed fondness for white-tie occasions.

The next day disputed the spring of the day before. It dawned grudgingly and was cold, foggy, and dark. At four o'clock, without being quite sure of why or how he got there, Mr. Constant found himself ascending the rather steep steps leading to Ben Dojoue, Importer.

A heavy, smoke-laden fog hung over the Loop and had crept into the shadowy, crowded aisles of the long showroom, making the shaded lights seem diffuse and dim and masking the smile of a bronze Buddha at Mr. Constant's elbow.

Mr. Dojoue, clad in a morning coat with a pearl in his tie, recognized him at once and greeted him with a grotesque flash of white teeth in a face that looked yellow and ghostly in the dim light.

Contrary to Mr. Constant's expectations, there were not many people there. So few indeed had come to the auction that the room in which it was held—the small, paneled back room that Mr. Constant already knew—was not at all crowded. Besides Ben Dojoue and Cecile, who recognized him also but greeted him less affably, there were only four other people: two men who were obviously dealers, and a tall woman in furs and a youthful hat, sitting with a youngish man in the front rank of chairs.

There was an almost churchly air of silence and solemnity while Mr. Dojoue stood at the long table intently studying a list and Cecile ranged along the table a few small gray velvet jewelers' boxes. The other chairs remained vacant in what Mr. Constant would have considered somewhat discouraging emptiness, but this did not seem to trouble the importer.

The details of the auction were, of course, to become immediate newspaper history, although there was, as far as Mr. Constant saw, nothing out of the ordinary. He did smile when he saw the jade cup at one end of the table, placed carefully on a tray with the silver pitcher and a box that he recognized as being the innocuous container of soda. So Mr. Dojoue was going to perform his small trick of showmanship! Later Mr. Constant remembered that he did just then pause to speculate on the—Cecile's word again—childishness of it.

Then Mr. Dojoue cleared his throat. Cecile sat down with an account book and pen, and the auction began. Several pieces—an antique screen, two embroidered panels, and a peachblow vase (which caught Mr. Constant's eyes only because it was so beautiful)—were put up and immediately sold to the two dealers. Everything was quiet except for the tiny, steady scratching of Cecile's pen noting each item.

Voices were somewhat hushed, and only one of the dealers had the temerity, in that ecclesiastical atmosphere, to smoke a very vile-smelling pipe.

Once, the lady sitting in the front turned her head in a stately fashion and quite audibly sniffed. Mr. Constant, absently thinking again how very pretty Cecile was in spite of her businesslike absorption, saw that the woman was someone he vaguely recognized; a little while later when Mr. Dojoue took up the jade cup and began expounding on the virtues of jade, he remembered that she was Mrs. Carter Muir.

The dealers, seated just in front of Mr. Constant, had grown restive. "He always does this," one dealer whispered scornfully to the other. "Silly, I call it."

And the other nodded and replied: "Wish he'd get to the cabochon. I've an appointment in half an hour."

Mr. Constant stirred and wished so, too; it was chilly in the little room, and the air was somehow heavy and cold.

There was certainly a feeling of tension and of approaching climax, but that was because the importer had come at last to jade and to the high point of the sale, the cabochon. Quite suddenly, Mr. Constant realized that the scarcity of possible buyers emphasized the rarity and value of the cabochon. There were few who would buy or wish to possess the thing. He felt a quickening of the subtle, unacknowledged, and indefinable thing—deeper than curiosity, stronger than intellectual interest—that had brought him there.

He had, however, except for a slight feeling of tension, no premonition at all of what was to occur. Rather indulgently he watched Mr. Dojoue complete his preparation, lift the smooth green cup to his lips and drink the bubbling liquid, smiling so that all his white teeth were exposed. He did not see that smile become a fixed and ugly grin, because in the sudden, deathly silence he had glanced at Cecile. He did, however, hear that queer stertorous gasp for breath, and he looked back at the importer in time to see him clutch at the table and fall, still clutching, behind it.

Probably the importer was dead before he reached the floor.

Mr. Constant was on his feet. So was everyone else, as if jerked by a string, and someone—Mrs. Carter Muir, possibly—screamed.

Curiously there wasn't much confusion. One of the dealers swore and started forward, knocking over a chair as he did so; the young man with Mrs. Muir was kneeling on the other side of the table, and the dealer knelt beside him, his overcoat sweeping out along the floor. Cecile was bending over, too, looking chalk white and still, as if her face had frozen.

Mrs. Muir cried in a strange, high voice: "What's the matter? What's the matter? Is he ill?"

And the other dealer—a short, squat German with a broad, shrewd face—said oddly: "He's dead. And it's murder, or I'm a—"

"Murder!" screamed Mrs. Muir.

The other dealer looked up. "You'd better call the police, Fritz," he said.

Mr. Constant sat down again, feeling very sick. The dealer was right. It *was* murder. And he had a sudden, horrible conviction that he knew who had murdered Ben Dojoue.

After a moment, while they were talking and telephoning and milling in the kind of shocked confusion around Cecile, who had hidden her face in her hands and was moaning, he rose again, looking rather white, and went to the table. It was as if something outside himself compelled him to do what next he did. No one noticed him.

He returned to his place. *The absentminded professor to the life,* he thought with a pale and sickly attempt to smile, and hunted through his pockets until he found what he was looking for: a half-empty package of cigarettes.

"Then his business affairs," said the policeman, "were all in order?" He addressed Cecile Dojoue.

Mr. Constant sank lower into his topcoat and wished that

he had never seen or heard of Ben Dojoue, of jade, of an auction. He also wished they would remove the body. Any number of people had looked at it; it had been photographed and examined and consulted over. Well, then, why didn't they take it away?

And what more could they ask? For there had been a steady fire of questions; the names of those present at the auction had been taken, along with their individual descriptions of the auction and of Ben Dojoue's death. Also their fingrprints, their life histories, and their connection or lack of connection with the importer.

It was murder. A fat little man who proved to be the medical examiner had said so, after one sniff at the murdered man's still-grinning lips. Mr. Constant had been an unwilling witness to that. He thought again of those two hours of separate and collective grilling. He recalled the questions and the innumerable repetitions. Again and again, Cecile Dojoue had shown them exactly how she had placed the soda and cup and water on the tray.

Lieutenant Murphy would question her. "Then he shook the soda into the cup himself?"

"Yes. Everyone saw it."

"But *you* had placed the things on the table?"

"Certainly. But I did not poison him."

"Who else had access to the soda—or the cup?"

"No one," said Cecile, as she looked around the room. "No one, until I had removed it from the cupboard. After I placed it on the table I suppose anyone in the room could have put poison in the cup. Or in the soda. Everyone here knew my brother's trick with the cup."

"When did you place it on the table?"

"About three-thirty, I think."

"Was anyone in the room besides yourself at the time?"

Her silken black eyelashes had made a shadow on her cheeks for a moment. Then she said thoughtfully: "I'm not sure. I—"

Here Mrs. Carter Muir had interrupted suddenly. "I was the first to arrive. I and Mr. Walsh. This—girl—was arranging things on the table."

"Did you see the jade cup?"

"I—no. Yes. I don't know. I suppose so. But if I did I thought nothing of it. Anyway, Mr. Walsh can swear that I did not approach the table. Can't you, Jimmy?" She shot a demanding glance at the blond and rather shrinking young man who accompanied her. He—the bored young man of the opera, Mr. Constant had discovered, who now looked very upset and anything but bored—gave a rather convulsive start and opened his mouth, and Mrs. Muir repeated sharply, "*Can't* you?"

"Oh—ah. Yes. That is—" He brought himself up abruptly, gave the lieutenant a nervous glance, and added hurriedly, "that is, I don't think so."

"You know I didn't," said Mrs. Muir with force and turned upon Lieutenant Murphy. "I demand a lawyer. And I can swear that no one—no one, mind you—but that girl approached the table."

It was then that Murphy had spoken a mysterious word to the policeman, and immediately the suspects found themselves herded together and under guard in the auction room, while Murphy interviewed one after the other, secretly and relentlessly, in the small office.

He kept Cecile the longest. And one of the dealers—the fat German one, Fritz Shosteen—was heard also demanding a lawyer.

Lieutenant Murphy's interview with Mr. Constant was brief and unpleasant.

"You're a professor?"

"I teach, yes."

"Know anything about poisons?"

"No."

"Know he was going to drink out of that jade cup?"

"I—no. That is, yes—"

"Make up your mind."

"I thought it highly probable."

"Oh, so you'd seen him do it before today?"

"Yes," said Mr. Constant grimly. "Yesterday. I did not murder him, however."

"Remains to be seen," Lieutenant Murphy had said and

beckoned a policeman. "Get that other woman in here. That Mrs. Muir."

Mr. Constant sighed and with a start recalled himself to the immediate inquiry. Lieutenant Murphy had asked again about Ben Dojoue's business affairs, if they were all in order.

That was, of course, their method, thought Mr. Constant. First they got from each one a kind of résumé of what had happened and why one was there and what, if anything, one thought of the matter. Then they kept repeating themselves, asking questions and questions and questions, trying to catch one in a discrepancy.

They were beginning again, now, upon Mrs. Carter Muir, who was angry but very stately and dignified.

Cecile, sitting in one of the brocade-and-teakwood chairs at the end of the table, was like a cold white statue in a sleek satin dress. The two dealers appeared resigned to the delay; one—the thin, dark one—was chewing a cigar savagely, and the broad-faced German, Fritz Shosteen, was sitting beside him, an expression of woe and bewilderment on his face. Jimmy Walsh, still looking very upset, had retreated to a corner of the room where he gnawed his blond mustache and denied all knowledge of the importer, jade, and poison.

"Certainly I came to buy, if the price was right," Mrs. Carter Muir said in a hoity-toity voice.

"Anything in particular?" asked Lieutenant Murphy.

"No," said Mrs. Carter Muir, after a very slight pause. The girl, Cecile, lifted her heavy white eyelids and shot one liquid glance at Mrs. Muir.

"You sat within reach of the table?"

"I've already told you I sat right there!" Mrs. Muir pointed vigorously. "Near the table and near that silly box of soda, but I assure you that I did not put poison in the jade cup or poison in the soda, if that's what it is."

Lieutenant Murphy looked thoughtfully at the small tray. The box, the water remaining in the pitcher, and the jade cup had been carried away for analysis.

"But you had seen him drink out of the jade cup before?"

"Certainly," said Mrs Muir scornfully. "He always did that at an auction when he had some jade to sell. Everybody knew it. You can't suggest that because I knew he was likely to—to perpetrate this very silly little trick that I came prepared to spill some poison in the cup."

"I'll suggest," said Lieutenant Murphy, "what I please. And certainly," he added with truth, "somebody poisoned him. Professor Constant—"

Mr. Constant started guiltily. "Yes."

"This—er—" He made a gesture toward the body lying under the morning coat. "He didn't put a cigarette to his mouth? Or, say, a pencil?"

"No."

"What do you say, Mr. Shosteen?"

Fritz Shosteen crossed his fat legs. "Everything, Lieutenant Murphy, is exactly as we have told you. We were all sitting here watching Ben. We saw him drink the stuff and fall to the floor. Our stories agree, don't they?"

"Oh, yes," said Lieutenant Murphy rather unhappily. "Your stories agree, all right. That's just the trouble. Look here, Shosteen. Why did you come to the auction? I mean, was there anything in particular that brought you here? I know something of you; I know you deal in pretty valuable stuff."

"If you know something of me," said the big German imperturbably, "you know I am honest. Yes, there was something in particular. It was the cabochon."

It was the first time, to Mr. Constant's knowledge, the cabochon had been mentioned. His pulse gave a queer little jump. Odd, that instant of silence before Mrs. Muir spoke quickly and jerkily.

"A particularly fine cabochon was to be sold today," she said. "I expect we were all rather interested in it. But not to buy—at least, I didn't intend to buy. Really, Lieutenant, you aren't getting anywhere with all these questions. I should think that it would be perfectly clear, although I say it with regret, had only one person had the opportuniy to poison Mr. Dojoue.''

Cecile had risen slowly to her feet.

''You mean me,'' she said in a low voice that was thick with rage and a queer impatience. ''Me!'' she cried and turned to the lieutenant. ''Do you think I would dare even if I—if I had the wish to do so? Dare to hand him poison with my own hands before all of you—publicly. Dare to put poison in a cup that was in my care?'' She turned to Shosteen, flinging out her hands toward him. ''Tell them, Fritz,'' she cried. ''Tell them I wouldn't be such a fool.''

Shosteen eyed her rather sadly, but with a certain respect, and spoke to the lieutenant: ''No,'' he said shaking his head. ''Cecile is nobody's fool. I'll admit it looks bad for her, giving him the poison herself, so to speak—''

''I didn't! I didn't give him poison! I didn't know there was poison.''

But Shosteen went on heavily, as if he had not heard her. ''Mrs. Muir's right when she says Cecile had the opportunity to give it. But Cecile—well,'' he said with a certain frankness, ''if Cecile Dojoue undertook to murder anybody, she'd fix it so nobody ever knew she did it. She'd never do it openly, in front of everybody.''

But the lieutenant had doggedly avoided what might or might not have been an adroitly dangled red herring on Mrs. Muir's part.

''What about this cabochon?'' he said. ''What is it, and why is it so valuable, and where did he get it?''

The silent, pipe-smoking dealer moved uncomfortably and looked at Shosteen. Mrs. Muir bridled and spoke with a suggestion of taking the bull by the horns.

''The cabochon belonged to my—my husband,'' she said crisply. ''My late husband was a collector of jade. After his death I was obliged to dispose of some of his pieces, and the cabochon was one of them. It's a piece of gem jade—''

Cecile interrupted again. ''Mrs. Muir has not told you quite all,'' she said. ''Her husband owed my brother a large sum of money when he died. My brother was obliged to take over a number of pieces of jade; he did so to oblige Mrs.

Muir, who had no money to pay the debts. She was very reluctant to give him the cabochon and did not want him to sell it. In fact, he had wished to sell it a number of times, and each time she had come to him and begged him to wait, telling him that she would soon have the money to repurchase the stone. She never did have—unless, of course," said Cecile, "she has today. Have you, Mrs. Muir?"

Mrs. Muir's thin, sallow face had gone a soft mauve. "The girl is impertinent," she said. "Certainly I wished to buy back the stone. But I didn't poison Ben Dojoue to keep him from selling it. Who inherits his property? Not I, certainly."

"I inherit, I suppose," said Cecile calmly, "if there is anything to inherit when the debts are paid. But perhaps Lieutenant Murphy should know that the list price of the cabochon is only three thousand dollars. It seems to me that three thousand dollars would not be exactly a cause for murder."

"But that isn't—" Mrs. Muir burst out furiously and then shut her mouth so suddenly it clicked.

And the lieutenant said, looking at the small gray velvet boxes on the table, "Just where is this—cabochon?"

Mr. Constant sank a little lower into his topcoat. Surreptitiously he looked at his watch. Seven o'clock—good heavens! Otto was waiting out in front. He glanced around the room. Funny how people betrayed themselves. One had only to sit back and look and listen quietly to see such queer things.

Mrs. Muir was standing, craning her long neck forward, watching with her eyes shining like marbles and both hands pressed across her heart. The blond young man was standing, too, watching. Shosteen was a big, rigid bulk in his chair, with his blue eyes coldly observant in his broad, shrewd face, and the other dealer was as still as if he had stopped breathing, his dark eyes beady with excitement. Cecile's hands were flying now among the boxes, opening, closing, spilling out carved pieces of green and white, going like lightning through them again. She was panting a little, her face as white as the dead man's and her red mouth parted, showing a white gleam of teeth.

And something had happened at the table.

"It's gone, then," said Lieutenant Murphy with a throb of heavy satisfaction under his suddenly brisker manner. "It's gone and that's the motive. Well, we've got something at last. You are sure the cabochon was here before the auction began, Miss Dojoue?"

"Yes, yes," cried Cecile Dojoue. "Oh, yes, it was here. I put it here myself. I'm perfectly certain, Lieutenant. Someone, someone in this room has taken it. Someone has stolen—you are all thieves, all of you! Thieves and murderers and—"

Shosteen got heavily to his feet and went over to Cecile, putting his hand on her shoulder. "Now, now, Cecile," he said, "Don't say something you'll regret. We know the cabochon was here. I saw it myself. It was in that box."

"Yes, yes," cried Cecile, showing him the empty, square velvet box. "It was here."

"The girl took it," said Mrs. Muir suddenly, hoarsely. "The girl—"

"I," cried Cecile bitterly, and pushed her lovely hands through her soft black hair. "Oh, I wouldn't be such a fool!"

It was just then that someone knocked loudly at the door and called out, "Lieutenant, the men are here with the stretcher. And the report from the laboratory's come."

There began a strange and painful little interlude, for which Mr. Constant should have been grateful, as he was very worried and did not at all know what to do. He had not, he realized with the most poignant feelings of alarm, thought quite far enough. Knowing himself innocent, he had been too ready to feel that the police would immediately recognize his innocence. He cursed himself inwardly and listened to the report.

It was brief enough. There was no poison in the box of powder, which actually proved to be soda and nothing else. No poison in the water.

"And the cup?" said Lieutenant Murphy.

"Traces of nicotine," said the policeman, reading from a paper in his hand. "That's all they've found yet, sir. That and a lot of soda. Shall we take the body now, sir?"

An ugly little silence fell on the room as the two men, carrying a curious basketlike conveyance between them, advanced. There was the sound of heavy feet, muffled by the thickness of the rug. Then the door closed, and Lieutenant Murphy spoke again, in a new voice. He looked all at once powerful, quite certain of himself and of the power he represented.

"Murder has been done here," he said. "And I'm going to find out which one of you killed him. And the first thing I'm going to do is to search you. O'Brien, send for a police matron. Mawson, take these people into that little office and keep them under close guard. We'll search 'em after we've searched this room. I'll take the keys, miss. Thank you. All right, Mawson."

Mr. Constant reluctantly followed the others into the office, where he lighted a cigarette, let the crumpled package drop unobtrusively to the floor, and sought a quiet corner. He was very troubled.

The minute search of the auction room was a lengthy business, and a disappointing one. The search of the suspects immediately followed. The police were swift, thorough, and businesslike.

After being searched, Mr. Constant went back through the dingy passage leading from the storerooms and into the office. Another policeman looked in and said, "Oh, it's you," and vanished again. No one was in the office now; both doors were closed. Mr. Constant thought, *What now?* His hands had reached out for the discarded package of cigarettes.

When the door opened, Mrs. Muir surged into the room and cried stormily, "Indecent, I call it! Outrageous! They'll hear from—" She perceived him and stopped. "Oh—" she said.

Mr. Constant's fingers closed on the crumbled package. He rose calmly and faced her.

"Oh," said Mrs. Muir again softly, and came toward

him, her glittering eyes on the package in his hand. "You have the cabochon." She came quite close to him, her face thrust forward, her mouth working a little. Then she said in the thinnest, coldest of whispers, "How much do you want for it?"

He muffed it a little there. He faltered and said, "How much—"

"I'll give you anything for it. Anything I've got. It's not much—not now—but I'll pay. I'll pay. I—"

"I know," said Mr. Constant wearily. "It was in the book."

"The—book—"

"The book your husband wrote about jade. He dedicated it to you. He said—"

"I know what he said."

"He said, 'To my wife,'" quoted Mr. Constant softly, "'who not only loves jade but worships it.'"

"Oh. Yes, of course. Yes—it's more than that, really. You see, it brings me health. It has always done so. That piece more than any other. Health and youth and—oh, I know you think it is superstition. Perhaps it is. Perhaps it was superstition that made it the Dowager Empress's favorite stone—perhaps it was superstition that kept her strong and young. That made her live—" The woman whispered, suddenly hoarse and gasping for breath, "That made her live years and years beyond her allotted time.

"If I could only make you see—if I could only make you understand. I'm ill, I'm growing old. And I . . . I'm in love—in love with a younger man. A man who—oh, you don't know what I am suffering. I must have that cabochon. I tell you. I—" Her fierce, hot strength went suddenly, and she put out both hands and clutched at Mr. Constant. "I must have it."

"Hush, there's someone at the door."

"Mrs. Muir, please," said the policeman named O'Brien. "The lieutenant wants you."

She went, giving Mr. Constant a strange, pleading look. He touched his face with his handerchief and looked at the crumpled, half-empty package of cigarettes in his other hand. He wondered suddenly if he could escape; but even if he managed to get past the police on guard, they knew who he was, where to find him. And besides, there were police all over the place. There was no possible chance—the door opened suddenly again and Cecile Dojoue entered.

"Mr. Constant," she said. "She put her hand to her forehead and swayed a little. He went forward.

"You'd better sit down, Miss Dojoue," he said. "Here's a chair—" Her hand on his own was deliciously soft and sweet. "Can I—is there anything—"

"You are so good. If I could have a glass of water. . . ."

"I'll ask a policeman."

Her eyelids fluttered. "Oh, no," she said. "I'm . . . quite all right." She would not sit down. Instead, she freed herself and went to the flat-topped desk and stood there thoughtfully.

Mr. Constant took a long breath and spoke gently, "I have the cabochon, you know."

For the first time her eyes blazed full upon him. "You!"

"Yes," said Mr. Constant. "I have it. Why did you—"

Her lovely white hands made a motion or two below the desk and came suddenly into view. "Put up your hands," said Cecile Dojoue, and Mr. Constant looked into a very large, very efficient revolver. "Put up your hands," said Cecile, still in the softest, silkiest of tones. "But first give me the cabochon."

Mr. Constant put up his hands.

"You killed him?" he said.

"Does it matter? *You* cannot accuse me. I didn't—"

"Oh, yes, I know you killed him," said Mr. Constant softly. "I was watching you, you see. You'd been writing steadily, and all at once, when he lifted the cup to his lips, it was very still, while you stopped writing to listen. You would not look. You listened—because you expected it. I saw you."

"Oh, what do I care what you say! I killed him. Why not? He was about to sell it. He sold everything; he had no joy in the possession of a perfect thing. Such a cabochon has never been known before; there will never be another. It is—oh, this is nothing to you. It's nothing to you that I hated him. Give the ring to me.''

"Aren't you afraid I'll tell what you've just admitted?''

"No one else heard it. My word is as good as yours. No one would ever believe that I would do it so openly. There were a hundred hidden ways, but none so certain to acquit me as the bold way. There is no proof. I was very careful about getting the poison. No one saw me put it in the cup. And no jury would believe I would place myself in such obvious danger.'' She was whispering rapidly but not nervously; the revolver was remarkably steady and purposeful.

"I shall tell them you had the ring, that I made you give it up to me. I am now its rightful owner. I'll tell them you murdered Ben. The absentminded professor,'' the girl said mockingly and added with the swift venom of a snake, "I'm going to count; on the third count I shoot. And I'm a good marksman. So you see why I'm not afraid of your telling—''

Something beyond her satin shoulder was moving stealthily; it was the door into the showroom, and there was a face in the slowly widening aperture.

"Duck—quick—'' cried Mr. Constant.

The lights went out.

Mr. Constant was never sure just what happened next. There were shouts and the heavy discharges of a revolver, again and again in that small room; there were pounding, running feet and thunderous commotion; there was the smell of gunpowder and a stinging, sharp pain in his shoulder. After what seemed a long time, somebody turned on the lights again, and Mr. Constant found himself on the floor, with Otto bending anxiously above him and Lieutenant Murphy shaking Otto's shoulder.

"Oh, go to hell,'' said Otto. "Want me to slug anybody, Mr. Constant?''

"No,'' said Mr. Constant weakly and sat up. "The cabochon, Lieutenant Murphy, is in this cigarette package. I took it on the principle of stirring up muddy waters. It was the only thing I could think of that might have or more than its money value. The only thing that might furnish a motive for murder. Its disappearance, then, would be unexpected to the murderer. It might be—only the spoke in the machinery, the thing that wasn't planned. I—I happened to be watching her, you see, when he put the cup to his lips. And that look of expectancy, of waiting—oh, I knew. It was unmistakable. But that was not proof."

"Urrgh," observed Lieutenant Murphy, who coughed and said kindly, "Suppose you tell me all about it."

Mr. Constant did so briefly, but with neatness. "You see," he concluded apologetically, "I spent the morning reading about jade. The tradition, the superstition—the rarity of so beautiful a stone and its meaning to a lover of jade."

Otto interrupted him without compunction. "He's beginning to talk like a professor," he said to Lieutenant Murphy with disapproval. "And he's got a bullet scratch—a deep one. I'm going to take him home."

Three hours later, Otto turned on a small night-light in Mr. Constant's bedroom, put a tray holding hot milk and crackers on the bedside table, and looked at Mr. Constant truculently.

"You ought've had me with you," he said with deep annoyance. "You're all right, Doc, when it comes to books and things, but there's times when a good fast right comes in handy. Especially," he added, "with women. And revolvers."

Mr. Constant opened his eyes, met Otto's stern gaze, and closed them again. "Yes, Otto," he said, and meant it.

*My affection for Mr. Wickwire is quite as firm*
*and remarkable as his affection for his dog.*
*But also I firmly like the careful*
*administration of banks that do their best*
*to protect depositors, and succeed.*

❏

# The Blonde from Sumatra

"It was a terrible experience," she said. "There we were in the middle of Sumatra. Daisy had had some vague sort of fever, but she seemed better and she had chartered a plane, so we took off. We ran into bad weather and there was a tiny landing field near a dreadful guesthouse. We stopped there, and she had a heart attack." She took a second helping of lemon pie and said, "I didn't know banks had such good cooks."

My name is James Wickwire; I am a senior vice president of the bank that had administered Daisy Fortescue Bell's affairs during her lifetime. I am a bachelor. Flora Fortescue (Daisy's cousin), Cal Vickers (Daisy's lawyer), and I were lunching in one of the small dining rooms at the bank. Flora had arrived from Manila the previous day. She had cabled me at once of Daisy's death, but when she told me of Daisy's will, I had suggested inviting Cal Vickers to lunch, too—and wished I hadn't when I met Flora. She was an utterly charming woman.

I said, "And did Daisy—that is, Mrs. Bell—die immediately?"

"No. But that was when she made the will leaving everything to me. Then she felt better and went to sleep, and she died very quietly during the night. The doctor didn't get there until the next afternoon. He made all the arrangements.''

I addressed Cal Vickers. "This will, then, cancels all previous wills?''

Flora replied, "Daisy never made another will. She was superstitious about it, I think.''

The slender, ivory-handled cane she carried slid to the floor, and Cal Vickers nearly broke his neck picking it up. I said, "But surely, Vickers, you advised her to make some sort of will.''

He tore his fascinated gaze from Flora and drew himself up pompously; his white hair, noble profile, and gallant manner were all very Kentucky colonel in effect. "Daisy came to me only once and about an entirely different matter. In fact, she intended divorcing her husband, and since much of her real estate is in California, there was some question of the community property law of which her husband intended to take full advantage. They were reconciled, however, and took a trip to Africa—''

Flora nodded. "I went, too. It was sad. Her husband died very suddenly.''

"That's right,'' Cal Vickers said. "It was a heart attack. On safari.''

It struck me that the Bells chose peculiar places in which to die. Cal Vickers's blue eyes were liquid and hazy. "But I remember Daisy. Dark, thin woman,'' he said with distaste. "Hard look in her eyes—but charming, very charming,'' he added quickly. "You knew her, Wickwire?''

"As a matter of fact, I never met her. I inherited her account from my predecessor. I had correspondence with her, of course.'' As I remembered them, her terse letters did not suggest charm.

Flora said, "Will it take long to have the will probated?''

"Now, now, we lawyers have to earn our living, you know.'' Cal Vickers almost chortled.

Flora smiled and lowered her eyelashes in a delightful way.

I said, "There'll be no complication about the will?''

"Oh, no,'' Colonel Cal said fruitily, watching Flora's

eyelashes. "It's a holograph will, of course, in Daisy's writing, but perfectly clear and legal. No other heirs to dispute it."

Flora sighed gently. "We were quite alone in the world, Daisy and I. She had inherited all that money, and I had none; but I lived with her. Since her husband died we have traveled almost constantly."

Ye olde Kentucky colonel gave a chivalrous start. "See here, Wickwire, if this little lady needs money, surely the bank can advance it."

"Oh, no," Flora said. "Daisy was very generous. There's no hurry about the will."

Cal Vickers beamed. "My dear Miss Fortescue—or may I say Miss Flora—just leave it all to me."

We both escorted her to a side entrance, where a car was waiting for her—each of us offering an arm, for she walked with a pronounced limp; I was on her right hand in which she carried her cane, so she took the colonel's arm, and it was something to see Cal Vickers strut across the sidewalk, his chest out and Flora on his arm.

"Ah," he sighed, as the traffic swallowed up Flora and the car, "a truly womanly woman. I'm a bachelor myself," he added, not too obliquely.

"So am I," I said, at which he turned abruptly away, bumped into a hydrant and said, "Oh, I beg your pardon, madam. I do indeed—" He got out his spectacles, put them on, checked himself in the middle of a bow, and looked at his watch. "Afraid I have to run along—phone call to make . . . See you later, Wickwire."

He departed with haste. I returned to my office and kept an eye on my own watch. When I thought Flora had time to reach her hotel, I telephoned and invited her to dinner—beating Cal Vickers, I was sure, by a eyelash. Indeed, the other telephone in her suite rang while I was talking to her.

But after I had put down the telephone, Flora lingered in my office as intangibly and provocatively as her perfume, which had mysteriously suggested a rose garden in June.

Or possibly in October, when roses are sweetest, for she was not young. She was also extremely plump; she was indeed a Rubens woman on a small scale, all curves and dimples. She had golden hair and features whose fine carving was softened by pink-and-white flesh. She was not beautiful. Yet she had that ineluctable quality of charm that cannot be defined and cannot be learned. I was overcome by a desire to do everything I could for her. So I got out the Daisy Fortescue Bell file and sent for the microfilms concerning her account. These microfilms are in fact photographs that record the daily business of the bank and are sent daily to storage (at some distance from the city in the event of emergency) and are kept indefinitely.

In short, I did everything possible to rival Cal Vickers as a *parfait gentil* knight—in this instance, to facilitate the will probate.

"There'll be a large inheritance tax, I expect," Flora said that night at dinner. She was wearing one of the pink roses I had sent her. There were soft lights, soft music, and excellent wines.

"I'm afraid so. Daisy was a very rich woman."

She said softly, "It's cheap at the price—" At least it sounded like that, but the music blurred her words.

"You said—I'm sorry. The music—"

"I said it's such a surprise," she smiled and sang softly with the music something about dancing all night, which struck me as an excellent idea, but Flora didn't dance. "I injured my right knee—oh, long ago, riding," she said wistfully. "But I love the music—and New York. I'm sorry I'm going to France in a few days."

Disappointment was like a pang. "But surely you'll want to see some of your old friends."

"No. Daisy and I have been away so long that I have lost touch. Besides,"—she adjusted her rose with a lingering, plump white hand—"sometimes new friends are best. Don't you think so, Jim?"

Very few women have ever called me Jim. After I deposited her at her hotel, I walked home, feeling twenty years old.

When I reached my house, its lighted windows were oddly lacking in welcome. Happy, my dog (who has been wickedly referred to as the Hound of the Wickwires) sprang upon me with customary zeal, which I have thus far survived only by resorting to football tactics, developed far too long ago—but even that failed to convey a welcome. There was something missing. Perhaps, in truth, a bachelor's life was not a happy one.

Yet during the night a faint uneasiness came from somewhere and nagged at my banker's sense. Since I could not pin it down, I dismissed it.

The next morning, however, when Daisy's microfilms arrived, I spent some time looking at them—a very long time, indeed, since the records for over fifteen years back had been sent. In the end I went down to the rank of tellers' cages and eventually found Miss Sharp, who did not remember Daisy but did remember Flora. "Blond hair? Walks with a limp? I didn't like her," Miss Sharp said surprisingly.

*"Why not?"*

Miss Sharp didn't know. I made one regrettable but necessary request, returned to my office, and very thoughtfully telephoned to Flora and then to Cal Vickers, asking them to come to my office.

Cal Vickers said, "I'll stop at Flora's hotel and bring the little lady."

I had barely concluded a conversation with the head of our safe deposit department—with a result that was satisfactory in one way but very lowering to my spirits in another— when Colonel Cal arrived with the lady on his arm. She was wearing another of my roses amid sables on her trim suit jacket.

I braced myself. "I've found some papers that I'd like you to put in your safe deposit box immediately," I said to Flora. "I asked Vickers to come as your lawyer, so he can witness the transfer. We'll go down to the safe deposit department at once."

Flora's long eyelashes touched her pink cheeks. "I'm afraid I've lost the key. Stupid of me. But I'll just take the papers with me—" She broke off as Miss Sharp came into my office, put some papers on my desk, and, at the door as she was leaving, made a slight negative motion of her head.

Cal Vickers blustered, "Why, there's nothing that has to

go into Miss Flora's safe deposit box this minute, Wickwire! Keep them in your own safe.''

I sighed. The magic fragrance of roses strangely vanished. I said, ''There's another question—only a formality—but we have to have someone identify Miss Fortescue. Some old friend, or perhaps someone here in the bank.''

Cal Vickers's eyes flashed with angry chivalry. ''This is outrageous! Of course, she's Miss Flora. Why—why—'' he spluttered, ''she showed me her passport—''

I said to the lady, ''What did Flora have that you had to have?''

Her eyes blazed up at me, then, hard and cold as steel. Her soft pink-and-white complexion retreated, leaving her features ruthless and deadly. Cal Vickers stared, got out his spectacles, put them on with a shaking hand, stared again, and shouted, ''*Good Heavens! You are Daisy!*''

I had to end it. ''Daisy, you were generous with Flora— too generous—beginning ten years ago with a check for twenty thousand dollars at about the time of your husband's death. Since then you have continued your remarkable generosity with even larger checks. I suggest that Flora was blackmailing you. I suggest that there is something in her safe deposit box, which is here in this bank, that is danger-ous to you. I submit that you had no intention of ever opening it. Access to Flora's box is too dangerous—forging Flora's name, running the risk of some official remembering Flora too well. It was no risk with Vickers, who is too vain to wear his spectacles. It was no risk with me—I had never met Daisy. But Miss Sharp, who was in here a moment ago, informed me that you are not Flora.'' Daisy's face was as still as marble; her eyes blazed murderously. I said, ''Did you murder your husband? And did Flora know it?''

I was then thankful to Cal Vickers; his face was purple, but his behavior as a lawyer and a citizen was exemplary. He got Daisy out of my office, and what he did then I didn't know and didn't want to know.

He came to see me that night, however. Happy playfully nipped his calf, but like a gentleman and an old Kentucky colonel, he ignored the nip. ''How did you know?''

"She said her right knee had been injured—and carried her cane in her right hand, which was the wrong hand. The injury was supposed to be of long standing; any orthopedic doctor would have taught her to carry the cane in her left hand."

"That couldn't have been all!"

"She was a little too unconcerned about the money—it was as if she had had it all her life, as indeed she had. She was leaving for France and did not propose to see any of her old friends—who would have recognized her. We may presume a family resemblance between the cousins. Her disguise was simple. She changed her dark hair to gold and—"

"And ate herself fat!" he cried, his chivalry slipping. "It must have taken months. Or perhaps not so long. Did you see the way she tucked into that second piece of pie?"

"She also said the inheritance tax was cheap at the price. I knew that it was, after I had looked at the microfilms of her checks."

He mopped his red forehead. "The police say that her husband might have been smothered. It could pass for a heart attack if the doctor didn't see him for some time, when the—what do they call it?—cyanosis had subsided. I suppose she murdered Flora the same way. It'll be hard to prove."

"Why would she pose as Flora at a cost of a terrific inheritance tax if she hadn't murdered Flora?"

He had no answer to that. He rose to leave. At the steps he sighed, muttered, "So charming," and waddled away.

So charming—otherwise I doubt if I'd have exerted myself so thoroughly and fatally in her behalf.

Happy took advantage of my wistful reverie and knocked me down the steps by way of a gentle hint for a walk. He then strolled away into the darkness, and I pursued him. It would be hard to lose Happy; indeed, at first glance nobody in his senses could be induced to accept him as a gift. But to me, just then, he was far more beautiful than, say, a rose garden.

*This story belongs to Sarah Keate, who introduced me to writing. She has a sense of humor that pleased me, and I must also quote from the well-loved and well-remembered poet Ogden Nash, who gave me a copy of his first book and inscribed it thus: "For Mignon G. Eberhart, because I'd rather have created Sarah Keate than own a diamond paraquet."*

❑

# The Old Man's Diamond

"If anything happens to me on this trip," he said with the greatest effect of casualness, "just take this thing to my daughter in Rome, will you?"

I said, "Will you take this capsule, please?" and popped it into his mouth, put a glass of water in his hand, and closed the red plush case all in one motion. I felt much easier, which was curious, the instant the case was closed and the blaze of the large, pear-shaped unset diamond, alive and wickedly sentient, was shut inside the worn red plush.

It was that very night, while we were going through the swells and practically everybody on board was seasick, that someone entered the cabin and murdered Arthur Sidney.

*The* Arthur Sidney.

I am Sarah Keate, a registered nurse and, heaven knows, no detective. No detective—though I must admit that, on occasion, I have been persuaded to act in a kind of observatory capacity.

Regarding the case in point, however, I had all but leaped at the chance to take Arthur Sidney from New York to Cherbourg. It is the very essence of irony to recall that alacrity with which I accepted the case; he was ill but not seriously so, and my only qualm had to do with storms at

96

sea. It was to be my first trip to sea. It came very near to being my last.

But I did not know that then. And since we had barely got under way, I still felt tranquil. I just did not, however, like the notion of a jewel of such value—and, incidentally, of rather bloody history—roaming at large in my patient's stateroom. So, after giving him a sedative and settling him comfortably for the night, I quietly extracted the diamond from the case, returned the case to its place in a small bag, relocked the bag, and restored the key, all without my patient being the wiser. He was, in point of fact, gargling in the bathroom at that moment. I remained with him until he fell into a calm and heavy sleep; then I withdrew, leaving a small light and locking the door of the stateroom after me. If he roused and wanted anything, he had only to ring for the steward, who would call me.

I remember it all very clearly—even that I hesitated outside the door thinking that the carafe of water within reach of his hand was empty, and I had forgotten to refill it. I did not return, however, for I didn't wish to rouse him and thus undo the effect of the sedative, and I felt sure he would not rouse of his own volition. After all, if he wanted a drink, he had only to get it; he was quite able to do so.

It was only because I knew that he had money and various valuables with him that I locked the door. I knew, of course, something of the diamond; he had talked about it at length, and it was, in fact, the reason for my presence.

Once in my own stateroom I locked that door, too, and sat down to look at the diamond that blazed so incongruously from the depths of my white linen pocket. It was uncannily alive; for a queer instant it seemed to me I was holding a bit of crystallized life in my hand and was on the verge of making some tremendous discovery about it—it was the strangest feeling, not quite recognition and not exactly familiarity, but a little of both. I was full of excited suspense, as if the secret of all this whirling about through space was about to be disclosed to me.

Then it was gone, and I was only myself again—sitting

on the edge of a berth that was, disconcertingly, only a bed and not at all nautical—holding a jewel that blazed white fire and was worth thousands of dollars. And must be more carefully guarded than my patient seemed disposed to guard it. It was, I knew, insured. And it had been for years in the vault at his bank. And he was now taking it, quite casually, to his daughter, who was about to be married in Rome. It was to be her wedding present. The insurance company had requested that a detective travel with him, and he had needed a nurse. So the upshot was that I was there in a chameleonlike role.

I looked at the glittering gem and realized that I'd undertaken a rather heavy responsibility. I must guard the stone very carefully; there must be no chance of my turning up the next morning with no diamond. I looked around the stateroom thoughtfully. Beds, chairs, drawers—it was exactly like any hotel room and very disappointing. Even the porthole, which I had hopefully expected to be round with great screws to hold it tight when waves dashed upon it, had proved to be only a window with a curtain over it. It was about then that I rose in some haste and pulled the curtain snugly across it. There was a desk just outside. Could anyone have seen me? I studied the angle of my position relative to that of the window and decided that no one could have seen the jewel while I had examined it.

The trivial incident, however, roused me to the need for action. I considered and rejected any number of places about the room and finally wrapped it in a handkerchief, tied it securely, and put it, I suppose, in the worst possible place—under my pillow. But even supposing anyone knew of the diamond's presence on this boat (the insurance company had warned us someone might know: "Jewel thieves," they had said dryly, "have sources of information"), the thief would have no reason to suspect that the jewel was momentarily in my possession, especially since Arthur Sidney himself did not know it. *The thief,* I thought, and smiled. I amended the description to *the problematical thief.* Certainly we had had no reason actually to suspect there was one. I went to sleep calmly enough.

Once in the night I wakened to a strange and not at all pleasant feeling of insecurity. I turned on the light. After a moment of perplexity I noticed the curtains against the window swinging slightly, and strangely enough, the sight gave me a kind of vertigo.

*Ha,* I thought wisely, *we are leaving the land.* The salt flavor of the phrase rather pleased me, but the vertigo grew stronger, and I finally rose and took a capsule with which the more experienced Arthur Sidney had provided me. Indeed, I caught another glimpse of the swaying curtain and took two more capsules.

It was due, I suppose, to that remedy for seasickness that I slept late the next morning, awoke slowly, and was only stupidly and gradually aware of a commotion going on in the passage outside. It was the word *murder*—uttered loudly and in a tone of horrified incredulity that was quickly and vigorously hushed—that fully roused me.

Murder... what were they talking of? What had happened...? What were those voices? The diamond—my patient—*my patient*!

I was wide awake, snatching at clothes, staggering a bit as the floor seemed to move under me. The diamond was still under my pillow, and I snatched at it, hesitated, slipped it into the coil of my rather abundant hair, and anchored it securely with a hairpin. Then I was at the door, opening it; I was in the passage surrounded by uniforms.

Suddenly a man in a white uniform was at my side, calling me by name. And then I was through the subdued confusion in the passage and was in my patient's stateroom, with the door closed and the ship's doctor gripping my elbow. Several other men in authoritative uniforms were there, too. They were talking, asking me short, sharp questions. But I pulled away from the doctor's hand and went to the bed and pulled down the sheet that covered my patient.

I remember altogether too well what I saw. But there was a kind of misty hiatus before I found myself in a chair, facing away from the bed, with the sharp stinging of ammonia in my nostrils and the doctor's voice questioning me.

There was little I could tell them. I had left my patient sleeping at about eleven o'clock the previous night. I had locked the door because he had various valuables with him and I didn't care to rouse him to see to the lock himself. No, I had heard nothing during the night. Yes, I had given my patient a mild sedative; mild but sufficient to induce heavy slumber. No, I knew nothing of any enemy.

"But do you understand why the entire stateroom has been so violently ransacked?" It was the captain himself speaking.

I glanced about me. *Violently* and *ransacked* were exactly the words to use. I had never seen such an utter and complete abandonment of all order. Drawers were pulled out, bags emptied, the one trunk open with its contents flung this way and that. It was vehemently obvious that the place had been swiftly and thoroughly and, finally, frantically searched. Even the life preserver was cut and shredded with a knife.

"Quite evidently," the captain was saying in a taut, swift voice, "whoever murdered Mr. Sidney was after something, something of value—something of so great a value that he would commit murder in order to gain possession of it. Can you tell us, Miss Keate, what Mr. Sidney carried with him of so great a value? You mentioned things of value just now. What, exactly, did you refer to?"

I hesitated. Murder somehow always remains an inconceivable thing. It had not entered our calculations in the faintest degree. Theft, yes. But not murder.

My patient had been sick, drugged, defenseless. A tired, amiable old man taking his daughter a wedding present. And that wedding present had been of great value. And the thief had known of it and had followed us and had somehow entered that stateroom—after all, a locked door is not much of a barrier—and had sought through every square inch of space for the diamond. (I had no doubt from the first that it was the diamond.) During that search Arthur Sidney had awakened. Had awakened only to be forever silenced.

I said, "How was he killed?"

The doctor's face quickened with a kind of interest.

"With the water carafe. Curious, isn't it? Want to look again, Miss Keate? It fractured his skull. See—" He motioned, and I forced myself to look. "See, there's the broken bottle—it was thick and full of water. It made a formidable if impromptu weapon. The thief was, we think, surprised—possibly meant only to stun the old man."

I looked long. There was growing within me a slow, deep fire of anger. I turned, answering the captain's question swiftly. I knew now what to say and that I must keep my own knowledge of the diamond a secret.

"He had quite a sum of money," I said. "Also some traveler's checks and a letter of credit. He had, too, in the trunk a few jewels of his own; I believe there was a ring or two, some pearl studs. Not much. Are there fingerprints on the pieces of glass?"

There were, it developed, no fingerprints.

And neither were there, at the end of a long and inexpressibly tiring and difficult morning, any clues to the murderer.

An exhaustive survey proved that, as near as I could recall them, neither my patient's jewels nor money had been stolen. Everything, despite the search, was intact. That knowledge complicated matters; a motive would have made the task easier, but I dared not supply the motive.

Actually, indeed, grueling though the queerly telescoped inquiry was, there was very little I could do. Very little anyone could do on that small floating city. There were no police, there was no paraphernalia of crime detection, there were no witnesses.

There was an exhaustive inquiry, but no one had seen anything that by the remotest chance could be suspicious. The passenger lists were studied and our neighbors investigated fruitlessly. The stateroom next to mine was occupied by a widow from the South who babbled in a horrified, high-pitched voice and all but overflowed with feminine charm in the presence of the captain—who was certainly not bad to look at. It took only a moment or two to convince me, and I think the others, that she could be by no possible means other than what she purported to be. It was all too evident that her brain power, not perhaps of the strongest, was concerned with one thing only, and that, at base, was biological. The captain sighed when she was permitted to flutter from the room and turned to the man who had the stateroom beyond that occupied by my patient. He, too, was from the South—New Orleans, he said. His name was Powers. He was a slender, dark man with a yellow face; he was lame and walked with a crutch and a cane and had a copy of *Tristram Shandy* in the pocket of his very new and well-cut tweed coat. He had heard nothing, seen nothing, knew of nothing that could help us.

"After all," said the captain in a disgruntled way to the purser when the man Powers had gone, "we can't get anywhere this way. Practically anybody on the ship could have got to Sidney's stateroom, and with luck, unobserved."

The purser nodded gloomily, and the doctor said:

"It's time for lunch. Have you sent all the necessary cables, Miss—er—Keate?"

I nodded. I had told them everything I knew of Arthur Sidney and his journey. Everything, that is, except the presence of the diamond and my own role of nurse cum detective. I don't think that I made, even inwardly, any resolution. I knew only that my patient had been murdered and that I had the diamond for which I had no doubt he had been killed. And I knew that he had asked me to take that diamond to his daughter. "If anything happens to me on this trip . . ." he had said. Prophetically? A sick, tired old man. The anger deep within me did not subside; instead, it grew stronger and more implacable. He had needed me, and I had not been there; he was without defense, and there had been no one to help him.

Before that, during various experiences that (by way of my duty and a kind of loose *entente cordiale* with the forces of law and order) have been quite literally thrust upon me, I had been, except for the occasional and harrowing moments of danger to myself, something of an observer. A spectator more than a principal. Now, all at once, I was a participant. It was neither duty nor the lure of adventure that motivated me. It was perhaps something baser but far more compelling, and very deep and personal.

I knew, too, that my own life was none too secure so long as I carried the diamond. I must not tell of the diamond; I must permit no one to know even that the jewel was on board ship. Above all, I must give no hint by action or attitude of my knowledge.

After lunch the inquiry was resumed, but so far as I knew, it came to nothing. I was not summoned by the captain again—somewhat, I think, to the disappointment of my coquettish neighbor, who attached herself to me like a limpet directly after lunch and refused to leave me, even though, in an effort to conquer a tendency toward nausea, I walked furiously around and around the promenade deck. To this day I remember the way she stopped babbling and turned faintly green around her powdered nose every time we reached and were obliged to negotiate the bow of the ship—a portion of the vessel that always seems to me to have a peculiar and very lively behavior of its own, separate and distinct from the rest of the ship.

Not built for walking, she was, I believe, failing when Mr. Powers joined us, walking slowly but steadily and using his cane and crutch so dexterously that one was scarcely conscious of his lameness. Mrs. Bash (believe it or not, that was her name: Antoinette Bash) brightened at once and, owing to our more deliberate pace, was able to keep up for another half-hour, at the end of which tea appeared, and we settled in deck chairs, Mr. Powers between us. The events of the morning had brought us more than casually together, and I was glad enough of their company. Somehow, that day, I did not like being alone.

And I was, at every instant, conscious of my hair. Or, more accurately, of the diamond. Wrapped as it was in a scrap of handkerchief with the ends tied securely and a hairpin thrust through them, it made a very small roll and was not, I was sure, perceptible in the thick coils of my hair and under the close hat I wore all day. But still I was conscious of it and uneasy.

I have never known why I was told so little of the inquiry that the ship's officers conducted; possibly they felt that I knew nothing of it and could be of no assistance. For my own part, I was only too glad to be let alone to follow my own path, dangerous though it proved to be.

I have never known exactly what measures they took to ensure silence regarding the fact that a murder had been committed on board that ship. People knew that Arthur Sidney was dead and that I had been his nurse; that much I gathered from incidental remarks let drop as the time at sea passed and various fellow passengers began to say good morning and to comment about the weather. Mrs. Bash, however, knew it was murder and so did Mr. Powers. So did the stewardess who was nervous and tried to talk of it to me but had nothing of value to say. So, too, did the various stewards and boys belonging to the particular part of B deck in which Arthur Sidney's (and my own) stateroom was located. It had been one of them, indeed, who had cried "Murder" in the passage and been immediately hushed. And I daresay there were others who knew besides those few and the ship's officers. But it speaks well, almost alarmingly well indeed, for the crew's discipline that for the most part the passengers remained unaware of the murder. I wondered fleetingly what and how many secrets are kept by ships at sea.

There was, of course, no particular need to warn the other passengers, for they were not apt to be in danger. From the first it was evident that the focus was Arthur Sidney.

Arthur Sidney and the diamond. And I had the diamond.

That night, just before the dressing gong sounded along the corridors, the captain sent me an urgent message by way of the ship's doctor, who came himself to deliver it and stood there in the corridor with his handsome white uniform outlined against the dark, closed door of the stateroom in which Arthur Sidney had been murdered. The message was strong—almost a peremptory request that I say nothing of the fact that my patient had been murdered. I repressed a desire to say that it was rather late in the day to take such measures and that if I had wanted to talk, the whole ship would have known of it by then; but I contented myself by remarking that so far as I was concerned, the captain was entirely in charge of the investigation.

Dr. Tammy opened his eyes a bit at that, and I added hurriedly that I had had an answer to my cable to his daughter and that she would meet the boat train in Paris. Dr. Tammy then departed, and I went to my stateroom and looked into the wardrobe and bathroom before I locked the door and began to consider some safe disposal of the diamond.

I had not yet discovered it when the dinner gong rang, and half an hour later when I arrived at my table in the dining room, the diamond was still hidden in my hair.

The diamond worried me—worried me so much that, fortunately, perhaps it somewhat distracted me from the horror and ugliness of the situation in which I found myself. After all, it was no good thinking that I might have prevented it. My immediate and pressing problem was the care of that diamond and my own safety. And there was something else I wanted to do.

My eyes roved over the great room: tables, soft lights, waiters coming and going swiftly and quietly; a murmur of voices alternating pleasantly with the lilt of violin strings and piano; the scents of food, of flowers; the tall bottles of wine beginning to appear on the tables; the glimmer of white arms; the glitter of crystal and silver; the flash of color of the women's gowns, sharply accented by the men's black and white—and always under it all the faint pulsating tremor of the ship. The whole was a picture of subdued gaiety, pleasantly quiet, pleasantly polite.

Opposite me, at the table intended for two, Arthur Sidney ought to have been sitting. I let my eyes travel slowly in and out the tables and groups, wondering which face concealed the dark knowledge of his death. Which pair of eyes was alert and wary? Whom must I guard myself against?

After dinner Mrs. Bash hailed me again. With the approach of night she had grown, I think, more consciously aware of the fact of murder, for under her habitual flutter of femininity, she was a bit taut and nervous. She had got up a bridge game and wanted me to take a hand. Mr. Powers would play, she said and a Major Horathon ("such a nice man," she said, thrilling) would join us. Would I play?

I said I would, rather relieved at the prospect; after all, my own thoughts were not pleasant ones. But I played badly—very much, I think, to the annoyance of Major Horathon, who was my partner, a man of uncertain age and unbelievably sleek and pleasant manners. I discovered rather late in the game that we were playing for money and tried to retrieve my errors, but it was too late, for the cards turned suddenly very bad.

"Unlucky in cards," murmured Major Horathon, looking at Mrs. Bash's diamond-laden fingers.

We stopped only when sandwiches appeared, and then Major Horathon left us to take a turn around the deck.

"A nice game," he said, bowing. He looked at the plate of sandwiches on the table, smiled, said softly, *"Bon appétit"* (a wish that, in all conscience, neither Mrs. Bash nor I appeared to stand in direct need of), gave a parting look at Mrs. Bash's rings, and disappeared.

"Such a lovely man," said Mrs. Bash. "I'd like a turn around the deck myself."

"Do come," said Mr. Powers gallantly. "You, too, Miss Keate?"

I thought of the diamond in my hair and of the dark corners of the deck and the black mysterious depth of the Atlantic all about and beneath us and refused.

It was not an hour later that the first attempt to get the diamond from me was made.

Since then I have come to the conclusion that it was a chance shot on the part of the murderer. He couldn't have known that I had the diamond. He couldn't even have known that I had knowledge of the jewel at all. He knew only that it had not been in Arthur Sidney's stateroom. His purpose was, I think, to induce me to confess by word or action my possession of the jewel and, more important, its whereabouts. If not, then the only alternative was to chance the dangerous risk that, as it developed, was attempted that very night.

What happened then was devilishly simple.

I had lingered in the lounge for a time, ostensibly glancing through some magazines but actually studying the groups of my fellow passengers about me, and, to tell the truth, rather hoping for Mrs. Bash's return. I did not much care for her company, it was true. But I did not fancy going through the shadowy corridors toward my own stateroom alone, and any company was better than none at all. She did not return, however, so presently I rose and strolled out of the lounge and down the stairway leading to the deck where my stateroom was situated. I daresay there is some nautical name for both the stairway and the various corridors, but they were to me a stairway and corridors and nothing else. Indeed, had it not been for the curious and constant and not too pleasant feeling of giddiness that haunted me, I would have felt myself in a modern and very gay hotel rather than on an ocean liner whose staff was successfully (and with amazing self-assurance) concealing a murder.

At the foot of the stairs, I hesitated. The corridor branched away in every direction, and it seemed to me that the narrow passage leading to my own room was very dim.

And just then, quite suddenly, I fell victim to the unpleasant certainty that somewhere eyes were watching me.

I looked about but could see no one: softly carpeted halls, blank doors, dim passages, the black gleam of glass in the doors at the end of the main corridor, which on both sides led to the outside deck. But the doors gleamed blankly, reflecting only lights and corridor and a glint of green and silver. There was no face peering through the glass. Or was there?

I checked an impulsive step toward the nearer doors. I dared not investigate. Besides, there was probably no one. No one at all.

But the sixth sense to which I have learned to pay heed

continued to drum at my pulses and send swift little messages of warning along my nerves.

I moved toward my corridor, caught my breath at the blackness of it, and entered it. There was no one anywhere along it, and the doors were blank and dark.

It was just before I reached my door that suddenly, inexplicably, I tripped, snatched at the wall, floundered to my knees, and stopped, bracing myself with my arms outflung and my knee twisted.

Instantly, automatically, I was scrambling again to my feet, ignoring the pain of the twisted knee, whirling around to defend myself. To defend myself against—nothing. And my hand instinctively started upward to my hair.

I don't know what prompted the gesture; the instinct to guard, I suppose. And in that very instant I realized that I was about to reveal not only the possession of the diamond but also its hiding place.

It was too late to check the gesture upward. But I did manage merely to touch my hair and smooth it lightly and adjust my dress while I stared along the passage, trying to discover whether or not one of those blank doors was actually open a bit.

I now know that I was under observation. I now know that there was scarcely a moment during those days that I was not under surveillance.

But then I could see no one, could hear nothing.

I bent and looked closer and detached a slender black thread that had been quite simply and neatly strung taut across the passage.

Once in my own stateroom I looked long at that thread. It was very strong. And it was black. And it looked like tailor's thread.

After a while I put it away. That thread might become even stronger. It might possibly become as strong as a noose.

It was then that I set myself to map out a course of action and to discover a better hiding place for the diamond. The recent ugly incident emphasized that need all too clearly.

I had plenty of time to think that day, but my efforts brought me little in the way of reason and nothing at all as inspiration.

I felt strongly that it would be most unwise to trust the diamond to the safe in the purser's office; that was too obviously the next point of attack. And I definitely dared not carry it any longer myself. Therefore, I had to find some simple hiding place, so simple that the murderer would overlook it, so completely available that I could have it within sight night and day. Yet it must conceal the diamond safely.

And how among all those people could I discover the murderer? There was no clue. There was no way to begin the process of elimination. It did seem to me that we might eliminate the second- and third-class passengers, chiefly because the jewel thief would certainly travel first class in order to be as near his victim as possible. I thought, too, that I could eliminate the corps of servants; after all, had there been among them anyone strange or questionable in any sense, the captain's own investigation would have weeded him or her out.

But those were hopelessly inadequate eliminations. Even in a season of light travel it left altogether too many first-class passengers. It would be a sheer process of elimination. Therefore I must discover a clue. And I had none. None, that is, except the thread.

It was not an encouraging situation, look at it as I might. After a long time I rang for the stewardess. I told her what I wanted; presently a boy arrived, set a dish of fruit on a table, and departed. I locked the door again after him, saw to it that the curtains were pulled over the window, and then selected from the fruit a large red apple.

My hands—a nurse's hands—are fairly adroit. Still, it was some time before I had accomplished my purpose. When it was done, however, I stood back and regarded that dish of fruit with considerable satisfaction.

No one could suspect that the core of that apple had been carefully cut and lifted out and then replaced; the line was neatly drawn. I frowned, thinking of the drying effects of air;

by morning that line so recently cut just at the stem of the apple would be shriveled and drawn and perceptible. After a moment of perplexity I went to the dressing table and found a bottle of nail polish. It was very much like shellac, and I applied it most artistically.

Just before I turned out the light for the night, I double-checked the innocent-looking dish of fruit. An apple, a pear or two, grapes, and an orange. I congratulated myself on what I had done; no one, I thought, would dream that the apple held in its moist heart a large, pear-shaped diamond.

Yes, I really felt quite cozy and comfortable about the apple; I did not know that it was to give me a moment of absolute agony.

I believe I did manage to sleep some, though I was restless and kept hearing sounds that, in all probability, did not exist at all.

Day dawned bright and pleasant with a smooth sea. Things on shipboard, however, were not so smooth. In spite of the secrecy decided upon and maintained, there was in the very air a kind of feeling of unrest, a mysterious hint that the voyage had not, somehow, begun propitiously. Or perhaps the restlessness was due to the fact that the barometer was dropping and there was every indication of an approaching storm.

With my breakfast and with many warnings of secrecy, the stewardess conveyed to me the news that during the previous night, the safe in the purser's office had been broken into.

"Nothing was taken," she said. "Nothing was taken, but you mark my words, this is going to be a bad trip. First a murder, and now this. There'll be something else—things always go in threes. I'd change my stateroom if I were you. Shall I remove this fruit, miss?"

"No," I said with vehemence.

So the safe had been opened. But nothing stolen. The meaning of it was too clear. I glanced approvingly at the apple: round, rosy, blandly secretive.

The day began, too, with a very unpleasant experience of

my own, and that was being summond by the captain and questioned so exhaustively that I could not avoid the somewhat chilling conclusion that I was his only murder suspect.

It was not a nice thought. Especially in view of my possession of the diamond. But I still managed to keep the knowledge of the diamond from them; so far as they knew, nothing had been taken from Arthur Sidney's stateroom. My discreet cable to the insurance company had been followed by a still more discreetly worded reply, one that begged me to "spare no efforts" but did not mention the diamond in so many words.

I was finally permitted to go. During all the questioning, nothing had been said of the safe. The captain looked harassed, however, and his quarters and the purser's office were very busy. When I returned to my stateroom I found it had been searched, whether by the murderer or by ship's officers I have never known. The only thing that mattered to me was that, incredibly, the apple was still there.

On the surface, the day passed quickly. Mrs. Bash attached herself to me again, and we saw something of Major Horathon and Mr. Powers and several other passengers. Late in the afternoon the sea grew a bit rough, and we were obliged to walk a great deal around and around the decks. When I went down to dress for dinner, I came upon the stewardess in the very act of removing the plate of fruit from my room. It gave me quite a turn. I believe I managed to conceal my agitation, although I still remember her odd look as I explained that I liked stale fruit. She went away murmuring something about ptomaine, and I believe she cherished grave doubts as to my sanity from that moment on.

The apple itself was undisturbed. But that night came and passed, and still I knew no more of the murder of my patient.

The next two days were stormy—so violently stormy that I am bound to admit I was extremely preoccupied with very personal concerns and was beginning to entertain a hope that the ship would go to the bottom, murderer and all. The following day, however, the weather cleared, and by noon people were beginning to straggle somewhat weakly and pallidly on deck—I among them, with smelling salts in one hand and an apple in the other.

It was a new, fresh apple (for the original one had grown a bit withered, even for one who likes stale fruit), and I had hidden the diamond well. But the next day we were to dock at Cherbourg, and since surely the murderer knew that the remaining time was short and that it was now or never, I simply dared not leave the diamond, hidden though it was, in my stateroom unguarded.

But if the time was growing short for the thief, it was also growing short for me, and I still had no clue.

"Feeling better?" said Mrs. Bash, pausing beside my chair.

"Much," I said more cheerfully than I felt. "And you?" She sank down beside me.

"My dear, I've been through hell!" she groaned. I repressed a P.G. Wodehouse quote and did not say, "And how were they all?" she went on. "I've not had a meal in three days. And I'm going to have to live in France for the rest of my life, for I shall never cross the ocean again. They told me it would be a rest and I—" Her eyes fell upon my apple and an expression of acute pain crossed her face. "Oh—," she said faintly, and closed her eyes.

"Good morning, good morning." It was a man's voice, so she opened her eyes again and even smiled faintly.

"Oh, Major Horathon! How nice the storm is over!"

"Did you mind it much?" he asked. "And how about you, Miss Keate? You seem to have fared pretty well. Bright and saucy and eating apples."

"Ha, ha," I muttered hollowly. Saucy! A belated wave came along just then, and the boat quivered and I with it. I looked at the apple, which was to me at the moment a truly revolting sight, and forced myself to nibble gently at one side of it.

The effort was terrific, and Major Horathon said heartily, "Hello, hello, you're quite pale, you know. Better take a turn or two around the deck. Come along, both of you."

He was, it seemed, the kind of man who continually takes turns around the deck. I rose, however, and Mrs. Bash and I tottered along beside him. We were both beginning to feel less limp when Mr. Powers turned up and joined us. And it was shortly after that when the next incident happened, though to this day I don't know exactly how.

Just as we rounded the ever-treacherous bow, someone slipped and jolted against me—I think it was Mrs. Bash. But the only thing I remember distinctly was the red apple flying out of my hands.

Out of my hands, with all the gray Atlantic beyond it.

I clutched frantically for it. I may have screamed. But the thing fled from me, flew through blue space, curved—curved like a baseball, and fell.

And then I know I screamed.

It did not fall into the water.

But what happened was almost as bad.

It rolled gently onto the second-class deck immediately below and before us and brought up at the feet of a child standing there. And that child picked it up and looked at it and began to eat it!

I don't know what I said. I don't know how I got to that deck, though I have a faint memory of a guard trying to stop me. I do remember that the child howled when I wrested the apple from him, and his father came and a crowd immediately collected and there were words, at the end of which I retired with my purse lighter by several dollars and my face very warm. But I had the apple.

By that time, numerous interested faces were lining the railing above.

And Major Horathon and Mrs. Bash and Mr. Powers were still waiting when I returned to them. They all three looked very peculiar, however, as I tried lamely to explain and then, as there was nothing to explain, stopped abruptly. Major Horathon and Mr. Powers remembered dates in the bar, and Mrs. Bash suddenly recalled a book she wanted to return to the library. Well, of course, to them it was only an apple. But I must say, I felt rather uncomfortable. I retired to my stateroom at once.

The apple was damaged, but the diamond was undisturbed. I sat there looking at the apple, realizing that I had given away the whole secret. True, I could not remember just who had been strolling the deck or leaning on the railing, but I knew that the unfortunate affair had attracted some little attention. And if the thief was actually watching me as closely as I had felt certain he would, then he knew not only that I had the diamond, but where I had kept it hidden. I had never been entirely without suspicion in his mind, in spite of the failure of the little trap of the thread and his probable search of my stateroom. He must have been biding his time during the storm, lurking near my room, perhaps, seeing the stewardess come and go; uncertain, wondering if, after all, I had the diamond that he knew to be on the ship and yet had so signally failed to find.

Decidedly, I was in the gravest danger.

I could tell the whole story to the captain, of course, and throw myself upon his mercy. But it was rather late in the day for my story to be received with anything approaching confidence. And their methods of inquiry so far had not impressed me very favorably. I would almost certainly be arrested pending investigation, and in the meantime we would reach land and the murderer would go free. I and the diamond would be safe, however, which was no small matter.

But the murderer—I shook my head impatiently, reached for the water carafe to pour myself a drink, and tried again to arrive at a clue.

The water carafe and the apple were there on the table before me. A water carafe, just like the one with which Arthur Sidney had been killed. The blow could not have been premeditated. The blow that—

I straightened up suddenly, feeling as if an electric shock had run all along my elbows. But the water carafe in Arthur Sidney's room had held no water. I had remembered as I stood there locking his door that there was no water in it and had very nearly gone back to fill it!

It had been empty. I was sure of that.

Why, then, had water been spilled all over the pillow and floor?

There was some implication there, some strange and revealing hypothesis.

And suddenly I had it, like a flash, swift and strong.

Arthur Sidney had been sleeping and so thoroughly drugged that I was sure that he had not filled that carafe himself. And he had not roused and rung for the steward to do it, as I would have known, owing to the locked door. Therefore, the carafe was empty. Therefore, the water had been spilled to lend an air of verisimilitude to the broken carafe on the floor. Therefore, the murderer had wanted it to appear that the carafe had been used as a weapon of murder. Therefore, the true weapon must be something else.

I sat there, staring at the carafe; what next, then? So far the hypothesis was reasonable, entirely possible though not by any means proved. But to what did it lead? What weapon had been used? What did I know of it?

First and foremost, it was something present at the scene of crime that would in some manner identify the criminal. Second, it was heavy, sufficient to fracture an old man's skull. Third—I was obliged to feel my way slowly toward the third qualification, and I arrived at it only after long thought. But once arrived, it was impregnable and exciting.

The weapon was something the murderer could not dispose of. Something that, with all the gray depths of the Atlantic about him, he dared not throw overboard and thus lose forever. For if he had dared throw it into the sea he would have done so without this elaborate pretense of the water carafe.

It must be so convincing that there would be no searching about for the real weapon.

Slowly I went all over my chain of reasoning again and arrived at exactly the same conclusion. But what was the object the murderer dared not throw into the sea?

It was just then, I think, that I saw the handle of the door into the passage move slowly up and down. Slowly, with incredible stealth. Then it moved again.

Something brought me up and across the room. And a voice that was not my own said huskily:

"Who is there?"

There was no answer. I listened and could hear nothing.

After a long time my heart stopped pounding in my throat. All at once I heard voices and footsteps coming along the corridor, Mrs. Bash's high-pitched giggle, and then the bang of her door. She was there, then, in the next room. I had no great faith in Mrs. Bash's resources, it is true, but the mere fact of her presence gave me courage, and I opened my door.

I opened it straight upon Mr. Powers. He steadied himself quickly, laughed, brushed away my murmured apology, and said something of packing.

"—for we reach Cherbourg early in the morning," he went on conversationally. "Are you glad the voyage is nearly over, Miss Keate? It's not been very pleasant for you."

"Yes," I said idiotically. "No."

He was looking curiously at me. The passage was utterly quiet and deserted.

Suddenly he leaned toward me and said in a clear, low voice, "I'll take that apple. Don't scream, for it will be with your last breath, I promise you."

I did not move or breathe. I couldn't have done either.

He leaned nearer, whispering hoarsely:

"Give it to me. Do you see that my hand's in my pocket? There's a revolver there. Now, then—the apple."

I think I moved backward, under the deadly clear light in his eyes.

At that very instant there was a rush of footsteps in the next room. Then Mrs. Bash's door swung quickly open and she stood on the threshold.

"Oh, there you are, Mr. Powers," she said. "I thought I heard your voice. See here, you bad man, I want my thread back again." She giggled. "I loaned him some tailor's thread to sew a button on with," she said to me, "and the naughty man has not returned it. I shall leave a trail of buttons all over Europe. You ought to have let me sew it on," she prattled reproachfully, rolling her eyes in a manner intended to call attention to her qualifications as a permanent button-sewer-on.

"Thread—" I said numbly. And in the same instant I knew what it was that the murderer could not throw into the sea. And that was a crutch.

Leaded, I supposed, and thus something from which investigation had to be convincingly diverted.

I shrank back.

He said, watching me, "It's on my writing table, Mrs. Bash. Do get it now so you can pack it. So sorry—"

She fluttered past us, giggling and entirely unconscious that a murderer stood there in the passage. She disappeared in the room beyond Arthur Sidney's.

The murderer leaned toward me.

"Get back into your room—say nothing—"

I saw in his eyes what he intended to do. I saw, indeed, that there was only one thing he could do, for he must have read my knowledge in my face.

I had no gun—I had nothing. I dared not scream.

I backed into the room. In another moment, what would I be? He would manage cleverly to cover his trail with the only possible witness, who was a fool. A curious surge of anger against Mrs. Bash for being a fool sang through my blood. And with it came defiance.

I would not be murdered like a rat in a trap. I would not. And I knew what to do.

I swayed.

"I'm . . . going . . . to faint," I gasped, and leaned against the wall. I leaned firmly and with all my strength against the little row of bells. I remained where I was until all at once there were feet running along the passage—feet and voices and people. Stewards and boys and no fewer than three stewardesses came in a hurry, and then doors opened all along the passage to discover the cause of the commotion.

I still think that he did not realize what I was doing until it was too late. I think he was only conscious that behind him someone was coming, for he did not take his eyes from mine to look, and I suppose he intended to keep me covered with the revolver until they had gone on past.

But the steward, a big, burly fellow, cried, "Madame rang—Madame is ringing—" and then I shrieked the truth and there were gunshots and a struggle, and somehow or other I made them understand.

And that is, of course, the end.

Except that as we docked at Cherbourg the next day, Mrs. Bash, who was standing beside me, watching the baggage being unloaded, sighed petulantly and said, "He was such a nice man. . . . To think of that crutch being loaded with lead. . . . Dear, dear—the more I see of the world the less I . . ."

She prattled on.

The boat train was waiting, and the diamond was in my bag. In another three hours I would be safe in Paris and the diamond would be in its owner's hands. The gangway was put down, and in a very few moments I would be off that accursed boat and on my way. Away from giddiness, away from murder, away from apples. Apples—how I should loathe all the rest of my life the sight of that bland and rosy fruit.

"Miss Keate."

I turned. A boy was standing there.

"With the captain's compliments," he said, bowing. "The captain fears that the restaurant car may be inadequate." And he thrust into my hands an enormous and beribboned basket of fruit, freshly procured at Cherbourg, with a horrid preponderance of great red apples.

Mrs. Bash turned, too, and looked. And, inspired either by an unexpected brainwave or by the ready influence of France, she said the only words possible to say, *"Quelle horreur!"*

*Sometimes I think that it is almost impossible for me to write a story without including dogs or a cat, or both.*

# Mr. Wickwire's Gun Moll

She was a singularly attractive lady with a singularly unattractive dog, and naturally I had no idea that either of them was involved in murder. While the dog looked capable of any perfidious crime, the lady did not. She was as fresh and charming as a rose.

A rather full-blown rose it is true, slightly middle-aged, but lovely with her blue eyes, her blond hair, her trim little figure in a trim blue suit. She carried a blue raincoat over one arm. She had white bare wrists and hands—and no wedding ring, which pleased me. A delightful perfume, like flowers, drifted from the corner where she sat opposite me. We were both waiting for the vet to return to his office; it was about seven o'clock on a rainy spring night. I held my dog, Happy, firmly by the leash and eyed the lady. She held her dog absently and eyed the door to the street.

Now I do not wish to give a wrong impression. I am and intend to remain a bachelor; I am also rather on the elderly side, being a senior vice president of a bank. My name is James Wickwire. If the ringless state of the lady's left hand pleased me, it was not due to any motive of amorous dalliance. The fact is merely that my duties in the bank include the care of too many widows—or rather, to the care of their estates and to the task of dissuading the widows all too frequently from the purchase of uranium lands that to date have provided no uranium, or from the financing of such urgently required items as space shoes. I am referring to yesterday's engagement book in offering these examples. Many of my widows are lovely and intelligent; I only say that the absence of a wedding ring on this lovely lady's hand did not detract from her charm.

It was different with Happy. Amorous dalliance was preeminent in his mind; quite clearly he had taken one look at the dog opposite and fallen madly in love. He gave a frenzied lunge in her direction, and I wound his leash around my wrist and pulled hard. The lady said absently, "Down, Lola," and watched the door.

Lola, being the kind of dog she was, did not obey; she flopped an ungainly paw in a lumberingly coquettish gesture that appeared to drive Happy out of his few wits with delight. I restrained him and glanced at my watch; it was twelve minutes after seven. I said politely to the rose, "Dr. Sherman is late."

She nodded absently. "It's twelve minutes after seven," she said as she watched the door anxiously and, I then perceived, nervously.

I took her anxiety to concern Lola, difficult though it was to comprehend, for I have never seen so revolting a creature. Lola was a long, brown, ungainly animal with the jowls of a bloodhound, the nose of a terrier, and the ears of a German shepherd—except that one of them slanted backward while the other slanted forward in an indescribably raffish way. There is no accounting for the vagaries of human affection, however, especially when it comes to dogs.

I said, "Dr. Sherman is an extremely fine vet. I'm sure he'll see to your dog—"

She gave me a surprised glance. "Oh, I'm only going to board Lola here. She's not got anything wrong with her."

There was, of course, everything wrong with her. I winced as I looked at Lola again and saw that she was rolling a waggish eye at Happy. He had just made another lunge when the door opened and a man came in.

It was not the vet. He was a thin, small man in a raincoat with a hat pulled low over dark, shifty eyes. He carried a lady's handbag, bright red, which with no ado he thrust at the lady. Happy then conceived one of his swift and whimsical dislikes. I do not really think that Happy would in fact dismember anybody and crunch the bones, but when overtaken by an aversion he gives the impression of such an intention. Consequently there arose a sudden, ear-splitting commotion in which Lola joined with a high-pitched, yoicks-and-at-'em series of yells. These cheers from the grandstand egged Happy on to the extent that I was violently occupied in preventing mayhem and thus had only a kaleidoscopic but odd impression that the man in the raincoat was trying to give the lady the red handbag and that she was fervently resisting it. Upon which the man in the raincoat snatched from it a billfold, amazingly stuffed with bills. This, too, the lady rejected with equal vehemence, drawing back until she pressed against the wall. Lola yelped, and I rather think got a nip in on her own account, for the man in the raincoat uttered a violent expletive and aimed a kick at Lola that instead encountered Happy's nose. It was a glancing blow but an unfortunate one, for Happy surged the leash out of my grasp as the man shoved the money back in the handbag and leaped for the door, closing it behind him just as Happy thudded against it. The door quivered, and the man disappeared into the rainy night. I snatched up Happy's leash again, and the lady turned to me. "What is your name? Please—"

I replied automatically. "Wickwire. James—"

"Thank you," said the rose and, to my chill dismay, thrust Lola's leash into my hand and whipped out the door herself, leaving nothing of her presence save a fragrance of flowers. And Lola. The dogs instantly lolloped wildly around my legs, and as I was endeavoring to disengage myself from the tangle of leashes, a sudden crash of sound from the street outside froze the dogs—and me, too, as a matter of fact—for it was undeniably a gunshot.

Before I could unfreeze and extricate myself, the door

flung open again and Dr. Sherman dashed in, shouting, "There's a man shot—" and dashed wildly out again. He made the mistake of leaving the door open, and as Happy is devoted to the vet, Happy raced out after him. Happy being a very large and vigorous dog, I shot after him with Lola, unwilling to miss anything, after me. A little crowd had already collected in the street about thirty feet away. It parted as Happy thundered upon it. I had a swift glimpse of the small dark man in the raincoat, huddled now in the gutter.

The streetlight shone down brightly through silver slivers of rain. There was no red handbag anywhere. The lady, like the handbag, was nowhere to be seen.

I am strongly opposed to murder, so I exerted all my influence over Happy and got him—and Lola, like the end of a remarkably animated kite—back into the vet's office. And presently the vet returned.

"Guy's dead," he said. "Patrolman on the job. Squad car on the way. Now, then, what's Happy's eaten this time?"

I was listening to the shriek of the approaching squad car, thinking of a lady who had refused to take a handbag stuffed with money, run into the street scarcely a moment before murder, and left her dog behind. I replied that a box of carpet tacks had disappeared in Happy's immediate vicinity.

Then the vet saw Lola and put a hand to his head. "*What's that*?" he demanded.

I replied that to the best of my belief it was a dog.

"Your dog?" The vet pointed an outraged finger at Lola, who grinned cozily at him. "Mr. Wickwire, have you gone out of your head?"

"Certainly not," I snapped and described the rose, the incident, and then made the mistake of trying to put the leash in the vet's hand.

"No!" he cried in a voice of anguish. "A thousand times no! I never saw that creature before. I don't know who the lady was. And I'm not going to keep that dog here!"

I daresay a career of inducing dogs with gleaming white teeth to swallow pills they do not wish to swallow develops a certain iron in a man's nature. An hour later, when I went home, I took Lola with me. It was an hour not without incident, for we had scarcely got Happy under the fluoroscope—which revealed no carpet tacks in his capacious interior—when the police arrived to inquire if either of us had seen or knew anything of the murder.

It was a triumph of my civic nature that I conquered a sneaking reluctance to share my information and told them all about the rose, the handbag, and the dog. Lola wore no tags as a reasonable and low-abiding dog would do—no license tag, no rabies tag, no address tag, nothing. There was no possible way of identifying the lady. After making various notes, the police went away. And so did I, taking Lola with me; it was that or the pound for Lola, owing to the lack of tags and the vet's stubborn intransigence. And while I'm sure Lola would have been happy in the pound, rollicking with other dogs—for there was nothing of the snob in her makeup, still—well, I took her home. Besides, the rose had asked me for my name.

I passed over the greeting Wilkins, my only servant, gave Lola; she was unaffected by it save to give him a hardy look and a nip in the calf as he passed the soup, which went over on Lola's head. Wilkins executed a vigorous ballet step in the air, and Lola howled pettishly and made a fretful dash at Wilkins when he came down. He then displayed another feat of remarkable agility in ascending to the top of the table, from whence he bitterly remarked that either he or Lola would depart from the house immediately.

In the end we locked Lola in a bathroom and Happy in my bedroom. After dinner I endeavored to ignore the sound of howls, moans, thuds, and what I was almost sure was the sound of rending pipes; listened for the telephone; and searched the evening papers—to no avail, of course, for the murder outside the vet's had occurred too late for the evening edition.

At ten o'clock, however, I turned on the radio and heard not one but two items of news. The murdered man's name was Sol Brunk. And Sol Brunk together with one or two confederates—the police were uncertain about this—had held up a payroll messenger at six o'clock that evening and got away with what I believe is called the swag, amounting in this instance to fifty thousand dollars. One of them had shot the messenger, who had lived long enough to identify a photograph of Sol Brunk—an item with which the police were supplied owing to former and intimate acquaintance with the late Mr. Brunk. The other robber, or robbers, had escaped; the messenger was vague about the number and identity of the accomplice or accomplices, for it had been Sol Brunk who assailed him directly, and he had been shot from behind; so Sol Brunk was not his murderer. The murderer of Sol Brunk was not known. It was known that on occasion a woman, a gun moll, so to speak, accompanied Sol Brunk on his nefarious excursions.

There was no description of the gun moll. There was no mention at all of a red handbag stuffed with money. There was no mention of the dog Lola.

Something went over upstairs—a small table, judging by the splintering crash—after which both dogs fell into silence and I hoped contrite slumber. After some thought only one sound conclusion emerged: there was some tie between robbery and murder and my rose. She had rejected the handbag, but with such resolution that I was sure it belonged to her; she had also rejected what looked to be a very large sum of money. She had hurried out into the street and disappeared altogether too coincidentally, and thieves have been known to fall out.

It boiled down to that, and it depressed me. I felt indeed a little cheated; a gun moll should not properly possess such ineffable charm and delicacy. Such white little hands and wrists, to aim a revolver so very efficiently! The revolver, of course, could have been concealed in the pocket of her raincoat.

Wilkins set out my mild evening highball in a foreboding manner and went to bed. And it was about then that it struck me that there was something odd about my rose's—or rather the gun moll's—pretty white wrists, something inconsistent yet puzzling. I could not pin it down and analyze it.

In fact, as the clock ticked on, I fell into a very curious sort of reverie in which blossoms of some kind formed a very agreeable background, not orange blossoms exactly but blossoms and sunlit paths and most delightful company; the company was not precisely identifiable either, except that it was definitely not that of a gun moll. Indeed, the faint ting of a distant bell blended so suggestively with my dream that for some time I did not rouse to the fact that it was not, say, something resembling a wedding bell but the ting of the back-entrance doorbell, touched lightly but repeatedly. I hurried back through the dining room and opened the kitchen door.

The lady flung herself into my arms—and had the presence of mind to reach out behind her and close the door firmly upon the rainy, dark night. The scent of flowers surrounded me most delectably; a soft strand of hair brushed my cheek.

"Somebody's trying to kill me," she cried.

Since it seemed more than likely that she had killed somebody herself, I steeled myself against the scent of flowers and the kitten warmth and softness of her clinging figure, disengaged myself from her embrace (strangely difficult, as a matter of fact), and forced her to look at me.

"It *was* your handbag," I said sternly.

Her blue eyes were amazingly sweet. "Of course! Where is Lola?"

I ignored that. "Where have you been?"

"Riding the subways. I had some change in my pocket. Then I looked up your name in a phone booth and had just enough money for a taxi here. If you'll lend me taxi fare—"

"You can have Lola and welcome," I said austerely. "But your handbag—"

"I left it in the bar Lola likes . . . at 6:43, before I took her to the vet's."

While nothing in the way of dissolute behavior on Lola's part would have surprised me, still it is a little unusual for a dog, even Lola, to crave alcoholic refreshment. I said, "Lola's bar?"

"But then, you see, the bartender didn't give her peanuts and then they saw me, so I had to get away. And I forgot my handbag, but he followed me, and my name and address are in my handbag and I'm afraid to go home. And they'll not take Lola in a hotel, at least they'll not keep her," she said candidly. "I don't suppose you'd—see to her for a few days, Mr. Wickwire?"

This really horrendous request brought me to my senses like an electric shock, with the result that I shortly extracted the story—or *a* story, at least. According to the rose, at one time she had visited a bar not far from the vet's—"with friends," she said hastily, fluttering her eyelashes at me—and the bartender had had the shocking lack of foresight to give Lola peanuts. The rose had been walking Lola that evening and had attempted to lead her past the bar; Lola had been of another mind. Quite logically they had entered the bar and settled themselves in a booth. "And, you see, there are high partitions between the booths. Nobody can see you unless they pass right by." Two men had entered at 6:33 and settled themselves in the next booth and talked.

They had talked in low but, to the rose, audible voices about their successful coup in robbing a payroll messenger; they were concerned not about shooting him but about establishing an alibi for themselves, which they believed they had done by coming into the bar. "And I was terri-fied!" she cried, opening her blue eyes wide. "I didn't know what to do. And then they saw me."

And that, too, as I might have guessed, was due to Lola, who had grown impatient with no peaunuts forthcoming and made shrill and penetrating complaint. So one of the men had peered over the partition, and the rose had seized Lola's leash and dragged her out of the bar, forgetting her red handbag. "I'd seen the vet's sign; it wasn't far away. So I thought I'd leave Lola there and then go to a hotel and phone the police. I couldn't go home because my name—charge tags, club cards, everything—was in my handbag. They knew I had heard them. They couldn't let me get away. And one of them followed me, you saw him, so I had to hurry, and you have such a kind face I knew you'd see to Lola and—"

"That man was shot."

"Oh, yes, I know. I was hurrying for the subway. I heard the shot behind me. I turned and saw him on the sidewalk and all the people running and—"

"Who shot him?"

"Why, the other man, of course," she said simply. "The other robber. They were quarreling about the—the loot. One of them said he was going to keep it and the other said no, he'd have half of it and it—really, it was quite dreadful. And then they heard Lola. And the one who shot the man who came into the vet's must have seen me in the street, and of course he had to get away fast, too, but he followed me. In the subways. Took every train I took. Brown coat and hat. Young. Nice-looking, really—but dreadful! Of course, there were always people around. He couldn't do anything. But he's outside now."

I may have uttered a startled word or two. She nodded firmly. "Another taxi was behind the one I took. So I ran around your house, along the areaway, and rang the back doorbell."

I told myself to count to ten. When I got to three I said, "How do you know that the men were in the bar at—you said they came into it at 6:33. Was there a clock? How could they expect to establish an alibi?"

"Oh, that was easy. There's a clock near the door, set rather low. One of them must have turned it back while the other talked to the bartender. And then, you see, they must have intended to set it up again, the same way, when they left. I saw the clock as I ran out of the bar, and it was half an hour slow."

"Did you—*see* him turn the clock back?"

"Oh, no. It wasn't necessary to see it. I knew. I have a perfect sense of time. It's like perfect pitch. I always know exactly what time it is. Like—like dogs, you know, when it's dinnertime. Or time for a walk or—I knew that it was 6:33 when they came into the bar."

This, to speak bluntly, finished me; being a banker, approached in the course of duty for loans, I have listened to some preposterous stories, but none as preposterous as this.

I said sternly, "What about all that money in your handbag? There were at least five thousand dollars—"

"Twenty," she said simply. "It's mine. But I couldn't claim it, could I? I did so hope he'd think I was the wrong woman and go away. But, of course, he'd remember Lola."

That was true enough; once seen, Lola could never be forgotten. But the story was preposterous—a perfect sense of time, indeed! There was no accounting for her motive in telling me such nonsense unless, in a confused way, it was intended to enlist my sympathy since already, because of Lola, I knew some of it. There was clearly only one thing for me to do and that was to call the police. I had started for the kitchen telephone when someone knocked at the back door.

"No, no!" she cried, but I opened the door.

A man came in swiftly. He wore a brown hat and coat; he was young, handsome, slick, and polite. "Oh, there you are, Aunt Masie," he said. "I've come to take you home. I'm sorry if she's troubled you, sir. She's quite all right, really; doesn't need to be in a sanitarium or anything like that. But she does let her fancy run away with her, especially if she gets into a bar and has a drink or two—"

"You've been listening at the door," the rose—and almost certainly the gun moll—cried with unexpected spirit. She clutched my arm with both white hands. "He's the other man. The one who shot the man with my handbag—"

And he had told a good story, too, I reflected skeptically; a story that was almost certain to get his accomplice out of my house. There were probably wheels within wheels, a complex situation between the two of them to which I had no key, except the maxim that thieves do fall out.

"Come now, Aunt Masie," the young man said and advanced upon us. The lady clutched my arm practically to the bone and cried, "He's got a gun!" I looked down, naturally, to see if she had broken my arm, saw her bare white wrist—and suddenly saw the truth.

And there wasn't anything I could do about it. Undoubtedly he did have a gun. The telephone was at least five feet away. Wilkins was asleep on the third floor, and the dogs were locked up on the second floor.

At that point, the lady gave a high and piercing shriek. "*Lola*," she shrieked. "*Lola*—"

I have read the phrase *pandemonium broke loose*, but I never fully comprehended its meaning until the house rocked with it. Howls, yells, and thuds broke out, along with the rending crash of doors from above; somewhere there were many madly running feet. I thrust the lady under the kitchen table and, since I am not a brave man, ducked under it myself. Happy hurtled through the kitchen door, swinging it back against the murderer, who went skittering across the floor. Lola flashed into view and into the corner whence savage growls, thumps, and curses arose, and suddenly two revolver shots crashed through the melee.

Peering out from under the table, I perceived a ghostly figure in white in the doorway that proved to be Wilkins in a nightshirt.

He shouted in a quavering voice, "Shall I shoot to kill, Mr. Wickwire? Or merely to maim?"

A panting, hoarse voice from the corner replied, "Don't shoot—don't shoot! Get these damned dogs off me! I give up!"

He did give up; Happy saw to that, with Lola assisting zestfully. He had no gun; it developed later—after Wilkins and I had trussed him up with roller towels and the police had got there—that he had dropped the gun with which he shot the payroll messenger and Sol Brunk in the river. But he did have the lady's handbag under his coat. And although he turned sullen and stubborn about confessing, my suggestion to the police that Happy—also leashed by that time—be let loose proved efficacious. "Oh, my God, don't let that dog loose!" he cried. "I'll confess! Yes, I shot the payroll messenger. Yes, I shot Sol Brunk. I had the loot and I intended to keep it. Why share with Sol? No, there were only the two of us in on it. Sol's girlfriend is serving a term in—" Happy growled at this point, and the murderer turned quite livid. "Take me to jail, too," he pleaded. "Anywhere. But get me away from that dog."

They departed—police, murderer, and all—sometime later. Lola sat down and rolled a complacent eye at Happy, who was still a little upset and snuffing at the back door in a menacing manner. Wilkins, the hero of the incident, draped a blanket modestly around himself, made chocolate and sandwiches for us, and went back to bed.

The rose said softly, "It was so sweet of you to believe me, Mr. Wickwire. About my sense of time, I mean. Some people don't."

I glanced at her white wrists, neither of which bore a watch. "Oh, yes," I said. "When we were at the vet's, you said it was twelve minutes after seven. I had looked at my watch. I knew that you were right. But there was no clock in the vet's office, and you didn't wear a watch." I didn't add that I had not believed her until I remembered that small fact—and that its oddity had nudged at me earlier in the evening without making itself clear. I said instead, "It's a very unusual gift. I've never heard of anyone—any person, that is—possessing it."

"I know," she said. "Sometimes it's convenient. But somehow it rather annoyed my late husband—"

"*Your late*—" I swallowed hard. During the chat with the police I had of course learned her name, which was Masie Blane. But that was all.

"I'm a widow," she said. "That's why it was so hard to know what to do. A man's advice—why, what's the matter, Mr. Wickwire?"

"Nothing," I said. "A slight touch of vertigo."

"Oh. That money, Mr. Wickwire, that twenty thousand—you see, I'm going to buy an oil well. That is, there's no oil discovered there yet, but I feel sure there will be. And my banker opposed it so strongly that I—I just drew out the cash, and—Mr. Wickwire, really you look quite ill."

"Not at all. It's nothing," I said, controlling a shudder. But I was conscious of a kind of emptiness somewhere within me as a pleasant little dream of blossoms and sunlit paths whisked itself away.

I took her home, with Lola sitting in the taxi between us. She is an utterly delightful woman—Masie, I mean. She is also now a very rich woman, as not one but two oil wells came in on the land she bought.

But the fragrant little dream of unidentifiable blossoms has never returned. Besides, there is Lola. I really cannot permit Happy to make so shocking a *mésalliance*.

*This story is taken from a not unusual occurrence in bank vaults—that is, not murder, dear me, but the storage of good pearls.*

◼

# The Wagstaff Pearls

At midnight the telephone rang, and a woman's voice said, "Mr. Wickwire?"

I had been asleep and was now only half-awake. I said, "Yes . . ."

She cried in an agitated, incoherent way, "This is Frances Dune. I'm sorry to call you now but—I couldn't sleep. I can't wait. I've got to tell you. My conscience—" She took a long rasping breath and said, "It's the Wagstaff pearls—" There was a thud and a clatter—as if the telephone had dropped—a kind of dull crash, and then a scream. It was a terrible scream, which gradually, as if from an increasing distance, died away. Then there was nothing.

I pressed the telephone against my ear. Frances Dune was my secretary, and the Wagstaff pearls were in my care. I knew that something was very wrong, and I didn't like that scream. Suddenly I heard rapid breathing into the telephone, and somebody began to dial.

I cried, "Miss Dune! What is it? Miss Dune!"

The dialing stopped. A strange woman gasped, "Police—police!"

"This is not the police! What's wrong?"

"Oh, Mr. Wickwire, I didn't know you were still on the phone. Frances Dune, she . . . I tried to stop her—I couldn't—"

The woman sounded hysterical. I snapped, "Who is this?"

"I'm—I'm Muriel Evans. I work in the bank. Mr. Wickwire, she killed herself—"

The scream echoed horribly in my ear. The terror of it put an edge to my voice. "Where are you?"

"Her apartment. I'm in her apartment—"

"Give me the address."

She gave it to me, unsteadily but clearly.

"Call the police. I'll be right there. Don't let anybody else come into the place. Call them—wait a minute. How did she kill herself? Are you sure she's dead?"

Miss Evans seemed to swallow hard. "She jumped out the window. It's the ninth floor—"

With another cold wave of horror I realized that there wouldn't be much use in calling a doctor. Again, I told Miss Evans to telephone the police and that I'd be there at once.

Fifteen minutes later I was dressed and in a taxi. My house is in the upper Sixties; we hurtled down Park Avenue. I was all too certain that I knew what had happened. Sometimes—rarely, but sometimes—things like that do happen in a bank. The trusted teller walks away with cash; the reliable cashier disappears with negotiable bonds. This time my perfect secretary had stolen the Wagstaff pearls.

My name is James Wickwire; I am a banker, a bachelor. I am indeed elderly enough to be one of the senior vice presidents. The Wagstaff pearls had been in my care for some twelve years, since Mrs. Wagstaff had died. Her estate was left to minors; its administration was in the care of trustees. I was one of them and, for the practical purposes of doing business, I had power of attorney for the estate. I was under the authority of the other trustees, but I could open the Wagstaff estate safe-deposit boxes. In one of those boxes, enclosed in a flat box of blue velvet, lay the Wagstaff pearls in their wasted beauty. They were rather a nuisance because twice a year, they had to be taken out of the vault and worn for one entire day.

Banks do many odd chores for old and valued clients, and this is one of those chores. Twice a year one of the girls in the bank was sent down to the vault, the pearls were clasped around her neck (next to her skin, one of Mrs. Wagstaff's requirements), and there she sat, reading a book for the entire day. At closing time, the pearls were returned to their blue box and to the vault for another six months. I could never see that their luster was in any way improved thereby, but that had been Mrs. Wagstaff's idea. She had charged me directly with the pearls.

It was a cold, raw night with the red-and-green traffic lights reflected in eerie streaks on the wet pavements; yet I could see Mrs. Wagstaff against the night almost as clearly as I had seen her during what proved to be my last talk with her. I could see her bedroom, luxurious with feminine fripperies. I could see her sitting up against the pillow, with her white hair neatly arranged and her veined, small hands caressing the pearls.

"They must be worn, you understand," she told me. "Otherwise they lose their luster. They must be worn by a woman and, Jim—" She was one of the few women who ever called me Jim. One hand went out to touch my arm pleadingly. "One of the girls in the bank will have to do it. I'm glad you have such pretty girls working in the bank."

Prettiness is not exactly a qualification for any bank employee. Perhaps my face showed perplexity, for she smiled.

"Pearls are meant for beautiful women. I was—they said I was beautiful once," she said, twinkling. A luminous quality of beauty flashed out and touched something in my heart. "My husband used to say that only beautiful women really love pearls. Beauty calls for beauty." She laughed, but rather sadly. "Of course, he didn't mean it, but he said that is why, sometimes, a beautiful woman will do anything for jewels, for pearls like these. . . ." She sighed. A nurse rustled forward. I kissed her small hand before I went away, but I don't know why.

It was my last talk with Mrs. Wagstaff. I had seen to it that her wishes about the pearls were observed. That is, they were worn regularly. I did not subscribe to her notion about beauty and pearls; I put that down to sentiment. Certainly I could not hold, in effect, beauty contests in the bank. Frances Dune had worn the pearls that day.

That too was my own direct responsibility. I had had occasion to be out of the office from noon till after the bank closed; I had returned to my own house about eleven. Miss Dune, looking at my calendar that morning, had reminded me of the pearls, and I had sent her to wear them because I would not require her services that day. Miss Dune had been my secretary for nearly ten years. She was a tall, extremely plain woman of about forty, very neat, rather meager somehow, fussy and overconscientious in a way, but efficient. I had trusted her.

Yet as soon as she spoke to me in that frenzied way over the telephone, I knew what had happened. I had left it to her to check in the pearls with Mr. Wazey, manager of the vaults; I had overstepped my power of attorney to the extent of giving him my key, without which he could not have opened the safe-deposit box. Obviously, Mr. Wazey had taken the velvet box, without looking inside it, returned it to the safe-deposit box, and gone home. But Miss Dune had taken the pearls.

And then, overcome by remorse, she had telephoned to confess her theft and had jumped out the window rather than face the consequences. It was tragic and pathetic: this plain, hard-working woman conquered by the beauty of a strand of pearls.

And they were beautiful; no question of that. But times have changed. When Mrs. Wagstaff—young then—had been given the pearls, her husband had paid nearly half a million for them; I knew that. I also knew that their value was nothing like that now. The old-time high market for pearls is no more. The popularity of cultured pearls, also flawless but plentiful, has done that.

We arrived at an apartment house not far from the river; already the street was lighted up. Police cars and an ambulance had come, and there were lights from windows all around and heads craning out of them.

A police lieutenant—a big, burly fellow who looked rather strained and white—asked me to identify the body and I did. The night seemed very cold; my gray topcoat was insufficient to keep out a chill that seemed to clutch my very bones. Then the ambulance moved closer. I went with the lieutenant to Miss Dune's apartment on the ninth floor.

It was a small apartment, a bedroom–sitting room with a tiny kitchenette; it was painstakingly neat and rather sparse and meager. Like Miss Dune.

A girl sat in a stiff chair; she rose as we came in. I recognized her only vaguely; she worked in the bookkeeping department of the bank, and I rarely saw her.

"I'm Muriel Evans, Mr. Wickwire," she said in a low voice. She was slender, dressed simply in gray; a cherry red coat lay across the chair back. She wore lipstick and matching nail polish, a custom I rather oppose in the bank, but certainly if the girls chose to wear nose rings outside the bank it was none of my business. However, she was quiet and well behaved in a very trying and indeed terrible situation.

I nodded. "This is the young lady who reported it," I told the lieutenant. I still felt cold and rather sick.

He removed his cap. "I'll have to ask you for a statement, miss," he said. "I realize it's been a shock but—" He was sorry for her; I could see that.

She began to talk, and I glanced around the room. She had replaced the telephone upon its cradle. A chair lay on its side, on the floor; it accounted for the dull crash I had heard. The window, a long window, too near the floor, was still open. "Miss Dune telephoned to me about eleven," Miss Evans was saying. "I live near here, two streets north. She said she couldn't sleep; she was nervous and she asked me to come. I didn't know her well, but she was rather important, you see, at the bank, being Mr. Wickwire's secretary. Of course, I came, and she told me she'd taken the Wagstaff pearls. They were in the vault and—"

"I'll explain that," I told the young lieutenant and did so briefly.

The lieutenant said, "Take it easy now, Miss Evans. Was she hysterical?"

"Yes! Oh, yes! I didn't believe her. She said she had to talk—it seemed to come out in spite of herself; she was crying and—well, I didn't believe her. I couldn't. I thought she was ill, nervous, something wrong. Anyway, I went into the kitchen. I intended to make some coffee. I didn't know what to do. While I was there I heard her at the telephone— she telephoned to Mr. Wickwire. I could hear her as she started to tell him what she'd done. But then she dropped the phone as if she couldn't go on. I ran from the kitchen and—and she was pulling up the window. I caught at the window and her and—I don't know what I did. But I couldn't stop her—" She put her hands over her face.

The lieutenant put a large hand kindly on her shoulder. "It's been tough. Take it easy. . . ."

I said, "Where are the pearls?"

The girl, Muriel Evans, looked up with a start. She had light brown hair, parted in the middle and drawn back into a heavy knot; it was the kind of hair, fine and soft, that seems to make a nimbus around a girl's face. She had blue eyes, set below finely arched hollows. It struck me that in spite of her pallor and shock she was rather attractive. "I don't know," she said. "She wouldn't show them to me. That's one of the reasons I didn't believe her."

"We'll find them," the lieutenant said. "The pearls or a pawn ticket," he added rather grimly.

I went to the telephone. "It is all right for me to use this?"

He hesitated. "Well, the fact is, Mr. Wickwire, it's suicide, but I have to go through some forms. Fingerprints and all that. Do you mind using another telephone?"

Miss Evans's blue eyes leaped to sudden darkness. "But it was suicide! I saw her—"

"I understand," the lieutenant said quickly. "Don't get scared, miss. It's not a question of murder. Besides, if you'd murdered her—"

"Oh—" Miss Evans gave a kind of gasp.

He patted her shoulder. "If you'd murdered her, you'd

have got the hell—that is, you'd have got out of here. Nobody knew you were here with her, did they?"

She moved her head slowly, saying no in a whisper.

"Well, there, you see! You'd have got out. You wouldn't have called the police. And we'd find the pearls all right. . . ."

A sergeant and another policeman came in from the hall as I went out. I took the elevator down to street level and used the telephone at the switchboard in the foyer, to rout out Mr. Wazey. The boy on duty watched me, pop-eyed.

"It's terrible," he said. "Miss Dune was sure upset when she phoned for the lady in the red coat. But I never thought of—"

I asked him to get me a taxi.

Banks are supposed to operate through masses of red tape, and in a sense they do; they have to. At the same time, in an emergency there are ways to cut some of that red tape. Mr. Wazey met me at the bank, and we went into the vaults and got out the flat velvet box. When we opened it, there were pearls lying on the yellowed satin lining. But the sight of those pearls shook me in a way that even Miss Dune's tragic confession had not done, for they were not the Wagstaff pearls. They were not pearls at all, but dull and waxy fakes; they proved that the theft had been planned. A moment of passionate impulse and a carefully planned theft were different things.

"I looked at them," Mr. Wazey panted, his round face very pale. "When I replaced the box, I glanced inside it. But I didn't notice—I'm no connoisseur of pearls. Besides, it was Miss Dune."

She had never been delegated to wear the pearls before that day; I was fairly sure of that, but we checked the records Mr. Wazey had kept. I could not remember when I had actually looked at the pearls myself so, for accuracy, I ran down the entire list of names. Some of the girls whose names appeared there had, of course, married or drifted to other jobs, and many of the girls had worn the pearls twice or even three times; but practically every girl in the bank had worn the pearls at some time. Miss Busch had worn them three times; Miss Smith, twice; Miss Evans (Muriel

Evans, the girl in the apartment), twice; Miss Williams, three times. Miss Dune, only once. But she'd have known all about them from my Wagstaff file, so she had prepared herself for an opportunity. And she had reminded me of the date and made the opportunity. My heart was heavy as I watched Mr. Wazey lock up the vaults; then I went back through the dismal, rainy night to Miss Dune's apartment.

I had been gone scarcely an hour, but the search of the apartment had been so thorough that it looked as if a hurricane had struck. Muriel Evans still sat in the armchair; she was pale, and something in the texture of her face made me think (although absently) of a magnolia petal.

The lieutenant had unbuttoned his blue coat and was wiping his forehead. "They're not here, Mr. Wickwire," he said rather desperately. "No pawn ticket. Nothing. We've searched everywhere."

I have never been one to shirk my duty, even if it proved to be unpleasant. I made my way past the debris of cushions, books, untidy heaps of clothing to the window and looked down—so far down to the street that I felt queerly dizzy and sick again. Poor, tragic Miss Dune, who had paid with her life for the pearls entrusted to me! Again I could almost see the lovely lady, the still beautiful woman, who had put her delicate old hand in mine and passed the pearls over to my safekeeping. I could almost see her smile and hear her voice.

I stood at the window for what seemed to me a long time; in fact, I suppose it was only a few seconds while I made up my mind to undertake the only course of action that I could determine. I turned back to the lieutenant "Is it all right for me to go now?"

The lieutenant nodded. "I'll report to you. We'll get started with the pawn shops and jewelers. We'll get the pearls back."

I thanked him. I said to Miss Evans, "Do you mind coming to my house with me? I have to dictate a full report of this."

The light fell fully on her magnolia-white face; it brought out a fine line of temple, a lovely shadow below her cheekbone, the soft fullness of her lips. She nodded and picked up her coat. The lieutenant sprang to assist her and she smiled, thanking him. While she preceded me to the elevator, I lingered to speak to the lieutenant. I made certain arrangements about the funeral, added a concise word or two of directions, and joined Miss Evans as the elevator came.

We found a taxi at once. Neither of us spoke all the way uptown. When we got to my house, I took out my latchkey. "My manservant is on his vacation," I said, and let her in to the hall. "I'm going to have a whiskey and soda. Will you join me?"

She refused but thanked me with a lift of her shadowed, lovely blue eyes. And I asked her something that had occurred to me in the taxi. "You might know. Did Miss Dune have a—well, I suppose one would say a boyfriend? Some man . . ."

She gave me a quiet but intelligent look. "That occurred to me, too. You mean someone who might have planned this and might have influenced her to take the pearls? Yes, I think so. Once or twice I've seen her with a man. I'm not sure that I could identify him; I might be able to. But I feel sure that she wouldn't have done that unless she was urged to do it. Some man, someone younger perhaps—but it seems cruel to say it or think it."

My study is at the right of the hall, and I took her there and told her to sit down. A tray with decanter and glasses stood on my desk. I mixed myself a rather strong whiskey and soda, then I opened a drawer of the desk and took out my revolver.

"What—" Miss Evans began, sitting upright.

I took out the box of shells and loaded the gun. "I don't like the idea of a man; by now he knows what has happened. He might be dangerous." I put the loaded gun down on the table and went into the hall to the street door. I opened it; the street was deserted. I went back to the study and closed the door. The house was extraordinarily quiet.

I picked up my glass and went to the window. The curtains had not been closed: the room behind me was reflected in the glittering, black windowpanes. I took rather a long drink. Then I said, "Where are the pearls?"

The figure in the cherry-red coat stiffened.

I said, "You've worn the pearls, twice; once six months ago, once a year and a half ago. One of those times you changed them for false pearls. No one saw the difference until today. Miss Dune saw that they were not the Wagstaff pearls; probably she looked up the record herself. She sent for you tonight to tell you to give them up, and you—"

Her head lifted. "I reported the suicide. I wouldn't have done that if—"

"You had to report it. The boy at the switchboard knew you were there."

The red coat flashed to one side. I had to go on. "You killed her."

I heard then a kind of metallic click behind me. I turned. She was standing beside the table, facing me. Her beauty leaped out like a flame. But she had my gun in her hand and it was pointed at me.

I am not a brave man and I decided rather swiftly that I wasn't very smart, either. "You can't do that!"

"I have to," she said. Her voice was low and melodious, her face as lovely as the stars and as fateful. "The pearls are in my apartment. I intended to hide them, but I'll not have time for that. You'd tell the police. But the pearls were your responsibility, and everyone knows how you feel about the bank and—they'll say this is suicide, too." She put her finger on the trigger.

I hadn't heard anyone enter the hall through the street door, which I had been at some pains to unlock. But the study door smashed wide open, and the room became flooded with policemen. The gun went off, but the bullet went straight through the ceiling. (Later I had to have the ceiling and the rug in the room above mended.)

"Of course she'd snatch at the idea of some man who might have the pearls. And you had to have an excuse for the gun. That was pretty fast work, sir," the lieutenant said some time later.

I said wearily, "I had no facts, nothing I could tell you. I could not make so serious a charge without facts. But I thought that if she was guilty, if I accused her and I gave her a chance to get hold of that gun, she'd try to get rid of me. Thanks for getting here as I asked you to, Lieutenant.''

He eyed me over his glass with, I will say, a certain respect. ''You are a real detective, Mr. Wickwire.''

''No. The detective in this case was—well, never mind.'' He wouldn't have understood, I thought. The detective was a lady who had once been a beauty, and who had smiled at me and said, ''Beauty calls for beauty. . . . That is why, sometimes, a beautiful woman will do anything for jewels.''

Yet perhaps he would have understood, for he said, a trifle wistfully, ''How that girl stacked up! A real beauty, wouldn't you say? You didn't exactly see it at first. But gradually—yes, sir, I guess that Helen of Troy dame might have looked something like her.'' He seemed to fumble deep down in his consciousness for an idea. ''I guess that's why she wanted the pearls. . . .'' With that, he gave me an abashed glance, murmured, ''So long as I'm off duty,'' and lifted his glass toward me.

I lifted my glass, too; but I toasted another, different but very beautiful woman.

# Introducing Susan Dare

Susan Dare watched a thin stream of blue smoke ascend without haste from the long throat of a tiger lily. Michela, then, had escaped also. She was not, however, on the long veranda, for the clear, broadening light of the rising moon revealed it wide and empty, and nothing moved against the silvered lawn that sloped gently toward the pine woods.

Susan listened a moment for the tap of Michela's heels, did not hear it or any other intrusive sound, and then pushed aside the bowl of lilies on the low window seat, let the velvet curtains fall behind her, and seated herself in the little niche thus formed. It was restful and soothing to be thus shut away from the house with its subtly warring elements and to make herself part of the silent night beyond the open windows.

*A pity*, thought Susan, *to leave*. But after tonight she could not stay. After all, a guest, any guest, ought to have sense enough to leave when a situation develops in the family of her hostess. The thin trail of smoke from the lily caught Susan's glance again, and she wished Michela wouldn't amuse herself by putting cigarette ends in flowers.

A faint drift of voices came from somewhere, and Susan shrank farther into herself and into the tranquil night. It had been an unpleasant dinner, and there would be still an hour or so before she could gracefully extract herself and escape again. Nice of Christabel to give her the guesthouse—the small green cottage across the terrace at the other side of the house, and through the hedge and up the winding green path. Christabel Frame was a perfect hostess, and Susan had had a week of utter rest and content.

But then Randy Frame, Christabel's young brother, had returned.

And immediately Joe Bromfel and his wife, Michela, guests also, had arrived, and with them something that had destroyed all content. The old house of the Frames, with its gracious pillars and long windows and generous dim spaces, was exactly the same—the lazy southern air and the misty blue hills and the quiet pine woods and the boxed paths through the flowers. None of it had actually changed. But it was, all the same, a different place.

A voice beyond the green velvet curtains called impatiently: "Michela—Michela—"

It was Randy Frame. Susan did not move, and she was sure that the sweeping velvet curtains hid even her silver toes. He was probably at the door of the library, and she could see, without looking, his red hair and lithe young body and impatient, thin face. Impatient for Michela. *Idiot, oh, idiot,* thought Susan. *Can't you see what you are doing to Christabel?*

His feet made quick sounds on the parquet floor of the hall and were gone, and Susan herself made a sharply impatient movement. Because the Frame men had been red-haired, gallant, quick-tempered, reckless, and (added Susan to the saga) abysmally stupid and selfish, Randy had accepted the mold without question. A few words from the dinner conversation floated back into Susan's memory. They'd been talking of fox hunting—a safe enough topic, one would have thought, in the Carolina hills. But talk had veered—through Michela, was it?—to a stableman who had been shot and killed by one of the Frames. It had happened a long time ago, had been all but forgotten, and had nothing at all to do with the present generation of Frames. But

Christabel said hurriedly it had been an accident; dreadful. She had looked white. And Randy had laughed and said the Frames shot first and inquired afterward and that there was always a revolver in the top buffet drawer.

"Here she is," said a voice. The curtains were pulled suddenly backward, and Randy, a little flushed, stood there. His face fell as he discovered Susan's fair, smooth hair and thin lace gown. "Oh," he said. "I thought you were Michela."

Others were trailing in from the hall, and a polite hour or so must be faced. Queer how suddenly and inexplicably things had become tight and strained and unpleasant!

Randy had turned away and vanished without more words, and Tryon Welles, strolling across the room with Christabel, was looking at Susan and smiling affably.

"Susan Dare," he said. "Watching the moonlight, quietly planning murder." He shook his head and turned to Christabel. "I simply don't believe you, Christabel. If this young woman writes anything, which I doubt, it's gentle little poems about roses and moonlight."

Christabel smiled faintly and sat down. Mars, his broad face shining, was bringing in the coffee tray. In the doorway Joe Bromfel, dark and bulky and hot-looking in his dinner coat, lingered a moment to glance along the hall and then came into the room.

"If Susan writes poems," said Christabel lightly, "it is her secret. You are quite wrong, Tryon. She writes—" Christabel's silver voice hesitated. Her slender hands were searching, hovering rather blindly over the tray, the large amethyst on one white finger full of trembling purple lights. It was a barely perceptible second before she took a fragile old cup and began to pour from the tall silver coffee pot. "She writes murders," said Christabel steadily. "Lovely, grisly ones, with sensible solutions. Sugar, Tryon? I've forgotten."

"One. But isn't that for Miss Susan?"

Tryon Welles was still smiling. He, the latest arrival, was a neat gray man with tight eyes, pink cheeks, and an affable manner. The only obvious thing about him was a rather finicky regard for color, for he wore gray tweed with exactly the right shades of green—green tie, green shirt, a cautious green stripe in gray socks. He had reached the house on the heels of his telephoned message from town, saying he had to talk business with Christabel, and he had not had time to dress before dinner.

"Coffee, Joe?" asked Christabel. She was very deft with the delicate china. Very deft and very graceful, and Susan could not imagine how she knew that Christabel's hands were shaking.

Joe Bromfel stirred, turned his heavy dark face toward the hall again, saw no one, and took coffee from Christabel's lovely hand. Christabel avoided looking directly into his face, as, Susan had noticed, she frequently did.

"A sensible solution," Tryon Welles was saying thoughtfully. "Do murders have sensible solutions?"

His question hung in the air. Christabel did not reply, and Joe Bromfel did not appear to hear it.

"They must have," Susan said. "After all, people don't murder just—well, just to murder."

"Just for the fun of it, you mean?" said Tryon Welles, tasting his coffee. "No, I suppose not. Well, at any rate," he went on, "it's nice to know your interest in murder is not a practical one."

He probably thought he was making light and pleasant conversation, reflected Susan. Strange that he did not know that every time he said the word *murder,* it fell like a heavy stone in that silent room. She was about to wrench the conversation to another channel when Michela and Randy entered from the hall; Randy was laughing and Michela smiling.

At the sound of Randy's laugh, Joe Bromfel twisted bulkily around to watch their approach, and, except for Randy's laugh, it was entirely silent in the long, book-lined room. Susan watched, too. Randy was holding Michela's hand, swinging it as if to suggest a kind of frank camaraderie. *Probably,* thought Susan, *he's been kissing her out in the darkness of the garden. Holding her very tight.*

Michela's eyelids were white and heavy over unexpectedly

shallow dark eyes. Her straight black hair was parted in the middle and pulled severely backward to a knot on her rather fat white neck. Her mouth was deeply crimson. She had been born, Susan knew, in rural New England, christened Michela by a romantic mother, and had striven to live up to the name ever since. *Or down,* thought Susan tersely, and wished she could take young Randy by his large and outstanding ears and shake him.

Michela had turned toward a chair, and her bare back presented itself to Susan, who saw the thin red line with an angle that a man's cuff, pressing into the creamy flesh, had made. It was unmistakable. Joe Bromfel had seen it, too. He couldn't have helped seeing it. Susan looked into her coffee cup and wished fervently that Joe Bromfel hadn't seen the imprint of Randy's cuff, and then wondered why she wished it so fervently.

"Coffee, Michela?" said Christabel, and something in her voice was more, all at once, than Susan could endure.

She rose and said rather breathlessly, "Christabel darling, do you mind—I have some writing to do—"

"Of course." Christabel hesitated. "But wait—I'll go along with you to the cottage."

"Don't let us keep you, Christabel," said Michela lazily.

Christabel turned to Tryon Welles and neatly forestalled a motion on his part to accompany her and Susan.

"I won't be long, Tryon," she said definitely. "When I come back—we'll talk."

A clear little picture etched itself on Susan's mind: the long, lovely room, the mellow little areas of light under lamps here and there, one falling directly upon the chair she had just left, the pools of shadows surrounding them; Michela's yellow satin, and Randy's red head and slim black shoulders; Joe, a heavy, silent figure, watching them broodingly; Tryon Welles, neat and gray and affable; and Christabel, with her gleaming red head held high on her slender neck, walking lightly and gracefully amid soft mauve chiffons. Halfway across the room she paused to accept a cigarette from Tryon and to bend to the small flare of a lighter he held for her, and the amethyst on her finger caught the flickering light of it and shone.

Then Susan and Christabel crossed the empty flagstone veranda and turned toward the terrace.

Their slippered feet made no sound upon the velvet grass. Above the lily pool the flower fragrances were sweet and heavy on the night air.

"Did you hear the bullfrog last night?" asked Christabel. "He seems to have taken up permanent residence in the pool. I don't know what to do about him. Randy says he'll shoot him, but I don't want that. He *is* a nuisance of course, bellowing away half the night. But after all, even bullfrogs have a right to live."

"Christabel," said Susan, trying not to be abrupt, "I must go soon. I have—work to do—"

Christabel stopped and turned to face her. They were at the gap in the laurel hedge where a path began and wound upward to the cottage.

"Don't make excuses, Susan honey," she said gently. "Is it the Bromfels?"

A sound checked Susan's reply—an unexpectedly eerie sound that was like a wail. It rose and swelled amid the moonlit hills, and Susan gasped and Christabel said quickly, though with a catch in her voice, "It's only the dogs howling at the moon."

"They are not," Susan said, "exactly cheerful. It emphasizes—" She checked herself abruptly on the verge of saying that it emphasized their isolation.

Christabel had turned in at the path. It was darker there, and her cigarette made a tiny red glow. "If Michela drops another cigarette into a flower I'll kill her," said Christabel quietly.

"*What*—"

"I said I'd kill her," said Christabel. "I won't, of course. But she—oh, you've seen how things are, Susan. You can't have failed to see. She took Joe—years ago. Now she's taking Randy."

Susan was thankful that she couldn't see Christabel's

face. She said something about infatuation and Randy's youth.

"He is twenty-one," said Christabel. "He's no younger than I was when Joe—when Joe and I were to be married. That was why Michela was here—to be a guest at the wedding and all the parties." They walked on for a few quiet steps before Christabel added, "It was the day before the wedding that they left together."

Susan said, "Has Joe changed?"

"In looks, you mean," said Christabel, understanding. "I don't know. Perhaps. He must have changed inside. But I don't want to know that."

"Can't you send them away?"

"Randy would follow."

"Tryon Welles," suggested Susan desperately. "Maybe he could help. I don't know how, though. Talk to Randy, maybe."

Christabel shook her head.

"Randy wouldn't listen. Opposition makes him stubborn. Besides, he doesn't like Tryon. He's had to borrow too much money from him."

It wasn't like Christabel to be bitter. One of the dogs howled again and was joined by the others. Susan shivered.

"You are cold," said Christabel. "Run along inside, and thanks for listening. And—I think you'd better go, honey. I meant to keep you for comfort. But—"

"No, no, I'll stay—I didn't know—"

"Don't be nervous about being alone. The dogs would know it if a stranger put a foot on the place. Good night," said Christabel firmly, and was gone.

The guest cottage was snug and warm and tranquil, but Susan was obliged finally to read herself to sleep and derived only a small and fleeting satisfaction from the fact that it was over a rival author's book that she finally grew drowsy. She didn't sleep well even then and was glad suddenly that she'd asked for the guest cottage and was alone and safe in that tiny retreat.

Morning was misty and chill.

It was perhaps nine-thirty when Susan opened the cottage

door, saw that mist lay thick and white, and went back to get her rubbers. Tryon Welles, she thought momentarily, catching a glimpse of herself in the mirror, would have nothing at all that was florid and complimentary to say this morning. And indeed, in her brown knitted suit, with her fair hair tight and smooth and her spectacles on, she looked not unlike a chill and aloof little owl.

The path was wet, and the laurel leaves shining with moisture, and the hills were looming gray shapes. The house lay white and quiet, and she saw no one about.

It was just then that it came. A heavy concussion of sound, blanketed by mist.

Susan's first thought was that Randy had shot the bullfrog.

But the pool was just below her, and no one was there.

Besides, the sound had come from the house. Her feet were heavy and slow in the drenched grass—the steps were slippery and the flagstones wet. Then she was inside.

The wide hall ran straight through the house, and away down at its end Susan saw Mars. He was running away from her, his broad hands outflung, and she was vaguely conscious that he was shouting something. He vanished, and instinct drew Susan to the door at the left, which led to the library.

She stopped, frozen, in the doorway.

Across the room, sagging bulkily over the arm of the green damask chair in which she'd sat the previous night, was a man. It was Joe Bromfel, and he'd been shot, and there was no doubt that he was dead.

A newspaper lay at his feet as if it had slipped there. The velvet curtains were pulled together across the window behind him.

Susan smoothed back her hair. She couldn't think at all, and she must have slipped down to the footstool near the door, for she was there when Mars, his face drawn, and Randy, white as his pajamas, came running into the room. They were talking excitedly and were examining a revolver that Randy had picked up from the floor. Then Tryon Welles came from somewhere, stopped beside her, uttered an incredulous exclamation, and ran across the room, too.

Then Christabel came and stopped, too, on the threshold, and became under Susan's very eyes a different woman—a strange woman, shrunken and gray, who said in a dreadful voice, "*Joe—Joe—*"

Only Susan heard or saw her. It was Michela, hurrying from the hall, who first voiced the question.

"I heard something—what was it? What—" She brushed past Christabel.

"*Don't look, Michela!*"

But Michela looked—steadily and long. Then her flat dark eyes went all around the room and she said, "Who shot him?"

For a moment there was utter shocked stillness.

Then Mars cleared his throat and spoke to Randy.

"I don' know who shot him, Mista Randy. But I saw him killed. An' I saw the han' that killed him—"

"*Hand!*" screamed Michela.

"Hush, Michela." Tryon Welles was speaking. "What do you mean, Mars?"

"They ain't nothin' to tell except that, Mista Tryon. I was just comin' to dust the library and was right there at the door when I heard the shot, and there was just a han' stickin' out of them velvet curtains. And I saw the han' and I saw the revolver and I—I don' know what I did then." Mars wiped his forehead. "I guess I ran for help, Mista Tryon."

There was another silence.

"Whose hand was it, Mars?" said Tryon Welles gently.

Mars blinked and looked very old.

"Mista Tryon, God's truth is, I don' know. I don' know."

Randy thrust himself forward.

"Was it a man's hand?"

"I reckon it was maybe," said the old servant slowly, looking at the floor. "But I don' know for sure, Mista Randy. All I saw was—was the red ring on it."

"A red *ring*?" cried Michela. "What do you mean—"

Mars turned a bleak firm face toward Michela; a face that rejected her and all she had done to his house. "A red ring, Miz Bromfel," he said with a kind of dignity. "It sort of flashed. And it was red."

After a moment Randy uttered a curious laugh.

"But there's not a red ring in the house. None of us runs to rubies—" He stopped abruptly. "I say, Tryon, hadn't we better—well, carry him to the divan. It isn't decent to—just leave him—like that."

"I suppose so—" Tryon Welles moved toward the body. "Help me, Randy—"

The boy shivered, and Susan quite suddenly found her voice.

"Oh, but you can't do that. You can't—" She stopped. The two men were looking at her in astonishment. Michela, too, had turned toward her, although Christabel did not move. "But you can't do that," repeated Susan. "Not when it's—murder."

This time the word, falling into the long room, was weighted with its own significance. Tryon Welles's gray shoulders moved.

"She's perfectly right," he said. "I'd forgotten—if I ever knew. But that's the way of it. We'll have to send for people—doctor, sheriff, coroner, I suppose."

Afterward, Susan realized that but for Tryon Welles the confusion would have become mad. He took a quiet command of the situation, sending Randy, white and sick-looking, to dress, telephoning into town, seeing that the body was decently covered, and even telling Mars to bring them hot coffee. He was here, there, everywhere: upstairs, downstairs, seeing to them all, and finally outside to meet the sheriff . . . brisk, alert, efficient. In the interval Susan sat numbly beside Christabel on the love seat in the hall, with Michela restlessly prowling up and down the hall before their eyes, listening to the telephone calls, drinking hot coffee, watching everything with her sullen, flat black eyes. Her red-and-white sport suit, with scarlet bracelets and earrings, looked garish and out-of-place in that house of violent death.

And Christabel. Still a frozen image of a woman who drank coffee automatically, she sat erect and still and did not speak. The glowing amethyst on her finger caught the light and was the only living thing about her.

Gradually the sense of numb shock and confusion was leaving Susan. Fright was still there and horror and a queer aching pity, but she saw Randy come running down the wide stairway again, his red hair smooth now above a sweater, and she realized clearly that he was no longer white and sick and frightened; he was instead alert and defiantly ready for what might come. And it would be, thought Susan, in all probability, plenty.

And it was.

Questions—questions. The doctor, who was kind; the coroner, who was not; the sheriff, who was merely observant— all of them questioning without end. No time to think. No time to comprehend. Time only to reply as best one might.

But gradually out of it all certain salient facts began to emerge. They were few, however, and brief.

The revolver was Randy's, and it had been taken from the top buffet drawer—when, no one knew or, at least, would tell. "Everybody knew it was there," said Randy sulkily. The fingerprints on it would probably prove to be Randy's and Mars's, since they picked it up.

No one knew anything of the murder, and no one had an alibi, except Liz (the bleak second girl) and Minnie (the cook), who were together in the kitchen.

Christabel had been writing letters in her own room: she'd heard the shot but thought it was only Randy shooting a bullfrog in the pool. But then she'd heard Randy and Mars running down the front stairway, so she'd come down, too. Just to be sure that that was what it was.

"What else did you think it could be?" asked the sheriff. But Christabel said stiffly that she didn't know.

Randy had been asleep when Mars had awakened him. He had not heard the sound of the shot at all. He and Mars had hurried down to the library. (Mars, it developed, had gone upstairs by means of the small back stairway off the kitchen.)

Tryon Welles had walked down the hill in front of the house to the mailbox and was returning when he heard the shot. But it was muffled, and he did not know what had happened until he reached the library. He created a mild sensation at that point by taking off a ring, holding it so they could all see it, and demanding of Mars if that was the ring he had seen on the murderer's hand. However, the sensation was only momentary, for the large, clear stone was as green as his neat green tie.

"No, suh, Mista Tryon," said Mars. "The ring on the han' I saw was red. I could see it plain, an' it was red."

"This," said Tryon Welles, "is a flawed emerald. I asked because I seem to be about the only person here wearing a ring. But I suppose that, in justice to us, all our belongings should be searched."

Upon which the sheriff's gaze slid to the purple pool on Christabel's white hand. He said, however, gently, that that was being done, and would Mrs. Michela Bromfel tell what she knew of the murder.

But Mrs. Michela Bromfel somewhat spiritedly knew nothing of it. She'd been walking in the pine woods, she said defiantly, glancing obliquely at Randy, who suddenly flushed all over his thin face. She'd heard the shot but hadn't realized it was a gunshot. However, she was curious and came back to the house.

"The window behind the body opens toward the pine woods," said the sheriff. "Did you see anyone, Mrs. Bromfel?"

"No one at all," said Michela definitely.

Well, then, had she heard the dogs barking? The sheriff seemed to know that the kennels were just back of the pine woods.

But Michela had not heard the dogs.

Someone stirred restively at that, and the sheriff coughed and said unnecessarily that there was no tramp about, then, and the questioning continued. Continued wearily on and on and on, and still no one knew how Joe Bromfel had met his death. And as the sheriff was at last dismissing them and talking to the coroner of an inquest, one of his men came to report on the search. No one was in the house who didn't belong there; they could tell nothing of footprints; the French windows back of the body had been ajar, and there was no red ring anywhere in the house.

"Not, that is, that we can find," said the man.

"All right," said the sheriff. "That'll be all now, folks. But I'd take it kindly if you was to stay around here today."

All her life Susan was to remember that still, long day with a kind of sharp reality. It was, after those first moments when she'd felt so ill and shocked, weirdly natural, as if, one event having occurred, another was bound to follow, and then upon that one's heels another, and all of them quite in the logical order of things. Even the incident of the afternoon, so trivial in itself but later so significant, was as natural, as unsurprising, as anything could be. And that was her meeting with Jim Byrne.

It happened at the end of the afternoon, long and painful, which Susan spent with Christabel, knowing somehow that, under her frozen surface, Christabel was grateful for Susan's presence. But there were nameless things in the air between them that could be neither spoken of nor ignored, and Susan was relieved when Christabel at last took a sedative and, eventually, fell into a sleep that was no more still than Christabel waking had been.

There was no one to be seen when Susan tiptoed out of Christabel's room and down the stairway, although she heard voices from the closed door of the library.

Out the wide door at last and walking along the terrace above the lily pool, Susan took a long breath of the mist-laden air.

So this was murder. This was murder, and it happened to people one knew, and it did indescribable and horrible things to them. Frightened them first, perhaps. Fear of murder itself came first—simple, primitive fear of the unleashing of the beast. And then on its heels came more civilized fear, and that was fear of the law, and a scramble for safety.

She turned at the hedge and glanced backward. The house lay white and stately amid its gardens as it had lain for generations. But it was no longer tranquil—it was charged now with violence. With murder. And it remained dignified and stately and would cling, as Christabel would cling and had clung all those years, to its protective ritual.

Christabel: Had she killed him? Was that why she was so stricken and gray? Or was it because she knew that Randy had killed him? Or was it something else?

Susan did not see the man till she was almost upon him, and then she cried out involuntarily, though she as a rule was not at all nervous. He was sitting on the small porch of the cottage, hunched up with his hat over his eyes and his coat collar turned up, furiously scribbling on a pad of paper. He jumped up as he heard her breathless little cry and whirled to face her and took off his hat all in one motion.

"May I use your typewriter?" he said.

His eyes were extremely clear and blue and lively. His face was agreeably irregular in feature, with a mouth that laughed a great deal, a chin that took insolence from no man, and a generous width of forehead. His hair was thinning but not yet showing gray and his hands were unexpectedly fine and beautiful. *Hard on the surface*, thought Susan. *Terribly sensitive, really. Irish. What's he doing here?*

Aloud she said, "Yes."

"Good. Can't write fast enough and want to get this story off tonight. I've been waiting for you, you know. They told me you wrote things. My name's Byrne. James Byrne. I'm a reporter. Cover special stories. I'm taking a busman's holiday. I'm actually on a Chicago paper and down here for a vacation. I didn't expect a murder story to break."

Susan opened the door upon the small living room.

"The typewriter's there. Do you need paper? There's a stack beside it."

He fell upon the typewriter absorbedly, like a dog upon a bone. She watched him for a while, amazed at his speed and fluency and utter lack of hesitancy.

Presently she lighted the fire already laid in the tiny fireplace and sat there quietly, letting herself be soothed by the glow of the flames and the steady rhythm of the typewriter keys. And for the first time that day, its experiences—noted and stored away in whatever place observations are stored—began to arouse and assort and arrange themselves and march in some sort of order through her conscious thoughts. But it was a dark and macabre procession, and it frightened Susan. She was relieved when Jim Byrne spoke.

"I say," he said suddenly, over the clicking keys, "I've got your name Louise Dare. Is that right?"

"Susan."

He looked at her. The clicking stopped.

"Susan. Susan Dare," he repeated thoughtfully. "I say, you can't be the Susan Dare that writes murder stories!"

"Yes," said Susan guardedly, "I can be that Susan Dare."

There was an expression of definite incredulity on his face. "But you—"

"If you say," observed Susan tensely, "that I don't look as if I wrote murder stories, you can't use my typewriter for your story."

"I suppose you are all tangled up in this mess," he said speculatively.

"Yes," said Susan, sober again. "And no," she added, looking at the fire.

"Don't commit yourself," said Jim Byrne dryly. "Don't say anything reckless."

"But I mean just that," said Susan. "I'm a guest here. A friend of Christabel Frame's. I didn't murder Joe Bromfel. And I don't care at all about the rest of the people here except that I wish I'd never seen them."

"But you do," said the reporter gently, "care a lot about Christabel Frame?"

"Yes," said Susan gravely.

"I've got all the dope, you know," said the reporter softly. "It wasn't hard to get. Everybody around here knows about the Frames. The thing I can't understand is why she shot Joe. It ought to have been Michela."

"*What*—" Susan's fingers were digging into the wicker arms of her chair, and her eyes strove frantically to plumb the clear blue eyes above the typewriter.

"I say, it ought to have been Michela. She's the girl who's making the trouble."

"But it wasn't—it couldn't—Christabel wouldn't—"

"Oh, yes, she could," said the reporter rather wearily.

"All sorts of people could do the strangest things. Christabel could murder. But I can't see why she'd murder Joe and let Michela go scot-free."

"Michela," said Susan in a low voice, "would have a motive."

"Yes, she's got a motive. Get rid of a husband. But so had Randy Frame. Same one. And he's what the people around here call a Red Frame—impulsive, reckless, bred to a tradition of—violence."

"But Randy was asleep—upstairs—"

He interrupted her.

"Oh, yes, I know all that. And you were approaching the house from the terrace, and Tryon Welles had gone down after the mail, and Miss Christabel was writing letters upstairs, and Michela was walking in the pine woods. Not a damn alibi among you. The way the house and grounds are laid out, neither you nor Tryon Welles nor Michela would be visible to one another. And anyone could have escaped readily from the window and turned up innocently a moment later from the hall. I know all that. Who was behind the curtains?"

"A tramp—" attempted Susan in a small voice. "A burglar—"

"Burglar nothing," said Jim Byrne with scorn. "The dogs would have had hysterics. It was one of you. *Who?*"

"I don't know," said Susan. "*I don't know!*" Her voice was uneven, and she knew it and tried to steady it and clutched the chair arms tighter. Jim Byrne knew it, too, and was suddenly alarmed.

"Oh, look here, now," he cried. "Don't look like that. Don't cry. Don't—"

"I am not crying," said Susan. "But it wasn't Christabel."

"You mean," said the reporter kindly, "that you don't want it to be Christabel. Well—" He glanced at his watch, said, "Golly," and flung his papers together and rose. "There's something I'll do. Not for you exactly—just for— oh, because. I'll let part of my story wait until tomorrow if you want the chance to try to prove your Christabel didn't murder him."

Susan was frowning perplexedly.

"You don't understand me," said the reporter cheerfully. "It's this. You write murder mysteries, and I've read one or two of them. They are not bad," he interpolated hastily, watching Susan. "Now, here's your chance to try a real murder mystery."

"*But I don't want*—" began Susan.

He checked her imperatively.

"You do want to," he said. "In fact, you've got to. You see—your Christabel is in a spot. You know that ring she wears—"

"When did you see it?"

"Oh, does it matter?" he cried impatiently. "Reporters see everything. The point is the ring."

"But it's an amethyst," said Susan defensively.

"Yes," he agreed grimly. "It's an amethyst. And Mars saw a red stone. He saw it, it has developed, on the right hand. And the hand holding the revolver. And Christabel wears her ring on her right hand."

"But," repeated Susan. "It *is* an amethyst."

"M-m," said the reporter. "It's an amethyst. And a little while ago I said to Mars: 'What's the name of that flowering vine over there?' And he said: 'That red flower, suh? That's wisteria.'"

He paused. Susan felt exactly as if something had clutched her heart and squeezed it.

"The flowers were purple, of course," said the reporter softly. "The color of dark amethyst."

"But he would have recognized Christabel's ring," said Susan after a moment.

"Maybe," said the reporter. "And maybe he wishes he'd never said a word about the red ring. He was scared when he first mentioned it, probably; hadn't had a chance to think it over."

"But Mars—Mars would confess to murdering rather than—"

"No," said Jim Byrne soberly. "He wouldn't. That theory sounds all right. But it doesn't happen that way. People don't murder or confess to having murdered for somebody else. When it is a deliberate, planned murder and not a crazy drunken brawl, when anything can happen, there's a motive. And it's a strong and urgent and deeply personal and selfish motive, and don't you forget it. I've got to hurry. Now, then, shall I send in my story about the wisteria?"

"Don't," said Susan choking. "Oh, don't. Not yet."

He picked up his hat. "Thanks for the typewriter. Get your wits together and go to work. After all, you ought to know something of murders. I'll be seeing you."

The door closed, and the flames crackled. After a long time Susan moved to the writing table and drew a sheet of yellow manuscript paper toward her, and a pencil, and wrote: *Characters; possible motives; clues; queries.*

It was strange, she thought, not how different real life was to its written imitation, but how like. How terribly like!

She was still bent over the yellow paper when a peremptory knock at the door sent her pencil jabbing furiously on the paper and her heart into her throat. It proved to be, however, only Michela Bromfel, and she wanted help.

"It's my knees," said Michela irritably. "Christabel's asleep or something, and those women in the kitchen are scared of their shadows." She paused to dig savagely at first one knee and then the other. "Have you got anything to put on my legs? I'm nearly going crazy. It's not mosquito bites. I don't know what it is. Look!"

She sat down, pulled back her white skirt and rolled down her thin stockings, disclosing just above each knee a scarlet blotchy rim around her fat white legs.

Susan looked and had to resist a wild desire to giggle. "It's n-nothing," she said, quivering. "That is, it's only chiggers—here, I'll get you something. Cold cream."

"Chiggers," said Michela blankly. "What's that?"

Susan went into the bathroom. "Little bugs," she called. Where was the cold cream? "They are thick in the pine woods. It'll be all right by morning." Here it was. She took the cream jar in her hand and turned again through the bedroom into the tiny living room.

At the door she stopped abruptly. Michela was standing at

the writing table. She looked up, saw Susan, and her flat dark eyes flickered.

"Oh," said Michela. "Writing a story?"

"No," said Susan. "It's not a story. Here's the cream."

Under Susan's straight look Michela had the grace to depart rather hastily, yanking up her stockings and twisting them hurriedly, and clutching at the jar of cream. Her red bracelets clanked, and her scarlet fingernails looked as if they'd been dipped in blood. Of the few people who might have killed Joe Bromfel, Susan reflected coolly, she would prefer it to be Michela.

It was just then that a curious vagrant memory began to tease Susan. Rather, it was not so much a memory as a memory *of* a memory—something that sometime she had known and now could not remember. It was tantalizing. It was maddeningly elusive. It floated teasingly on the very edge of her consciousness.

Deliberately, at last, Susan pushed it away and went back to work. Christabel and the amethyst. Christabel and the wisteria. Christabel.

It was dark and still drizzly when Susan took her way down toward the big house.

At the laurel hedge she met Tryon Welles.

"Oh, hello," he said. "Where've you been?"

"At the cottage," said Susan. "There was nothing I could do. How's Christabel?"

"Liz says she is still asleep—thank heaven for that. God, what a day! You oughtn't to be prowling around alone at this time of night. I'll walk to the house with you."

"Have the sheriff and the other men gone?"

"For the time being. They'll be back, I suppose."

"Do they know any more about—who killed him?"

"I don't know. You can't tell much. I don't know of any evidence they have unearthed. They asked me to stay on." He took a quick puff or two of his cigarette and then said irritably, "It puts me in a bad place. It's a business deal where time matters. I'm a broker—I ought to be going back to New York tonight—" He broke off abruptly and said, "Oh, Randy—" as young Randy's pale, thin face above a shining mackintosh emerged from the dusk—"let's just escort Miss Susan to the steps."

"Is she afraid of the famous tramp?" asked Randy and laughed unpleasantly. He'd been drinking, thought Susan, with a flicker of anxiety. Sober, Randy was incalculable enough; drinking, he might be dangerous. Could she do anything with him? No, better leave it to Tryon Welles. "The tramp," Randy was repeating loudly. "Don't be afraid of a tramp. It wasn't any tramp killed Joe. And everybody knows it. You're safe enough, Susan, unless you've got some evidence. Have you got any evidence, Susan?"

He took her elbow and joggled it urgently.

"She's the quiet kind, Tryon, that sees everything and says nothing. Bet she's got evidence enough to hang us all. Evidence. That's what we need. Evidence."

"Randy, you're drunk," said Susan crisply. She shook off his clutch on her arm and then, looking at his thin face, which was so white and tight-drawn in the dusk, was suddenly sorry for him. "Go on and take your walk," she said more kindly. "Things will be all right."

"Things will never be the same again," said Randy. "Never the same—do you know why, Susan?"

*He's very drunk*, thought Susan; *worse than I thought*.

"It's because Michela shot him. Yes, sir."

"Randy, shut up!"

"Don't bother me, Tryon. I know what I'm saying. And Michela," asserted Randy with simplicity, "makes me sick."

"Come on, Randy." This time Tryon Welles took Randy's arm. "I'll take care of him, Miss Susan."

The house was deserted and seemed cold. Christabel was still asleep, Michela nowhere to be seen, and Susan finally told Mars to send her dinner on a tray to the cottage and returned quietly like a small brown wraith through the moist twilight.

But she was an oddly frightened wraith.

She was alone on the silent terrace, she was alone on the dark path—strange that she felt as if someone else was there, too. Was the bare fact of murder like a presence hovering, beating dark wings, waiting to sweep downward again?

"Nonsense," said Susan aloud. "Nonsense—" and ran the rest of the way.

She was not, however, to be alone in the cottage, for Michela sat there, composedly awaiting her.

"Do you mind," said Michela, "if I spend the night here? There's two beds in there. You see—" she hesitated, her flat dark eyes were furtive—"I'm—afraid."

"Of what?" said Susan, after a moment. "Of whom?"

"I don't know who," said Michela, "or what."

After a long, singularly still moment, Susan forced herself to say evenly, "Stay if you are nervous. It's safe here." Was it? Susan continued hurriedly, "Mars will send up dinner."

Michela's thick white hand made an impatient movement.

"Call it nerves—although I've not a nerve in my body. But when Mars comes with dinner—just be sure it *is* Mars before you open the door, will you? Although as to that—*I* don't know. But I brought my revolver—loaded." She reached into her pocket, and Susan sat upright, abruptly. Susan, whose knowledge of revolvers had such a wide and peculiar range that any policeman, learning of it, would arrest her on suspicion alone, was nevertheless somewhat uneasy in their immediate vicinity.

"Afraid?" said Michela.

"Not at all," said Susan. "But I don't think a revolver will be necessary."

"I hope not, I'm sure," said Michela somberly and stared at the fire.

After that, as Susan later reflected, there was not much to be said. The only interruption during the whole queer evening was the arrival of Mars and dinner.

Later in the evening Michela spoke again, abruptly. "I didn't kill Joe," she said. And after another long silence she said unexpectedly: "Did Christabel ask you how to kill him and get by with it?"

"*No!*"

"Oh." Michela looked at her oddly. "I thought maybe

she'd got you to plan it for her. You—knowing so much about murders and all.''

"She didn't," said Susan forcefully. "And I don't plan murders for my friends, I assure you. I'm going to bed.''

Michela, following her, put the revolver on the small table between the two beds.

If the night before had been heavy with apprehension, this night was an active nightmare. Susan tossed and turned and was uneasily conscious that Michela was awake and restless, too.

Susan must have slept at last, though, for she woke up with a start and sat upright, instantly aware of some movement in the room. Then she saw a figure dimly outlined against the window. It was Michela.

Susan joined her. "What are you doing?''

"Hush," whispered Michela. Her face was pressed against the glass. Susan looked, too, but could see only blackness.

"There's someone out there," whispered Michela. "And if he moves again I'm going to shoot.''

Susan was suddenly aware that the ice-cold thing against her arm was the revolver.

"You are not," said Susan and wrenched the gun from Michela's hand. Michela gasped and whirled, and Susan said grimly, "Go back to bed. Nobody's out there.''

"How do you know?" said Michela, her voice sulky.

"I don't," said Susan, very much astonished at herself but clutching the revolver firmly. "But I do know that you aren't going to start shooting. If there's any shooting to be done," said Susan with aplomb, "I'll do it myself. Go to bed.''

But long after Michela was quiet, Susan still sat bolt upright, clutching the revolver and listening.

Along toward dawn, out of the mêlée of confused, unhappy thoughts, the vagrant little recollection of a recollection came back to tantalize her. Something she'd known and now did not know. This time she returned as completely as she could over the track her thoughts had taken in the hope of capturing it by association. She'd been thinking of the murder and of the possible suspects; that if Michela had not murdered Joe, then there were left Randy and Christabel and Tryon Welles. And she didn't want it to be Christabel; it must not be Christabel. And that left Randy and Tryon Welles. Randy had a motive, but Tryon Welles had not. Tryon Welles wore a ring habitually, and Randy did not. But the ring was an emerald. And Christabel's ring was what Mars called red. Red—then what would he have called Michela's scarlet bracelet? Pink? But that was a bracelet. She wrenched herself back to dig at the troublesome phantom of a memory. It was something trivial—but something she could not project into her conscious memory. And it was something that somehow she needed. Needed now.

She awoke and was horrified to discover her cheek pillowed cosily upon the revolver. She thrust it away. And realized with a sinking of her heart that day had come and, with it, urgent problems. Christabel, first.

Michela was still silent and sulky. Crossing the terrace, Susan looked at the wisteria winding upward over its trellis. It was heavy with purple blossoms—purple like dark amethysts.

Christabel was in her own room, holding a breakfast tray on her lap and looking out the window with a blank, unseeing gaze. She was years older; shrunken somehow inside. She was pathetically willing to answer the few questions that Susan asked, but added nothing to Susan's small store of knowledge. She left her finally, feeling that Christabel wanted only solitude. But she went away reluctantly. It would not be long before Jim Byrne returned, and she had nothing to tell him—nothing, that is, except surmise.

Randy was not at breakfast, and it was a dark and uncomfortable meal. Dark because Tryon Welles said something about a headache and turned out the electric light, and uncomfortable because it could not be otherwise. Michela had changed to a thin suit—red again. The teasing ghost of a memory drifted over Susan's mind and away again before she could grasp it.

As the meal ended Susan was called to the telephone. It was Jim Byrne saying that he would be there in an hour.

On the terrace Tryon Welles overtook her again and said: "How's Christabel?"

"I don't know," said Susan slowly. "She looks—stunned."

"I wish I could make it easier for her," he said. "But—I'm caught, too. There's nothing I can do, really. I mean about the house, of course. Didn't she tell you?"

"No."

He looked at her, considered, and went on slowly.

"She wouldn't mind your knowing. You see—oh, it's tragically simple. But I can't help myself. It's like this: Randy borrowed money from me—kept on borrowing it, spent it like water. Without Christabel knowing it, he put up the house and grounds as collateral. She knows now, of course. Now I'm in a pinch in business and have got to take the house over legally in order to borrow enough money on it myself to keep things going for a few months. Do you see?"

Susan nodded. Was it this knowledge, then, that had so stricken Christabel?

"I hate it," said Tryon Welles. "But what can I do? And now Joe's—death—on top of it—" He paused, reached absently for a cigarette case, extracted a cigarette, and the small flame from his lighter flared suddenly clear and bright. "It's—hell," he said, puffing, "for her. But what can I do? I've got my own business to save."

"I see," said Susan slowly.

And quite suddenly, looking at the lighter, she did see. It was as simple, as miraculously simple as that. She said, her voice to her own ears marvelously unshaken and calm: "May I have a cigarette?"

He was embarrassed at not having offered it to her: He fumbled for his cigarette case and then held the flame of the lighter for her. Susan was very deliberate about getting her cigarette lighted. Finally she did so, said, "Thank you," and added, quite as if she had the whole thing planned, "Will you wake Randy, Mr. Welles, and send him to me? Now?"

"Why, of course," he said. "You'll be in the cottage?"

"Yes," said Susan and fled.

She was bent over the yellow paper when Jim Byrne arrived.

He was fresh and alert and, Susan could see, prepared to be kind. He expected her, then, to fail.

"Well," he said gently, "have you discovered the murderer?"

"Yes," said Susan Dare.

Jim Byrne sat down quite suddenly.

"I know who killed him," she said simply, "but I don't know why."

Jim Byrne reached into his pocket for a handkerchief and dabbed it lightly to his forehead. "Suppose," he suggested in a hushed way, "you tell all."

"Randy will be here in a moment," said Susan. "But it's all very simple. You see, the final clue was only the proof. I knew Christabel couldn't have killed him, for two reasons: one is, she's inherently incapable of killing anything; the other is—she loved him still. And I knew it wasn't Michela, because she is, actually, cowardly; and then, too, Michela had an alibi."

"Alibi?"

"She really *was* in the pine woods for a long time that morning. Waiting, I think, for Randy, who slept late. I know she was there, because she was simply chewed by chiggers, and they are only in the pine woods."

"Maybe she was there the day before?"

Susan shook her head decidedly.

"No, I know chiggers. If it had been during the previous day they'd have stopped itching by the time she came to me. And it wasn't during the afternoon, for no one went in the pine woods then except the sheriff's men."

"That would leave, then, Randy and Tryon Welles."

"Yes," said Susan. Now that it had come to doing it, she felt ill and weak; would it be her evidence, her words, that would send a fellow creature over that long and ignominious road that ends so tragically?

Jim Byrne knew what she was thinking.

"Remember Christabel," he said quietly.

"Oh, I know," said Susan sadly. She locked her fingers together, and there were quick footsteps on the porch.

"You want me, Susan?" said Randy.

"Yes, Randy," said Susan. "I want you to tell me if you owed Joe Bromfel anything. Money—or—or anything."

"How did you know?" said Randy.

"Did you give him a note—anything?"

"Yes."

"What was your collateral?"

"The house—it's all mine—"

"When was it dated? Answer me, Randy."

He flung up his head.

"I suppose you've been talking to Tryon," he said defiantly. "Well, it was dated before Tryon got his note. I couldn't help it. I'd got some stocks on margin. I had to have—"

"So the house actually belonged to Joe Bromfel?" Susan was curiously cold. Christabel's house. Christabel's brother.

"Well, yes—if you want to put it like that."

Jim Byrne had risen quietly.

"And after Joe Bromfel, to Michela, if she knows of this and claims it?" pressed Susan.

"I don't know," said Randy. "I never thought of that."

Jim Byrne started to speak, but Susan silenced him.

"No, he really didn't think of it," she said wearily. "And I knew it wasn't Randy who killed him because he didn't, really, care enough for Michela to do that. It was—Tryon Welles who killed Joe Bromfel. He had to. For he had to silence Joe and then secure the note and, probably, destroy it in order to have a clear title to the house himself. Randy—did Joe have the note here with him?"

"Yes."

"It was not found on his body?"

It was Jim Byrne who answered: "Nothing of the kind was found anywhere."

"Then," said Susan, "after the murder was discovered and before the sheriff arrived and the search began, only you and Tryon Welles were upstairs and had the opportunity to search Joe's room and find the note and destroy it. Was it you who did that, Randy?"

"*No—no!*" The color rose in his face.

"Then it must have been then that Tryon Welles found

and destroyed it." She frowned. "Somehow, he must have known it was there. I don't know how—perhaps he had had words with Joe about it before he shot him and Joe inadvertently told him where it was. There was no time for him to search the body. But he knew—"

"Maybe," said Randy reluctantly, "I told him. You see—I knew Joe had it in his letter case. He—he told me. But I never thought of taking it."

"It was not on record?" asked Jim Byrne.

"No," said Randy, flushing. "I—asked him to keep it quiet."

"I wonder," said Susan, looking away from Randy's miserable young face, "just how Tryon Welles expected to silence you."

"Well," said Randy dully, after a moment, "it was not exactly to my credit. But you needn't rub it in. I never thought of this—I was thinking of . . . Michela. That she did it. I've had my lesson. And if he destroyed the note, how are you going to prove all this?"

"By your testimony," said Susan. "And besides—there's the ring."

"Ring," said Randy. Jim Byrne leaned forward intently.

"Yes," said Susan. "I'd forgotten. But I remembered that Joe had been reading the newspaper when he was killed. The curtains were pulled together back of him, so, in order to see the paper, he must have had the light turned on above his chair. It wasn't burning when I entered the library, or I should have noted it. So the murderer had pulled the cord of the lamp before he escaped. And ever since then he has been very careful to avoid any artificial light."

"What are you talking about?" cried Randy.

"Yet he had to keep on wearing the ring," said Susan. "Fortunately for him he didn't have it on the first night—I suppose the color at night would have been wrong with his green tie. But this morning he lit a cigarette and I saw."

"Saw what, in God's name," said Randy burstingly.

"That the stone isn't an emerald at all," replied Susan. "It's an Alexandrite. It changed color under the flare of the lighter."

"Alexandrite!" cried Randy impatiently. "What's that?"

"It's a stone that's a kind of red-purple under artificial light and green in daylight," said Jim Byrne shortly. "I had forgotten there was such a thing—I don't think I've ever happened to see one. They are rare—and costly. Costly," repeated Jim Byrne slowly. "This one has cost a life—"

Randy interrupted: "But if Michela knows about the note, why, Tryon may kill her—" He stopped abruptly, thought for a second or two, then got out a cigarette. "Let him," he said airily.

It had been Tryon Welles, then, prowling about during the night—if it had been anyone. He had been uncertain, perhaps, of the extent of Michela's knowledge—but certain of his ability to deal with her and with Randy, who was so heavily in his debt.

"Michela doesn't know now," said Susan slowly. "And when you tell her, Randy—she might settle for a cash consideration. And, Randy Frame, somehow you've got to recover this house for Christabel and do it honestly."

"But right now," said Jim Byrne cheerily, "for the sheriff. And my story."

At the doorway he paused to look at Susan. "May I come back later," he said, "and use your typewriter?"

"Yes," said Susan Dare.

# The Calico Dog

It was nothing short of an invitation to murder.

"You don't mean to say," Susan Dare said in a small voice, "that both of them—*both* of them are living here?"

Idabelle Lasher—Mrs. Jeremiah Lasher, that is, widow of the patent medicine emperor who died last year (resisting, it is said, his own medicine to the end with the strangest vehemence)—Idabelle Lasher turned large pale blue eyes upon Susan and sighed and said:

"Why, yes. There was nothing else to do. I can't turn my own boy out into the world."

Susan took a long breath. "Always assuming," she said, "that one of them is your own boy."

"Oh, there's no doubt about that, Miss Dare," said Idabelle Lasher simply.

"Let me see," Susan said, "if I have this straight. Your son Derek was lost twenty years ago. Recently he has returned. Rather, two of him has returned."

Mrs. Lasher was leaning forward, tears in her large pale eyes. "Miss Dare," she said, "one of them must be my son. I need him so much."

Her large blandness, her artificiality, the padded ease and softness of her life dropped away before the earnestness and

176

honesty of that brief statement. She was all at once pathetic—
no, it was on a larger scale; she was tragic in her need for
her child.

"And besides," she said suddenly and with an odd
naïveté, "besides, there's all that money. Thirty million."

"*Thirty*—" began Susan and stopped. It was simply not
comprehensible. Half a million, yes; even a million. But
thirty million!

"But if you can't tell, yourself, which of the two young
men is your son, how can I? And with so much money
involved—"

"That's just it," said Mrs. Lasher, leaning forward earnestly
again. "I'm sure that Papa would have wanted me to be
perfectly sure. The last thing he said to me was to warn me.
'Watch out for yourself, Idabelle,' he said. 'People will be
after your money. Impostors'."

"But I don't see how I can help you," Susan repeated
firmly.

"You *must* help me," said Mrs. Lasher. "Christabel
Frame told me about you. She said you wrote mystery
stories and were the only woman who could help me, and
that you were right here in Chicago."

Her handkerchief poised, she waited with childlike anxiety to see if the name of Christabel Frame had its expected
weight with Susan. But it was not altogether the name of
one of her most loved friends that influenced Susan. It was
the childlike appeal on the part of this woman.

"How do you feel about the two claimants?" she said.
"Do you feel more strongly attracted to one than to the
other?"

"That's just the trouble," said Idabelle Lasher. "I like
them both."

"Let me have the whole story again, won't you? Try to
tell it quite definitely, just as things occurred."

Mrs. Lasher put her handkerchief away and sat up briskly.

"Well," she began. "It was like this. . . ." Two months
ago a young man called Dixon March had called on her; he
had not gone to her lawyer, he had come to see her. And he
had told her a very straight story.

"You must remember something of the story—oh, but, of course, you couldn't. You're far too young. And then, too, we weren't as rich as we are now, when little Derek disappeared. He was four at the time. And his nursemaid disappeared at the same time, and I always thought, Miss Dare, that it was the nursemaid who stole him."

"Ransom?" asked Susan.

"No. That was the queer part of it. There never was any attempt to demand ransom. I always felt the nursemaid simply wanted him for herself—she was a very peculiar woman."

Susan brought her gently back to the present.

"So Dixon March is this claimant's name?"

"Yes. That's another thing. It seemed so likely to me that he could remember his name—Derek—and perhaps in saying Derek in his baby way, the people at the orphanage thought it was Dixon he was trying to say, so they called him Dixon. The only trouble is—"

"Yes," said Susan, as Idabelle Lasher's blue eyes wavered and became troubled.

"Well, you see, the other young man, the other Derek—well, his name is Duane. You see?"

Susan felt a little dizzy. "Just what is Dixon's story?"

"He said that he was taken in at an orphanage at the age of six. That he vaguely remembers a woman, dark, with a mole on her chin, which is an exact description of the nursemaid. Of course, we've had the orphanage records examined, but there's nothing conclusive and no way to identify the woman; she died—under the name of Sarah Gant, which wasn't the nursemaid's name—and she was very poor. A social worker simply arranged for the child's entrance into the orphanage."

"What makes him think he is your son, then?"

"Well, it's this way. He grew up and made as much as he could of the education they gave him and actually was making a nice thing with a construction company when he got to looking into his . . . his origins, he said—and an account of the description of our Derek, the dates, the fact that he could discover nothing of the woman, Sarah Gant, previous to her life in Ottawa—''

"Ottawa?"

"Yes. That was where he came from. The other one, Duane, from New Orleans. And the fact that, as Dixon remembered her, she looked very much like the newspaper pictures of the nursemaid, suggested the possibility that he was our lost child.''

"So, on the evidence of corresponding dates and the likeness of the woman who was caring for him before he was taken to the orphanage, he comes to you, claiming to be your son. A year after your husband died."

"Yes, and—well—'' Mrs. Lasher flushed pinkly. "There are some things he can remember."

"Things—such as what?"

"The—the green curtains in the nursery. There *were* green curtains in the nursery. And a—a calico dog. And—and a few other things. The lawyers say that isn't conclusive. But I think it's very important that he remembers the calico dog."

"You've had lawyers looking into his claims."

"Oh, dear, yes," said Mrs. Lasher. "Exhaustively."

"But can't they trace Sarah Gant?"

"Nothing conclusive, Miss Dare."

"His physical appearance?" suggested Susan.

"Miss Dare," said Mrs. Lasher. "My Derek was blond with gray eyes. He had no marks of any kind. His teeth were still his baby teeth. Any fair young man with gray eyes might be my son. And both these men—either of these men—might be Derek. I've looked long and wearily, searching every feature and every expression for a likeness to my boy. It is equally there—and not there. I feel sure that one of them is my son. I am absolutely sure that he has—has come home."

"But you don't know which one?" said Susan softly.

"I don't know which one," said Idabelle Lasher. "But one of them *is Derek*."

She turned suddenly and walked heavily to a window. Her pale green gown of soft crepe trailed behind her, its hem touching a priceless thin rug that ought to have been in a museum. Behind her, against the gray wall, hung a small Mauve, exquisite. Twenty-one stories below, traffic flowed unceasingly along Lake Shore Drive.

"One of them must be an impostor," Idabelle Lasher was saying presently in a choked voice.

"Is Dixon certain he is your son?"

"He says only that he thinks so. But since Duane has come, too, he is more—more positive—"

"Duane, of course." The rivalry of the two young men must be rather terrible. Susan had a fleeting glimpse again of what it might mean: one of them certainly an impostor, both impostors, perhaps, struggling over Idabelle Lasher's affections and her fortune. The thought opened, really, quite appalling and horrid vistas.

"What is Duane's story?" asked Susan.

"That's what makes it so queer, Miss Dare. Duane's story—is—well, it is exactly the same."

Susan stared at her wide green back, cushiony and bulgy in spite of the finest corseting that money could obtain.

"You don't mean *exactly* the same!" she cried.

"Exactly," the woman turned and faced her. "Exactly the same, Miss Dare, except for the names and places. The name of the woman in Duane's case was Mary Miller, the orphanage was in New Orleans, he was going to art school here in Chicago when—when, he says, just as Dixon said— he began to be more and more interested in his parentage and began investigating. And he, too, remembers things, little things from his babyhood and our house that only Derek could remember."

"Wait, Mrs. Lasher," said Susan, grasping at something firm. "Any servant, any of your friends, would know these details also."

Mrs. Lasher's pale, big eyes became more prominent.

"You mean, of course, a conspiracy. The lawyers have talked nothing else. But, Miss Dare, they authenticated everything possible to authenticate in both statements. I know what has happened to the few servants we had—all, that is, except the nursemaid. And we don't have many close friends, Miss Dare. Not since there was so much money. And none of them—none of them would do this.''

"But both young men can't be Derek,'' said Susan desperately. She clutched at common sense again and said: "How soon after your husband's death did Dixon arrive?''

"Ten months.''

"And Duane?''

"Three months after Dixon.''

"And they are both living here with you now?''

"Yes.'' She nodded toward the end of the long room. "They are in the library now.''

"Together?'' said Susan irresistibly.

"Yes, of course,'' said Mrs. Lasher. "Playing cribbage.''

"I suppose you and your lawyers have tried every possible test?''

"Everything, Miss Dare.''

"You have no fingerprints of the baby?''

"No. That was before fingerprints were so important. We tried blood tests, of course. But they are of the same type.''

"Resemblances to you or your husband?''

"You'll see for yourself at dinner tonight, Miss Dare. You will help me?''

Susan sighed. "Yes,'' she said.

The bedroom to which Mrs. Lasher herself took Susan was done in the French manner with much taffeta, inlaid satinwood, and laced cushions. It was very large and overwhelmingly magnificent, and gilt mirrors reflected Susan's small brown figure in unending vistas.

Susan thanked fate that the only dinner gown she had brought was a new and handsome one, and felt very awed and faintly dissolute in a great, sunken, black marble pool that she wouldn't have dared call a tub. After all, reflected Susan, finding that she could almost swim a stroke or two, thirty million was thirty million.

She got into a white chiffon dress with silver and green at the waist and was stooping in a froth of white flounces to secure the straps of her flat-heeled silver sandals when Mrs. Lasher knocked.

"It's Derek's baby things,'' she said in a whisper and with

a glance over her fat white shoulder. "Let's move a little farther from the door."

They sat down on a cushioned chaise longue, and between them, incongruous against the suave cream satin, Idabelle Lasher spread out certain small objects, touching them lingeringly.

"His little suit—he looked so sweet in yellow. Some pictures. A pink plush teddy bear. His little nursery-school reports—he was already in nursery school, Miss Dare— prekindergarten, you know. It was in an experimental stage then, and so interesting. And the calico dog, Miss Dare."

She stopped there, and Susan looked at the faded, flabby calico dog held so tenderly in those fat diamonded hands. She felt suddenly a wave of cold anger toward the man who was not Derek and who must know that he was not Derek. She took the pictures eagerly.

But they were only pictures. One at about two, made by a photographer; a round baby face without features that were at all distinctive. Two or three pictures of a little boy playing, squinting against the sun.

"Has anyone else seen these things?"

"You mean either of the two boys—either Dixon or Duane? No, Miss Dare."

"Has anyone at all seen them? Servants? Friends?"

Idabelle's blue eyes became vague and clouded.

"Long ago, perhaps," she said. "Oh, many, many years ago. But they've been in the safe in my bedroom for years. Before that in a locked closet."

"How long have they been in the safe?"

"Since we bought this apartment. Ten—no, twelve years."

"And no one—there's never been anything like an attempted robbery of that safe?"

"Never. No, Miss Dare. There's no possible way for either Dixon or Duane to know of the contents of this box except from memory."

"And Dixon remembers the calico dog?"

"Yes." The prominent blue eyes wavered again, and Mrs. Lasher rose and walked toward the door. She paused then and looked at Susan again.

"And Duane remembers the teddy bear and described it to me," she said definitely and went away.

There was a touch of comedy about it, and, like all comedy, it overlay tragedy.

Left to herself, Susan studied the pictures again thoughtfully. The nursery-school reports, written out in beautiful "vertical" handwriting. *Music:* A good ear. *Memory:* Very good. *Adaptability:* Very good. *Sociability:* Inclined to shyness. *Rhythm:* Poor (advise skipping games at home). *Conduct:* (this varied; with at least once a suggestive blank and once a somewhat terse remark to the effect that there had been considerable disturbance during the half-hours devoted to naps and a strong suggestion that Derek was at the bottom of it). Susan smiled there and began to like baby Derek. And it was just then that she found the first indication of an identifying trait. And that was after the heading *Games*. One report said: Quick. Another said: Mentally quick but does not coordinate muscles well. And a third said, definitely pinning the thing down: Tendency to use left hand, which we are endeavoring to correct.

Tendency to use left hand. An inborn tendency, cropping out again and again all through life. In those days, of course, it had been rigidly corrected—thereby inducing all manner of ills, according to more recent trends of education. But was it ever altogether conquered?

Presently Susan put the things in the box again and went to Mrs. Lasher's room. And Susan had the somewhat dubious satisfaction of watching Mrs. Lasher open a delicate ivory panel that disclosed a very utilitarian steel safe set in the wall behind it and place the box securely in the safe.

"Did you find anything that will be of help?" asked Mrs. Lasher, closing the panel.

"I don't know," said Susan. "I'm afraid there's nothing very certain. Do Dixon and Duane know why I am here?"

"No," said Mrs. Lasher, revealing unexpected cunning. "I told them you were a dear friend of Christabel's. And that you were very much interested in their—my—our situation. We talk it over, you know, very frankly, Miss

Dare. The boys are as anxious as I am to discover the truth of it."

Again, thought Susan feeling baffled, as the true Derek would be. She followed Mrs. Lasher toward the drawing room again, prepared heartily to dislike both men.

But the man sipping a cocktail in the doorway of the library was much too old to be either Dixon or Duane.

"Major Briggs," said Mrs. Lasher. "Christabel's friend Susan, Tom." She turned to Susan. "Major Tom Briggs is our closest friend. He was like a brother to my husband and has been to me."

"Never a brother," said Major Briggs with an air of gallantry. "Say, rather, an admirer. So this is Christabel's little friend." He put down his cocktail glass and bowed and took Susan's hand only a fraction too tenderly.

Then Mrs. Lasher drifted cross the room where Susan was aware of two pairs of black shoulders rising to greet her, and Major Briggs said beamingly:

"How happy we are to have you with us, my dear. I suppose Idabelle has told you of our—our problem."

He was about Susan's height; white-haired, rather puffy under the eyes, and a bit too pink, with hands that were inclined to shake. He adjusted his gold-rimmed eyeglasses, then let them drop the length of their black ribbon and said:

"What do you think of it, my dear?"

"I don't know," said Susan. "What do you think?"

"Well, my dear, it's a bit difficult, you know. When Idabelle herself doesn't know. When the most rigid—yes, the most rigid and searching investigation on the part of highly trained and experienced investigators has failed to discover, ah, the identity of the lost heir, how may my own poor powers avail!" He finished his cocktail, gulped, and said blandly, "But it's Duane."

"What—" said Susan.

"I said, it's Duane. He is the heir. Anybody could see it with half an eye. Spittin' image of his dad. Here they come now."

They were alike and yet not alike at all. Both were rather tall, slender, and well made. Both had medium-brown hair.

Both had grayish blue eyes. Neither was particularly handsome. Neither was exactly unhandsome. Their features were not at all alike in bone structure, yet neither had features that were in any way distinctive. Their description on a passport would not have varied by a single word. Actually they were altogether unlike each other.

With the salad, Major Briggs roused to point out a portrait that hung on the opposite wall.

"Jeremiah Lasher," he said, waving a pink hand in that direction. He glanced meaningly at Susan and added: "Do you see any resemblance, Miss Susan? I mean between my old friend and one of these lads here."

One of the lads—it was Dixon—wriggled perceptibly, but Duane smiled.

"We are not at all embarrassed, Miss Susan," he said pleasantly. "We are both quite accustomed to this sort of scrutiny." He laughed lightly, and Idabelle smiled, and Dixon said:

"Does Miss Dare know about this?"

"Oh, yes," said Idabelle, turning as quickly and attentively to him as she had turned to Duane. "There's no secret about it."

"No," said Dixon somewhat crisply. "There's certainly no secret about it."

There was, however, no further mention of the problem of identity during the rest of the evening. Indeed, it was a very calm and slightly dull evening except for the affair of Major Briggs and the draft.

That happened just after dinner. Susan and Mrs. Lasher were sitting over coffee in the drawing room, and the three men were presumably lingering in the dining room.

It had been altogether quiet in the drawing room, yet there had not been audible even the distant murmur of the men's voices. Thus the queer, choked shout that arose in the dining room came as a definite shock to the two women.

It all happened in an instant. They hadn't themselves time to move or inquire before Duane appeared in the doorway. He was laughing but looked pale.

"It's all right," he said. "Nothing's wrong."

"—*Duane*," said Idabelle Lasher gaspingly, "*what*—"

"Don't be alarmed," he said swiftly. "It's nothing." He turned to look down the hall at someone approaching and added, "Here he is, safe and sound."

He stood aside, and Major Briggs appeared in the doorway. He looked so shocked and purple that both women moved hurriedly forward.

Idabelle Lasher said, "Here—on the divan. Ring for brandy, Duane. Lie down here, Major."

"Oh, no—no," said Major Briggs stertorously. "No. I'm quite all right."

Duane, however, supported him to the divan, and Dixon appeared in the doorway.

"What happened?" he said.

Major Briggs waved his hands feebly.

Duane said, "The Major nearly went out the window."

"O-h-h-h—" It was Idabelle in a thin, long scream.

"Oh, it's all right," said Major Briggs, shaken. "I caught hold of the curtain. By God, I'm glad you had heavy curtain rods at that window, Idabelle."

She was fussing around him, her hands shaking, her face ghastly under its makeup.

"But how could you . . ." she said jerkily, "what on earth—how could it have happened?"

"It's the draft," said the Major irascibly. "The confounded draft on my neck. I got up to close the window and—I nearly went out!"

"But how could you—" began Idabelle again.

"I don't know how it happened," said the Major. "Just all at once—" A look of perplexity came slowly over his face. "Queer," said Major Briggs suddenly, "I suppose it was the draft. But it was exactly as if—" He stopped.

Idabelle cried, "As if what?"

"As if someone had pushed me," said the Major.

Perhaps it was fortunate that the butler arrived just then, and there was the slight diversion of getting the Major to stretch out full length on the divan and sip a restorative.

And somehow in the conversation it emerged that neither

Dixon nor Duane had been in the dining room when the incident had happened.

"There'd been a disagreement over—well, it was over inheritance tax," said Dixon flushing. "Duane had gone to the library to look in an encyclopedia, and I had gone to my room to get the evening paper, which had some reference to it. So the Major was alone when it happened. I knew nothing of it until I heard the commotion in here."

"I," said Duane, watching Dixon, "heard the Major's shout from the library and hurried across."

That night, late, after Major Briggs had gone home, and Susan was again alone in the paralyzing magnificence of the French bedroom, she still kept thinking of the window and Major Briggs. And she put up her own window so circumspectly that she didn't get enough air during the night and woke struggling with a silk-covered eiderdown under the impression that she herself was being thrust out the window.

It was only a nightmare, of course, induced as much as anything by her own hatred of heights. But it gave an impulse to the course she proposed to Mrs. Lasher that very morning.

It was true, of course, that the incident may have been exactly what it appeared to be, an accident. But if it was not accident, there were only two possibilities.

"Do you mean," cried Mrs. Lasher incredulously when Susan had finished her brief suggestion, "that I'm to say openly that Duane is my son! But you don't understand, Miss Dare. I'm not sure. It may be Dixon."

"I know," said Susan. "And I may be wrong. But I think it might help me if you will announce to—oh, only to Major Briggs and the two men—that you are convinced that it is Duane and are taking steps for legal recognition of the fact."

"Why? What do you think will happen? How will it help things to do that?"

"I'm not at all sure it will help," said Susan wearily. "But it's the only thing I see to do. And I think that you may as well do it right away."

"Today?" said Mrs. Lasher reluctantly.

"At lunch," said Susan inexorably. "Telephone to invite Major Briggs now."

"Oh, very well, " said Idabelle Lasher. "After all, it will please Tom Briggs. He has been urging me to make a decision. He seems certain that it is Duane."

But Susan, present and watching closely, could detect nothing except that Idabelle Lasher, once she was committed to a course, undertook it with thoroughness. Her fondness for Duane, her kindness to Dixon, her air of relief at having settled so momentous a question, left nothing to be desired. Susan was sure that the men were convinced. There was, to be sure, a shade of triumph in Duane's demeanor, and he was magnanimous with Dixon—as, indeed, he could well afford to be. Dixon was silent and rather pale and looked as if he had not expected the decision and was a bit stunned by it. Major Briggs was incredulous at first, and then openly jubilant, and toasted all of them.

Indeed, what with toasts and speeches on the part of Major Briggs, the lunch rather prolonged itself, and it was late afternoon before the Major had gone and Susan and Mrs. Lasher met alone for a moment in the library.

Idabelle was flushed and worried.

"Was it all right, Miss Dare?" she asked in a stage whisper.

"Perfectly," said Susan.

"Then—then do you know—"

"Not yet," said Susan. "But keep Dixon here."

"Very well," said Idabelle.

The rest of the day passed quietly and not, from Susan's point of view, at all valuably, although Susan tried to prove something about the possible left-handedness of the real Derek. Badmintion and several games of billiards resulted only in displaying a consistent right-handedness on the part of both the claimants.

Dressing again for dinner, Susan looked at herself ruefully in the great mirror.

She had never in her life felt so utterly helpless, and the thought of Idabelle Lasher's faith in her hurt. After all, she ought to have realized her own limits: the problem that Mrs. Lasher had set was one that would have baffled—that, indeed, had baffled—experts. Who was she, Susan Dare, to attempt its solution?

The course of action she had laid out for Idabelle Lasher had certainly, thus far, had no development beyond heightening an already tense situation. It was quite possible that she was mistaken and that nothing at all would come of it. And if not, what then?

Idabelle Lasher's pale eyes and anxious, beseeching hands hovered again before Susan, and she jerked her satin slip savagely over her head—thereby pulling loose a shoulder strap and being obliged to ring for the maid, who sewed the strap neatly and rearranged Susan's hair.

"You'll be going to the party tonight, ma'am?" said the main in a pleasant Irish accent.

"Party?"

"Oh, yes, ma'am. Didn't you know? It's the Charity Ball. At the Dycke Hotel. In the Chandelier Ballroom. A grand, big party, ma'am. Madame is wearing her pearls. Will you bend your head, please, ma'am."

Susan bent her head and felt her white chiffon being slipped deftly over it. When she emerged she said:

"Is the entire family going?"

"Oh, yes, ma'am. And Major Briggs. There you are, ma'am—and I do say you look beautiful. There's orchids, ma'am, from Mr. Duane. And gardenias from Mr. Dixon. I believe," said the maid thoughtfully, "that I could put them all together. That's what I'm doing for Madame."

"Very well," said Susan recklessly. "Put them all together."

It made a somewhat staggering decoration—staggering, thought Susan, but positively abandoned in luxuriousness. So, too, was the long town car that waited for them promptly at ten when they emerged from the towering apartment house. Susan, leaning back in her seat between Major Briggs and Idabelle Lasher, was always afterward to remember that short ride through crowded, lighted streets to the Dycke Hotel.

No one spoke. Perhaps only Susan was aware (and suddenly realized that she was aware) of the surging desires and needs and feelings that were bottled up together in the tonneau of that long, gliding car. She was aware of it quite suddenly and tinglingly.

Nothing had happened. Nothing, all through that long dinner from which they had just come, had been said that was at all provocative.

Yet all at once Susan was aware of a queer kind of excitement.

She looked at the black shoulders of the two men, Duane and Dixon, riding along beside each other. Dixon sat stiff and straight; his shoulders looked rigid and unmoving. He had taken it rather well, she thought; did he guess Idabelle's decision was not the true one? Or was he still stunned by it?

Or was there something back of that silence? Had she underestimated the force and possible violence of Dixon's reaction? Susan frowned: it was dangerous enough without that.

They arrived at the hotel. Their sudden emergence from the silence of the car, with its undercurrent of emotion, into brilliant lights and crowds and the gay lilt of an orchestra somewhere, had its customary tonic effect. Even Dixon shook off his air of brooding and, as they finally strolled into the Chandelier Room, and Duane and Mrs. Lasher danced smoothly into the revolving colors, asked Susan to dance.

They left the Major smiling approval and buying cigarettes from a girl in blue pantaloons.

The momentary gaiety with which Dixon had asked Susan to dance faded at once. He danced conscientiously but without much spirit and said nothing. Susan glanced up at his face once or twice; his direct, dark blue eyes looked straight ahead, and his face was rather pale and set.

Presently Susan said, "Oh, there's Idabelle!"

At once Dixon lost step. Susan recovered herself and her small silver sandals rather deftly, and Idabelle, large and pink and jewel-laden, danced past them in Duane's arms.

She smiled at Dixon anxiously and looked, above her pearls, rather worried.

Dixon's eyebrows were a straight dark line, and he was white around the mouth.

"I'm sorry, Dixon," said Susan. She tried to catch step with him, for the moment, and added, "Please don't mind my speaking about it. We are all thinking of it. I do think you behave very well."

He looked straight over her head, danced several somewhat erratic steps, and said suddenly, "It was so—unexpected. And you see, I was so sure of it."

"Why were you so sure?" asked Susan.

He hesitated, then burst out again, "Because of the dog," he said savagely, stepping on one of Susan's silver toes. She removed it with Spartan composure, and he said: "The calico dog, you know. And the green curtains. If I had known there was so much money involved, I don't think I'd have come to—Idabelle. But then, when I did know, and this other—fellow turned up, why, of course, I felt like sticking it out!"

He paused, and Susan felt his arm tighten around her waist. She looked up, and his face was suddenly chalk white and his eyes blazing.

"Duane!" he said hoarsely. "I hate him. I could kill him with my own hands."

The next dance was a tango, and Susan danced it with Duane. His eyes were shining and his face flushed with excitement and gaiety.

He was a born dancer, and Susan relaxed in the perfect ease of his steps. He held her very closely, complimented her gracefully, and talked all the time, and for a few moments Susan merely enjoyed the fast swirl of the lovely Argentine dance. Then Idabelle and Dixon went past, and Susan saw again the expression of Dixon's set white face as he looked at Duane, and Idabelle's swimming eyes above her pink face and bare pink neck.

The rest of what was probably a perfect dance was lost on Susan, busy about certain concerns of her own, which involved some adjusting of the flowers on her shoulder. And the moment the dance was over she slipped away.

White chiffon billowed around her, and her gardenias sent up a warm fragrance as she huddled into a telephone booth. She made sure the flowers were secure and unrevealing upon her shoulder, steadied her breath, and smiled a little tremulously as she dialed a number she very well knew. It was getting to be a habit—calling Jim Byrne, her newspaper friend, when she herself had reached an impasse. But she needed him. Needed him at once.

"Jim—Jim," she said. "It's Susan. Listen. Get into a white tie and come as fast as you can to the Dycke Hotel. The Chandelier Room."

"What's wrong?"

"Well," said Susan in a small voice. "I've set something going that—that I'm afraid is going to be more than I meant—"

"You're good at stirring up things, Sue," he said. "What's the trouble now?"

"Hurry, Jim," said Susan. "I mean it." She caught her breath. "I—I'm afraid," she said.

His voice changed.

"I'll be right there. Watch for me at the door." The telephone clicked, and Susan leaned rather weakly against the wall of the telephone booth.

She went back to the Chandelier Room. Idabelle Lasher, pink and worried-looking, and Major Briggs and the two younger men made a little group standing together, talking. She breathed a little sigh of relief. So long as they remained together, and remained in that room surrounded by hundreds of witnesses, it was all right. Surely it was all right. People didn't murder in cold blood when other people were looking on.

It was Idabelle who remembered her duties as hostess and suggested the fortune-teller.

"She's very good, they say," said Idabelle. "She's a professional, not just doing it for a stunt, you know. She's got a booth in one of the rooms."

"By all means, my dear," said Major Briggs at once.

"This way?" She put her hand on his arm and, with Duane at her other side, moved away, and Dixon and Susan followed. Susan cast a worried look toward the entrance. But Jim couldn't possibly get there in less than thirty minutes, and by that time they would have returned.

Dixon said: "Was it the Major who convinced Idabelle that Duane is her son?"

Susan hesitated.

"I don't know," she said cautiously, "how strong the Major's influence has been."

Her caution was not successful. As they left the ballroom and turned down a corridor, he whirled toward her.

"This thing isn't over yet," he said with the sudden savagery that had blazed out in him while they were dancing.

She said nothing, however, for Major Briggs was beckoning jauntily from a doorway.

"Here it is," he said in a stage whisper as they approached him. "Idabelle has already gone in. And would you believe it, the fortune-teller charges twenty dollars a throw!"

The room was small: a dining room, probably, for small parties. Across the end of it a kind of tent had been arranged with many gaily striped curtains.

Possibly due to her fees, the fortune-teller did not appear to be very popular; at least, there were no others waiting, and no one came to the door except a bellboy with a tray in his hand who looked them over searchingly, murmured something that sounded very much like Mr. Haymow, and wandered away. Duane sat nonchalantly on the small of his back, smoking. The Major seemed a bit nervous and moved restlessly about. Dixon stood just behind Susan. Odd that she could feel his hatred for the man lolling there in the armchair almost as if it were a palpable, living entity flowing outward in waves. Susan's sense of danger was growing sharper. But surely it was safe—so long as they were together.

The draperies of the tent moved confusedly and opened, and Idabelle stood there, smiling and beckoning to Susan.

"Come inside, my dear," she said. "She wants you, too."

Susan hesitated. But, after all, so long as the three men were together, nothing could happen. Dixon gave her a sharp look, and Susan moved across the room. She felt a slight added qualm when she discovered that in an effort probably to add mystery to the fortune-teller's trade, the swathing curtains had been arranged so that one entered a kind of narrow passage among them, which one followed with several turns before arriving at the looped-up curtain that made an entrance to the center of the maze and faced the fortune-teller herself.

Susan stifled her uneasiness and sat down on some cushions beside Idabelle. The fortune-teller, in Egyptian costume, with French accent and a Sibylline manner, began to talk. Beyond the curtains and the drone of her voice Susan could hear little, although once she thought there were voices.

But the incident, when it happened, gave no warning.

There was only, suddenly, a great dull shock of sound that brought Susan taut and upright and left the fortune-teller gasping and still and turned Idabelle Lasher's broad pinkness to a queer pale mauve.

"*What was that?*" whispered Idabelle in a choked way.

And the fortune-teller cried, "It's a gunshot—out there!"

Susan stumbled and groped through the folds of draperies, trying to find the way through the entangling maze of curtains and out of the tent. Then all at once they were outside the curtains and staring at a figure that lay huddled on the floor, and there were people pouring in the door from the hall, and confusion everywhere.

It was Major Briggs. And he'd been shot and was dead, and there was no revolver anywhere.

Susan felt ill and faint and after one long look backed away to the window. Idabelle was weeping, her face blotched. Dixon was beside her, and then suddenly someone from the hotel had closed the door into the corridor. And a bellhop's voice, the one who'd wandered into the room looking for Mr. Haymow, rose shrilly above the tumult.

"Nobody at all," he was saying. "Nobody came out of the room. I was at the end of the corridor when I heard the shot, and this is the only room on this side that's unlocked and in use tonight. So I ran down here, and I can swear that nobody came out of the room after the shot was fired. Not before I reached it."

"Was anybody here when you came in? What did you see?" It was the manager—fat, worried, but completely keeping the door behind him closed against further intrusion.

"Just this man on the floor. He was dead already."

"And nobody in the room?"

"Nobody. Nobody then. But I'd hardly got to him before there was people running into the room. And these three women came out of this tent."

The manager looked at Idabelle—at Susan.

"He was with you?" he asked Idabelle.

"Oh, yes, yes," sobbed Idabelle. "It's Major Briggs."

The manager started to speak, stopped, began again. "I've sent for the police," he said. "You folks that were in his party—how many of you are there?"

"Just Miss Dare and me," sobbed Idabelle. "And"—she singled out Dixon and Duane—"these two men."

"All right. You folks stay right here, will you? And you, too, miss"—indicating the fortune-teller—"and the bell-hop. The rest of you will go to a room across the hall. Sorry, but I'll have to hold you till the police get here."

It was not well received. There were murmurs of outrage and horrified looks over slender bare backs and the indignant rustle of trailing gowns, but the scattered groups that had pressed into the room did file slowly out again under the firm look of the manager.

The manager closed the door and said briskly, "Now, if you folks will be good enough to stay right here, it won't be long till the police arrive."

"A doctor," faltered Idabelle. "Can't we have a doctor?"

The manager looked at the sodden, lifeless body.

"You don't want a doctor, ma'am," he said. "What you want is an under—" He stopped abruptly and reverted to his professional suavity. "We'll do everything in our power to save your feelings, Mrs. Lasher," he said. "At the same time, we would much appreciate your—er—assistance. You see, the Charity Ball being what it is, we've got to keep this thing quiet." He was obviously distressed but still suave and competent. "Now then," he said, "I've got to make some arrangements—if you'll just stay here." He put his hand on the doorknob and then turned toward them again and said quite definitely, looking at the floor, "It would be just as well if none of you were to try to leave."

With that he was gone.

The fortune-teller sank down into a chair and said, "Good gracious me," with some emphasis and a midwestern accent. The bellhop retired nonchalantly to a corner and stood there looking very childish but very knowing in his smart white uniform. And Idabelle Lasher looked at the man at her feet and began to sob again. Duane tried to comfort her, while Dixon shoved his hands in his pockets and glowered at nothing.

"But I don't see," wailed Idabelle, "how it could have happened!"

*Odd*, thought Susan, *that she didn't ask who did it. That would be the natural question. Or why? Why had a man who was—as she had said, like a brother to her—been murdered?*

Duane patted Idabelle's heaving bare shoulders and said something soothing, and Idabelle wrung her hands and cried again, "How could it have happened! We were all together— he was not alone a moment—"

Dixon stirred.

"Oh, yes, he was alone," he said. "He wanted a drink, and I'd gone to hunt a waiter.

"And you forget to mention," said Duane icily, "that I had gone with you."

"You left this room at the same time, but that's all I know.

"I went at the same time you did. I stopped to buy cigarettes, and you vanished. I don't know where you went, but I didn't see you again. Not till I came back with the crowd into this room. Came back to find you already here."

"What do you mean by that?" Dixon's eyes were blazing, and his hands were working. "If you are accusing me of murder, say so straight out like a man instead of an insolent little puppy.''

Duane's face was white but composed.

"All right,'' he said. "You know whether you murdered him or not. All I know is when I got back I found him dead and you already here.''

"*You*—''

"*Dixon!*'' cried Idabelle sharply, her laces swirling as she moved hurriedly between the two men. "Stop this! I won't have it. There'll be time enough for questions when the police come. When the police—'' She dabbed at her mouth, which was still trembling, and at her chin, and her fingers went on to her throat, groped, closed convulsively, and she screamed: "*My pearls!*''

"Pearls?'' said Dixon staring, and Duane darted forward.

"Pearls—they're gone!''

The fortune-teller had started upward defensively, and the bellhop's eyes were like two saucers.

Susan said, "They are certainly somewhere in the room, Mrs. Lasher. And the police will find them for you. There's no need to search for them now.''

Susan pushed a chair toward her, and she sank helplessly into it.

"Tom murdered—and now my pearls gone—and I don't know which is Derek. I—*I don't know what to do. . . .*'' Her shoulders heaved, and her face was hidden in her handkerchief, and her corseted fat body collapsed into lines of utter despair.

Susan said deliberately, "The room will be searched, Mrs. Lasher, every square inch of it—ourselves included. There is nothing,'' said Susan with soft emphasis, "nothing that they will miss.''

Then Dixon stepped forward. His face was set, and there was an ominous flare of light in his eyes.

He put his hand upon Idabelle's shoulder to force her to look up into his face and brushed aside Duane, who had moved quickly forward, too, as if his defeated rival had threatened Idabelle.

"Why—why, Dixon,'' faltered Idabelle Lasher, "you

look so strange. What is it? Don't, my dear, you are hurting my shoulder—''

Duane cried: "Let her alone. Let her alone." And then to Idabelle: "Don't pay any attention to him. He's out of his mind. He's—" He clutched at Dixon's arm, but Dixon turned, gave him one black look and thrust him away so forcefully that Duane staggered backward against the walls of the tent and clutched at the curtains to save himself from falling.

"Look here," said Dixon grimly to Idabelle, "what do you mean when you say as you did just now, that you don't know which is Derek? What do you mean? You must tell me. It isn't fair. *What do you mean?*"

His fingers sank into her bulging flesh. She stared upward as if hypnotized, choking. "I meant just that, Dixon. I don't know yet. I only said I had decided in order to—"

"In order to what?" said Dixon inexorably.

A queer little tingle ran along Susan's nerves, and she edged toward the door. She must get help. Duane's eyes were strange and terribly bright. He still clutched the garishly striped curtains behind him. Susan took another silent step and another toward the door without removing her gaze from the tableau.

Idabelle Lasher looked up into Dixon's face, and her lips moved flabbily, and she said the strangest thing, "*How like your father you are, Derek.*"

Susan's heart got up into her throat and left a very curious empty place in the pit of her stomach. She probably moved a little farther toward the door but was never sure, for all at once, while mother and son stared revealingly and certainly at each other, Duane's white face and queer bright eyes vanished.

Susan was going to run. She was going to fling herself out the door and shriek for help. For there was going to be another murder in that room. There was going to be another murder, and she couldn't stop it, she couldn't do anything, she couldn't even scream a warning. Then Duane's black figure was outlined against the tent again. And he held a revolver in his hand. The fortune-teller said: "Oh, my

God" and the white streak that had been the bellhop dissolved rapidly behind a chair.

"Call him your son if you want to," Duane said in an odd, jerky way, addressing Mrs. Lasher and Derek confusedly. "Then your son's a murderer. He killed Briggs. He hid in the folds of this curtain till the room was full of people, and then he came out again. He left his revolver there. And here it is. *Don't move.* One word or move out of any of you, and I'll shoot." He stopped to take a breath. He was smiling a little and panting. "Don't move," he said again sharply. "I'm going to hand you over to the police, Mr. *Derek.* You won't be so anxious to say he's your son then, perhaps. It's his revolver. He killed Briggs with it because Briggs favored me. He knew it, and he did it for revenge."

He was crossing the room with smooth steps; holding the revolver poised threateningly, and his eyes were rapidly shifting from one to another. Susan hadn't the slightest doubt that the smallest move would bring a revolver shot crashing through someone's brain. He's going to escape, she thought, he's going to escape. I can't do a thing. And he's mad with rage. Mad with the terrible excitement of having already killed once.

Duane caught the flicker of Susan's eyes. He was near her now, so near that he could have touched her. He cried, "It's you that's done this! You that advised her! You were on his side! Well—" He'd reached the door now, and there was nothing they could do. He was gloating openly, the way of escape before him. In an excess of dreadful triumphant excitement, he cried, "I'll shoot you first—it's too bad, when you are so pretty. But I'm going to do it."

*It's the certainty,* thought Susan numbly; *Idabelle is so certain that Derek is the other one that Duane knows it, too. He knows there's no use in going on with it. And he knew, when I said what I said about the pearls, that I know.*

She felt oddly dizzy. Something was moving. Was she going to faint—was she—something *was* moving, and it was the door behind Duane. It was moving silently, very slowly.

Susan steeled her eyes not to reveal that knowledge. If

only Idabelle and Derek would not move—would not see those panels move and betray what they had seen.

Duane laughed.

And Derek moved again, and Idabelle tried to thrust him away from her, and Duane's revolver jerked and jerked again, and the door pushed Duane suddenly to one side and there was a crash of glass, and voices and flashing movement. Susan knew only that someone had pinioned Duane from behind and was holding his arms close to his side. Duane gasped, his hand writhed and dropped the revolver.

Then somebody at the door dragged Duane away; Susan realized confusedly that there were police there. And Jim Byrne stood at her elbow. He looked unwontedly handsome in white tie and tails but very angry. He said, "Go home, Sue. Get out of here."

It was literally impossible for Susan to speak or move. Jim stared at her as if nobody else was in the room, got out a handkerchief and wiped his forehead with it.

"I've aged ten years in the last five minutes," he said. He glanced around. Saw Major Briggs's body there on the floor—saw Idabelle Lasher and Derek—saw the fortune-teller and the bellhop.

"Is that Mrs. Jeremiah Lasher over there?" he said to Susan.

Mrs. Lasher opened her eyes, looked at him, and closed them again.

Jim looked meditatively at a revolver in his hand, put it in his pocket, and said briskly, "You can stay for a while, Susan. Until I hear the whole story. Who shot Major Briggs?"

Susan's lips moved and Derek straightened up and cried, "Oh, it's my revolver all right. But I didn't kill Major Briggs—I don't expect anyone to believe me, but I didn't."

"He didn't," said Susan wearily. "Duane killed Major Briggs. He killed him with Derek's revolver, perhaps, but it was Duane who did the murder."

Jim did not question her statement, but Derek said eagerly, "How do you know? Can you prove it?"

"I think so," said Susan. "You see, Duane had a

revolver when I danced with him. It was in his pocket. That's when I phoned for you, Jim. But I was too late."

"But how—" said Jim.

"Oh, when Duane accused Derek, he actually described the way he himself murdered Major Briggs and concealed himself and the revolver in the folds of the tent until the room was full of people and he could quietly mingle with them as if he had come from the hall. We were all staring at Major Briggs. It was very simple. Duane had got hold of Derek's revolver and knew it would be traced to Derek and the blame put upon him, since Derek had every reason to wish to revenge himself upon Major Briggs."

Idabelle had opened her eyes. They looked a bit glassy but were more sensible.

"Why—," she said, "why did Duane kill Major Briggs?"

"I suppose because Major Briggs had backed him. You see," said Susan gently, "one of the claimants had to be an impostor and a deliberate one. And the attack upon Major Briggs last night suggested either that he knew too much or was a conspirator himself. The exact coinciding of the stories (particularly clever on Major Briggs's part) and the fact that Duane turned up after Major Briggs had had time to search for someone who would fulfill the requirements necessary to make a claim to being your son, seemed to me an indication of conspiracy; besides, the very nature of the case involved imposture. But there had to be a conspiracy; someone had to tell one of the claimants about the things upon which to base his claim, especially about the memories of the baby things—the calico dog," said Susan with a little smile, "and the plush teddy bear. It had to be someone who had known you long ago and could have seen those things before you put them away in the safe. Someone who knew all your circumstances."

"You mean that Major Briggs planned Duane's claim— planned the whole thing? But why—" Idabelle's eyes were full of tears again.

"There's only one possible reason," said Susan. "He must have needed money very badly, and Duane, coming into thirty million dollars, would have been obliged to share his spoils.''

"Then Derek—I mean Dixon—I mean," said Idabelle confusedly, clutching at Derek, "this one. He really is my son?"

"You know he is," said Susan. "You realized it yourself when you were under emotional stress and obliged to feel instead of reason about it. However, there's reason for it, too. *He is Derek*."

"He—is—Derek," said Idabelle catching at Susan's words. "You are sure?"

"Yes," said Susan quietly. "He is Derek. You see, I'd forgotten something. Something physical that never changes all through life. That is, a sense of rhythm. Derek has no sense of rhythm and has never had. Duane was a born dancer."

Idabelle said: "Thank God!" She looked at Susan, looked at Derek, and quite suddenly became herself again. She got up briskly, glanced at Major Briggs's body, and said calmly, "We'll try to keep some of this quiet. I'll see that things are done decently—after all, poor old fellow, he did love his comforts. Now, then. Oh, yes, if someone will just see the manager of the hotel about my pearls—"

Susan put a startled hand to her gardenias.

"I'd forgotten your pearls, too. Here they are." She fumbled a moment among the flowers, detached a string of flowing beauty, and held it toward Idabelle. "I took them from Duane while we were dancing."

"Duane," said Idabelle. "But—" She took the pearls and said incredulously, "They *are* mine!"

"He had taken them while he danced with you. During the next dance you passed me, and I saw that your neck was bare."

Jim turned to Susan.

"Are you sure about that, Susan?" he said. "I've managed to get the outline of the story, you know. And I don't think the false claimant would have taken such a risk. Not with thirty million in his pocket, so to speak."

"Oh, they were for the Major," said Susan. "At least, I

think that was the reason. I don't know yet, but I think we'll find that he was pretty hard-pressed for cash and had to have some right away. Immediately. Duane probably balked at demanding money of Mrs. Lasher so soon, so the Major suggested the pearls. And Duane was in no position to refuse the Major's demands. Then, you see, he had no pearls because I took them; he and the Major must have quarreled, and Duane, who had already foreseen that he would be at Major Briggs's mercy as long as the Major lived, was already prepared for any opportunity to kill him. After he had once got to Idabelle, he no longer needed the Major. He had armed himself with Derek's revolver after what must have seemed to him a heaven-sent chance to stage an accident had failed. Mrs. Lasher's decision removed any remaining small value that the Major was to him and made Major Briggs only a menace. But I think he wasn't sure just what he would do or how—he acceded to the Major's demand for the pearls because it was at the moment the simplest course. But he was ready and anxious to kill him, and when he knew that the pearls had gone from his pocket he must have guessed that I had taken them. And he decided to get rid of Major Briggs at once, before he could possibly tell anything, for any story the Major chose to tell would have been believed by Mrs. Lasher. Later, when I said that the police would search the room, he knew that I knew. And that I knew the revolver was still here.''

"Is that why you advised me to announce my decision that Duane was my son?'' demanded Idabelle Lasher.

Susan shuddered and tried not to look at that black heap across the room.

"No,'' she said steadily. "I didn't dream of—murder. I only thought that it might bring the conspiracy that evidently existed somewhere into the open.''

Jim said, "Here are the police.''

Queer, thought Susan much later, riding along the Drive in Jim's car, with her white chiffon flounced tucked in carefully and her green velvet wrap pulled tightly about her throat against the chill night breeze, and the scent of gardenias mingling with the scent of Jim's cigarette—queer how often her adventures ended like this: driving silently homeward in Jim's car.

She glanced at the irregular profile behind the wheel and said, "I suppose you know you saved my life tonight."

His mouth tightened in the little glow from the dashlight. Presently he said, "How did you know he had the pearls in his pocket?"

"Felt 'em," said Susan. "And you can't imagine how terribly easy it was to take them. In all probability a really brilliant career in picking pockets was sacrificed when I was provided with moral scruples."

The light went to yellow and then red, and Jim stopped. He turned and gave Susan a long look through the dusk and then slowly took her hand in his own warm fingers for a second or two before the light went to green again.

# Bermuda
# Grapevine

The hotel lay in rambling, irregular levels against a hillside and above a blue lagoon. The Bermuda sun was about to sink, tranquil and rosy after its blazing day, and the Bermuda moon was about to rise, huge and white. It was the quiet hour between daylight and night.

It was hot, for it was August. Back of the hotel and around the hill behind it wound a narrow white road along which carriages and bicycles made their patient way to Hamilton or to St. George. The bus was some miles from the hotel, which increased its inaccessibility and remoteness from all things urban.

It was a substantial, well-built old hotel, so much remodeled that its present owner and manager had had some difficulty, at first, finding his own way among its winding corridors and unexpected changes in level. That was James Fanfare Smith, and he sat, as he always did at sunset, on the strip of lawn above the lagoon, drank barley water, and pretended he did not know that light footsteps, presumably feminine, had crossed the veranda and the strip of lawn and halted at the white balustrade above the lagoon not far behind him.

For Jim was the victim of his own efficiency; after a few years of struggle his hotel had become inordinately successful. It was with some dismay that he found he had got the lion by the tail and couldn't let go. He became more and more choice about the guests he accepted. He gave them excellent rooms and a gourmet's cuisine and boosted his prices. He could not stop being a gracious and friendly host, and the popularity of his hotel only increased.

He was a tall man, youngish, and, now that he could afford to be, was very lazy. He had dark hair and a brown face, which wore, as a rule, an extremely bland and disingenuous expression. He had light, clear blue eyes that were extraordinarily discerning but by habit and nature friendly. He wore a small, clipped black mustache and affected tropical and informal attire—usually a white linen jacket and perhaps a nonchalant bright scarf tucked in the neck of his jacket. He affected this mode because it was cool and comfortable and because in this, as in many other things, he had a shrewd eye for effect. It went with the tropical surroundings—the hat, the planter's punches he always had waiting for arriving guests, the blazing suns and opal seas.

He had not yet heard departing footsteps. He permitted a thin, blue slit to show beneath his heavy upper eyelids.

A young woman with smooth dark hair was standing at the balustrade a few feet away, looking out to the purpling sea beyond the lagoon opening. She wore a tailored shirt and shorts, and her bare, lightly tanned legs were slender. The blue slit below Jim's eyelids vanished.

If her legs were good they were no better than hundreds that had marched through his lobby during the past five years. He'd been polite to a great many lady guests in shorts. He had, however, a strong sense of taste and propriety and could be, if it became necessary, a master of gentle renunciation, gently implied. Twice a week during at least eight months in the year he went conscientiously into Hamilton to wave farewells to departing guests from the balcony of the Twenty-One Club and perhaps, now and then, to ignore at that safe distance from the rails of departing boats sundry handkerchiefs pressed to eyes.

Absently he lifted the barley water to his lips, and the young woman must have perceived the slight motion, for she came nearer. He screwed his eyes shut, feeling that this one hour out of the day (when, as a rule, all his guests were dressing for dinner) belonged to him. It made no difference. She said in an extraordinarily lovely voice, "You are Mr. Smith?"

He opened his eyes and got to his feet, and in the instant of rising searched his memory for the names of guests who had arrived that day. There had been two boats, one from England and one from New York, and he had met both, but in the confusion some of the guests had escaped him. He granted at once that if he had seen this guest before he would have remembered her. It was his habit to remember, but no one could forget this particular face. For it was, James Fanfare Smith was obliged to admit, even over his prejudices, lovely. She had large deep gray eyes, extraordinarily luminous, and a slender, beautifully planed face and sensitive, crimson lips, which, when she smiled as she was now doing, were very sweet and gay.

She said again, "You *are* Mr. Smith?"

What was the girl's name? He made a small and almost imperceptible gesture with his left hand, a gesture that a young man in beige porter's uniform, standing at the entrance to the hotel some two hundred feet away, nevertheless perceived and understood.

"Won't you join me?" he said to the young woman.

"No, thank you. The desk clerk told me I couldn't have a key."

"A key—oh, you mean a key!" Her sweet mouth and his own failure to select her special card in the index his mind usually carried disconcerted him a little.

"Yes, a key. To our rooms, you know. I want a key."

"You—but . . ." The porter reached his elbow. Mr. Smith said, "Excuse me . . ." and bent his ear.

Along with other qualities of the Bermuda scene that James Fanfare Smith had perceived, adopted, and successfully utilized was the grapevine telegraph, which in its accuracy and incredible swiftness is peculiarly Bermuda's own. He ran his hotel by it, as a matter of fact, for every detail, every small complaint, every idiosyncrasy, every desire was thus reported to him. He knew what a guest had for breakfast, and he knew it if one quarreled with his wife. There were a great many other things he knew. If a guest closed his door at midnight and pulled down the shades and sneezed, Jim was quite likely to ask that guest, the next morning, how his cold was.

The porter murmured. His words were altogether indistinguishable twelve inches away but perfectly clear to Mr. Smith's attentive ear. That too had been carefully worked out, and thus were behind-the-scene emergencies, as well as relevant and irrelevant news items, reported.

The porter said in the habitual mixture of good English and dialect of the Bermuda native, "Wife of Mr. Peter Blake. Rich. Suite twenty-one. Lots of baggage, foreign labels. Honeymoon. Lawyer man Mr. Pusey, friend. Arrive on New York boat to meet Mr. Blake. All come this morning. Orders, boss?"

Smith replied, "Table three. Tell the headwaiter to serve them my own Napoleon brandy after dinner with my compliments. That's all."

His words, too, had been completely unintelligible to the young woman (Mrs. Peter Blake, on her honeymoon with her rich husband), who now was sitting on the balustrade and had turned a rather chilly and very pretty profile toward him. Her slender figure silhouetted itself against the blue water of the lagoon. All around them the tropic night was gently, softly, and a little threateningly, drawing closer.

The porter vanished. Jim Fanfare Smith said, frowning a little, "We don't have keys. We never lock doors. Our employees are honest. There's no crime in Bermuda. The only objects ever . . . removed . . . are flashlights. They are irresistible, because of bicycle riding at night. But anything else—money, jewelry, clothing—is perfectly safe. However, if you really want a key . . ."

"I do want a key. It isn't a flashlight."

He said, "Oh, very well. I'll send one up to you at once. Now, won't you have a cocktail? . . ."

"No, thank you. I'll expect the key." She gave a pleasant but brief little nod and walked away.

It left him feeling a little flat. His advice was not, as a

rule, flouted nor his conversation brought coolly to a close. However, the silence of her departure was soothing. Again he sat relaxed, sipping from the tall glass. Behind him in the far-flung wings of the old hotel, lights appeared; his guests were changing for dinner. A night bird stirred somewhere and cried eerily. Faint and far away along the road beyond the hotel a native strolled and touched a guitar softly.

Jim Fanfare Smith closed his eyes and let the deep, mysterious night enfold him.

When he roused and entered the hotel at last, guests had already filled the bar with the flutter of voices and women's gowns, the light clash of glass and ice and the scent of cigarettes and perfumes. Men were immaculate, if informal, in white silk or linen jackets; women showed smooth, brown shoulders and arms above bright chiffons and satins.

He stopped at the desk. One of the two desk clerks (both college men well content with their summer jobs) looked up brightly. "Yes, sir?"

"Find a key for Mr. Blake's suite. Send up a skeleton key if you can't find the key that belongs to that number."

"Yes, sir. Say, Mr. Smith, did you know he's *the* Peter Blake who invented and manufactures gold-processing equipment and machinery? He won't sell the equipment; leases it. What an income that man must have!"

"Has the fellow in eighteen got over his drunk?"

The clerks' eyebrows went up. "Nine Tom Collinses went to his room this afternoon. By actual count; it's on the bar list."

"Don't let him come into the dining room."

"No, sir. But he does carry it well. He's done nothing but order up drinks for the last four days; ever since he arrived, in fact. And I've not seen him drunk. Even his eyes are clear."

"Don't let him bother anybody. What's his name?"

"James Smith. The same as yours, you know, sir."

"It's not," said James Fanfare Smith a little haughtily, "an uncommon name. We'd better ship him home. Has he got money?"

"Yes," said the clerk economically; "fifteen hundred or more in the safe."

"Well—we'd better get him out before he sobers up."
"Yes, *sir*."

James Fanfare Smith went to his own rooms. Below and around him the hotel accommodated itself to the night. Out in the gardens, tables were laid and candles in hurricane glasses were lighted upon them. A native orchestra aligned itself under a canopy and began to play a rumba with a soft, insistent beat. A great yellow moon outlined palms and hibiscus in deep black and shone goldenly on the water and on the garden. The whole was curiously theatrical, as if the stage were set for some mysterious, secret drama. As, indeed, it was, though not even the actors knew it.

Later there was dancing under the rising golden moon. Jim, joining his guests, did not see or think of the Blake party. He danced with a pretty, jeweled English woman. He ordered a special dessert—crepes suzette, rolled with a light hand—for a stockbroker from New York. He paused to chat with a rich cattleman from the Argentine and his fat, worldly wife, and to order for them, with his compliments, a light, fragrant claret that bore a label: LAID DOWN 1842. BOTTLED 1929 FOR JAMES FANFARE SMITH, ESQ.

By one o'clock the hotel was quiet. Night became deeper, the moon passed its height and began to descend, and the shadows of tall cacti here and there about the grounds made sprawled, stark arms across silvery lawn. Crickets droned; now and then a horse trudged monotonously along the road. By two o'clock the hotel slept—peacefully, one would have said. Very quietly, at any rate, with its quota of human passions, human desires, human good and evil, lulled and slumbering.

Suite 21 was quiet, too; it opened on the long terrace that ran along the second-floor length of the narrow southern wing, and it was the finest suite in the hotel. But in one of its two bedrooms Lana Blake, the young woman with smooth, dark hair, lay awake. Oddly, somewhere in the vague and cloudy nimbus of her thoughts hovered the tall figure of James Fanfare Smith.

The moon went down at last.

Morning came, bright, tranquil, sunny and hot, with the water aquamarine. Mr. Smith, refreshed by the night, automatically set about making his guests comfortable and went to pay his respects to Mr. Peter Blake. That was at exactly 10:30. Breakfast for two, the elevator man told him, had gone to suite 21 some time ago and the trays had come down again. "Eighteen," continued the young man audibly (since only his employer was in the car), "had black coffee and whiskey. Second floor, sir." He opened the door and opened it on a very curious scene.

Two corridors branched from the elevator well; one to the left into the main and northern section of the building, and one to the right, which bisected the southern wing. There were two stairways in the main part of the hotel, but none for the south wing; thus, the instant the elevator door was opened, Jim had a full and complete view of the south-wing corridor.

A porter at that very instant plunged from a doorway along it and ran heavily toward the elevator, and beside the elevator stood a buxom, pretty maid. She had two stacks of sheets in her arms and she was perfectly rigid, with her face ashen, her eyes bulging.

The porter all but fell upon Jim and gibbered, "Murder! Boss! Murder!"

The corridor behind him was empty; Jim was forever after sure of that.

The maid screamed and dropped the sheets.

"What do you mean? Stop that noise, you! Now then, what's all this?"

"He shouted, 'Murder! Help!' In there...." The porter's hands were shaking as he gestured down the corridor behind him. The other man gaped over Jim's shoulder. The maid sat down on the floor amid tumbled sheets.

Jim grasped the porter's shoulder. "Not so much noise! Who? Where?"

The porter choked. "The room hummed. Then he yelled, 'Help—murder...' I think he's dead." Under the blazing blue eyes of his employer he achieved an instant's lucidity. "The man in twenty-one," he gurgled.

All of them followed Jim down the corridor. He was conscious of their presence behind him as he opened the door of the living room of suite 21. "You stay here," he ordered the elevator man. "Watch the corridor."

He didn't knock. The room was empty, and the door opposite, which led upon the long terrace, was open. The porter gasped, "In there," and Jim ran across the room toward the bedroom that the porter's shaking hand indicated. He ran across and stopped dead still in the doorway.

For the porter was right. A man lay face down on the floor. There was red all across the back of the dressing gown he wore and on the floor, and his head was twisted at an odd angle. The young woman—Mrs. Peter Blake—in pajamas, with her dark hair disheveled, knelt beside him and held something in her hands and looked up at Jim. She didn't say anything, just looked at him dazedly. The thing in her white hand was a knife.

The knife was long, slender, and oddly domestic in appearance; it was a plain kitchen knife with a wooden handle, and its nine-inch blade was wet. The girl's white hands were stained.

The porter breathed heavily over Jim's shoulder. Something about the pose of the man on the floor convinced Jim that he was quite dead.

He said, the words sounding harsh in that utter stillness, "Why did you kill him?"

He addressed Lana Blake. She did not appear to realize it; her face was perfectly white, her dark gray eyes were enormous and completely without expression.

Jim stepped nearer, bent and took the knife out of her hands, and laid it on the table. There was a red smear on the sleeve of her lounging pajamas. He said, "Get up."

She had given up the knife without question. Now stumbling a little, she got to her feet and stood there looking down. Jim said, "Louise."

The maid, still ashen and open-mouthed, stepped forward.

"Put a sheet over him. No, wait."

The maid waited, arrested in motion; they all waited while Jim, steeling himself to the task, knelt beside the man on the floor. After a moment or two he got up again. No one had moved. He said, "He's dead. There's not a flicker of a pulse or breath.... All right, Louise."

The maid skirted the body cautiously, took a sheet from the bed nearby and laid it shrinkingly across the murdered man.

Jim looked at the girl. "I've got to call the police, you know."

She still did not speak; did not, indeed, appear to hear him. And he heard himself saying again, still harshly, "Why did you kill him?"

At last she looked up at him. Her eyes had lost their dazed, blank look and were focused upon him. "What—what did you say?"

"I said, why did you kill him?"

"Kill him! Kill *him*? I didn't kill him. I..."

Jim's face tightened. His eyes were bright and clear and had hard black pupils. He said, "If you didn't kill him, who did?"

She put out her hands in a helpless gesture. "I don't know! I don't know what could have happened. I—he was just there, you see. When I came in. I don't know...."

"Madam, you had the knife in your hands when I entered the room."

"But I—why, yes, of course. I..." She struggled to get the words out. "I had to take it out. He ... I didn't think he was dead. Of course, I tried to pull it out and..." She stopped and said, "How could it have happened! He ..."

"You claim you didn't kill him, then?"

"But I didn't kill him. I didn't. You are wicked—cruel—you ...!"

"Don't scream." He motioned to Luzo, the porter. Together, swiftly, they searched the suite. There was no one. It took perhaps sixty seconds to make sure of that. They looked everywhere.

The young woman was still standing rigid, as if frozen, when he returned to her. "There is no one else in the suite," he said.

"I tell you I didn't—I don't know who—there was nobody—he had no enemies. I had to take the knife..." She was trembling and incoherent. Her voice all at once became faint. "I couldn't have murdered..." she whispered and swayed.

Jim caught her in his arms. She didn't faint, but she was perfectly limp and nerveless against him and startlingly white. He said to Louise, "Help me. Get water. I'll put her on the bed in the other bedroom."

The young woman walked, stumbling and supported by his arm, across the living room and into her own bedroom. He put her on the bed and took the pillow from under her head and put it under her feet. Her eyes were still open and very dark and followed him in an anguish of appeal as he went to the door again.

He said, "Louise will stay with you. I'll call the police."

In the living room the porter Luzo waited, and outside in the hall the elevator man stood against the door. He stepped quickly aside when Jim opened the door. His eyes were popping with excitement. Jim glanced along the row of closed doors on a line with suite 21.

"Has anyone come into the hall, George?"

"No, sir."

"All right. Let me know if anyone comes out, and stay here and keep your mouth shut if anybody inquires. If anything—frightens you—shout."

"Yes, boss."

In the living room of 21 again, Jim took the telephone. The desk clerk answered at once, in a polite voice.

"Get the police at Hamilton. Tell them there's been an accident. Don't let anyone hear you."

He could hear the clerk's excited gasp: "Yes, sir."

"Be quick about it.... Oh, yes. Put Mark on the elevator." He put down the instrument sharply.

"Now then, Luzo, what about it? Quick. Exactly what happened?"

With a sheet properly over the body and the bedroom door closed, the porter was more lucid. Still, it took ten minutes to get the story straight, brief though it was. For Luzo had been in the living room of the suite when sounds of voices in the next room attracted his attention.

"What were you doing in this room?"

"The umbrella, sir. The one for the terrace. I was going to put it out for the day. I knocked on the door of this room, and as no one answered I knocked again and then entered. It is the only door onto the terrace."

"Was anyone in here when you came in?"

"No, sir, and the bedroom doors were closed. So I went quietly across the room and then I heard voices in the bedroom. Loud voices. Quarreling."

"Who was it?"

"I don't know, boss."

"Did you hear words?"

"No, sir, not until he yelled 'Murder' and 'Help.' No words, just voices and—and a queer sound, too, sir. The room"—he paused, searched for a word, did not find it, and concluded with an effect of inadequacy—"hummed."

"The room hummed!" Jim frowned. "You said that before. What on earth do you mean?"

The porter made a helpless gesture with his hands. "I don't know, sir. Just a—a humming sound. Like it was hollow."

"But can't you . . . ?" Jim paused. The porter was evidently perplexed and evidently had done his best at what, in all probability, was an unimportant bit of description. "What did you do then?"

"I heard it, boss. I heard a sort of yell—a scream maybe it was, but not very loud. But he screamed 'Help' and 'Murder' and then stopped as if—as if he'd choked or something. It wasn't very loud, any of it. I ran to tell you."

"Why didn't you go into the bedroom?"

Luzo looked frightened. "I—I thought I'd better tell you, sir. The scream sounded—sounded bad, sir. Dreadful. I . . ." He stopped and passed his hands across his glistening black forehead. "It sounded like death."

"You didn't see anyone go into or come from the bedroom?"

"No, sir. There was only the voices."

"Men's voices?"

"Oh, yes, sir. Men's. Low and deep. And then the room hummed. . . ."

"Listen. Stop talking about the room humming. Stay with facts. Did you hear a woman's voice in there, too?"

Luzo was uncertain; he said doubtfully he wasn't sure.

"But you are sure you heard men's voices."

"Yes, sir."

"How many?"

"Two, at least."

Jim took a turn up and down the room. The door onto the terrace was open, and outside soft morning sunlight made a light pattern on the old stone floor. The woman had killed him, despite her white, stunned look, or the murderer had simply walked out that door and vanished while the porter had run to find help.

*But it would have been*, Jim thought suddenly, *a very natural thing to withdraw that knife. It would be your first, instinctive action, if you came upon the scene—a man dying with a knife in his back. If you could summon the courage to do it.*

The porter waited. Jim said, "All right. Stand at that door. On the inside of the room. Don't stir from it and don't let anybody come in, and don't tell anybody what has happened."

He went back to Mrs. Blake's bedroom door, knocked, and went in.

The maid was sitting on a chair watching the young woman; the maid's eyes were beginning to show a dark gleam of excitement. Mrs. Blake lay perfectly inert on the bed, her face as white as the sheet below it, and stared with great, dark eyes at the ceiling.

He spoke very clearly and distinctly, "Mrs. Blake. Please tell me as clearly as you can just what happened. Take your time, and don't be frightened."

"I don't know—who did it. I can't understand. There isn't anyone who would want to kill him."

"Tell me..." He paused and told himself to be patient. By this time the desk clerk had got the police and they were doubtless on their way. The hotel was a good hour from Hamilton but no more. He addressed Mrs. Blake. "When did you go into your husband's room?"

It was horror and pain, he decided, that made her eyes so dark.

She flinched a little and said, "Just before you came in. He was there—on the floor. There was blood and I saw the knife and I—I made myself pull it out. But it was too late—and then you came in."

"Why did you enter his room?"

"Because I thought I heard him call me. I wasn't sure. I was in this room. The door was closed and the door to his room was closed. But I thought I heard him call and I—I put on these pajamas and my slippers . . ."

"Immediately?"

"Yes, of course. That is, it took a moment or two because I couldn't find my slippers. I had to look around."

"Did you feel his voice was urgent?"

"No. I wasn't sure he had called."

"Had you heard any voices preceding his—calling you?"

"No. But there might have been voices. I had just got out of the shower. The sound of the water . . ."

Would have drowned the sound of the voices. That and two closed doors. He frowned and glanced at the windows, which opened onto the terrace.

"Did anyone pass the window?"

"I don't know. I don't think so. I believe I would have noticed it."

"I see." But did he? Well . . . "The police are coming." He paused, and then, rather to his own astonishment, heard himself giving orders: "The police are on their way here. When they come they'll question you. All of us. I think it would be better not to bring up the matter of your having— withdrawn the knife. Tell everything but that."

Her eyes seemed to take it in and understand it. He turned to the maid. "You heard me, Louise?"

"Yes, sir."

There was gratitude in Mrs. Blake's eyes. Or did he imagine it? He turned abruptly and left the room.

He would have to wipe the fingerprints—his own and Mrs. Blake's—off the knife. He would thereby destroy evidence and make himself an accomplice, an accessory after the fact. Well, he was a fool. And it would accomplish nothing; her presence beside the murdered man was almost as damning as the knife in her hands. But not quite. His hotel would be ruined; there existed among travelers a good, old-fashioned prejudice against murder.

Well—he'd better take a look at the terrace. The porter's eyes followed him as he opened the door to the terrace and went out.

It was a long terrace, running the full length of that particular wing of the second floor. The hotel was built against a hillside and, owing to a resultant irregularity of levels, there were no rooms below that particular portion of the second floor; the terrace itself rose sharply, with a high stone retaining-wall, from the very edge of the lagoon. One end of it was backed by an angle of the building, the other end rose above the water, as did the outward side. Thus, the only approach to the terrace (other than through the hotel) would have been accomplished by scaling the wall from the water and clambering over a high stone balustrade.

There were no footholds anywhere in the retaining wall; a hook and rope would have done the trick, with a boat anchored below, but the whole process in the bright light of that sunny morning would have been clearly visible, not only from overlooking windows and the opposite shore of the lagoon, but from the hotel's bathing beach some three hundred feet to the left.

Jim began to see that there was a certain scarcity of approaches and exits from the terrace room in which the murdered man lay, and consequently a definite isolation of any possible murder suspects.

For, if the only door to the terrace was the door from the living room of 21, still there were four other bedrooms along the terrace side of that wing, each of them having a window or windows onto the terrace. Reaching the terrace from any of those four bedrooms was only a matter of unhooking a screen and stepping out.

He frowned as he began to consider the implications of that particular situation. The porter had been in the living room almost certainly when the blow had been struck. Luzo had burst immediately from the door at an instant when Louise and Jim, himself, had commanded a view of the corridor leading to 21, and no one had escaped in that way. This meant that whoever had killed Peter Blake had had to escape by means of the terrace. Always provided the murderer was not actually Peter Blake's young wife.

He considered the occupants of those four rooms. Eighteen, nearest the elevator, was, of course, occupied by the man bearing his own name, James Smith. He had been drinking steadily and prodigiously ever since his arrival and ought to be in a stupor by this time.

The next room, 19, was occupied. It was a Mr. and Mrs. Fritz Von Holzen from New York. They were a vaguely pleasant middle-aged couple, quiet, placid. There was about them something faintly foreign, an accent perhaps.

Well, then, who was in the next room, 20? Yes, of course, John Tovery, the actor; a handsome fellow in his forties, fresh from a Broadway success that had closed merely for the summer and was to open again in the fall. He was by way of being a pal of Jim's. They'd had drinks together and had gone sailing.

The next three rooms belonged to the suite, 21, and were a bedroom (in which the murder occurred), a living room, and the bedroom in which Mrs. Blake lay and stared with great, dark eyes at the ceiling.

He went on swiftly in his mind to the next and last room along the terrace wing. That was room 22, and it was occupied—he gave a little start as he remembered—it was occupied by Ernest Pusey, who had come from New York expressly to meet the Blakes and was a lawyer.

Well, then he was obviously the man to be informed of the murder and to represent young Mrs. Blake in all the troublesome details to follow. There was certainly no need for him, Jim, to undertake the unaccustomed and reluctant role of knight-errant. Unless, of course, it was Pusey himself who had murdered his client. On the face of it, it sounded unreasonable; for, even aside from the probably friendly relations existing between them, murdering your client was in the nature of killing the goose that laid the golden egg. And yet, as decidedly, the lawyer must fall within the range of suspects, because his room lay along the terrace and because, which was as important, he knew Peter Blake.

As important? It was, Jim saw at once, far more important. For in all probability the only people in the hotel who knew Peter Blake were, naturally, his wife and this lawyer who had come to meet him. And total strangers do not as a rule walk up and plunge a knife into you. No, it was clear that this Pusey was not only a suspect; he was, outside of the widow, the prime and only suspect. Well, then, Jim had better take steps.

The whole point, of course, lay in the fact that no one had escaped by the corridor during that time. From the moment the alarm was given, it had been utterly impossible for anyone to have entered the corridor from the wing without being seen. And since then he had had the porter on guard. That meant that whoever had murdered Peter Blake was almost certainly still bottled up within that wing.

He turned, jerkily and instinctively, to look along the screened, blank windows, and a man was sitting quietly in one of the steamer chairs, watching him. It was Fritz Von Holzen, and he held a newspaper in his hands. "Good morning," he said affably.

He was perhaps fifty or fifty-five, plump and slightly bald. His eyes were very sharp behind his glasses. And he commanded a full view of the terrace.

*Queer,* thought Jim, *that I didn't notice his presence when I came out on the terrace.* Still, perhaps it wasn't queer. He'd been thinking hard and fast. He had been only vaguely aware of the terrace itself, with its clusters of brightly painted tables and chairs and the gay red-and-white umbrella at the south end. He walked now toward Fritz Von Holzen.

"Good morning. I didn't see you when I came out just now," Jim said.

"I beg your pardon," said Von Holzen, cupping a hand around one ear. Evidently he was deaf. Jim repeated his remark in a louder voice, and Von Holzen replied, "No. You were in what is called a brown study, Mr. Smith."

"Oh, you saw me?"

"Why, certainly. I'm deaf but I'm not blind. I've been sitting here for—oh, since nine-thirty or so."

Nine-thirty. Here, then, was a witness. Jim said tensely, "Has anyone else been on the terrace?"

"No. At least not within the past hour or so. Unless— yes, it seems to me there was a porter with an umbrella. That's all."

"Are you sure of that? Hasn't anyone else come out of that door over there?"

"No one but you, Mr. Smith," said Von Holzen cheerily. "I've been sitting here without moving for the last hour and would have seen anyone."

"You—I suppose you heard nothing?"

"Heard nothing?" Von Holzen's sharp eyes were now definitely aware of purpose back of this inquiry. "What do you mean—heard nothing? If you mean anything—out of the way or unusual, no, I have not."

"You didn't hear—anyone call out—for help?" persisted Jim.

"No. You'd better tell me just what has happened."

"A hotel crisis. You are altogether sure that no one passed you?"

"Well, yes. I'm certain. Who called for help and why?"

It was Lana Blake, then. It had to be Mrs. Blake who had murdered Blake, for there was no one else. Yet, despite Von Holzen's story and its clinching evidence against Lana Blake, Jim was still loath to believe her guilty.

The main, indeed the only, evidence to the contrary was Luzo's statement that there had been two voices—loud voices—in Blake's room.

He said, "It's a police affair. I'm afraid my guests are going to be questioned and annoyed. I'm sorry."

"You must mean murder," observed Von Holzen coolly. "Who was murdered?"

"The man in there," admitted Jim. "Now, if you'll excuse me. . . ."

He had expected a flood of questions and commotion and was prepared to cut it short. But Von Holzen took it without the faintest change of expression. He said, "In that case your hands are full, Mr. Smith. I'm afraid I'm delaying you. If I can be of any assistance..."

"Thank you—I'll try to keep it as long as possible from my guests..." (His guests; there would be trouble there.)

There was courteous understanding in the gesture of a small hand that promised discretion. Jim left Von Holzen and went into the living room of 21.

He entered the bedroom and closed the door behind him and lifted the sheet. There was no more to be seen than he had already seen. A middle-aged man, florid and heavy, with a mouth that suggested temper, violently done to death. He replaced the sheet somewhat hurriedly and turned again to the knife, lying on a table nearby.

Jim had the usual layman's respect and fear for the evidence of fingerprints. He did not know that police expect to find innocent fingerprints, with—if they are in luck—one guilty one among them. Jim in that instant was convinced that the discovery of Lana Blake's fingerprints on that knife would be proof of her guilt.

He wiped the knife.

Then he put the knife on the table again, shoved his handkerchief back in his pocket, and went swiftly through the living room into the corridor.

George still remained on guard and no one, he said, had entered the corridor. Jim looked at his watch and started with room 18.

The man in that room, James Smith, his namesake, did not respond when Jim knocked. When he opened the door the man seemed dead to the world and would not rouse. There were six empty glasses on the table.

In room 19 Mrs. Von Holzen, a stout, placid woman of fifty or so, came promptly and cheerily to the door. Obviously her husband had not yet told her the news, for she was altogether calm, said she had not left her room yet that morning, and thanked him for a hastily concocted inquiry as to the comfort of the room.

John Tovery, the actor, in room 20, had also been in his room all morning. Jim's cautious inquiry as to persons on the terrace brought a prompt confirmation of Von Holzen's story. For Tovery had been writing letters for the past half-hour at a table facing the window and the terrace, and Von Holzen had been in full view all the time.

"He's been there the full time. I'm sure I would have known it if he had moved a foot away from the chair. You know how a movement attracts one's eyes. Why?"

"Did you know Peter Blake?"

"Who's Peter Blake?"

Jim murmured and went on, passing suite 21 again, to room 22. "My prime suspect," he thought, knocking.

But when the lawyer, Ernest Pusey, came to the door Jim's heart sank. For Ernest Pusey was a dry, gray, upright man in his middle fifties and the very personification of a corporation lawyer. Probably, reflected Jim ruefully, he didn't brush his teeth without first considering any possible legal consequences of the action.

"Mr. Pusey?"

"Yes?"

He wore neat, coffee-colored trousers and coat, and his shirt, as a slight concession to the heat, was open at the throat. His thin gray hair was brushed neatly back and his pince-nez glittered.

"Mr. Blake is your client?"

"Yes, of course."

There was a commotion at the elevator—feet marching toward them and voices.

Jim risked a rebuff. "You've been in your room all the morning?"

Pusey's precise eyebrows lifted. "Yes. Why do you ask?"

"You've—heard nothing—out of the way?"

"See here—what's the meaning of this?"

"Mr. Pusey—do you know of any reason for Peter Blake's . . ."

"Blake's—what? What do you mean?"

The feet came closer. Jim swallowed hastily and said, "For Peter Blake's murder. Here are the police . . ."

Ernest Pusey stared at him, rigid and gray and wordless, for the moment it took the police to reach suite 21. Then he said in a harsh, deep voice that sounded rusted, "Murdered! My God!" and thrust Jim out of the way and went to meet the police. Jim followed. . . .

By seven o'clock that night the commotion induced by the arrival of the police and the subsequent investigation had in a measure died down. Somewhat to Jim's surprise, his guests did not arise and depart in a body at first word of the murder. Instead, they submitted with the best possible grace to the prolonged inquiry, which embraced a statement from every single one of them. But Jim would have expected a complaint or two, and so far he had none—none from his guests and none from his staff, who were also questioned.

It had taken time and a steady, patient sifting of facts. But in the end, so far as Jim knew, the police still had only the few initial facts he, the maid and two other employees, and Lana Blake herself had been able to give them. Von Holzen's story remained firm (regrettably, Jim felt), and John Tovery gave Von Holzen himself a sound alibi.

There was only one item that Jim knew and the police did not know. That was the fact that Lana had had the knife actually in her hands.

Unfortunately, the omission did not much lighten the weight of evidence against Lana Blake. Yet, too, it might have proved to be the deciding factor.

The inspector in charge was one Willaker, a man whom Jim knew and liked. He was extremely thorough, extremely deliberate, and he left no stone unturned. It was he, indeed, who found that the knife had been removed, when or by whom no one could say, from the hotel kitchen. At night there was no one, as a rule, in the kitchen. Thus anyone in the hotel might have removed the knife.

However, there still were, when all evidence and stories were sifted, only six people, besides the porter himself, who had had access to the room in which Peter Blake was murdered. And of those people there was only one who they could prove had been in Peter Blake's bedroom, and that was, of course, Lana.

"Von Holzen himself could have murdered Blake," said

Inspector Willaker to Jim, "and then walked out onto the terrace and made of himself a witness instead of an obvious culprit. But since they themselves (Von Holzen and his wife, I mean) both say they had never laid eyes on Blake—at least, knowingly—there's the question of motive. John Tovery backs up Von Holzen's story, anyway. Yes, it all simmers down to the question of escape. If no one left the suite, then the person remaining there must have murdered Blake."

"Mrs. Blake?"

"Yes."

"Somehow—I don't think she did it."

"There's nobody else. Don't let a pretty face carry you away, Jim, my boy."

Jim shook his head impatiently. "Are you—arresting her?"

"Not tonight," said Willaker cautiously. "Not so long as there's the faintest loophole in our case."

"What's the loophole?"

"Your porter's story of the voices. Men's voices, he said. He thinks there were two voices only. But he swears neither of the voices he heard was a woman's voice. If he heard two men talking, then what happened to the other man?"

"Exactly," said Jim with a little too much enthusiasm.

Willaker looked at him sharply. "I take it you're willing to give us every possible assistance on this case?"

"Why, certainly. The sooner it's over, the better for my hotel."

"Right. I'm leaving a couple of policemen on guard in the suite. By the way, are your employees superstitious?"

"Not inordinately. Why?"

"The porter who heard Blake call for help keeps saying something about the room humming. He implies a kind of death song. Know anything about it?"

Jim searched his knowledge of Bermuda—of the secret order the natives call Gombies, of night ceremonies along deserted coves. "No. He may have heard some coincident sound. A motorboat or a vacuum cleaner . . ."

"He would have recognized those sounds. This special thing seems to worry him. Well, our investigation may take time. We've had to cable in order to check the stories these people tell of themselves." Willaker sighed. "It's a bad business, but I think it'll be cleared shortly. We have opportunity and motive."

"Motive? I suppose you mean he leaves his widow with plenty of money?"

"Certainly. She . . ." Willaker looked at his watch and rose. "She was his secretary, you know; he'd only known her six weeks before he married her. His only living relative is a nephew with whom he quarreled over the marriage. The nephew's name is Sandy Blake. We've cabled him."

"Did she tell you that?"

"No. Pusey—against his will. He's her lawyer, and right on the job. She denied knowledge of the quarrel with his nephew. Pusey advised her to say nothing. . . . Oh, that reminds me. Give your barman orders not to send any more drinks to the fellow in eighteen. We haven't been able to get a word out of him."

"All right, Inspector."

"And you might keep after your kitchen help a bit about that knife. In case one of them remembers anything. Although, as a matter of fact, there's something phony about that knife. It doesn't seem just right somehow to find it there on the table, wiped free of fingerprints."

"Seems quite natural to me. Fellow sticks another fellow with knife—pulls it out and wipes off his fingerprints, puts it down on the handiest table."

Inspector Willaker's intelligent eyes looked a little too intelligent. "Um," he said. "Sound natural to you, does it?" And went away, without—which was the important thing—arresting Lana Blake.

Jim sighed. The lobby and lounge had gradually cleared, for, come what may, life and meals went on and people still dressed for dinner. It was sunset, with the water in the lagoon tranquil again and blue. He went out to his favorite seat above the lagoon, and a waiter instantly produced a tall, cold drink and withdrew.

Jim closed his eyes wearily. The affair gave every indication of putting him to very much more energy and effort than he ever willingly expended. He wished for his own sake he could find a quick and easy way out of it. And one, said a small voice within him, that would clear a young woman with the loveliest face and sweetest mouth Jim had ever seen. A young woman who was frightened and helpless and all too definitely on the spot.

Twenty-four hours ago Lana Blake had sat there on the balustrade and had looked steadily at him and asked for a key.

A key!

He sat up abruptly. She'd asked for a key, and she'd said, what? Something that, even then, struck him as unusual, for she'd said firmly that ''it'' wasn't a flashlight. . . . What wasn't a flashlight?

And why had she wanted a key? Did it argue fear? Or merely that she'd wanted to lock the door?

Or—he sank back suddenly. The police would say she'd wanted the key in order to insure that there would be no interruption during a certain half-hour that morning. And thus would argue a cool, devilish premeditation.

But it wasn't premeditation. And the door had not been locked when Luzo entered it that morning. Well, then, why? He half rose, and a voice behind him said, ''Mr. Smith.''

It was the lawyer, Ernest Pusey. He said, ''May I sit down? . . . No, thank you, no cocktail. I—I only wanted to say, Mr. Smith, that I'm sorry I was so obtuse when you came to break the news to me this morning. It was good of you to try to spare me some of the shock, and I appreciate it.''

''How is Mrs. Blake?''

''Poor girl. It's a dreadful thing. But if it had to happen I suppose it's lucky I was here to take over. Peter was my oldest friend—since school days—and my best client. Well, so the world goes. Lana will be well provided for.''

''I suppose this makes her an extremely rich woman.''

''Well, yes and no. There's a rather odd—still, not at all an unusual—situation involved. Lana is not actually Peter's heir and yet will certainly inherit a great deal of money. Peter was a very rich man. The income from his leases alone . . .''

"Leases?"

"You don't know his business? Not leases in the ordinary sense; I referred to the leasing of the gold-smelting equipment and machinery that Peter long ago invented and on which he held patents, and which he also manufactured. If he had sold the equipment, you see, he would have had money from the outright sale, but that's all. By retaining possession and only leasing equipment and machinery, he assured himself a steady income; in fact, he had almost a monopoly. He had only a few competitors, and not many of them lasted very long. So long as no similar process is discovered, Peter (and Peter's heirs) will be very rich.

"Well, as I was saying, his heir is his nephew Sandy. Peter never really expected to marry and was very fond of Sandy always. In fact, the only quarrel I ever knew them to have was about—well, never mind. The fact remains that his will has been unaltered since his marriage. He did, however, write a letter on the day of his wedding, requesting Sandy, if the need arose, to provide generously for Lana. He intended to make a new will as soon as he returned from his honeymoon; in fact, that is the main reason for my meeting him here. Peter cabled, asking me to come."

"That's putting a lot of faith in this man Sandy."

"Peter trusted Sandy. And I'm sure Sandy will be generous with Lana."

"At any rate, it removes a motive for your client's having murdered her husband."

"My client? Oh, you mean Lana Blake. Unfortunately, she believed Peter had already changed his will. And when the police questioned her, before I could persuade her not to talk, she admitted it. The letter to Sandy, of which I knew, was a shock to her. I don't mind saying—to you, Mr. Smith, because I believe you are inclined to be friendly . . .''

"She told you about the knife."

"She . . .'' Pusey glanced quickly around, but they were alone. "Yes, she did. It was kind of you, Mr. Smith."

"But not much help. You are going to get her out of it, aren't you?"

"I hope so. She . . ." He took off his glasses and polished them. "I hope so, I'm sure, Mr. Smith. But I don't mind telling you it's a bad business. However, I'm going to do my very best."

Jim rose with the lawyer and they walked together back to the veranda.

That night, too, there were candles on the tables and a native orchestra playing rumbas and its own version of pop tunes. There were women with soft, brown shoulders and bright gowns and men very festive in white dinner jackets. But there was a subtle difference between that night and the night before.

During the daytime the guests had been good sports. They had talked of the murder with interest and speculation and excitement. It had seemed, however, quite remote, an impersonal thing.

But by night murder became a different matter. It assumed gradually, with the darkness, its own sinister and hideously personal property. Where there is murder there is also a murderer.

Not a nice thought.

It induced an early going to bed and an unprecedented number of requests at the desk for keys.

Jim Fanfare Smith, on his way to the elevator, was accosted by the actor, John Tovery. "Look here, Jim."

"Yes."

"This murder. I—well, gosh, I don't like it, Jim. Do you realize that the police seem to regard me as a suspect, merely because my room has a window on that damn terrace? They won't let me leave. I'm due in New York on Monday of next week. I've got to be there for rehearsals."

"I thought you were going to stay another two weeks."

"Yes, I was. But I just had word from my manager. I've got to go. I can't hang around here until this thing is settled. It may be weeks. Say a good word for me, will you, Jim?"

"Von Holzen wouldn't much like your leaving just now. You are his alibi."

John Tovery ran expressive hands through his fine and beautifully waved dark hair. "If I had known I was going to be anybody's alibi I'd have kept my mouth shut," he said. "Do help me out."

"There's nothing I can do. However, I don't imagine they'll keep you here long."

Out of the corner of his eyes he perceived the chef waiting at the door leading from the main hall into the kitchen passage. The chef was standing perfectly immobile but his eyes were fixed on Jim, and Jim knew the chef, Jean, wanted to speak to him. He disengaged himself from Tovery. "I'll do my best."

"But you . . ." Tovery stopped and listened. "Hey, what's that?"

An eerie, rhythmic sound of drums, beating in a curiously quick and stirring tempo, was growing out of the dark night somewhere at a distance. The drumbeats thudded in the air like an intangible pulse and grew more distinct rapidly, and all at once you heard, besides, and high above the beat of the drums, shrill, confused whistles and the rattle of horses' hoofs and wheels going a a furious pace.

"What, under heaven . . . ?"

"Gombies. It hasn't rained for a while, and they're praying all over the island for rains. Holding ceremonies."

The drums came quickly nearer. Obviously, the center of the tumult was rapidly moving past the hotel and along the white, moonlit road beyond. Drums, whistles, shouts, the rattle of the omnibus, the sounds of voices, the thud and patter of feet running after the horse-pulled vehicle.

"Aren't they dangerous?"

"No. It's all right. The police watch them. They hold their ceremonies and then go home."

"Gombies, did you say?"

"So they call themselves. It's some obscure, mysterious relation, I imagine, to the African zombi—that is, the living dead. If you want to see them you'll have to hurry; they'll soon be out of sight."

The actor hesitated, looked at Jim, and then hurried out onto the veranda.

The chef still waited. Jim approached him.

"Well?... Why, Jean, what's wrong?" He saw, on closer view, that the chef was very pale.

Jean whispered. "The knife. Another knife. It's gone. And I saw her in the kitchen passage."

Jim glanced quickly about. No one was within earshot. "What do you mean?"

"Another knife has been taken. I counted this morning when the police inquired. There were eleven altogether. Now there are ten. And I saw her."

"Saw who?"

"The woman. The fat woman with the German name. In the terrace wing..."

"Do you mean Mrs. Von Holzen?"

"Yes! Yes, that's the woman. She was hurrying away when I came into the kitchen."

"When?"

"About fifteen minutes ago. I had gone to the kitchen to see that all was closed for the night. After I saw her I looked around my kitchen and I—the knife is gone, sir."

Jim's heart constricted. "All right. Thanks, Jean."

The chef gave him an uneasy, irresolute look and scurried out of sight.

The clerk sprang to attention. "Yes, sir."

"Is Louise still with Mrs. Blake?"

"Yes, sir."

Jim hesitated. The police were in the living room of 21, and a telephone was in 21. The sensible thing, of course, was to tell the police—well, tell them what? That the chef was frightened. That he'd counted kitchen knives and said one was missing. That he'd seen a woman he believed to be Mrs. Von Holzen scurrying away.

He decided not to telephone to them. The desk clerk leaned forward.

"Mr. Smith. I heard that the only people in the hotel who were acquainted with the man who was murdered were, of course, his wife and the lawyer, Pusey."

"So I understand. Why?"

"Well, that's wrong, sir. Mr. Blake knew Von Holzen."

*"What's that?"*

"I saw them meet, here in the lobby, right in front of the desk. They spoke. . . ."

"What did they say?"

"Well, not much, I guess. Didn't seem very friendly. Called each other by their first names, though."

"Did you tell the police?"

"No, sir. I didn't think of it until after they had questioned us."

"All right. I'll telephone Willaker."

Jim took the elevator upstairs, walked briskly to the living room of suite 21 and knocked.

Two minutes later he was walking a little less briskly toward the elevator again, having been denied an audience with Lana Blake. "Inspector Willaker's orders," said one of the two policemen. "He said only her lawyer could see her."

Jim could accept it. "I'd better tell you," he said, "that my chef believes there's another knife missing from the kitchen."

The two policemen looked at each other and back at Jim. "Is he sure?"

"So he says."

The policeman acting as spokesman looked a little skeptical. "Well—I don't imagine there'll be any trouble. Not with us here. Maybe that knife's been lost for months. Maybe it isn't lost."

"But . . ."

"Don't worry, Mr. Smith. I'll tell the inspector about it in the morning."

There was nothing to do but retreat, leaving the two policemen to their interrupted game of cribbage at the little table with its checked cloth.

Jim passed the door to 20, John Tovery's room, and, rather to his surprise, saw a light in the crack of the closed transom. Tovery had come upstairs, then, almost immediately after the Gombies had passed the hotel. The door to 19 was closed, too. The picture of Adelaide Von Holzen stealing surreptitiously out of the kitchen wing with a knife in her hand was, now that he was removed from the chef's convincing earnestness, patently absurd. He recalled her bland, middle-aged hausfrau's face. Yet Blake had known Von Holzen.

He passed 18, stopped, and cautiously opened the door. It was dark inside. There was no movement in the room. His namesake in all probability was sleeping off the effects of four days of uninterrupted bar orders.

Jim listened, and then tiptoed quietly across the room; the screen, which opened on a hinge, was already unhooked; he opened it carefully. The bed was in a mass of shadow in one corner, and there was no motion or voice. He closed the screen gently and was on the terrace.

It was yet in deep shadow; later it would be flooded with moonlight. Upon the flat, black floor lay areas of light from the window of Tovery's room, the living room of 21, and (less well defined, for the shades were drawn) Pusey's room at the south end of the terrace. By going along the balustrade he skirted the rectangles of light, and a moment later reached the black windows of Lana Blake's room and, mindful of police in the next room, scratched lightly on the screen.

There was a movement in the room. Someone approached the window cautiously and tiptoed away again, and there was a murmured colloquy.

"Mr. Smith . . ." It was Lana herself. "Louise said it was you."

"Can you come out on the terrace?"

The screen clicked a little and opened. She was a slender, shadowy figure, dressed in something soft and silky.

"This way," he said, and guided her into the area of deep shadow at the end of the terrace. They leaned against the balustrade. No one was about. He caught himself watching the shadows and was annoyed to discover a small sense of danger tweaking at his nerves.

"No one can hear," he said, "if we talk low."

"You were right about the—the knife," she said. "Thank you. I didn't know how difficult—how horrible it was going to be."

"I'm sorry."

"Louise stayed with me all day—at your orders, I suppose. It's good of you. Mrs. Von Holzen came and asked the police if she could stay with me tonight. They refused, but I thought it was awfully kind."

Mrs. Von Holzen! He said, "Look here. Why did you ask me for a key?"

"Peter told me to get one."

"But why did he want a key? You said, 'It isn't a flashlight.' "

She hesitated and then spoke: "Yes, there was a special reason. Peter had some work with him; there is a new process he was perfecting, and he brought all the papers along with him in a briefcase."

"Did you get the key?"

"Yes. It's in the door now, I think. Or was. But I had unlocked the door to the living room this morning in order to let the waiter bring the breakfast trays into the suite."

"Where is the briefcase containing the papers?"

"It's in my room. Peter had left it there because he wanted me to copy some notes he had made. I . . . was his secretary, you know, before he married me." Her voice faltered. "He was so good. So kind. He had a temper, but he always controlled it. He had no enemies. It's so cruel . . ."

"Don't." She was trembling; he could sense it.

"He was good to me. No one was ever so good to me." She was crying softly.

He put his arms around her lightly and thought she was scarcely aware of it. Presently she stopped crying and wiped her eyes.

"Do you know what this process Blake was perfecting consisted of?" Jim asked.

"Oh, yes. He told me. I was the only person who knew anything about it. I think. Unless he told Sandy."

"Sandy? That's his nephew?"

"Yes."

"You know him, of course."

"No. I've seen him only once. He came into the office once before I was married; I don't think he saw me. He didn't come to our wedding. Peter loved Sandy dearly. He wanted us to be friends.''

She didn't know then that Peter had quarreled with his nephew, or why.

''About the process . . .''

''Oh, yes. Well, it was nothing Peter could ever use, you see. He was only doing it in order to take out patents himself on it, and thus prevent anyone else (who might have the same idea) from using it.''

''Why couldn't he use it? Was it something about gold smelting?''

''Yes, of course. He couldn't use it, because it was a new way to refine gold—a chemical process that was very cheap and readily available, and would have put Peter out of business altogether. You see, a long time ago he invented a gold-smelting process, and then invented and manufactured the machinery for that process, and leased the machinery . . .''

''Yes, I know. So this new process would have put him out of business.''

''Yes, of course. Oh, he could have patented it and sold it for a big sum of money, but the factory and business he had already established would have been a total loss, as well as the income from leasing his machinery. It's . . . a little ironical, I suppose—to discover such a process, I mean, and then in order to protect yourself be obliged to bottle it up.''

''It isn't unusual,'' said Jim slowly. ''It happens fairly frequently with big manufacturing concerns. He thought this new process was cheap and successful?''

''Oh, yes; he knew it was.''

''And you—you still have the papers in your room?''

''Yes. Isn't it safe? I mean . . .'' She leaned forward. ''Do you think that was a motive for his murder?''

''You say he had no enemies.''

''And he had none. But there is no one here who would know . . .''

''Did he know this Von Holzen?''

''I don't know.''

''Did Pusey know of this new process?''

"No. He said he'd never heard of it until I told him this morning."

"Did he offer to keep the papers for you?"

"No."

"Look here. Do you want me to put them in the safe?"

"Why—why, yes. If you think . . ."

"I think it's just as well."

"I'll get the briefcase."

She vanished into the rim of shadow and presently was briefly and dimly silhouetted against the light from 21.

He wanted to light a cigarette and stopped in the act, lest the little flame betray his presence on the terrace. The night was no longer clear. Clouds had gradually obscured the moon. He could barely discern along the terrace solid shapes of deeper black that were occasional chairs and tables, and the umbrella, closed and thus tall and slender like a man; it ought to have been taken in for the night as usual, he thought absently.

He turned and leaned his elbows upon the balustrade and waited. Lana ought to be returning. The thick, dark night was laden with scent—salt water and flower fragrances mingled. Vague shapes loomed out of the shadows below.

Lana ought to have returned.

Struck by the notion that a very long time had elapsed, he turned abruptly. The area of light from the living room of the suite still lay flat and empty upon the terrace floor. No one moved. Nothing had changed. Except the umbrella had moved. Its vague, dark shape was at least three feet nearer the wall of the building than it had been. And it was moving again.

It was moving again, and it wasn't an umbrella, for now he saw that the umbrella's dark silhouette remained stiff and straight beside the balustrade.

And it wasn't Lana.

Instinct alone told him that. The shadow outlined itself for an instant against the path of light fifty feet away. It was a fleeting glimpse, but certain. Someone—a man—was on the terrace and was moving stealthily toward Pusey's window.

Jim started forward, and then drew back again. Better

watch and make certain. He could always shout and attract the attention of the police in 21.

There was, except for the murmuring water below, utter silence. Then quite suddenly there was the slight scuffle of a footstep, and a shadow outlined itself definitely against Pusey's lighted window. A shadow that hesitated. And then Jim heard a rasp of fingers against the screen. He said, "What are you doing there?"

But he was not prepared for what happened. For the shadow jerked away from the window, was momentarily lost in the darkness all about, and then became solid muscle that hurled itself upon him. He clutched, tried to get a grip, and missed. A fist shot hard at his chin, and Jim quietly and neatly sat down, bumping his head hard against the balustrade. There was a soft patter of footsteps and then utter silence.

He rubbed his chin and swore under his breath. For his fingers had encountered the smooth, cool leather of a briefcase.

And his assailant had gone as unexpectedly and much more swiftly than he had come. But he had given up his attempt to break into Pusey's room. That was certain. Jim got to his feet and ran along the terrace. He passed Lana's darkened window and stopped at the door of 21. To his intense astonishment, the policemen were not there. The table was bare; the cribbage board and cards were strewn on the floor, and the room was bare of human presence.

Lana's window was beside him. He pulled at the screen and it opened. The room was dark, and he stepped over the sill quickly and whispered, "Lana! Lana!"

No one answered.

It was very still and very black. He took a step into the room, and another, and trod on something inert and soft.

He stumbled—knelt—groping into the blackness at his feet.

He had an instant of cold panic. Then his hands encountered the crisply starched folds of a maid's uniform. It was Louise. It must be Louise. He spoke to her softly, and she did not answer, but she was breathing.

He turned on the light. By its soft glow he saw that the room had been ransacked and that Lana was not there. Louise lay in a huddle near the window. He bent over her again. He thought she must have been struck.

There was an adjoining bathroom, empty, for the door was open, and a long, narrow clothes closet. Obviously Lana was not in the room, but nevertheless he went to the closet. Rows of gowns hanging like fragile, fragrant ghosts confronted him. He stepped inside in order to thrust aside the soft folds, bent, groping among them, and all at once heard a small, cautious motion behind him in the bedroom. He whirled around and was too late.

Darkness came upon him and the door was closed and fastened. Probably by a chair under the knob, for when he hurled himself against it, it did not budge an inch.

He was capable of sudden, tempestuous rages, and one overtook him now. He'd be damned if he'd let anyone bottle him up in a closet in his own hotel. He'd be—a chill, cold little wind seemed to cut through his anger. What was going on out there? He must get out of that closet.

The door was stubborn against his repeated onslaughts, and in the end it was Louise who released him. She looked and probably felt dizzy and was very wild-eyed.

She put her hand to a rapidly swelling temple and asked him as he emerged why he hit her.

"I didn't. What happened? Where's Mrs. Blake?"

Louise moaned and sank into a jabbering heap on the bed. She didn't know. She didn't know anything at all.

He questioned her swiftly. She'd been sitting beside the window waiting for Mrs. Blake to return. Maybe she dozed. The first thing she knew, something came out of the dark and struck her, and that was all.

"Where are the police?"

She shook her head. She'd heard them talking over the telephone just before she dozed off. She'd heard a door close somewhere, too.

"What door?"

She didn't know. It might have been the window. And she didn't know who had silently entered the room after Jim and closed the door into the closet and propped a chair under the knob. She didn't know anything except that her head hurt.

"Can you get to your room?"

"Yes, sir."

Jim went with her through the living room of the suite, still oddly empty of police, and watched her wavering progress as far as the elevator. Then he went back to the living room of 21 and got the desk clerk on the telephone.

"Where are the police?"

"They went out. Received a telephone call from outside . . ."

"Well, what was it?" demanded Jim impatiently, brushing aside the fiction that the desk clerk who handled the switchboard at night wouldn't know.

"Gombies, sir. It was a bad connection, but I heard enough. Willaker heard there was going to be some trouble and sent the two police who were here because they were nearest."

Jim swore. "How long ago?"

"Eleven-forty exactly, sir. It's now twelve forty-one."

"Get Willaker. Tell him—there's trouble here. Have you seen Mrs. Blake?"

"No, sir."

"Never mind. Call Willaker. Tell him I told you to tell him to hurry."

He put down the telephone. Odd that the racket he'd made had not waked the hotel. But perhaps not so odd, because the suite above was empty and the rooms on the back of the terrace wing were undesirable and hot, and tenanted only when the hotel was full.

He turned, and Ernest Pusey, in a dressing gown, stood on the threshold.

"What is all the noise about? Has anything happened?" His eyes took in the room and he said, "Where are the police?"

"Have you seen Mrs. Blake?"

"Mrs. Blake! Heavens, no! I've been in bed."

"Asleep?" asked Jim, thinking of his lighted window.

"Reading. I was just going to sleep when somebody dropped a number of bricks in Lana's room."

"It wasn't bricks," said Jim and told him briefly what had happened.

"Good Lord!" said Pusey, looking white. "Who was the man who attacked you?"

"I tell you I don't know who the fellow was, except he's got good biceps. I've just called the police. Those who were here were very stupidly called away by their superior. But it'll be an hour before the police can get here, and in the meantime anything can happen to Lana."

"Yes, certainly. We must find Lana at once. I suppose the search leads first to the rooms in this wing and . . ." Pusey strode to the Von Holzen door and knocked.

Von Holzen himself, in pajamas, opened the door and blinked.

"There's been a little trouble in the hotel," began Pusey smoothly. "Mr. Smith is obliged to ask to search the guests' rooms . . ." He broke off suddenly, adjusted his eyeglasses, peered at the face of the man in the doorway, and said, "Ah—so you are Von Holzen!"

"What do you mean? Of course I'm Von Holzen," began Von Holzen, blustering a little.

"You know what I mean," said Pusey. "I take it you didn't tell the police of your connection with Mr. Blake."

"I had no connection with Blake. I don't know what you're talking about."

"Don't be a fool. You may as well admit it. I never forget a face. I was in Blake's outer office one day three years ago when you came in, and Blake refused to see you. I never knew your name, but I know your face and I know why you were trying to make trouble, because he told me."

"You're crazy."

Pusey turned to Jim.

"This man was once president of the Consolidated Ore Company. He was at that time a competitor of Mr. Blake's. He failed, and blamed Peter for it, and wrote some threatening letters and tried to see him a few times." He turned to Von Holzen. "I'd have recognized you this morning when the police were here if you hadn't taken care not to let me have a good look at you."

"Listen, Pusey. I'm telling you the truth. It is sheer, unlucky coincidence—our being here. I'd forgotten my quarrel with Blake long ago. I'm in no sense a competitor of his now. Do you have to tell the police?"

"Fritz . . ."

Adelaide Von Holzen, her hair disheveled, a robe caught around her, and her plump face distraught, was at Von Holzen's side. "Fritz, I told you you ought to tell them. You had nothing to do with Peter Blake's murder. My husband is perfectly innocent—as innocent as I, myself. What motive— what possible motive . . . ?"

Jim interrupted: "Mrs. Von Holzen—were you near the kitchen wing tonight?"

She said, "No—yes. Yes, I asked one of the kitchen help for some baking soda. Fritz has nervous indigestion and he's been so worried. It's—it's only a coincidence, our being here. It's . . ."

Jim interrupted again: "Can't we thrash this out later, Pusey? Lana . . ."

"Yes, of course. If Mr. Smith may search your room . . ."

"What for? If you think you can implicate me in this thing . . ." began Von Holzen truculently.

His wife, weeping, watched a search that was as rapid as it was futile. As they turned toward the corridor again Adelaide Von Holzen grasped Pusey's arm pleadingly. "Must you tell the police?"

"You ought to have told the truth in the first place. They'll find out for themselves," said Pusey, and knocked at Tovery's door.

Lana was not in that room, either, and Tovery, roused from sleep, was indignant.

"I came here for rest," he said, glaring at Jim. "Not to step into the position of a prime suspect in a murder investigation. My advice to you both is to leave this to the police and let innocent people alone. If you must pry, look in the next room?"

"Eighteen? Why?" demanded Jim.

"Why?" said Tovery. "Because he's wearing a black wig, that's why."

The two men in the corridor looked at each other a little blankly.

"What does he mean, a wig?"

"Just that, likely," said Jim. He looked at Pusey thoughtfully. "Did you see the man in eighteen?"

"No. I understood he was dead drunk an couldn't be roused. What about him?"

"I think," said Jim slowly, "it's Sandy. And I think he's the man with the briefcase."

"Sandy! Sandy Blake! Impossible."

Jim shrugged. "Perhaps." He knocked at the door of 18.

"But Sandy..." gasped Pusey.

Jim opened the door of 18 and snapped on the light. The bed was tumbled; there were the usual empty glasses on the table, and no one was in the room.

"It can't be Sandy Blake," said the lawyer.

"All right," said Jim. "Maybe it isn't. This fellow's got dead black hair and Tovery spotted it as a wig. Since he's arrived he's kept completely out of sight—sending a constant stream of orders to the bar. Probably the drinks went down the drain. What color's Sandy's hair?"

"Red."

"Well—a fellow with black hair, registered as James Smith and staying in his room on a bender, wouldn't sound, by the description, like Sandy, would it?"

"I suppose you're right."

"Then what's he done with Lana?"

Pusey's face was gray and deeply troubled. "He'd be the heir," he said. "If Peter was murdered before he had time to make a new will. And it was no secret at Peter's office why I was coming down here.... Where are you going?"

"To the terrace...."

Pusey said slowly and reluctantly, "If it is Sandy—if he did get past Von Holzen on the terrace and murder Peter Blake, and Lana—Lana knew it—you see, both of them stand to profit."

"You mean they could be together on this thing? But she said she didn't know him—Sandy!"

"Didn't know him!" Pusey looked startled. "Did she say that?"

"Yes."

"I see. Well, I suppose it may be true. There would be no special point in her denying it if she does know him. We'd better continue our search. I feel sure they are not escaping together. I do not for a moment credit my own suggestion; it was forced upon me. Please forget it. I think, really, that they are both innocent."

Triple fool, thought Jim wryly to himself. To be taken in by a pair of shining, deep gray eyes and a lovely face. And yet, stubbornly, he believed in her.

"Von Holzen," he said aloud, "could so easily have murdered Blake. He was there on the terrace all the time."

Pusey gave the suggestion a moment of thought and agreed.

"Tovery might have failed to observe Von Holzen leaving his chair. And grudges have been cherished as long as this. Or Von Holzen might have had a stronger motive than a long-ago hatred."

The new process was what he meant, of course. He thought Jim didn't know. But then, that would be a motive for Sandy, too. And where was Sandy? Odd how strong and certain was his conviction that the man in eighteen was actually Sandy Blake.

"You stay here," he said to Pusey. "If the man calling himself James Smith comes back, nab him. Make sure whether or not it's Sandy and whether or not he has a briefcase belonging to Peter Blake."

"Where are you going?"

"To look for Lana."

He let himself into the corridor again and paused. A search for Lana resolved itself simply into a room-to-room check. There were still those untenanted and undesirable bedrooms along the back of the wing; the corridor that night had not been under observation as it had been at the time the murder occurred. Therefore, anybody could have crossed it to take advantage of the varied hiding places offered by those empty, small rooms.

There were seven of them, each with an adjoining bath. He started at the end nearest the elevator and opposite room 18 and covered them swiftly. It didn't take long; the rooms were starkly empty of human occupancy. It was a simple and quick procedure that involved only a glance at each.

Until he came to a door about midway along the corridor. He went through the same procedure. He opened the door, snapped on the light, glanced about—and stopped, unbelieving and frightened. For a long, shining kitchen knife lay on the bureau.

His heart got up into his throat and his shoulder blades prickled. The knife had no place in that room. It couldn't have been taken there and left by accident.

A little gingerly he picked up the knife and went to the corridor. And, as he did so, somewhere along that dimly lighted hall a door closed softly.

He heard it distinctly, for the hotel was as silent as a house of the dead. But in the corridor he had no way of knowing what door it was. A row of blank, closed panels confronted him.

Holding the knife under his coat, he concluded his rapid survey of the unoccupied rooms at the back of the wing. He closed the last one, opposite Pusey's room, and wiped his wet forehead. It hadn't been easy—looking in those rooms with that knife at hand and knowing what he might find.

Now what? He hesitated. There was still the darkened terrace; he's been so sure it was empty. Yet, after all, it was on the terrace that he'd last seen Lana. Perhaps by now she had returned and was waiting for him.

Pusey's room offered the quickest exit to the terrace. He opened the door and entered. The light burned over the bed and no one was in the room. He started toward the window, unpleasantly conscious of the knife under his coat. . . . And someone moved outside the window.

Jim jerked backward and took up a position at one side of the window. He wished he'd had time to turn off the light. But he couldn't do so now, for the screen was being opened, and a man crept cautiously through the aperture and stood looking about him, his back to Jim. It was the man calling himself James Smith. His hair was startlingly black, and he carried a leather briefcase under his arm.

What did one say at such a time?

"Hands up," said Jim, reverting to childhood games with a feeling of incredulity.

The man whirled and put up his hands, and the briefcase dropped.

"What—who are you?" he said coolly enough after staring at Jim for a moment. He glanced at the fallen briefcase and started to lower his hands.

"Keep 'em up there." Jim's hand was under his coat. He said, with truth, "I have a weapon here. Move over there, across the room. Sit on the bed."

The man from room 18 hesitated and finally did so, backing cautiously away. The leather case lay on the floor. Above it the two James Smiths stared at each other.

James Smith, the second, was a young fellow. He had the kind of very pale blue eyes that go sometimes with red hair. Just now his face was sullen.

Jim said, "Take off your wig."

"My—say, who are you?"

"Take it off. Hurry."

Jim made what he trusted was a threatening gesture. James Smith, the second, looked still more sullen and finally reached up and yanked off an extremely luxuriant black wig. Red hair, damp and disheveled, lay below where the wig had been.

"You're Sandy Blake," said Jim.

"Not much use my denying it, I suppose."

"Not in the least. Why didn't you come out and admit your identity this morning? The police will know tomorrow, anyway; by that time they'll have had answers to their cabled inquiries."

Sandy Blake's eyes narrowed. "What's it to you?"

"I'm the owner of this hotel; you came here under a false name. I've caught you making a burglarious entrance into a guest's room. . . ."

"Pusey?" Blake eyed him for a moment and then said, "Look here. Pusey's my lawyer. I came for—for advice."

"Surreptitiously. As you came to my hotel."

"No, I—okay, I'll tell you . . . the truth," said Sandy Blake, eyeing Jim. "I came to Bermuda because I wanted to—to see my uncle. I knew he was going to be here."

"Apparently you didn't want him to see you."

"I didn't. Not, at least, until I had satisfied myself about this—this marriage. After all, when an elderly man—"

"Fifty—if you mean Peter Blake . . ."

". . . Marries his pretty secretary after six weeks' acquaintance, don't you think it's the—er—duty of his nearest relative to do something about it?"

"What did you propose to do?"

"It's none of your business." He changed suddenly and became communicative: "Look. I know I've got into a mess. I wanted to ask Pusey what to do."

"Are you trying to make me believe that your coming here was inspired by sheer affection for your uncle?"

Blake nodded quickly. "Yes. Yes, that's exactly it. It was an impulse. I thought if I could see them together, without their knowing I was here, I could tell whether she was really . . . fond of him. Whether or not he was happy. If she was sincere and he was happy, it was all right. It was fine. But I wanted to be sure."

"I suppose you're going to tell me next you were bringing this briefcase to Pusey to ask him what to do about it—after you knocked out the maid and searched Mrs. Blake's room and barricaded me in the closet."

Young Blake's wary eyes became more guarded, as if a shutter had dropped down. "That's—that's exactly what I was doing. Bringing it to Pusey. Certainly. I—I thought it would be safe. And naturally I—I wanted legal advice before . . ."

"Before the police got on to you. Where is Lana?"

The look in Blake's pale blue eyes instantly became sheer, cold hatred. "I don't know and I don't care, and you won't get another word out of me."

Jim touched his chin meditatively. Then he bent cautiously, eyes on Blake, and picked up the briefcase.

"What are you doing? This is no concern of yours. Where are you going?"

"To the telephone. I wouldn't move if I were you." Jim felt nervously behind him for the telephone.

Blake edged forward a little, looking tense and white. "I didn't murder him. If you're going to call the police . . ."

Jim got the telephone in his hand and a voice said instantly, "Desk clerk . . . Come up to room 22," said Jim into the telephone, and as he said it Blake sprang. Jim dropped the telephone and Blake jerked the screen aside and was out on the terrace and was gone. But Jim still had the briefcase. And he still had the knife.

He checked himself on the verge of pursuit. First, get that briefcase safely put away. And put the knife where it could do no harm. He opened the briefcase, thrust the knife into folds of papers, and closed it again. His own fingerprints would be on it but there might be others, too. He met the desk clerk at the elevator.

"Yes, sir."

"Here." Jim glanced along the corridor and whispered. "Take this down to the safe. Don't let anybody see you. . . ."

"Yes, sir." The clerk took it quickly and, impressed by Jim's manner, thrust it under his coat.

"And listen. I need help. Call Mark and Luzo to help, and tell Tom to take the desk and switchboard. Then get my revolver out of my right-hand desk drawer and get some flashlights and come back here. I may be on the terrace. Step on it."

The clerk closed the elevator door. Jim ran lightly back into Pusey's room. He would have preferred to see the briefcase and knife in the safe himself. But he didn't dare leave Sandy Blake at large. Sandy Blake, who had the only sound motive for murdering Peter Blake (if you excepted revenge on Von Holzen's part as a motive) that they had yet uncovered. Sandy Blake, who had quarreled with his uncle and who stood to lose a considerable sum of money when the new will was drawn and signed. Well, now that will would never be made. Sandy Blake, who must have known that the briefcase held papers of value.

Was it Blake who had taken that knife from the kitchen and placed it in the unoccupied room, thinking it would be safe there until it was needed?

Blake hated Lana and had been unable to disguise it. No, Jim didn't dare leave him at large. However, he couldn't go far. And the briefcase was safe. But where was Lana?

He went through the window of Pusey's room onto the terrace. The whole sky was heavily overcast with clouds, so it was as if a pitch-black blanket closed upon him.

With a stubborn hope that Lana might have returned to the end of the terrace where they had talked (an hour ago, now), he felt his way in that direction. He found the balustrade unexpectedly by bringing up sharp against it, and called softly, "Lana—Lana . . ."

Well, she wasn't there. She wasn't anywhere in the wing. And so much can happen in an hour. He began to feel as if he were caught in the endless, peculiarly baffling gyrations of a nightmare. Even the failure of the police and of his hotel staff to materialize was a recognizable quotient of nightmare. He listened to the water below but could not see it, and he thought how shallow the lagoon was just below the terrace.

But she'd have screamed! Surely she'd have screamed or made some outcry if anyone molested her.

It must be, by that time, after one. The only thing left to do was to get lights and make an organized search of the whole place. And by this time the hotel staff ought to have reached the second floor—the staff and his revolver. He went through Pusey's room again, along a still corridor, and rang for the elevator. There was no answering rumble, and he rang again.

Impatiently, feeling that everything in his hotel had set itself for his own bafflement, he ran down the branching corridor through the main body of the hotel and down a twisting flight of stairs to the lobby.

He stopped short. The lobby was entirely empty; no one was at the desk. No one was on the elevator bench, and the elevator was not, as it was usually, standing idle with its door open.

The emptiness and silence were ominous. He turned and ran up the stairs again, convinced that the desk clerk had never reached the safe with the briefcase and the knife. He reached the elevator and the clerk lay in a huddled heap on the bottom of the cage. There was no briefcase anywhere.

But the silence was gone. For there was somewhere a trembling and agitation of the air that grew into a deep, muffled beat. It grew louder, and Jim recognized it. The Gombies had finished their brief ceremonies and were returning along the same route. Then the two police sent by Willaker to watch the Gombies would be returning, too—or so he hoped.

He felt the clerk's head and pulse. He was only stunned, as Louise had been stunned. Blake had swift and hard fists. And he wouldn't give up the briefcase without a struggle.

The beat of the drums was confusing. It seemed to fill the air, to hover just over your heartbeats, to suck you into its own quick rhythm.

Jim considered. He'd better try to carry the clerk out of harm's way, but he . . .

Another sound rose in the air, piercing the waves of drumbeats. A shrill, high sound that rose horribly to the very roofs of the old hotel sobbed and swelled shrilly and stopped at its very height.

It was a woman's scream.

It was not far from him. Shrill and high with terror though it was, in all probability no one in the hotel beyond that wing heard it; or, if they did and awoke, the sound was submerged instantly by the tumult of whistles and drums and horses' hoofs that was reaching its peak along the road behind the hotel.

And, oddly, in the very moment of hearing it, Jim knew it was not Lana. It wasn't because he instinctively felt that she couldn't—wouldn't—scream. It wasn't because of any recognizable timber in that strained pitch of stark terror.

But it wasn't Lana. And it was somewhere in the wing;

therefore it must be Mrs. Von Holzen. He ran into the corridor.

It was. The door to 19 flew open and Adelaide Von Holzen surged out, her dressing gown swirling around her. She saw Jim and clutched at him with shaking hands.

"Addie, for heaven's sake . . . !" It was Von Holzen himself, flinging himself out from 19 also and grasping his wife's heaving shoulders. "What happened? What's the matter?" Her eyes bulged and she tried to speak and couldn't, and Von Holzen shook her briskly. "Now speak up. What's wrong?"

"A man," she gasped, her head jerking under her husband's somewhat strenuous propulsion. "With a knife. On the terrace. I saw him. . . ."

"You're dreaming. She's had a nightmare, Mr. Smith. Don't pay any attention to her."

His wife turned the color of milk and put shaking hands on Jim's arm. "I did see him. It wasn't a nightmare. I was upset about Fritz's being recognized. I couldn't sleep, and I got up quietly, so Fritz in the other bed wouldn't hear me, and went to the window. And there was a man with a knife. . . ."

"It was dark," cried Von Holzen. "You couldn't see a man with a trunk, let alone a knife. . . ."

"I had my little flashlight. The one I keep on the bed table when I'm traveling. I had it in my hand, and it flashed over him and . . ."

Jim detached himself from her grasping fingers and, halfway through the door of 19, jerked back. "Who was it? Quick!"

"I don't know. I only saw the knife. Long and sharp. The light shone on it and . . ."

He left them. Two strides took him through 19, and he jerked open the screen over one of the windows. Blackness and the eerie retreating throb of drums fell upon him. The nearest window beyond led to the bedroom of suite 21, in which Peter Blake had been murdered.

It gave him the queerest shock to realize suddenly that, searching the wing as he had, still he'd missed that room.

How? There was no time to think. He felt along the wall, listening for a sound near at hand. Here was the screen. But it was in the wrong place—it was standing directly before him. It was standing open, of course.

He swung around it, and the long rectangle of the window made a deeper patch of blackness before him. There was no sound at all inside the room. He stepped cautiously over the sill and stepped on something small and hard that clattered along the floor and was a knife. He bent, groping, and found it.

He plunged into the blackness of the room, heard no sound at all except the great pounding of his own heart, and halted smartly by a chair. Where was the electric switch? By the door, of course. He made himself pause and reflect, grope for the wall, follow the cool touch of painted plaster to the panels of the door, and then explore up and down.

He found the switch, and bright, hard light flooded the room.

There was nothing and no one there. No one, except—a closet door was barely open. A small foot and a wisp of silk showed in the slight aperture.

It was Lana. And if he had been any kind of a detective, he'd have guessed what had happened. Lana was huddled on the floor of the closet, half-sitting, half-lying, wholly helpless, because a checked tablecloth was wound around her head and her arms and tied at the back. A towel was stuffed in her mouth, and another very efficiently secured her ankles.

"Lana . . ."

But she was alive and uninjured. He untied the cloth and jerked away the towels and lifted the young woman in his arms; and then others reached the room.

"Are you hurt?"

"No." She said it wearily, as if the word came from some great distance, and looked with great, dazed dark eyes at the people crowding into the room. All at once her inert body tautened in his arms, and she lifted her head from his shoulder and gasped, "Sandy—Sandy Blake."

Jim looked up.

The Von Holzens were there, very much in dishabille; Pusey and Sandy Blake were in the doorway, Sandy staring with cold, pale eyes at Lana.

"My dear child!" cried Pusey. "What on earth—how did you find her?"

"Sandy Blake," said Lana again.

"My poor child," said Adelaide Von Holzen, advancing. "Let me take her, Mr. Smith. What happened, dear?"

She put out her arms and Lana pressed a little closer against Jim; her eyes looked enormous in her white face, and she watched Sandy Blake.

"Why did you come here?" she demanded. "What have you done?"

John Tovery, his hair smooth and wavy, himself clad in a handsome dressing gown, strolled through the door and stopped just behind Pusey and Sandy Blake. "Good grief!" he said, eyeing the disheveled group. "More murder? Or is it a love scene?"

No one seemed to hear him. Fritz Von Holzen's shrewd eyes were like little jewels peering behind his glasses. Jim could just see his wristwatch across Lana's small shoulder, and it said twenty minutes after one. If he could hold the fort another twenty minutes the police would be there. One of those people had murdered Peter Blake—cold-bloodedly, brutally; and one of them, without any reasonable doubt, had tried to murder the girl in his arms.

He'd got to keep them together. And he'd got to hear Lana's story. She must know who had attacked her, who had flung that tablecloth over her head and arms and dragged her into that closet, and then—why?—had gone away, intending to return. He must get Lana alone.

He said, "I'll take you to your room. Will you others stay here, please."

He couldn't count on it, of course, but he had to make them stay together. He didn't dare let any of them leave before the police came. A knife was silent and thus more desirable, but it was perfectly possible that the murderer was also armed with a gun. Not so silent, but swift.

He urged Lana toward the door. The living room was still empty, and the cards and cribbage pegs flung on the floor. If he hadn't been an idiot he would have noted the significance of those tossed cards and pegs; it meant that someone had snatched off the table cover. Letting Blake go was another blunder.

Sandy Blake, still looking at Lana with that look of distilled hatred, stood aside to permit her to pass out of the door.

Jim paused. "Suppose you all come into the living room; there are chairs here. You'll have to wait. . . ."

"Wait!" cried Tovery. "What do you mean? What for?"

How to keep them together? Jim, as always, found the truth less of an effort than any other course. "Because one of you murdered Peter Blake. Because one of you tried to murder—Lana. And because the police are on their way and you've got to stay in this room together until they arrive."

Would they do it? Probably not. Jim wore authority like a cloak, but he couldn't force them to wait. He added thoughtfully, "I am assuming—as you are—that of the five people here, four must be innocent of murder. Therefore, I ask those four to . . . to cooperate."

Tovery burst out, "Don't be an idiot, Jim! I'm not going to stay here and get mixed up any further with this thing. The police questioned every one of us this morning. If they had anything against any one of us, they would have held him for further questioning. They'd have arrested him. You can't go around saying one of—of us murdered Blake. That's criminal—well, libel or something . . . slander?"

"All right," said Jim. "I'll put it this way. If one of you leaves this room, you'll have me to reckon with." He was about to say more, but observed in time that there was a cryptic lack of explanation as to his meaning that caught their attention and held it. He could almost read the successive speculations in Tovery's handsome eyes. Had Jim a revolver? Had he a hotel staff armed and ready to back him up? Did he mean only his not inconsiderable strength of muscle?

In any case, Tovery drew back a little. He said, "Now, don't get all worked up about this, Smith. Don't do anything rash. I've got my looks to consider, you know. After all, an actor..."

Pusey said dryly, "He'll stay here, Jim. Take her into her bedroom. Don't worry, Lana...."

"Take her into the bedroom! Don't worry, Lana," burst out Sandy Blake. "Take care of the little helpless dear—she's only killed her husband!"

"Shut up!" said Jim, and led Lana into her bedroom. Once out of sight of the others he put his lips to her ear. "Tell me quickly. Who took you in there?"

"I don't know. I—did one of them kill him?"

"What happened after you left me?"

She stared at him, swallowed hard, and told him in an incoherent little whisper. Her room had been dark when she entered it after leaving him on the terrace. She'd found, as he had, the maid senseless on the floor. As soon as she realized that it was Louise and that she'd been struck, she flung open the door to the living room, expecting to find the police there. They were gone, and she'd hurried across to the opposite bedroom, thinking they must be in that room. And then someone had come from somewhere behind her and jerked something dark and binding over her head and thrust a gag into her mouth and warned her not to scream. "He said Peter had called for help. He said..."

"Who said, for heaven's sake?"

But she didn't know. "Everything was confused. I was struggling, scared..."

"What was his voice like?"

She put her white hands to her head and stared at him blankly. "I don't know. Very low—deep, I mean. I didn't recognize it. But it—I don't think it was his normal voice. I think I came very near to fainting—it's all confused in my mind. Except I knew I mustn't scream. Even when he was gone it was as if his voice kept saying it over and over again in my ears, but I knew it wasn't, because the room didn't—hum."

Jim started violently. "What did you say?"

"I said—I don't know who . . ."

"You said the room didn't hum."

"Oh. That. It was the room—or my ears. . . . I felt as if there was a kind of—vibration. A hollow sort of hum. As if the room . . ."

Jim stared back at her. His eyes narrowed until they became lazy blue slits, except they were not lazy, for all at once he was thinking furiously. Thinking back to college physics classes.

"What is it? You look so . . ."

Jim's eyes snapped. "Listen. If anybody comes in this room—so much as puts his foot over the threshold—no matter who it is, you scream like hell. I'll be in the other bedroom."

He went into the living room and singled out Tovery. "Come in here, will you, Tovery. I want to talk to you."

"Certainly not," said Tovery. "I have nothing to do with this affair. You can't pin this thing on me. You . . ."

"Get the hell in that room over there," said Jim, and Tovery went. Jim closed the door. Their voices could be heard by those in the living room, but not what they said.

"See here, what do you mean?" began Tovery, blustering.

"You killed Peter Blake."

"I didn't. I didn't kill him. You can't . . ." Tovery, as white as the counterpane behind him, was pressing backward away from Jim. His cultivated voice rose to a thin, high squeal.

"I say you did. You came in here with a knife when Von Holzen wasn't looking. You . . ."

"I tell you I didn't." The actor's voice rose another shrill pitch. "Don't look at me like that! I had nothing to do with murder! I—"

"All right," said Jim in a low voice, "you didn't. Now then, I want you to tell me something. . . ."

Two minutes later the closet door closed cautiously upon Tovery. The actor opened it an inch to peer at Jim. "You say you want me to listen?" whispered Tovery.

"Just listen. I need a witness who knows what to listen for."

Tovery nodded and closed the closet door quietly. Jim went to the door to the living room. It seemed fruitless, but he'd got to make four direct, definite accusations of murder. Adelaide and Fritz Von Holzen; Sandy Blake and Ernest Pusey. And it was quite in the cards that he would have to make a fifth.

Again the need for haste possessed him. The police would not believe the small thing he knew; it was too tenuous a clue, they would say; too airy and unsubstantial. But it led to murder.

"Von Holzen—will you come in here, please."

Again he closed the door between. "You killed Peter Blake, Von Holzen. You wanted the invention—the chemical process that would put him out of business. It would be priceless in the hands of a competitor. You—"

"I . . . !" cried Von Holzen. "You're crazy! What chemical process?"

Shrewdness and quick interest struggled with fright in his eyes. Jim was annoyed. He came nearer threateningly. "You came in here and stabbed him, and I've got proof of it. You were on the terrace. No one else could have done it. And you—"

It was convincing. Von Holzen's protestations rose in earnestness and tone: "You're nuts. I didn't know there was a new process. I didn't explain I'd ever known Peter or had had a grudge. . . ."

"Why?"

"Because I didn't want to be mixed up in it. If I'd thought twice I'd have realized it was bound to come out soon as the police got going on their investigation. But I didn't like the idea of being a suspect. There I was on the terrace, and grudge was a motive and—but I didn't do it, I tell you! You can't prove!" He was at last frightened. It was in his lifted voice and his sparkling, bright little eyes.

Jim thought, and said a little dubiously. "Okay."

"What do you mean, okay?"

"I mean, get out. Anywhere. On the terrace. And keep your mouth shut."

He scuttled away. Jim turned back to the living-room

door. Suppose he was all wrong? Suppose his tenuous, fleeting little clue wasn't a clue at all? Suppose . . .

Lana was standing in the bedroom door, tall and slender. She'd pulled her lovely hair together so it looked smooth.

"Pusey," said Jim. "Will you help me a moment?"

"Why—certainly. But what . . . ?"

"In here."

It meant leaving the girl and Sandy Blake together, but Adelaide Von Holzen was there, too. And it wasn't conceivable that Adelaide Von Holzen and young Blake could have leagued together for any purpose whatever. One would serve as a check to the other.

He closed the door and began again: "You killed Peter Blake."

"What on earth do you mean?"

"I mean, you killed him. You knew of his invention—this chemical process—and you wanted it. All your life you've seen Peter Blake making tons of money, and you were jealous. Possession of the chemical process meant money for you and failure for him. You came in here this morning and killed him. You came into this room to talk to him before Von Holzen came out on the terrace. You talked to him and you—you quarreled, and you had a knife and you suddenly realized the thing had to be done. . . ."

Pusey said, "Now, now, Mr. Smith." He was quite composed; his voice was, if anything, deeper and altogether unagitated.

Driven, Jim went on: "You escaped." He stopped.

Pusey smiled. "Escape? That's the problem, isn't it? With Von Holzen on the terrace, nobody could have escaped. You're a good fellow, Jim, and you're trying to get the girl off, and I'm going to try to save her, too. But it's no go."

Jim didn't answer. There was a small memory nagging at him. A memory of something said, something done or implied, something later disproved. What? A small discrepancy, noted at the time, but not put in its proper alignment. He stared at Pusey, caught in the meshes of recollection.

"By golly!" said Jim.

He was right. He knew he was right. An umbrella out on the terrace where it ought not to have been. Beige uniform and coffee-colored legs.

"By golly!" said Jim Smith. "You *did* do it!"

Pusey's gray eyes retreated; the conviction in Jim's surprised voice became a living thing, charging the very air about them.

Pusey said deeply, harshly, "You fool, you! How dare you . . . !"

His voice was curiously deep under excitement. Deep and very vibrant—and suddenly a small, queer vibrance answered it, deep and hollow and low in pitch. It stopped when Pusey stopped speaking. Footsteps ran across the living room, and Lana Blake jerked open the door and cried, "That's it! That's the sound I heard!" Adelaide Von Holzen and Sandy Blake were behind her.

Ernest Pusey said, still low and harsh, so that the betraying hum rose again hollowly, "You fool! Do you think I'm going to stay here and answer such absurd accusations?"

All Jim's attention was suddenly riveted upon a revolver, black and ugly, that came like magic from a pocket of Pusey's bathrobe. Pusey was ten feet from him, and he had nothing whatever in the way of defense. The police ought to be rounding Castle Point about now. Five more long minutes.

"This revolver," said Pusey—odd how the steel-and-concrete walls answered him—"this revolver does not mean that I'm guilty. It means only that I'm going to defend myself against a—a madman."

But he held the thing pointed at Lana. Jim was afraid to move. One touch of that neat, precise finger would send a quick messenger of death, and he knew it. Self-defense would be Pusey's plea. What . . . ? Jim was suddenly aware that the closet door behind Pusey was moving. Tovery was about to undertake his first heroic role.

Would Blake's eyes shift? Jim prayed they wouldn't. Would Adelaide Von Holzen scream? No, she was like a wooden woman—eyes bulging, face rigid. Would Pusey . . . ?

Tovery leaped, and Jim leaped, revolver shots thudded, Adelaide Von Holzen screamed, and in the middle of a writhing, shouting, smoke-filled melee, a heavy voice shouted authoritatively from the doorway. "Here, here! What's all this?"

The water in the lagoon was clear and gray, the graying sky very soft and gentle, and the treetops were beginning to show faint gold touches when Jim and Lana stood again beside the balustrade.

"It was the tone pitch of the room," said Jim, throwing away his cigarette. It hissed gently as it struck the water. "College physics. The same principle as a tuning fork. If your voice happens to strike the tone pitch of a room, it sets up a vibration. Sounds like someone humming—at a short distance, at any rate. It's not uncommon, especially with concrete-and-steel structures. I asked Tovery—when I remembered it suddenly—and he said yes, it happened often. That it was one of the problems of construction in modern theatres, because there was not so much wood as formerly used in their construction. He says especially in an opera house they do all kinds of things to make sure that their basso profundo doesn't get a neat little vibration hum. It happens mainly with a very deep, very harsh voice. Pusey's voice roughened and deepened under excitement. Tovery's and Von Holzen's went up—became thin and sharp—and there was no answering vibration." Jim yawned. "That's all."

"But the umbrella and Von Holzen."

"Oh, that. Well, I ought to have known that right away. It was so simple and so obvious. It was a case of not seeing the forest for the trees. Von Holzen said nobody had passed but a porter with the umbrella. The porter said he had entered the living room for the purpose of putting out the umbrella but had immediately heard the voices and then Blake's call for help, and had instantly run for help. Well, the umbrella ought to have been in the living room (where presumably Luzo dropped it), but it wasn't. It was in its place on the terrace. And then all at once I remembered the coffee-colored suit Pusey wore this morning; it was almost exactly the color of the porters' uniforms.

"Pusey had simply walked out of the living room of the suite carrying the umbrella, holding the handle of it down and the umbrella itself between him and Von Holzen. Von Holzen had glanced up, seen an umbrella and beige-colored legs below it, assumed it, naturally, to be a porter, and had gone back to his paper. Then, as soon as Von Holzen became absorbed in reading, Pusey was able to slip into his own room through the window." Jim yawned again. "The police have checked Luzo's story, and it's right; he dropped the umbrella where he stood in the living room and ran for me. But a little later the umbrella was in place on the terrace."

"But Sandy..."

"Sandy's reasoning seems a little muddled. But I do think he was simply telling the truth when he explained himself and his motives."

"Sandy loved Peter," said Lana. "As I did. Peter had told him of the new process, and Sandy had actually worked with Peter on it, so it was part Sandy's. Peter had told Pusey about it, too. And each of us thought he was the only person in whom Peter had confided. Peter was—like that. A little secretive, I mean."

"Then this morning—yesterday morning, I mean—when Peter Blake told Pusey he was ready to take out patents, Pusey knew he had to act then or not at all. Queer to think of the jealousy and hatred that must have been seething in Pusey all these years. Perhaps he and Blake quarreled, first. Certainly there were violent words. Then Pusey struck. It's queer, too," said Jim thoughtfully, "that if Pusey had waited in his room, Sandy would have brought him the briefcase. But it might have cost Sandy his life."

Lana gave a little shiver. "It's not nice," she said, "feeling that somebody has wanted to murder you."

Footsteps crossed the terrace, and Willaker, solid and thick as a column in the gray dawn, stood beside them. He had heard Lana's last words, for he said coolly, "Pusey had to murder you or give up his whole project. We've got the thing put together, I think, Jim."

He leaned on the balustrade and talked. "Tonight's ructions really began yesterday when Mrs. Blake told Pusey that she knew of the new process and that she actually had the notes relating to it in her own possession. He had been disappointed in not finding them in Blake's room after the murder, and in being obliged to make a quick and expedient escape when the porter gave the alarm. Her knowledge of the notes meant that mere possession of them would not be enough for him; he would have to silence Mrs. Blake before he could patent and sell the invention as his own. Having murdered once successfully, it was easy to decide to murder again. It was to be in almost every detail like the first, with the important exception that, this time, he would make sure of the briefcase before the murder was done.

"He secured another knife and placed it where it would be near at hand but not incriminating. Then he took advantage of the uproar caused by the passing Gombies to send a message to the police (purporting to be from me) from the telephone booth in the store below the hotel. You know how successful that was," said Willaker a little dryly. "But, while Pusey was gone from the hotel, Sandy Blake entered Mrs. Blake's room, knocked the maid senseless, discovered the briefcase, and removed it. So, when Pusey returned and searched Mrs. Blake's room, the briefcase was already gone. And while Pusey was searching, Mrs. Blake came back to the room. He didn't want to murder her until he had the briefcase; yet he must have her where he could later—"

Lana uttered a stifled little cry.

Willaker said hurriedly, "Well, well—you know all about that. And then you came on the scene, Jim, after having scared young Blake away at his first attempt to reach Pusey. When you came into Mrs. Blake's room, Pusey again had to retire hurriedly and watch, and when you gave him a chance by entering the closet, he fastened the door and searched the room again, this time in the light. Again he failed to find the briefcase, and when the maid showed signs of returning consciousness, Pusey left. Then, as you remember, you met him in the corridor. You talked, and he very cleverly led you to suspect Mrs. Blake and Sandy Blake. He leaped at the chance to make a scapegoat of either or both of them; you couldn't have given him a more welcome bit of news than that of Sandy's presence, for he didn't know, then, that Sandy also had been taken into Blake's confidence about the new process.

"When you continued your search for Mrs. Blake, Pusey remained in room eighteen ostensibly to wait for Sandy, who was still lurking about in the shadows of the terrace and about to make another attempt to reach Pusey. Pusey probably was watching you, Jim, when you found the knife. Certainly he was watching when you gave the case to the desk clerk. He rang the elevator bell as soon as you entered his room again, and the clerk, naturally, thought it was you ringing and came back. It was simple for Pusey to get the briefcase, and when he reached his room with it at last, the knife was there. So he hid the case in his room and went back to Mrs. Blake and—and that's all," said Willaker. "He failed."

Lana looked slowly at Jim through the soft, gray light. "Thanks to you," she whispered. . . .

Two days later a boat left, and Lana and Sandy Blake went away on it. The sun was very bright, the sea very blue, and the coral roofs of the houses looked newly scrubbed. Jim rode to Hamilton alone with Lana Blake, in the back seat of a swaying victoria. Lana seemed sad, and her profile was clear and beautiful against the blue sea beyond them.

She turned and caught his eyes. "I can't thank you enough."

He had been thinking how desirable and sweet her mouth was. He murmured that he hadn't done anything, really.

She smiled a little wistfully. She put a small hand on his own. "I've not known many men. I—I've never known anyone like you."

Jim took the hand. It was a nice hand, small and warm and clinging gently to his stronger one. He put it down rather quickly. "Things will be happier for you after a while. When all this is over. You'll meet people and . . ."

She was shaking her head. Her eyes were the candid eyes of a child. She said, as if it must be so, "No one like you."

Jim stirred uneasily. He heard himself say, "You'll come back. Sometime."

The girl turned and looked deeply at him again. She said slowly, "Yes. I'll come back. Sometime."

An hour later from the balcony of the Twenty-one Club he watched her boat go to sea. Lana Blake was standing at the rail and she did not have a handkerchief pressed to her eyes. Gradually her slender figure became indistinct. Jim sighed a little sadly and lifted his glass.

On the boat Lana leaned against the railing. The tall, brown figure on the balcony became smaller and farther away. Green shores and white houses and opal bays slipped past her. They were heading for the open purple seas.

Well, she would see those opal bays and green shores again.

Sometime.

# The Crimson Paw

Kings Manor Lady-in-Waiting was my last hope, and at seven-thirty that night I gave up. It's impossible to say whether or not an hour-old puppy is going to be a fine dog, but I looked at the wriggling black mites and faced the fact that even if every one of the litter proved to be a prize winner, still they couldn't pull Kings Manor Kennels out of the red and fast enough. Lady looked at me proudly, and I patted her loving head and started to town.

Some three hours later I was accused of murder.

My name is Patricia Bennet. I own and had signally failed to operate successfully the Kings Manor Kennels. I love the kennels and the dogs—beautiful, intelligent French poodles—and perhaps I had spent more on their care than I ought to have done. In any event, the Kings Manor Kennels were on the rocks and so was I.

It was the only thing I could think of, all the way to town, on a trip I had to make that night. In order to provide some needed cash I had undertaken, months before, a sort of sideline, that of clipping and grooming other people's poodles. I had that night an unexpected chore of clipping to do, and I had left my tools—clippers, scissors, brushes, and all that—at John Ransome's house in town the previous day. I had to get my tools and proceed to clip one Maurice, a little fiend that bit when I worked around to his mustache. But the only thing in my mind was the fact I had finally accepted, after months of dimming hope: I'd have to give up the kennels, which were my livelihood.

It was a wet, gusty night, and it seemed a long, tiring drive from Dunham Woods to the rear North Side of Chicago. When I reached John Ransome's house it was lighted, but when I rang at the door no one answered. I rang again and looked at my watch. It was close to nine; so if I finished my chore by eleven I could telephone to Bill—that is, Dr. William Ransome—at the sanitarium and meet him somewhere for a few minutes before I started the long drive home.

I put my thumb on the bell and held it there. John Ransome wouldn't answer; he was slightly deaf, and also he would let the house burn down before he'd bring himself to perform his houseman's duties. But where was Everett, the houseman?

It was only when I had a startling glimpse of the Steathways' butler down the street, hurtling out of their door, dressed to his false teeth in evening clothes, that I remembered. It was the night of the Chauffeurs' Ball.

The Chauffeurs' Ball is a Chicago institution, an annual festivity when all the best chauffeurs and their friends gather for a bang-up but dignified gala. So there was no one to answer the bell; John's houseman and his cook had gone to the ball. I opened the door.

I didn't intend to open it; it is not my custom to walk into other people's houses. But I was cold and exasperated and I put my hand on the brass doorknob, turned it, and the door opened.

I was surprised. Residents of Chicago's Gold Coast do not leave doors unlocked to invite burglars. However, I went into the hall, which was lighted. It was very hot. Nobody was there, but there was a sort of whine from the stairs and I saw Harpo standing perfectly still at the top of them, eyeing me. Harpo was a standard black poodle, from my own kennels; I had given him as a puppy to John Ransome, and later wished I hadn't.

Harpo didn't move, and I could hear a muffled murmur of voices from John's study upstairs. I didn't want to see John. The simplest thing for me to do was go back to the laundry, gather up my two brown duffel bags, and leave.

So I did. I passed a mirror and caught a fleeting glimpse of myself, certainly not at my best in the worn tweed coat that looked out of place against the opulent setting of John's house; and my face looked tired and pale. I went on back, through the dining room and pantry and kitchen, turning on lights as I went and encountering nobody. My duffel bags were on a table in the tiny laundry off the kitchen, exactly as I had left them the day before, when I finished trimming Harpo, and just before the ugly and painful interview I had had with John. I gathered up the two bags and went back to the hall.

Harpo was standing again at the top of the stairs, watching me. The murmur of voices above had stopped, and indeed the house was extremely quiet. I started for the door, and suddenly Harpo whimpered. It was an uneasy and troubled sound. He ran down a few steps toward me, his black eyes very bright and anxious, and gave another beseeching kind of murmur that wasn't a bark but said in so many words, "I'm in trouble."

I didn't want to see John. But I put down my duffel bags and tried to coax Harpo to me, silently, with my hands. Harpo only whined. I thought he had been somehow hurt, so I started up the stairs, and he flung himself down to meet me, pawing at my coat. I tried to calm him, so John wouldn't hear. And then I saw on my sleeve a red smear of blood. So Harpo had cut his foot.

I knelt on the stairs and caught him by the collar. He wriggled and pulled as I reached for his paws to discover which one was cut. Then he stopped wriggling and burst into a fusillade of barks, and the front door opened. A man in a mackintosh, with a rosy face below a uniform cap, came into the hall and stopped to stare at me and Harpo. He said loudly over Harpo's barks, "The door is unlocked!"

I nodded, angry with myself, for John couldn't fail to hear the tumult, and I'd have to see him.

The man said, "I'm Brannigan, Mr. Ransome's private watchman. I want to see Mr. Ransome." He eyed me. "Aren't you the young lady that trims the dog—Miss Bennet?"

I nodded again. "The dog's got a cut on his paw," I said. "I think Mr. Ransome is in his study."

"I'll report to him."

Brannigan knew the way. He started for the stairs, and I drew Harpo aside. Brannigan's mackintosh swished past us. I thought I could still get away without seeing John. I gave Harpo's paws and head a quick look, found no cuts, and released him. I went quickly down the steps, and Harpo followed me. I gathered up my duffel bags and had my hand on the doorknob when Brannigan shouted, "Miss Bennet!" He was leaning over the banister, his face no longer rosy. "Come up here!"

Something in his voice excited Harpo, who charged for him, barking wildly. I clutched Harpo's collar, dragged him into the coatroom, and shut him in, then ran up the stairs. Brannigan caught my arm and pulled me into John Ransome's study. "Look."

I looked. The room was lighted. John Ransome sat in his deep armchair. Rather, he sagged there—that big, gray-haired man with his heavy and arrogant face—like a bag of sand. There was a blotch of bright red on his white shirtfront.

I had known John Ransome all my life.

The man in the mackintosh cried, "Don't touch him!" but I couldn't have touched him. There was a gun on the floor beside John's chair, shining on the thick carpet. I stooped over, I don't know why, and Brannigan snapped, "Don't touch that, either! Don't touch anything. Where's the telephone?"

"Is he dead?"

The watchman gave me a queer look. "Oh, he's dead."

"A doctor! We should call a doctor."

"Nothing a doctor can do." Then he saw the telephone on the desk beside the radio. But he watched me—and the room and the hall behind me—while he dialed and told somebody that John Ransome had either killed himself or been murdered, and gave the house number. He put down the telephone, and we looked at each other for a moment with John Ransome there between us. John Ransome, dead in his study, with its long rows of bookshelves, its thick red curtains, and the Cézanne above the mantel.

I had to get out of the room so I couldn't see John. I went into the hall, and Brannigan followed me. I thought of Bill. "I've got to phone to Bill. I mean, his nephew."

Brannigan had a gun. It was in his hand. "I know Dr. Ransome. And that other nephew, the one that drives the foreign job."

I hadn't thought of Jimmy.

"There's that young lady everybody said he was about to marry, too. Miss Candy. She'll have to be told. But we'll wait for the police."

Undoubtedly he knew them all. He said, oddly, "What's that on your hand?" His bright eyes quickened. "It's on your coat, too."

He was staring at the faint reddish smears from Harpo's paws. I got out a handkerchief and dabbed at my hand and told Brannigan how they got there, but all I could think of was John Ransome, dead. Why had he killed himself? *Would* he have killed himself? Not John Ransome!

Somebody had killed him.

The floor seemed uneven; I remember holding the newel post, which itself seemed unsteady, and then sinking down to the top step. You were supposed to put your head down when you felt dizzy. Bill had told me that one time. . . . Who had killed John? And then I remembered. "Somebody was here. In the study. They were talking."

I put my head back against the newel post and shut my eyes. If I had an enemy in the world it was John Ransome, but I wouldn't have wanted him to die. All I knew of him whirled like a kaleidoscope around me: Bill and me, and John Ransome. My father and John Ransome. Sugar Candy and John Ransome. Jimmy and John Ransome. John himself, sprawling out in the armchair, rich and successful—and miserly and cruel . . . John Ransome was the pivot for it all. And a burglar had shot him!

It seemed obvious. Everyone who read the papers knew of the Chauffeurs' Ball, and it was an ideal night for anyone so minded to break into a house and make a rich haul. John had seen the burglar, threatened to call the police, and had been shot. There was an ugly irony about John's money being the cause of his death.

I was only dimly conscious of Brannigan, prowling about, but watching me, too. But I became fully aware when Harpo began to bark wildly, someone pounded at the street door, and Brannigan ran past me down the stairs. The police had arrived.

They shut me into the coatroom with Harpo, with a policeman stationed in the hall.

It wasn't quite the way it sounds; the coatroom was a luxurious room, with French armchairs and a dressing table where the lady guests at John's dinner parties could primp themselves.

I don't know how long I was there, alone with Harpo. I went over Harpo mechanically and still found no cut. I think it was then that I realized where those smears of blood had come from. Harpo, frightened and puzzled, had pawed at John, trying to rouse him. I remember feeling sick and washing my hands, in the tiny adjoining lavatory, scrubbing them over and over. And then wiping at the stain on my coat sleeve with paper tissues and telling myself that cold water removed bloodstains. It didn't quite; the rusty wetness had soaked into the thick cloth. I washed Harpo's front paws, too.

And I thought of everything, of John and of Bill and me. They would find the burglar. They'd let me leave, and I would telephone to Bill then. Or I'd wait for him, because they would want him to come. They'd have to find Jimmy, too. And Sugar would be waiting for me to trim Maurice. I'd telephone her, unless of course they told her of John's death. Brannigan knew her name, the young lady John was going to marry. Her name was Caroline Candy, but everybody had always called her Sugar because it seemed to fit.

More cars arrived and more people entered the house. I looked out of the window, barred, as all the ground-floor windows were barred. There was an array of police cars and a little crowd of people who had gathered outside.

After a while, too, the house grew cooler, so someone must have turned down the thermostat that controlled the heat. And finally two policemen and Brannigan came to question me.

One of the policemen, a thin, bony man with a long lantern jaw, said, "I'm Lieutenant Wilkins. Now, then . . ." He spoke to the other policeman, who had a stenographer's tablet and a pencil in his hand. "Take her statement."

It was, of course, perfectly proper and in order but I said, "Have you talked to his nephew? Dr. William Ransome? He's at the hospital and . . ."

The lieutenant cut me off: "We'll see to all that. Your full name, please."

"Patricia Bennet."

"Where do you live?"

"Why, I—I live in the country, near Dunham Woods."

"Live out there alone?"

"Yes, since my father died three years ago. Except, of course, for the kennel man, Mike Reilly. I own a poodle kennel; Mike's got a room over the garage."

"What time did you come here tonight?"

"About nine. I left home about seven-thirty."

"Who let you into the house?"

"Nobody. I rang and rang, and then I remembered that the houseman wouldn't be here—tonight's the Chauffeurs' Ball. So I tried the door, and it was unlocked. I had to have my duffel bags tonight. I left them here yesterday when I clipped Harpo, because my car was in the garage for a new bearing; I had to come and go by train. I didn't want to carry the bags back home again. But then Sugar—that is, Miss Caroline Candy—was going away, on a Caribbean cruise. She was starting in the morning and intended to take Maurice—that's her dog—and she wanted him clipped to-night. So I came in the house to get the tools." I told him everything, nervously and quickly, and in full detail.

"Did you hear the shot?" he asked when I had finished.

I hadn't thought of that. "No! There wasn't any shot. I'd have heard it."

"You said you'd gone back to the laundry."

"I did. But I'd have heard a shot!" Suddenly the significance of that struck me. "Why, then it must have happened before I came into the house! After the houseman and cook left." I shivered, thinking of myself entering the house, with John dead in his armchair in the room above.

There was not a flicker of change in the lieutenant's face. "Did you see anybody? Besides Ransome, I mean."

"I didn't see John!"

"You said you heard somebody talking upstairs."

"Yes, I did. But I didn't hear a shot." That had its significance, too. I cried, "Was that the burglar? Was he in the house, then?"

Neither of them replied for a moment. Then Wilkins said slowly, "Certainly nobody got out of the house after Brannigan entered it and found you coming down the stairs. You say you were not in the study at all?"

"*No*, I told you. Harpo . . ."

Brannigan interrupted. "All the windows were bolted, Miss Bennet. Back door, too. Nobody left while I was in the study; I was facing the hall and the stairs, so I'd have seen him. There wasn't anybody but you in the house."

"You were on the stairway," the lieutenant said, "when Brannigan opened the door. You were trying to get away; you were at the door, when Brannigan made you come back. There was blood on your hand and on your coat."

"I got that off of Harpo's paws, I told you. I thought he was hurt."

The lieutenant picked up my coat. "You've been trying to wash off the blood," he said. "Why were you in such a hurry to leave, Miss Bennet?"

For all it was so clear, minutes seemed to pass before I got the idea. They were not talking of burglars. They were talking about murder. And I had a motive for killing John Ransome.

The lieutenant stooped over Harpo, but Harpo growled

and backed away. It was Brannigan who picked up his paws, one at a time, passing his hands over them.

"I washed it off," I cried. "He must have pawed at John and . . . But I washed his paws."

There was a queer kind of silence. Brannigan showed a clean, pink hand to the lieutenant and then, to make sure, brought dampened tissues from the lavatory and blotted at Harpo's paws with them. But I had washed them off thoroughly. The tissues came away clean. "I washed his paws . . ." I began again, and Lieutenant Wilkins said, "You saw the gun upstairs, Miss Bennet. Had you ever seen it before?"

"No!"

"Want to put that in your statement? Remember, I'm going to ask you to sign all this. Do you know what perjury means?"

"Of course."

The lieutenant said, "It was your gun, Miss Bennet."

The room rocked around me. I had to speak, but something seemed tight and paralyzing around my throat.

Wilkins had cold blue eyes, which never wavered. He said, "Don't try to deny it. We've checked your permit."

The tight band around my throat let go. "It's not! It couldn't be! I have a gun. I have a permit. It's the kennels'; we've got some fine dogs. Sometimes there are prowlers and . . . But that can't be my gun."

"Young lady," said the lieutenant then, "I'm arresting you on a murder charge. . . ."

The outside door opened with a crash against the wall. Bill came running into the coatroom, looked at me, looked at everybody, and shouted, "What are you doing to her?"

They had it all over again, with Bill getting whiter as he listened and the line of his jaw showing sharper. When they'd finished he came to me. "Is this exactly the way it happened, Pat?"

I had to say yes. He glanced at Harpo. "There must be traces of blood from the dog's paws on the stairs and on the rug in the library . . ." He stopped as Wilkins shook his head. An army of feet had tracked mud and wet over those stairs.

Lieutenant Wilkins said, "It'd be hard to find now, even if the dog actually did that. Will you come upstairs?"

Bill put his hand gently on my shoulder. "It'll be all right, Pat," he said quietly. "It'll be all right."

The lieutenant took my coat with the wet patch on the sleeve. Then I waited again, listening to the long murmur of voices from John's study. I don't know how long it was before Jimmy arrived, but I heard him question the policeman outside the door, and suddenly he came into the room.

When I was eighteen, three years before, I had been engaged to Jimmy, and I thought that in all the world there was nobody like him until, to put it with brutal frankness, Jimmy jilted me. He did it with a gay and charming insouciance and insisted, later, on seeing me. But one day I simply didn't care whether he came or not, and all at once I wasn't in love with Jimmy Ransome any more and couldn't understand why I ever had been. I didn't know how it happened; but that's exactly the way it happened. Bill came later, and that was very different.

Jimmy said, "They got me at the Knothole Club. I can't believe it. Darling, they said that you were here. What happened? They said he'd been shot, but that's all."

I told him briefly. But I didn't tell him I'd been arrested for murder and I didn't tell him about the gun; none of it seemed real. I stopped as a policeman put his head inside. "They want you upstairs, Mr. Ransome."

I was left alone again. I tried to think when I had last seen the gun. Bill had given it to me, long ago. My house was isolated and he thought I ought to have a gun. But I kept it in the filing cabinet along with pedigrees and bills. I couldn't remember having seen it for months, and in truth I was rather afraid of guns.

Sometime during that long wait a man came to take my fingerprints. And at last Bill came.

He opened the door and said, "All right; we can leave." He had a woman's raincoat that was too big for me. "It belongs to cook," he said, and put it around me. Jimmy came running down the stairs and went out the door with us.

I didn't question Bill; I didn't think of the duffel bags or anything but the miracle of getting out of the house. But at the last moment I turned back and let Harpo out of the coatroom; he'd have to be taken care of, and I didn't know what the police were going to do about the house. Harpo came bouncing after us and into the back seat of my small coupé.

Jimmy said, "You go ahead. My car is parked down the street."

Bill got behind the wheel. As we backed out away from the curb another police car drove up, and Everett, the houseman, and Rosie, the cook, who was Everett's wife, got out; they were dressed in evening clothes and escorted by police. Obviously, the police had found them at the Chauffeurs' Ball and brought them to the house for inquiry.

We shot away and turned left to Lake Shore Drive.

"Brannigan did it. I don't know what he told him, but the lieutenant said finally that you could leave."

"My coat . . ."

"They sent it to the laboratory. That and the gun. You didn't touch anything, did you?"

"No! Bill, it must have been a burglar!"

He drove on for a few moments in frowning and thoughtful silence. Finally he said, "Was it John you heard talking?"

"I don't know. It wasn't distinct. It was as if the door was closed and . . ."

"Men's voices? Could you tell that?"

"Yes. Yes, I'm sure of that."

"But you didn't hear a shot?"

"No! I heard voices, but that's all. I didn't see anybody. I didn't hear a door close or—or anything."

"Did they ask you how long you were in the laundry?"

"I told them. It couldn't have been more than two or three minutes at the most." My voice had wavered unsteadily.

He gave me a quick glance. "Pat, the trouble is, you told them the truth. And they think it's contradictory. I mean, if John was alive and talking to somebody when you arrived, then he was killed while you were there. Yet you didn't hear the shot."

"But I *didn't* hear it. And I would have!"

"I know. And I know you. But they..."

"They don't believe me."

Bill said gently, "You and I know that you didn't kill him. That makes the difference."

The difference between positive proof that anybody but me had been in the house, and my presence, my gun. Blood on my hand and coat.

Bill said, "I wish I'd got there sooner. I wish you'd had a lawyer. He wouldn't have let you..." He checked himself, and then went on quickly, "But it's only beginning. There's got to be an answer, and they'll find it. There's the whole routine of investigation. They asked me if anything had been stolen. As far as I could see nothing was missing, but there may not have been time for anybody to rob the place. He'd have had to get out as fast as he could. They asked if John had enemies. But I don't know of any special quarrel he'd had with anybody."

"He had one with me."

"That's not a motive. People don't murder people because a mortgage comes due."

He turned off the Drive, left again. "They'll find the note your father gave him. They'll not know that John intended to take over every stick of property you've got. Pat, I talked to him again last night; I went to see him. That was just before dinner. I tried again to persuade him to let up on you."

"He wouldn't! I saw him yesterday, too. He came just as I finished trimming Harpo. He said that I'd have to get out by the first." I shivered a little, thinking of John as he had been the day before and John as he now was.

The facts of the loan were simple. He'd lent my father money to start the kennels. It had seemed then an act of friendliness and generosity, and John had many times referred to it as such. It was also a business transaction; his security was the property itself. John had been, I think, a little awed by my father, who was in literal fact a scholar and a gentleman, even if impractical about business, and he had a fineness John sensed, yet lacked.

It was during the past year, just as I was beginning to get the worst of the muddle straightened out, that John had demanded his money.

Cars streamed beside us with a wet swish of tires. Bill turned into the narrow street behind the towering apartment house that fronted on the Drive, where Sugar lived. He stopped the car. "They told me to tell Sugar. They'll question her later."

He came around and opened the door on my side. As I got out he took me in his arms, and just for a moment I felt that somehow it was going to be all right. The whole world had to be all right, so long as Bill and I could be together. We had lived on that faith for a long time.

I stopped shivering, and Bill said, "If there's any need for it we can get the best lawyer there is. I can pay him."

With John Ransome's money. Jimmy and Bill, suddenly, because John Ransome was dead, were both rich men, for John had willed his money to them, equally. John had never made any secret about that, but then he had intended to live for a long time; he was only in his middle fifties. He had never helped Bill, but he had supplied Jimmy, often and lavishly, with money. In some ways they were alike, and I suppose John saw himself in Jimmy's handsome, charming youth. But Bill half starved himself trying to save money, and half broke his heart trying to stifle ambition.

For Bill was what they call a dedicated doctor. All his life he'd wanted to be a doctor, and all his adult life he'd wanted to do bone research and experiment, and the dream, the very top pinnacle of it, was to have his own hospital. Once or twice Bill had taken me to visit a charity ward where he managed to squeeze in some hours of extra work. It was a children's ward and when I saw the patient little figures, immobile because of casts or traction, and the way their faces turned and lightened when Bill came into the room, I understood what he wanted to do and why.

We went into the apartment house, where an elevator swooped us up to Sugar's apartment at the top. Jimmy was already there and he had told Sugar, and she was sitting on the sofa, dabbing at her eyes with a lacy handkerchief.

Sugar—Caroline Candy—and I had known each other, and Jimmy and Bill, too, all our lives. Sugar and I had gone to the same schools, but our paths had diverged immediately afterward. I had spent the intervening years at the kennels, loving it, too. Sugar, at eighteen, had come into a really stunning fortune, left by her grandfather, Thompson Candy. After that we didn't see much of each other, yet we kept in touch and she drove out to the kennels to see me fairly often.

There was another and a rather odd bond between me and Sugar. We had both, although at different times, been jilted by Jimmy Ransome. Her own engagement to Jimmy had followed mine, and when Jimmy jilted her she didn't take it as hard as I had; she was far more sensible about it, but she never forgave Jimmy. I knew that. Yet they saw each other frequently, even after Sugar began to go about with John Ransome. It was as if Jimmy felt a kind of obligation to her for having jilted her, which was an odd way of looking at it, but was Jimmy's.

I didn't think of all that, then.

Sugar dabbed at her eyes and said, "What happened? Jimmy said Pat was there."

Bill told her. Sugar, blond, with a childish face and candid, wide eyes, was always beautiful and very, very chic. A huge bracelet on her white wrist sparkled with sapphires and diamonds. The bracelet alone would have paid my debt to John.

She sprang up when Bill finished. "But you don't understand!" she cried. "John and I were going to be married! He was going to meet me at Montego Bay, and we were going to announce it then and be married as soon as we got back to Chicago. And tomorrow he was going to get my ring." She sighed and added, "A big emerald surrounded with diamonds."

That settled it; for John Ransome wouldn't have parted with money for a bag of peanuts if he hadn't expected to get value received, and all of us knew it.

Jimmy whistled. Bill said uncomfortably, "Well, I'm sorry," and Jimmy unexpectedly began to talk about alibis. "They'll look for a motive," he said, "and Bill and I had motives and I've got an alibi. I was at the Knothole Club, and at least three men can swear to it. I don't know about Bill."

Bill thought for a moment. He looked like Jimmy and yet unlike him; they were the sons of John's two brothers, and his only relatives. Jimmy was extremely handsome; Bill was handsome, too, but in a different, sort of solid way, and I'd rather have looked at his face any time and all my life than Jimmy's.

He said, "I was at the sanitarium, but I was in my office doing reports. I finished about nine-thirty and went out to get a sandwich; then I walked back to the sanitarium. I was there when I had the message from the police, and I went at once to the house. I was in my office around nine o'clock. But I'm not sure that anybody saw me there."

"But you don't need an alibi!" Sugar cried, dabbing at her eyes again. "Pat says nobody else was there!"

"Somebody was there," Bill said shortly, his gray eyes angry. "Pat didn't kill him."

"Oh, of course. I didn't mean . . . Oh, I can't believe it," Sugar wailed. "John . . ."

Jimmy passed a hand over his crisp, curling black hair, and waited until Sugar took her handkerchief from her eyes again. Then he said, "How about you, Sugar? The police are going to question you, you know."

"Question *me*!" She sat down and stared at Jimmy blankly. "Why?"

"They'll want to know whether you've got any information," Bill said. "Did John ever say anything to you that would give you an idea that he was—well, afraid of anybody? Or had quarreled with anybody, or anything at all like that?"

She shook her head. "He was going to take me to the plane in the morning and"—she dabbed at her eyes again—"he said he'd phone to me tonight about eleven. He always did. I went with the Rakeleys to see their show—you know, the Teen Show. It was on tonight, and they brought me home. I got home about an hour ago. I was waiting for John to phone."

The Rakeleys, a young couple, friends of Sugar's, owned the Teen Chocolate Bars, advertised everywhere.

Jimmy said, "Sugar's got an alibi, then. So have I. If we need it."

It was just then that Maurice entered the picture by giving a shrill yelp, and I started for the bedroom. Not that I liked Maurice, but it was a yelp of pain.

Sugar followed me. "He's been jumping," she said. "He always yelps when he jumps."

I knelt down and felt Maurice's tiny leg. Sugar closed the door and said suddenly in a kind of whisper, "Pat, who was in the study with John? You can tell *me*."

"I don't know." Maurice had only twisted his foot and there was nothing wrong with it. I released him, and he jumped up on Sugar's chaise longue. The room was so full of satin and lace pillows and perfume bottles and stuffed dolls that it seemed crowded, although it was orderly; Sugar flung things about, but she had two excellent maids.

Sugar said slowly, "If I'd married John—well, it would have made a difference to Bill and Jimmy. John's money . . ."

"Bill didn't kill John to keep him from marrying you!"

I started for the door, and Sugar caught my arm. "Wait, Pat! Suppose there was another woman? Somebody he— well, had to get rid of? Because he was going to marry me, I mean."

I knew nothing of John Ransome's love life, and cared less. I said so shortly and went back to the living room. Soon after that, Bill and I went home.

Harpo was asleep in the back of the car when we reached it. Bill drove. Since there was no late train we decided that Bill would drive my car back to town, and then drive out to see me again the next night. "Police permitting," he said tersely.

We talked all the way home and got nowhere. I told Bill of Sugar's charming little notion of another woman whom John had to get rid of, and Bill thought it over and shook his head. "If there was a woman in his life I didn't know it. Besides Sugar, that is." He drove for a while and added, "But the door was unlocked. He must have expected somebody. Did he know you were coming?"

"No. I was going to ask the houseman for the duffel bags."

"What did John say yesterday when you saw him?"

It wasn't very pleasant. "He said my father cheated him; he said my father had made him believe that the kennels would pay off, and of course they hadn't. He said I'd mismanaged and that his 'good money had gone down the drain' because I hadn't seen to things properly."

"It wouldn't have hurt him to cross off the debt. He's boasted about loaning it to your father. I suppose," he said, his voice tired, "it made him seem to be a good fellow, generous to his friends."

"He could have helped you, Bill. He could have started you in a private practice. He could have built your hospital, even."

"I got along." He put out his hand and caught mine for a minute, and I calmed down.

Eventually we turned into the little lane leading to Kings Manor. My father had named the place, and there was never a less suitable name. In fact, the house was a cottage, red brick with vines over it; there were five acres around it, grown to meadow and birches. Behind the house was a long building for the kennels; the runways stretched out back, and the garage, with a room for Mike, stood at one end.

Nothing could have been less like a manor. I think the kennel names for our dogs, which Kings Manor suggested, appealed to my father's romanticism and also his sense of humor. There were Kings Manor King and Queen, and Prince and Princess, and on down. I had lately been tempted to give the puppies such names as Kings Manor Debit and Kings Manor Scullery Girl as more befitting my circumstances, but I hadn't, and had worked right through all the conceivable noble titles. And I had sold the puppies, but not as well, perhaps, as I ought to have done, for I cared more about the kind of owner a puppy went to than the price he'd pay. Mike seemed to understand the dogs, and though he was rough in his manner the dogs all trusted him. I owed Mike both past wages and gratitude.

When we reached Kings Manor the dogs in the kennels heard us and barked, but politely, for they recognized the sound of my car. We let Harpo out and went into the cottage, where Kings Manor Exchequer greeted us warmly. Poor old boy, he was almost as thin and ragged as the present state of the real exchequer, but once he'd been a prizewinner, and was, indeed, the father of Harpo. He lived in the cottage now, as he was too old to be left in the kennels. He didn't like Harpo's entrance and showed what teeth he had left, so Bill put Harpo in my tiny office, once the dining room.

Then we looked for the gun, and it was not there. There were bills and pedigrees and odd bits of medicines for the dogs, and letters from past and future buyers, but no gun. I could not remember when I had last seen it. There had been a box of shells, and that was gone, too.

"You don't keep the filing cabinet locked?" Bill asked.

"Never. There's nothing anybody would want."

"Somebody wanted the gun."

It was not a pleasant thought. I moved to put my cheek against the warmth of Bill's coat sleeve, but it couldn't shut out horror. Whoever shot John had had to stand there, in the tiny office, search through my filing cabinet, secretly, when I was not in the office, and remove the gun and shells.

Bill said, "Look through your files. Who has come lately to look at or buy one of the dogs?"

We made the list together; it was short, and none of the names meant anything to either of us. Bill looked at it carefully and then put it in his pocket, and said what neither of us could have avoided thinking: "I've been here often. So have Jimmy and Sugar. Jimmy and I had motives for killing John."

"But somebody could have known that. Whoever shot John could have taken the gun to make the police suspect you or Jimmy or me."

I said that, and then there was a tumult of barking from

the kennels as a car came along the lane. I looked out the window and saw the station wagon, which surprised me, for Mike rarely left the place. "It's Mike," I said; and Bill said slowly, "Mike could have got into the filing cabinet at any time. Did he know John was about to take over the kennels?"

"Oh, yes. But Mike wouldn't have—"

"Mike would have been out of a job. He's too old to get another job very easily."

"He wouldn't have left my gun there."

"No. Not unless he got nervous and scared and . . . Did he and John ever quarrel?"

They had. About two weeks before, John had driven out to see me. Mike had overheard the whole conversation, for John had found me in the kennels, where I was cooking and stirring the great kettles of food, and Mike was there, too. John had said much the same things that he had said to me yesterday, and Mike had flown into a rage when John said we had mismanaged the kennels and wasted his money. Mike had sworn at John and told him to get off the place. John had said the place belonged to him, and in the end Mike had knocked him down. John had picked himself up, purple with anger, got in his car, and driven away.

I didn't want to tell Bill that. And just then Mike came thumping to the door and opened it. "I saw your light. . . . Hello, Doctor."

"Hello, Mike. Where have you been?"

"Went to the vet's to get some medicine. That new boarder, the dachshund puppy, looks to me like he's got distemper. Did you ask if he'd had all his shots?"

I had; there's a state law about hydrophobia shots, but you can never be sure the owner has complied. A woman had brought him only two or three days before; he was to board at the kennels while she went to Florida, and she had said certainly he'd had all his puppy shots. I told Mike.

Bill said, "Mike, something's happened. My uncle, John Ransome, was killed tonight."

Mike sat down slowly. He was a man of about sixty, heavyset, with powerful muscles. I saw his underlip come out and his eyes take on a guarded look as Bill told him the story. He told it all, about my gun and everything. When he'd finished, Mike sat in brooding silence. Finally he said, "He got what he deserved," and got up without another word and stalked out.

It was like him; he'd go away and think about it deeply, and the next day, or even the next week, he'd say something about it. It didn't strike me as anything unusual.

But Bill went quickly after him. "Wait, Mike. Miss Bennet's gun—can you remember when you last saw it?"

Mike didn't turn. He said over his shoulder, gruffly, "Never saw it," and banged the door after him.

Bill left shortly after that; it was very late, and when I saw the lights of the car vanish into the main road the cottage seemed very empty. I let old Exchequer into my bedroom, where he made himself comfortable in a chair and instantly began to snore. I envied him. I thought of everything during that night, half-awake, half-asleep. And sometime during those cold and weary hours I began to have an odd feeling that there was something I had forgotten and must remember. I didn't know what, but it nagged at me. It was as if some fact subtly did not fit into the design of other facts.

I realized that it was morning when I heard Mike come into the kitchen, and smelled the coffee he put on the stove. He was out again by the time I had got myself into dungarees and a sweater. I went to the kennels to see about the little dachshund. But he didn't have distemper. He looked up from his feed bowl, which he had licked clean, and sprang upon me with delight. His nose was cold and he had no temperature. I took a long breath of relief and went to work.

I didn't talk to Mike, who was cleaning the kennels at the other end of the long building. I expected Bill to telephone and kept listening for the ring, but he didn't call. About noon Mrs. Sales, the dachshund's owner, came and wanted to take her dog home. She had changed her mind, she said; she wasn't going to Florida, and she was in rather a hurry, so would I get the dog at once.

She was a tall, very thin woman, with dark eyes and

sleek black hair and a thin red mouth. She was dressed very smartly, although not expensively; and although there was a certain crispness and efficiency in her manner, she was also, that morning, obviously nervous. She looked, in fact, as if she'd been crying, for there were swollen, heavily powdered patches below her eyes. I got out the little dog; she clasped him in her arms, paid for three days' board, and hurried out to her car. As she reached it Harpo came dashing around the corner of the house and bounded over, tail wagging, to greet her.

It wasn't like Harpo; it wasn't, indeed, like any French poodle, for they are inclined to be reserved and a little shy of strangers. Mrs. Sales slid her thin and elegant legs into the car, and Harpo looked disappointed—Harpo, who was John Ransome's dog!

I said abruptly, "Harpo seems to know you."

Her dark eyes flickered toward Harpo. "He's very friendly, isn't he?" Her voice showed no recognition. Her car shot away down the lane.

I thought of the list Bill and I had made. I hadn't put Mrs. Sales's name on it because the dachshund was a boarder. Had Harpo really recognized her? I decided to tell Bill about it.

But when I tried to reach him at the sanitarium they said he was out, and by four I decided that I couldn't bear it any longer; I'd take the station wagon into town and find out what was happening. Then, just as I had showered and got myself into a fresh white blouse and my best tweed suit, Jimmy came, and he had news.

The police had spent the whole time sifting what clues there were, digging into John Ransome's life, questioning the servants, his friends, his office force; questioning Sugar and Jimmy and Bill. Bill had told them that he had bought and given me the revolver, and they had the record of it, the purchase and the transfer permits. Bill had also quarreled violently with John the night before John was murdered. He hadn't told me that.

"Everett—you know, the houseman—heard it all and put them on to it," Jimmy said. "But Bill admitted it frankly.

He tried to get John to renew your note, and then told John to take it out of anything he intended to leave to Bill in his will. John fired up and said if that's the way Bill felt about it he'd see that he didn't get anything—well, in short, there was a row. They didn't come to blows, but Everett said he thought they were going to. Bill left, and John caught Everett listening and nearly took his head off.... Well, that's the way it was. So the police think John intended to change his will so Bill wouldn't get a cent."

"Bill wouldn't have murdered him!"

"Take it easy, Pat. The upshot of it is, they've got Bill down at headquarters. They know that you and Bill want to get married and don't have the money. They know about the row. As it stands now, Bill inherits. And they say that if he shot John and you saw him in the house, you'd have protected him."

"He wasn't there!" I looked for my coat, remembered where it was and why, and snatched up a worn old leather coat instead.

"Where are you going?" Jimmy asked. "Nobody can do anything right now. They think it was somebody John knew and wasn't afraid of, because he was sitting in his chair; he hadn't made a move to struggle or get to the telephone or anything. They've got your note—that is, your father's. It was in his desk in the study. Everett heard you and John talking about that, too. He heard everything John said."

I put on my coat and went out to tell Mike I was going to town. When I got back to the house Jimmy was standing beside his car. "I'll take you in," he said, "but I don't see what you can do."

When we reached town Jimmy took me to Sugar's apartment, where I agreed to wait while Jimmy went on to police headquarters to see if I could talk to Bill. I caught his arm as he turned to go. "Tell Bill I'm here. Tell him I'll come the minute they'll let me."

"Of course, darling. I'll tell him—if they'll let me see him."

Sugar was at home, dressed in heavy black crepe that somehow suggested mourning, and there were newspapers all over the floor. She didn't know any more than I knew; Jimmy had told her about Bill and his quarrel with John, and the police had questioned her, and that was all.

"I couldn't tell them anything! I don't know who killed him or why—or anything. . . . You look terrible, Pat. You'd better stay here tonight."

I'd be nearer to Bill if I stayed in town, so I did.

It was a dreadful evening. Neither Bill nor Jimmy phoned, and there wasn't any way for us to know what was happening. Dinner was served and we tried to eat. Then we listened to the news. Much of it was about John Ransome's murder and none of it was news to us, except that the police had said they expected to make an arrest very soon. That meant Bill, I thought drearily, or me. Or both of us.

Sugar snapped off the radio, and the apartment seemed very quiet and empty. "The maids have gone," she said. "They don't live in. Tell me everything again, Pat, all of it. From the time you went to his house."

I didn't mind doing it; I was seeking some loophole, some small thread that might be a clue; anything to show them that Bill hadn't shot his uncle. But there was nothing.

"Who was talking to John?" Sugar said. "You must have heard something—you said it was a man."

"I said men's voices. I didn't hear anything distinctly. It was like a—oh, a radio, or a record or something. Only, it wasn't, because whoever was there must have shot him. Except I didn't hear the shot. So he could have been killed before I got there."

"Can't the police tell when he was killed?"

"I don't know. I think it's something to do with the temperature of the body. And the house was so hot . . ."

She shivered. "Don't!" She got up and wandered around the room.

I said, "Besides, they don't believe me. They don't even believe that there was blood on Harpo's paws."

It was then that I remembered Mrs. Sales, and I found out that Sugar knew her. She had stopped to stare out one of the great windows, and she turned a white, startled face to me when I told her of the woman's visit.

"Why, of course! That's Edith Busch. At least, she used to be Edith Busch, and then she married and left John's office. But you must remember her! She was John's secretary for years."

"Edith Busch!" Of course I remembered—that is, I had never seen Edith Busch, but I had heard her name. I had seen it many times signed to letters John had told her to write to me or to my father.

Sugar said slowly, "He got a man secretary after that. His name is Whiting. I always thought that Edith made a play for John, and that's why he fired her. She could have taken your gun. . . . Pat, are you sure you didn't hear a shot? It might have sounded like a—oh, a backfire or something."

I was sure, and she jerked the heavy curtains across the windows. It was again gusty, with a wind off the lake that stirred up rain that slashed violently at the great panes of glass, as if something out there in the night, high above the lighted city, wanted to get in.

"It's late," Sugar said. She led me to a small guest room, as lavishly appointed as the rest of the apartment, for Sugar spent money like water and always had. We passed her room and there were no trunks, and I said something about her trip. She said, "You don't think I'd leave now, do you?" and added thoughtfully, "I've got to get some black things and a veil for the funeral." I could see her, with a veil to the floor probably, going down the aisle with Jimmy and Bill. John Ransome's beautiful young fiancée, so the papers would say.

She put Maurice in the kitchen and brought a nightgown that needed only a belt to be a ball dress, and also a dressing gown and sleeping pills. I was turning down the bed, and she dumped the heap of chiffon upon it and put the bottle of sleeping pills on the table. Her bracelet flashed in the light from the lamp on the table; it flashed so oddly and flatly that I gave it a second look.

She saw me and laughed shortly. "Paste," she said. "It's a copy. The real one is in the safe. You'd better take a sleeping pill." She went away.

I didn't want a pill; I was so tired that I thought I didn't need it. But rain slashed against the windows and I couldn't sleep. What were the police doing? How soon would I hear from Bill?

Sometime, however, I slept, because I awoke abruptly. I sat up, my heart thumping. Something had roused me.

I listened. Away up there the wind surged and tore at concrete and steel and wailed around corners and whistled at the windows. After what seemed a long time I told myself it had been nothing, and settled back again. As I did so there was a sound of hammering somewhere in the apartment.

It was an irregular beat. It was muffled yet heavy. Somebody in the apartment was hammering on something, and since the maids were gone, it had to be Sugar. What was she doing? The hammering stopped.

I snapped on the bedside lamp and got into Sugar's dressing gown and opened the door. A hall ran back from the living room, past Sugar's bedroom and mine. It was lighted; no one was there. An icy breath of air swirled around me. Sugar's door was open; in the dim light streaming past me from the hall, I could see her figure humped up quietly in bed. The thin dressing gown swirled around my ankles, and suddenly I realized what had happened. The cold current of air was sweeping down the hall from the living room, so a window that had been insecurely latched must have blown open.

I ran to the living room and turned on the light. One of the windows, a huge casement window that opened like a door, was now wide open, the draperies swirling out and rain swishing across the carpet. I ran across to close it. I got the latch in my hand and pushed against the wind, and the lights went out.

There was a rush of motion, and someone pushed me hard from behind.

It happened that quickly. For a terrible instant I fought for balance over the low window sill, so low, so narrow, with a horrible depth of blackness below me. I clutched the thick draperies and screamed and screamed against the night and the cold rain and the black space below me.

The heavy draperies held. Somehow I braced myself

against the wall. Somehow I knew that the hands against me were gone. But I was still clutching the draperies, still screaming, still braced against the wall, when the lights sprang up and Sugar came running to me.

The first thing we did was close and bolt the window. Sugar was screaming at me, and I was shaking and trying to tell her what had happened. She cried, "But there's nobody here! You've been dreaming! You slipped. . . ."

"Somebody was here," I said.

Sugar went to the front door and came back. She was white. "The door was open. But I locked it! I locked it last night." Sugar's eyes widened. "The safe!"

She whirled around and ran into the next room, a kind of library whose shelves mainly held glass rabbits and little china figures. I could hear her moving, little clicks and rustles, and I went across to the door. The safe was set in the wall and she was closing it. She pushed a picture into place to hide the door of the safe. "No, it's all right. Nothing's gone. You must have been dreaming."

I hadn't been dreaming.

I went out into the smart foyer, and Sugar followed me; we looked at the door and opened it. The wide, carpeted corridor outside was blank and empty. There was a night latch on the door and a bolt inside, and Sugar turned it. She said, "I always lock it—I mean, it locks itself when I close it, but I always turn the bolt inside. But perhaps I didn't last night."

"Does anybody have a key?"

Her eyes flickered away from me; then she shook her head. And it suddenly and horribly occurred to me that perhaps whoever had been there was still there, hiding.

I called the police. And then we sat in the living room, with the carpet wet from the rain, and the heavy draperies sagging from the rod where I had pulled them. I was thankful she'd had heavy rods and heavy draperies, and I began to shiver again. Sugar said, again, that I had dreamed it. And in a very short time the police arrived.

The building was new, and so thoroughly soundproofed that nobody apparently had heard the commotion. We didn't hear the elevator or the police until they rang discreetly at the door.

There were two of them; they were from the nearest prowl car. They didn't then associate either of us with John Ransome's murder. But they searched the apartment quickly and thoroughly, and found the kitchen door locked and nobody anywhere except Maurice in the kitchen.

They examined the window and the door and finally told us indulgently that nobody was in the apartment now, and we'd better go back to sleep and forget about it. Clearly, they, too, believed that I had imagined the whole thing. They perked up, however, when one of them started to write out his report of the visit and asked for Sugar's name and mine. He gave a start when I told him mine was Pat Bennet.

"Bennet? Bennet! Say, are you the girl who was there when they found Ransome?"

I told him yes. He stared at me, but only wrote our names. Then both of them went away.

I had no doubt the report would reach Lieutenant Wilkins. Sugar closed the door after them and bolted it, and I telephoned to Bill, but he still wasn't in. I thought vaguely that if the police had let him go he might have gone to Jimmy's, so I tried Jimmy's number, and nobody answered there.

Sugar yawned. "It's three o'clock. Let's go back to bed."

We did, and sometime I must have slept, but I was sitting bolt upright in bed with the light burning when a maid knocked and entered with a tray in her hands.

She was neat and quiet, but shocked. "Good morning, Miss Bennet. I've brought your tray, and the—the police are here and wish to question you."

And so began a strange day, an overcast day during which the foghorn out in the lake sounded constantly, and fog wreathed Lake Shore Drive, far below. A day that brought in Mike Reilly and Mrs. Sales and Sugar herself as suspects.

It also was a day during which Jimmy's alibi was broken down, and a day during which a thing of horror was silently and secretly performed.

The interview was long. Lieutenant Wilkins began it by questioning me in detail about what had happened the night before.

"It did happen," I told him. "I didn't dream it."

He said flatly, "You say it happened. I have no reason to doubt it. On the other hand, if you could prove that someone tried to murder you, then it would go to prove that that same person murdered Ransome. And thus that you didn't kill Ransome. . . . Wait, please. I want to tell you exactly how things stand."

He told me, concisely ticking off the items, outlining the facts: Bill's quarrel with John and the reason for it. My own quarrel with John. It was then that he told me something I didn't know, which was why John Ransome had determined to give me no more time: It was not only because he wanted his money back, but because he wanted the property.

"He had bought the property adjoining it," Lieutenant Wilkins said, "and he intended to drill for oil."

It both surprised and didn't surprise me. As everybody knows, a few oil wells have been put down in the vicinity of the low-lying Fox River valley—that is, around St. Charles, Geneva, Elgin—a vicinity that took in my cottage and a few acres in the Dunham Woods section. As far as I knew, no one had expected to discover a great oil field, and everyone knew about the various wells that had so far been driven. But obviously John Ransome had been attracted by such a possibility.

The only point was that it was like John. It gave a consistency and logic to his determination to take over the kennels, or, more precisely, the acreage they stood on.

I thought for a moment. "I'm not surprised. There's no secret about oil out there. Who told you that John intended to do that?"

"Jimmy Ransome. His uncle had told him." And Jimmy hadn't mentioned it to me.

Lieutenant Wilkins said, "Now then, you realize that if Ransome and Miss Candy had married, the probability is that Ransome would have made a new will, certainly including his wife. This would have cut down both Jimmy's and

Dr. Ransome's inheritances. It might even have excluded them altogether."

"But that doesn't mean that either of them..."

He cut me off: "We'll get down to brass tacks, Miss Bennet. The night Ransome was murdered we had only one suspect; that was, clearly, you, and on your own testimony to the effect that no one was in the house except yourself and Ransome."

"But I went back to the laundry. He could have left then."

"Except for one thing, Miss Bennet: Brannigan was on his way to the house. He is watchman for several houses on that street, and was keeping a particularly careful eye on them that night, trying the doors and all that. He can't swear that nobody left the Ransome house. Nevertheless, he is reasonably sure that he would have seen anybody who left by the front door. Somebody could have left by the kitchen door."

"I would have seen him..."

"After which the kitchen door could have been bolted by someone in the house. You, Miss Bennet."

"I didn't! There wasn't anybody." He meant Bill, of course.

"Your—er—friend, Dr. Ransome, has no alibi for the time of Ransome's murder, and he had a very strong motive for that murder."

I tried to say something, and he said sharply, "Wait!" and went on. He knew all about Bill—his job, his salary, me. He knew that Bill wanted to do bone research and that John Ransome had never offered to help him. "Dr. Ransome bought the gun, Miss Bennet. It was that gun that killed Ransome, no question of it. And would you have accused Dr. Ransome?" He leaned forward and said very quietly, "Would you have told anyone that he was in Ransome's house that night?"

"But he wasn't there!"

Lieutenant Wilkins said in a sad and honest way that was curiously disarming, "A man with ability—and your doctor has that—a man with a dream, a man who wants something, not selfishly but for a high and humane reason—is that man likely to consider one man's life as weighing much against that of many?''

"Bill's not like that! He's not a man with an obsession. Yes, he wants to study. But he's—he's like anybody else. He takes things as they come, and he doesn't mind working, and he never asked John for a penny.''

"He asked John Ransome for money for you. He asked him to deduct the sum from whatever John Ransome had willed him.''

"But John had talked of it! It was no secret! He'd often said that Bill and Jimmy would have his money sometime.''

"And Dr. Ransome bought a gun and gave it to you.''

"Anybody could have taken it.''

"Jimmy Ransome? Mike Reilly? Miss Candy? All friends of yours. I'm not trying to frighten you, and I'm not trying to have you charged with murder if you didn't kill him. But I do want you to see that you must help yourself a little, too. . . . That is, if you didn't kill Ransome,'' he added in a flat and honest parenthesis that was more terrifying than any threats he could have made.

"Jimmy Ransome has no alibi for the time Ransome was shot. He was at the Knothole Club, which is, as you know, a cocktail lounge and restaurant, and he was with several friends; we have talked to all of them. The fact came out that for at least an hour, from about eight to something after nine, he was not there at all. He says that he went to the garage where he keeps his car, got it out, stopped at a drugstore for cigarettes, didn't find the brand he wanted, stopped at another drugstore—in short, spent roughly an hour walking to the garage and then driving around the near north side. Jimmy, too, is now a very rich man. We have read Ransome's will.''

He said unexpectedly, "Do you also know a Mrs. Sales?''

"What!'' I jumped to my feet, and his bony hand waved me down onto the sofa again.

"His will, briefly, reads thus: Two thousand apiece to his house servants, Everett and Rosie Lewson. They are out of it; they went early to the Chauffeurs' Ball because Everett had something to do about the decorations. They've both got hard-and-fast alibis from seven o'clock on, till one of our men picked them up there and brought them to Ransome's house. Other bequests are ten thousand to Miss Caroline Candy; a picture to Mrs. Edith Busch Sales. The remainder is divided equally between his two nephews, Dr. Ransome and Jimmy Ransome.''

I said, ''A picture . . .''

And he said, ''The picture over the mantel in the study where he was murdered. They say it can be sold for at least fifty thousand, maybe even sixty.''

''It's a Cézanne,'' I said absently, surprised beyond words. Yet it must mean that Sugar was right—Edith Busch Sales, who had worked so long for John and perhaps hoped in the end to marry him.

Lieutenant Wilkins said, ''Has Mrs. Sales ever visited the kennels? Could she have taken your gun?''

He must have seen something in my face. He said, ''When was she there?''

I explained it. And I thought, Harpo wouldn't have barked if she had come into John's house; Harpo knew her. He wouldn't have barked, and she could have entered the house while I was in the laundry and after whoever had been talking to John in his study had gone. But anybody could have entered the house while I was in the laundry; there was time—not much time, but enough. If Brannigan was checking other houses along the street, someone might have slipped in or out without his seeing. I told the lieutenant.

Lieutenant Wilkins said, ''Mrs. Sales has been questioned. She says she knew nothing of the picture or Ransome's will. She admitted, however, that she and Ransome were close friends for a long time and that Ransome may have felt in a sense obligated to her. She admitted that they had dinner together last week. Her husband, she said, is in New Orleans on business.''

Certainly Mrs. Sales had intended to go away, and had canceled her trip after the news of John's murder. It seemed to me that that cleared Edith Sales; she wouldn't have brought the little dachshund or made plans to leave if she had intended to kill John Ransome. But my notion collapsed, for perhaps she had killed him in anger, without having planned it. Because he had told her he was going to marry Sugar, and she had, in effect, had a moment of uncontrollable, berserk fury.

But that didn't quite account for it, either. If she had taken my gun when she brought the dachshund, it argued a certain premeditation.

"Was she left alone in your office when she brought the dog?" Lieutenant Wilkins asked.

For the life of me I couldn't remember and had to say so. "There are always things I have to dash out to see to. The filing cabinet was never locked. Anybody—"

He said again, "Jimmy? Dr. Ransome? Mike Reilly? Miss Candy? Can you definitely remember when any one of them had that opportunity? Within, say, the last month?"

And of course there had been many times; it was nothing unusual for me to come in from the kennels and find Sugar or Jimmy or Bill, or all of them, lounging around the fire in the tiny living room.

Wilkins nodded and went back to Mrs. Sales. He said he supposed that John Ransome had felt, because of their long friendship, an obligation to Mrs. Sales, and thus had willed her the picture. That was exactly like John Ransome, too. He would always have felt that he could pay off any human emotion with money, or its equivalent. I said that John had left money, too, to Sugar, and that didn't mean anything, and Wilkins said thoughtfully that ten thousand dollars meant something to anybody.

It didn't to Sugar, with all her money; and, besides, if her affection for John Ransome had been, as Jimmy had hinted once or twice, largely influenced by her affection for his money, she had lost far more than ten thousand dollars at his death.

But it was then that Lieutenant Wilkins brought Mike Reilly into the thing, and I forgot all about Edith Sales and Sugar. He asked me if Mike had quarreled with John Ransome, and before I could decide upon a reply he added that I might as well give him the facts, for he had been told that there had been a quarrel and that Mike had attacked Ransome and knocked him down. "Jimmy Ransome told me that, too," he said. "John Ransome had told him."

"But Mike wouldn't . . ."

Lieutenant Wilkins stood up. "Miss Bennet," he said solemnly, "I wish you'd get it into your head that somebody, and somebody who had a motive, killed Ransome. Consider your position. And consider mine. Do you think I want to see an innocent person—you or your young doctor—convicted for murder? That is, if you didn't murder him."

It was terribly true.

He went on. "A station wagon was parked for a long time two blocks from Ransome's house the night he was murdered. It was there from about nine o'clock to something after eleven. The cop on the beat saw it, and because it was there so long took the number. It was a Kane County license; in short, it was your station wagon. We sent a man to see Mike Reilly late yesterday afternoon; he admits having been away from your place that night, but he says he went to see the vet. The vet he named says that Mike did not come to see him at all."

I felt empty and queer inside. "What does Mike say?"

For the first time an exasperated look came into Lieutenant Wilkins's face. "He sticks to his story. He says it's his word against the vet's."

Lieutenant Wilkins strode out of the room then, and in a moment came back with Sugar.

She was in black again and had a handkerchief in her hand. I listened with only half an ear, for I was thinking of Mike and how the little dachshund hadn't been sick at all the morning after John's murder, and how Mike had driven the old station wagon into the lane so late. But I did hear Lieutenant Wilkins go over the whole thing again; he started out with my story of the previous night, and Sugar replied to his questions: No, she hadn't heard any sound of pounding or hammering or whatever it was; she had heard my scream, though, and had hurried down the hall and snapped on the lights, and there was nobody there. . . . Yes, the door was unlocked.

She hesitated there, and glanced at me and said that she'd really thought, though, that I'd had a nightmare. "We'd been talking about—about John, and the murder, and Pat was depressed, of course. We both were. I even wondered if she hadn't tried to . . . But the door was unlocked, and Pat is certain that somebody tried to push her out the window."

Somebody had tried to push me out the window and I said so, but the lieutenant went right on. When Sugar heard about Jimmy's lack of an alibi, she said that Jimmy hadn't wanted her to marry John. He questioned her about that, too. Why hadn't Jimmy wanted her to marry John? Because of the money, she supposed. Had he ever said so? Well, no, Sugar said, but his attitude showed it. How? Lieutenant Wilkins asked. But she wouldn't, or couldn't, be more specific. How about Bill Ransome; had he been against their marriage?

"Well," Sugar said, with a glance at me, "John had always said Jimmy and Bill would have all his money sometime. And if he married . . ." She shrugged.

"When were you to be married?" he asked Sugar.

"Soon. We hadn't set a date."

"Did either of the nephews know of it?"

"Everybody knew of it. That is, they must have guessed."

I began again to say that Bill wouldn't have killed John to prevent his marriage to Sugar.

Lieutenant Wilkins didn't even look at me; he asked Sugar if she had known that John had willed her money, and she sat up. "What do you mean? His will?" She caught her breath and cried, "*How much*?"

It was perfectly sure, from her look, that it was a surprise to her, even before she told the lieutenant that she had never heard of the bequest, never dreamed of it. Again she said, with her eyes wide and very bright, "How much?"

He told her, and she stared at him blankly. "Why did he do that, Miss Candy?"

"I don't know. He never said anything to me about it. I can't see why. . ."

She paused, and he urged it: "Can't see why? What do you mean?"

She shrugged. "It seems odd, doesn't it? We were going to be married and—well, it just seems odd, that's all. When did he do it?"

"The will itself is dated five years ago. The picture for Mrs. Sales is specified in a codicil dated about the time she left the office. The bequest to you is contained in a second codicil dated about a month ago."

She shook her head. "I didn't know about it. I can't see why."

"One reason," Lieutenant Wilkins said unexpectedly, "might be because he was afraid of murder."

"*John!*"

"He might have wished you to be, in some measure"—he glanced around the room with its rather overwhelming luxury—"not provided for exactly, but—well, to be—remembered in his will."

"He wasn't afraid of anything. And I didn't know anything about it," Sugar said flatly.

After a few more questions that were mainly repetition, Lieutenant Wilkins said that that was all now and left.

"Well!" Sugar closed the door after him and looked blankly at me. "Ten thousand. I can't see why John would do that!"

"He was always very orderly. Cautious. I suppose he thought that until you were actually married—well, anybody can step in front of a taxi."

"I suppose so," she said, and added suddenly, "So this makes me a suspect! I could see it, the way he looked at me!"

"We're all suspects," I said wearily, and the buzzer at the front door sounded. It was Bill.

The telephone rang, too, and Sugar went to answer it. I was glad, because Bill and I had a few minutes alone. Bill had been released about midnight, and he hadn't been charged with murder. Neither had I. So far. He looked white and tired, and I don't suppose I was any beauty, but just for a minute or two nothing mattered except we were there, together.

Then Sugar came back, flushed and angry. "Who do you

think that was? It was Lyda Rakeley, and the police have been after her! They have no right to question my friends.''

Bill said, ''Your alibi?''

Sugar stamped her foot. ''Yes! They asked her if I was really with her the night John was murdered. They asked her if she was sure that I was with her the whole time!''

''And were you?'' Bill asked.

''Of course I was! But that fool Lyda said she wasn't sure. I was sitting on the other side—I mean, her husband was between us. And that part of the room was dark, the lights were on the show, and she said she thought I was there, but I might have slipped out while the show was going on. There were only five or six people in the room, watching. She'd have known if I'd sneezed!'' She whirled around to me. ''You see! I told you they suspected me!''

Bill sat down and stretched out his long legs and eyed Sugar with a half-amused, half-exasperated gleam in his gray eyes. ''Well, that's all right. It's an exclusive club, you know. Pat and me. Jimmy. Now you.''

And Edith Sales, I thought. And Mike Reilly.

''But I *was* there!'' Sugar cried angrily. ''What a fool she is!''

''Never mind,'' Bill said wearily. ''They'd have to find somebody who saw you leave or saw you return. Aren't those television studios pretty closely shut in while a show is going on?''

She thought for a moment and calmed down a little. ''Of course. I never thought of that. They close the doors and don't let anybody in or out while the show is on the air.''

''Besides,'' I said, ''the Teen Show is a play, isn't it? You can tell the police all about it.''

''I could tell them if I'd watched the show on television,'' she said sulkily.

''If they hadn't managed to find somebody who could swear to it that nobody left or returned to the studio, they'd have questioned you about it,'' Bill said. He looked at me. ''I want to talk to you, Pat. Let's have lunch...''

The telephone rang again.

Sugar went into the next room to answer it, and this time

we could hear her. In fact, we couldn't have helped listening for she cried with a kind of terror in her voice, "What do you mean? Who is this?" Her voice was high and sharp. She rattled the instrument. "Who is this? Hello—hello." We heard her put down the receiver, and Bill got up and went to the door, and I followed him.

Sugar was sitting at the telephone, and she was so white I thought she had fainted. But when I ran to her, she opened her eyes. "Somebody said I killed John! Oh, Pat!" She gave a high-pitched kind of scream. "It was me he tried to kill last night! Not you, Pat! He thought it was me at the window!"

"What is all this? What is she talking about?" Bill caught me by the arm, his eyes blazing. "Did anybody touch you?"

I told him. Bill didn't say a word; he went into the next room and I knew he was looking at the window.

Sugar sprang up and followed him. "It could have been you last night, Bill! It could have been Jimmy! Pat tried to phone to both of you, and neither of you was at home. It was after two o'clock and . . ."

Bill said, "You're not making sense. Why should I try to kill you? Why would Jimmy try to kill you?"

"I don't know. But somebody was here. I didn't believe Pat. I thought she'd had a dream or . . ." She looked at me with wide eyes. "Well, I really thought that perhaps she— she intended to do it herself and got scared at the last moment and screamed."

Bill's black eyebrows lowered. "Let's get this straight. Do you mean that you thought Pat intended to jump out that window? Do you think she shot John? Is that what you're trying to say?"

"N-no."

"Who was it on the telephone?"

But Sugar only shook her head and stared at us.

Bill said, "Was it a man or a woman?"

Sugar said slowly, "It was a man's voice. I don't know who."

"Did he threaten you?"

Sugar blinked. "Not exactly. He said, 'You shot John Ransome.' And—and that was all."

"Then why do you think he tried to shove you out the window?"

Again she shook her head. "I don't know."

In the end it was all he could get out of her. But she still looked pasty gray when we left and didn't object to our leaving. In fact, we had barely got out the door when we heard her bolt it behind us.

"I suppose I ought to have told her to tell the police," Bill said, ringing for the elevator. "Probably, though, it was some crackpot. And probably he asked for money to keep his mouth shut and she didn't want to tell us."

The elevator came.

We made a mistake, both of us, but we weren't thinking very clearly then. Bill held my hand hard and tight in his own all the way down the long drop of twenty-one floors.

The morning fog had drifted out over the lake by that time, and we walked along the Drive, with the foghorn making a dismal sort of accompaniment. We went to a restaurant and Bill ordered a very expensive lunch, and we talked.

He didn't tell me much about the long hours of questioning at police headquarters the day before. He said only that they hadn't arrested him so far because Jimmy, too, had a motive for killing John. "And I've got a notion, Pat, that Brannigan knows something that they aren't telling."

He didn't know what. He knew about John's will; he knew about Mrs. Sales, although he didn't know about her visit to the kennels. He didn't know anything of Mike and my station wagon. When he heard that, he got up and said he was going to telephone.

I sat and looked around the room. It was a gay, warm little room, very smart; it seemed to me that every woman in the room wore a mink coat. And then I saw Jimmy and Mrs. Sales.

They were sitting in one of the semicircular alcoves, and I could see Jimmy's black head, turned away from me, and

Mrs. Sales sitting opposite him, her dark eyes looking feverish in her pale face.

Mrs. Sales saw me. She nodded, and said something to Jimmy. He turned, waved, and they came to my table.

Both of them were different. I couldn't say exactly how, except that if before I had felt grief like a kind of aura around Edith Sales, it was gone now; there was something excited about her, a kind of triumph and sparkle in those vehement dark eyes. And Jimmy called me darling, and smiled and patted my hand. He was full of charm and conversation, and somehow I felt that it was all forced.

Bill came back before we'd said more than a few words. He greeted them, and Mrs. Sales turned to me. "I have to apologize to you, Miss Bennet. I knew Harpo, of course. But I'd read about John. I was upset. I didn't want to talk to you about it. You do understand, don't you?"

I didn't exactly.

She continued smoothly, "A policeman came to question me about John yesterday afternoon—because of the picture, I suppose. I'm afraid I wasn't of much help. At the time John was shot I was playing canasta with a friend. My husband is out of town," she added in a perfunctory way.

I wondered briefly about the absent Mr. Sales and what he was like, and Jimmy said to Bill, "It's my turn now. They've been questioning me all morning."

Bill said nothing. Jimmy passed one hand nervously over his dark hair, smiled at me, and said, "Couldn't you possibly induce yourself to remember somebody that looked like a burglar?"

"They wouldn't believe it now, even if she could," Bill said shortly.

Mrs. Sales got up. "I have an appointment," she said. "Thank you for the lunch, Jimmy." She said goodbye politely but quickly to me and Bill.

Bill rose. "We've got a date, too," he said. "See you later, Jimmy."

Jimmy got his check and left before we did, but he was still at the checkstand getting his coat and hat when Bill and

I emerged. Bill said, "I didn't know that you and Edith Sales were so chummy."

Jimmy reached for his coat and shrugged. "She asked me to take her to lunch. Said she wanted to hear everything."

Bill stopped him as he turned away. "Wait, Jimmy. Have you heard what happened last night?"

Jimmy's smile became fixed, his eyes bright and narrow. "What do you mean?"

"Somebody tried to murder Pat," Bill said, and told him.

The fixed smile gradually left Jimmy's face, but his eyes did not change. "Who do you think it was?"

"Who do *you* think it was?" Bill asked. Jimmy lifted his eyebrows.

"How should I know? Sugar could have done it. Opened the window, hammered on the floor with something, and wakened Pat. She'd have known Pat would go to close the window."

"But why would Sugar try to . . . ?"

Jimmy's eyes flickered. "I only said she was there; she could have."

"It had something to do with John's murder," Bill said.

"Well, then what?" Jimmy's eyes were half-mocking and very bright. "What do you know, Pat? Do you know who shot John?"

Bill said, "She's told everything she knows about it."

"Have you, Pat?" Jimmy insisted. "Why didn't you call Lieutenant Wilkins last night? Instead of the police in the prowl car? Did you think then that this—attack on you might have a connection with John's murder?" His smile was indulgent, as if he didn't want to believe it.

I hadn't called Lieutenant Wilkins. I hadn't so much as thought of it, for the only thing in my mind then was safety and police to search the apartment. I said so. "But I phoned Bill," I added, "and you. Nobody was there."

Jimmy said, "Where were you, Bill?"

"I couldn't sleep. They'd questioned me till midnight. I got up and went for a walk. . . ."

"Sure you didn't go to Sugar's apartment?" Jimmy said, smiling.

"I wish I had," Bill said. "Where were you, Jimmy?"

The smile vanished. Jimmy said, "Oh, I was at home. Had my telephone turned off. . . . Well, I've got to get along. See you." He gave a debonair wave toward me and went quickly through the lobby and down the steps to the street. He had disappeared by the time Bill and I reached the street.

Bill hailed a taxi. "We do have a date," he said. "With Brannigan." He gave the driver an address.

"Brannigan! Why? And, oh, Bill, did you talk to Mike? What did he say?"

He answered my second question first. "Mike's a mule, but I think I got at least some of the truth out of him. He did come to town, Pat. He started just after you did, and he parked the station wagon a couple of blocks from John's house."

"Why?"

"Because he was going to talk to John. He said that he had a little money saved up, and he was going to offer it to John."

"Mike!"

"He says he had to drive slowly, because the station wagon isn't up to much speed. By the time he got to town, police cars were there at the house, and everything was lighted up and people standing around in the street outside. Somebody told him what had happened. He didn't want to get into the affair. He says he went over to Clark Street and sat around in a little restaurant for a while; then he walked around in the vicinity of John's house, to try to see what was going on, but didn't come close to it. Says he finally went to another restaurant and waited there for a long time; he didn't know what to do. Finally he drove home. Sounds like Mike. I think he's telling the truth. On the other hand . . ."

On the other hand, it might not be the truth. On the other hand, he hadn't told his story to the police. But I fell back on the premise I couldn't seem to escape: "Mike wouldn't have left my gun there. He wouldn't have given them reason to suspect me."

"Well, I don't think so, either. But there it is."

We crossed Clark Street and went on west. As in most cities, the entire character of a neighborhood may change within the space of two or three blocks. We had left the dignified atmosphere of the Gold Coast and were in a region of small stores that lined the streets, and narrow, huddled houses and flats.

"Brannigan's going to meet us here," Bill said, and stopped the taxi at a small German restaurant. We went past a shining counter to a table in the back. There was a red-and-white checked tablecloth and, on the wall above, an enormous elk's head peering glassily down at us. Bill ordered coffee. "Look here, Pat. Didn't it ever occur to you that you were—well, framed?"

"Framed?"

"It's got to be that way," he continued. "It was clear from the beginning. Your gun. You were in the house, too. But nobody knew that you'd be at John's, and even if somebody knew that, he wouldn't know when. . . . And now that thing last night." He looked at me. "That's not going to happen again, Pat. If you're in danger . . ." He stopped, his mouth very tight and hard.

"Why?" I said. "There's nobody who would try to murder me."

But there had been somebody.

A waitress put down coffee.

Bill said, "Who knew that you were going to John's house?"

"Nobody. Everett and Rosie knew I'd left the duffel bags there. I suppose John may have known it."

"How about Mike?"

"He'd have known that I didn't bring the bags home with me on the train, after I clipped Harpo. He met me at the station that night. . . . Bill, *could* Jimmy have shot him?"

"I don't think so. I don't want to think so, of course, but there are reasons to back it up. If it was money Jimmy wanted, he could have married Sugar. Marriage would certainly be safer than murder. And if he'd had some sort of emergency, John would have given him money. He always did."

"Maybe he wouldn't this time." I had thought of everything during the night. "Maybe sometime Sugar gave him a key to her apartment. He could have come in and—"

Bill gripped my hand so hard it ached, and for a long time neither of us said anything, but I began to feel better. Finally he said, "Drink your coffee, Pat. It's past now and it won't happen again."

A sudden thought struck me. "Bill! Do you think Jimmy could have been jealous of John?"

He looked surprised. "About Sugar, you mean?"

"He used to see Sugar often. Even after their engagement was broken off. Suppose—suppose he wanted her back again and she preferred John?"

"I don't think," Bill said slowly, "that jealousy is the motive."

But it carried me on to another hypothesis. I cried, "What about her husband? Edith's? Mr. Sales!"

He did consider it, while my mind raced through all sorts of possibilities. "The missing Mr. Sales," he said at last, but he shook his head. Then he looked up and said, "Here's Brannigan."

Brannigan, rosy-faced and brisk, was also a little nervous. But he sat down at Bill's invitation and asked for beer and was perfectly willing to answer Bill's questions.

"I'll tell you the truth, Dr. Ransome. I've seen Miss Bennet, times when she didn't know I'd seen her, and I don't think she'd kill him, that's all. Everything's against her. There wasn't anybody else, but . . ." He took a thirsty drink from the foaming glass before him.

Bill said, "How did you get Wilkins to let Miss Bennet go that night? What did you tell him?"

Brannigan wiped foam from his mouth. "That's what I decided to tell you. You see, somebody phoned me that night, just before I left home, and told me to be sure to stop in at Ransome's house about nine o'clock. So I did, and there she was, and Ransome was shot. It looked to me like a frame. That's all. But I told the lieutenant about the call that night.''

So that was why they let us go. Bill said, ''I knew it! It couldn't have been coincidence—your arrival at just that time, I mean. Brannigan, who phoned you?''

But Brannigan didn't know. ''I've thought and thought, Dr. Ransome. I think it was a woman's voice.''

*''Who?''*

Brannigan shook his head. ''I don't know. I'm not even sure it was a woman's voice; it was sort of high and queer. It could have been a man pretending to be a woman. You know, talking like this...'' He broke into a high and squeaky falsetto, and then shook his head gloomily again. ''The only point about it is that it wouldn't have been Miss Bennet; it could have been somebody that knew Ransome was going to be shot, and knew Miss Bennet might be there at about that time and tried to frame her. So that's what I told Wilkins, and that's why he let her go.''

He added, ''But it doesn't change things much. Because Miss Bennet *was* there and he was killed, and so far they haven't got anybody else. Unless...'' He looked at Bill rather reluctantly and said, ''Of course, you and the other nephew had motives. You can't get around that.''

He was right; we couldn't get around that.

Brannigan said suddenly, ''I thought for a minute it was that secretary—I mean the woman that used to be Mr. Ransome's secretary. She used to phone to me once in a while, to tell me to stop in for my check or to do something for Mr. Ransome or something like that. Anyway, whoever it was that called, it sure looks bad for Miss Bennet.''

Bill said to me suddenly, ''Did Sugar know that you were going to stop at John's to get the duffel bags before you went to her place?''

In other words, had Sugar framed me?

''No. She talked to me over the phone late in the afternoon. She was in a hurry and so was I. Lady's new litter was about to arrive. I'm sure I didn't tell her the tools were at John's.''

Bill got up. "I'll talk to Everett." He went up to a phone booth beside the cashier's cage.

Somebody had turned on very bright lights outside above the entrance, and their rosy glow lighted the room. It was by then late in the afternoon; we had lunched late and we had waited for Brannigan. Brannigan emptied his glass and Bill came back.

"Everett says John knew the bags were there. He didn't like it. Said his home wasn't a checkstand. But Everett didn't mention it to anyone else. Neither did Rosie. . . . Brannigan, more beer?"

Brannigan nodded and Bill ordered the beer, and said, "Brannigan, you've been close to the police about this. I've asked Wilkins, but he didn't give me much of an answer and . . . Do you know the medical examiner's report? I mean, when do they think that my uncle was shot?"

Brannigan looked surprised. "Why, about the time I found him."

"Yes, but . . . Well, this is what struck me. It isn't ever easy to establish the exact time of death. And in this case the house was very hot; there wouldn't have been the normal . . ."

Brannigan interrupted. "Miss Bennett says she heard him talking when she came in."

"She heard voices. She assumed it was John and somebody else."

I cried excitedly, "It could have been a radio! The voices were indistinct, and I thought the door was closed. A radio, turned low . . ."

Brannigan was shaking his head gloomily. "There wasn't a sound anywhere when I got there. No radio, nothing."

"There's an automatic switch on his radio," Bill said. "It was set to turn off at nine."

But Brannigan said that didn't mean anything. "I know about that, Dr. Ransome. But even if Miss Bennet heard a radio instead of somebody talking, it doesn't change anything. She was there and he was shot and . . ." He hesitated, but went on doggedly, "There was blood on her coat. *I* think it was that dog, but . . ."

Bill said, "Whoever murdered him wouldn't have known that Miss Bennet would be there at exactly that time. But suppose it was just a lucky break that worked?"

Brannigan eyed him over the glass. "Did you talk to Wilkins about it? What does he think?"

"Well," Bill said, "he says it's not important. I think it was a chance that worked. But it wouldn't have made any real difference, because you'd have come at nine, found John, and whether Miss Bennet was still there or had gone, it would be easy to prove she had been there. This is what I think, Brannigan: Somebody knew that the duffel bags were at John's house; somebody knew that Miss Bennet was going to need them that night and might be at John's house around nine o'clock. Somebody was let into the house by John himself, shot John—then turned up the thermostat so high that the heat in the house would prevent the body from cooling at a normal rate and thus confuse the exact time of death. This person set the radio switch, just for an extra touch that happened to work, left the door unlocked, and went away. Somebody planned so carefully that he had already telephoned to you and told you to stop at the house about nine, when either Miss Bennet was there or it could easily be proved that she had been there."

"Well," Brannigan said cautiously, "maybe." He got up. "There's still the question of motive, Dr. Ransome. I'm sorry, Miss Bennet."

He didn't want to believe that I had killed John Ransome, and he had followed the dictates of his honest heart, but he gave me a troubled look as we thanked him, and then he went away.

Of course, the only difference the radio with its automatic switch could have made was the difference in the possible time of John's murder. It couldn't alter the fact that I was there, with blood on my sleeve, and that the gun was mine. And Bill and I had motives.

"But it's a step in the right direction," Bill said. "I'm going to talk to Sugar and Mrs. Sales."

I waited while Bill telephoned. He tried Sugar first, but no one answered. Then he searched the telephone directory for Edith Sales, and as he didn't know the initials of the absent Mr. Sales, in the end he telephoned to John's office. Whiting, the new secretary, gave him Mrs. Sales's telephone number and address—rather haughtily, I gathered. Bill emerged from the telephone booth with a wry face. "Now for Mrs. Sales," he said.

"Do you think she telephoned Brannigan?"

"We'll ask her," Bill said.

We walked back to Sugar's apartment. It was by then almost dark; lights were on all along the streets. When we reached the apartment house, Bill called Sugar's apartment from the lobby, but still no one answered, so evidently the maids were out, too.

Bill had parked my little car behind the apartment house. "We'll go to Mrs. Sales's house," Bill said, and turned the car west.

It was by then the rush hour; we groped our way along, stopping for the jammed-up traffic at the corners, threading our way past trucks and taxis. Allowing for the slow traffic and the early darkness, it took us perhaps thirty minutes to reach the side street where Edith Sales lived. It was a quiet street, a street of two-flat houses, all much alike, close to the sidewalk, yellow or red brick, and very trim and neat.

It was so quiet, indeed, and so deserted in spite of scattered lights in the windows, that there was something rather unpleasant about it. The entrances were all alike, too, with glassed doors at street level and tiled vestibules beyond, but we finally found the number and went in.

The vestibule was lighted, but there were no lights in either rank of windows, and not a sound anywhere. There were too mailboxes with speaking tubes above them, and Mrs. Sales's apartment was on the first floor. Bill rang, but no one answered. Then we both saw that the varnished oak door was a little ajar. It was not open, but it had not been latched, either; it was as if someone leaving the flat had pulled the door hurriedly and not quite closed it.

It was odd. I thought of the door to John Ransome's house, unlocked so I could enter it.

Bill said in a queer voice, "Stay here," and pushed the door open.

The hall beyond it was almost dark; I could barely see a sort of settee with cushions on it. Bill went on into the flat.

I waited for a while in the hall, and when Bill turned on lights somewhere ahead, I followed him. I didn't close the door; I didn't think of it. By the time I got into the living room, a rather pleasant room, although furnished in a severe modern manner, Bill had gone on into a dining room and turned on lights there. A photograph of a man, the missing Mr. Sales, I thought, stood on a table near me; it showed a weak face, which just escaped being pretty, with a rabbity and rather cruel mouth. Then I saw Bill take a quick step or two across the dining room. I saw him stop and stand rigid.

I couldn't see what lay on the other side of the table. But Bill knelt, and all at once I was looking over his shoulder and had both hands over my mouth to keep from screaming. Mrs. Sales lay there, very quietly; her head was turned in a strange and terrible way, and her face was a bluish gray.

Bill put his hand on her wrist and then on her heart. He said, "She's been strangled. Only a few minutes ago. You've got to get out."

Bill was leaning over, examining her throat. He glanced around the room, under the table. "It was something soft, a scarf or . . ." There was nothing on the floor, nothing anywhere except that limp, terrible thing at our feet. Bill's eyes met mine. "Get out! And take your car. I'll report this. You've got to . . ."

Someone entered the vestibule. Bill caught my wrist.

There was a door across the room, and he drew me that way. We were in a bedroom; I couldn't see much, it was too dark, but there was a sort of fragrance like that of perfume and cosmetics. Bill had closed the door except for a thin crack of light and stood there listening. Someone entered the flat.

We could hear slow footsteps, as if whoever entered did so cautiously, pausing to look around, puzzled perhaps by the empty flat and the open door. The footsteps stopped, apparently in the living room, and then, incredibly, there was the sputter of a match and a drifting odor of tobacco smoke.

I had my hand on Bill's arm, holding tight. I could see the vaguest outline of furniture in the room, the shape of a bed, the pale rectangle of a window. Oddly, at that moment, the strong scent of perfume stirred something in my memory. Something small, subtly out of place . . .

"Stay here," Bill whispered, and opened the door. Light streamed into the bedroom. Then the door closed very quietly and Bill walked across the dining room and said clearly, "Jimmy . . ."

That was all I heard, for someone was in the room with me.

I knew it, and for a horrible second I couldn't move. Then I screamed, "Bill!" and flung open the door, and light streamed across the room full upon Sugar. Her blond head was bare; a coat was flung around her shoulders. Bill from the doorway cried, "Sugar! What are you doing here?" He turned on lights. Jimmy stood beside him.

Sugar's eyes were wide and dark in her white face. She cried shrilly, "She wanted to see me! Edith Sales! I came and—and she was like that! Then I heard someone come into the apartment and I was terrified. I didn't know it was you!"

"How did you get into the apartment?"

"I—I just came in. The door was open. Somebody left it open."

I didn't see the heap of crimson on the floor, where Sugar had dropped it, until Bill stooped and picked it up. It was a man's silk scarf. Sugar cried, "That was on the floor beside her!" Bill held it in the light and looked at Jimmy. "Yours."

"No, it can't be!" Jimmy snatched the scarf from Bill's hands, and Bill said, "It's got your initials on it. J.R."

"But I didn't—I lost this—I don't know where. I can't remember." Suddenly Jimmy dropped the deadly silk scarf and sat down on the bench and put his face in his hands.

"Jimmy," Bill said. He caught his shoulder. "Jimmy, tell me. What is it? What do you know?"

Jimmy wouldn't speak; he held his hands stubbornly over his face.

Bill said, "I've got to call the police."

Suddenly he spoke to Jimmy gently as if they were boys, friends and cousins again: "Why did you come here to see Mrs. Sales? Tell me, Jimmy, before the police come."

Jimmy wouldn't answer; his handsome face was lowered. The silk scarf, crimson as blood, lay at his feet.

Bill said, "Were you at Sugar's apartment last night?"

"No," Jimmy mumbled. "I was here. Mrs. Sales wanted to see me."

"Why? Did she tell you who killed John?"

Jimmy's dark head sunk lower, and gave a nod. And suddenly he broke. "It's all my fault!" he cried, and put his hands over his face again.

"What was your fault?" Bill urged.

"All that money," Jimmy mumbled, "I couldn't pay it."

"What money?"

"Close to a hundred thousand! She made me take it. She said to invest it, and I couldn't pay it back unless John died."

"Who . . . ?"

"Sugar," Jimmy said simply. "When we were engaged. She told me to invest it. But then she ran through her money. There wasn't as much in the beginning as everybody thought, but Sugar thought it was inexhaustible. She spent and spent, and then when she got to the bottom of the barrel she wanted me to pay her, and I couldn't. So she made a play for John. But John balked. He wasn't going to marry her and told her so."

The room was suddenly very still. Sugar's teeth were sunk into her lip.

Bill said, "How do you know that?"

Jimmy lifted his face. "Because John told Mrs. Sales, and she told me."

"That's not true," Sugar flashed, gripping the curtains beside her so that her hands were like fists.

"Oh, yes," Jimmy said. "That's why he left you that money. It was his idea of making it square with you. Like the picture he left Mrs. Sales. John was like that."

Sugar's wide eyes were blazing. "Yes, I had to have my money back. Jimmy hadn't invested it. He'd used it, all of it, himself. He said he'd pay me when John died. He told me that! He promised me! But I never thought he'd murder . . ."

"I didn't murder John!" Jimmy cried desperately. "I didn't murder him. Believe me, Bill."

Bill walked across the room and into the dining room. There was the click of a telephone dial. We all listened while Bill talked to the police. We heard him say, "Right. I'll keep them here." He came back. He looked white and queer.

It was very quiet; I think all of us were aware suddenly of the terribly quiet thing in the next room. The lights glimmered on the bottles and jars on the dressing table, and the scents touched my memory again with light perfumed fingers. And this time I knew why. I waited a second, to test the truth of my discovery, and Bill said, "Jimmy, did Mrs. Sales telephone to Sugar and threaten her?"

"Yes! Mrs. Sales hated her; she was jealous. I didn't know what to do."

"Did she know that you owed Sugar that money?"

A slow flush rose in Jimmy's face. "Yes. I'd told her one time when I thought maybe Mrs. Sales would get John to advance me some money. She wouldn't. She said it was no use asking John."

"Did Edith Sales tell John?"

"No. I'm sure she didn't. John would have blown up."

"But if John died, you could pay Sugar."

Sugar cried, "That's why Jimmy killed him! That's why he strangled Mrs. Sales! She'd have told. She guessed and—"

Bill said to me, "Pat, when Sugar phoned to ask you to clip Maurice, did you tell her when you would come to town?"

"No. No, I didn't know when I could leave. Lady's puppies . . ."

"Did you tell her about Lady's puppies?"

And I had. I'd said I was in a hurry because of Lady's new puppies. I knew that I had said that, and Sugar knew it; I could see it in the way her eyes flickered.

Bill knew it, too. "So she knew you wouldn't start to town right away."

Sugar cried in a high, shrill voice, "Jimmy killed him! He took Pat's gun and—"

"It's no use, Sugar," Bill said. "Wilkins knows. When you tried to make him think that Pat attempted suicide, he began to concentrate on you. You hadn't bought any plane tickets, so you hadn't intended to leave. You were in debt everywhere. You made a play for John, and he balked at marriage. You'd sold your jewelry. You had to have money now. Jimmy could wait. You couldn't. And there was only one way for you to get your money back from Jimmy. All Wilkins needs is the motive, and now. . ."

Sugar was panting. "I don't believe you!"

"He's found the shells for the gun."

"He couldn't! I threw them—" She flung both hands over her mouth.

"You threw the box out of your car on the way home from Pat's, after you had removed enough shells to load the gun. It was found this afternoon and turned in to a highway patrolman. They're working on the remaining shells now— for fingerprints."

For a second she stared at him. Then, like magic, everything about her changed. Her face was suddenly soft and lovely, her wide eyes appealing. She went to Jimmy and put her hands on his arm, coaxingly. "You'll help me, won't you, Jimmy?" She glanced at us. "You are all my friends. You wouldn't turn me over to the police. You couldn't do that to me. We'll forget all this. It was wrong, but I—"

Bill said, "You tried to murder Pat."

"But—but I *had* to!" Sugar cried, her eyes wide and childish. "I took the gun two weeks ago when John—when I began to realize . . . It was easy. Pat was in the kennels. She didn't even see me. . . . I had to keep Mrs. Sales from talking, too. She let me in, and she said she'd call the police and started for the telephone and I—I did it. You'd never have known it if I'd got the door closed. I thought I had. I was trying to get the scarf out of my pocket, and I just gave the door a shove and I—I didn't even think about it. . . . I *had* to! But it wasn't my fault! She told me I'd killed John and she knew why and—what else could I do? I didn't want to; I couldn't even think how until I found Jimmy's scarf in my car. He'd left it there sometime and I—I didn't mean to make anybody suspect you, Jimmy. It was the only thing I could use.''

Jimmy said, ''Why did you try to murder Pat?''

''I told you! I *had* to! Pat was getting too close to the truth. Talking about the radio and Harpo's behavior and how hot the house was. I was standing by the window, and all at once I saw how it would clear up everything if Pat . . . They'd say she was a suicide and she had murdered John and—''

She caught her breath; her wide eyes went to Bill and to Jimmy, and at what she saw there. She gave a queer scream and flung herself across the room and out the door.

I heard her high heels click on the floor. I knew Bill and Jimmy had gone after her. I knew, too, that there was a siren somewhere and men's shouts out in the street.

I sat down on the little bench. The scents of perfumes were nearer and reminded me again of Sugar's bedroom, the night John was murdered: the orderly bedroom, where there were no suitcases, signs of packing for the trip she'd said she was starting early the next morning. I was thankful that I hadn't had to tell them that; they already knew she had no plane tickets.

I thought of the bracelet; copied, she'd said. Her terror when Mrs. Sales telephoned her, and how after she'd had time to think she said it was a man's voice. The way Jimmy had showed her attentions, as if he were obligated to her—as indeed he was. Her suggestion to Wilkins: Pat was depressed. She must have known—perhaps John had told her—that my duffel bags were there. So she had ensured my visit to the house by getting me to promise to trim Maurice that night. It seemed strange that even Lady and her litter had been a small part of Sugar's careful plan; she'd known I wouldn't leave Lady and drive to town at once.

I remembered all of it, and I wondered if she had made a last appeal to John that night—and if John had sat arrogantly, contemptuously in his armchair, and told her there was no chance of marriage. She had killed him, and then she had gone blithely off to the Teen Show. . . .

I sat there for a long time while they did what they had to do in the house and outside. There was a small yard out back, and they found the dachshund and took him away with them. Finally, Bill took me home.

When we arrived, Mike already knew about it; Bill had telephoned him. He had a fire blazing and coffee and sandwiches waiting for us. He didn't say a word about Sugar; he gave me one look and put another log on the fire, and said over his shoulder that Exchequer and Harpo had got into a fight but he'd separated them. Exchequer came and put his head on my knee. And all at once there were tears on my face.

Bill came and put his arm around me. "Don't. There are people who would do anything—anything in the world for money. She's one of them." He stopped and held me tight. "It's in the past. Now we'll think ahead."

We didn't, of course. We just sat there with the fire dancing and flickering, and Bill's arms around me, and old Exchequer lying down with a contented thump before the fire.

□

# Murder in Waltz Time

It was a gusty night, with scudding clouds and a wind that hurled white-capped waves out of the blackness of the sea upon the beach. The orchestra played louder and faster, as it always did on such nights, as if to shut out the wind and the sea, and to distract the guests when Mr. Brenn, the owner-manager of the hotel, felt that the weather was letting him down.

At eleven promptly the lights above the dinner tables were turned out, spotlights shot onto the dance floor, and Fran and Steve emerged into the spotlights as the orchestra began a slow number. It was the first of what the hotel called, in its brochure, "Exhibition Dancing, in the club-house after dinner by representatives of the Garden School of Dancing. (Private lessons on request. Learn to Rumba.)"

Steve and Fran whirled and dipped and paused for a long beat, and then whirled again. Faces emerged dimly from the rim of shadow that marked the tables.

Miss Flora Halsey, looking like an elderly and rather troubled doll, her small face framed in white curls, smiled at them wistfully. Her nephew Henry Halsey opposite her, his face doll-like, too, but a sullen doll, stared at nothing. Fran and Steve turned and whirled again. This time Senator

322

Bude and his sister emerged from the surrounding shadow. The Senator smiled charmingly above his white dinner jacket; his elder sister knitted, her haughty face disapproving.

They vanished as Fran and Steve took a long, glorious swoop completely around the lighted oval of the dance floor. Fran wondered briefly, where was Nanette, the hotel siren, who had captivated first Henry and then the Senator? With a long, slow dip that brought them now into the very middle of the floor, the dance finished.

There was applause. They bowed. The orchestra swung into a fast rhythm. The next time they passed the Halsey table, Miss Halsey sat alone and didn't smile at them, didn't apparently see them; Henry probably had gone to the bar.

The one-step was followed by a rumba, with so many interpolated steps that Fran concentrated only upon following Steve. The rumba was followed by a romping, galloping samba. Sometime during the dances Miss Halsey went away. No one saw her leave.

After the seven-minute intermission, at eleven-thirty, during which Fran sat in the dressing room with her feet up on a chair, and Steve went outside for some fresh air and a cigarette, the arrangement of the tables had changed a little. The Senator sat alone, and must have gone during their next dance, for when applause arose at the end of it and they bowed, the Bude table was vacant.

At midnight precisely, the orchestra swung into their final number, a gay, fast waltz. As they danced, Fran's black chiffon skirt making flashing circles around her slippered feet, she felt the usual captivated and nostalgic approval of their audience from the darkness beyond the spotlighted circle within which she and Steve moved. There was always, Fran thought, something special about a waltz. The orchestra came to its throbbing, haunting climax, and Fran bent backward over Steve's supporting arm until her hair all but touched the floor.

It was supposed to suggest, thrillingly, a long and passionate embrace. So she was pleased to hear, in the abrupt silence, a kind of sigh from that rim of darkness. Somebody somewhere said quite audibly, "Oh, look; he's kissing her!"

Steve's brown face pressed against her own. In fact, however, he said unromantically, "Hold it, Fran. I've got my foot on your skirt."

She held her pose, panting and trying not to, until she felt Steve's almost imperceptible shift of balance. Then, hand in hand, they bowed, retreating toward the dressing room and trying not to gasp for breath.

The applause died away. Chairs slid back from tables; people were moving about, talking, drifting toward the elegance of the clubhouse. Steve released her hand. "I hope I didn't tear your skirt."

Mr. Garden's School of Dancing paid her a salary, her train fare south, and a percentage of the money paid by guests of the hotel for dancing lessons, but nothing for clothes, and Steve knew it.

"No, it's all right," she said.

"It was clumsy of me. Are you going over to the hotel?"

"Yes." She took her coat and wondered fleetingly if he intended to ask her to take a stroll along the sea, or drive into town for a supper of scrambled eggs in a patio restaurant. Sometimes he did.

But not this time. "Will you . . . ?" He dug into his pocket and fished out a small gold evening bag. "Will you take this to Miss Halsey? She's not at her table, so she must have gone to her room. She told me to put it in my pocket while I was dancing with her, and I forgot it."

Disappointment tweaked at Fran. Facing herself in the mirror above the dressing table, it seemed to her that her face was too thin and pointed, her eyes too large and bright, her beige coat far too shabby above the glamorous chiffons. Perhaps Steve had a date with Nanette. Not that it was anything to Fran. She and Steve were merely a dance team, Frances Allen and Steve Greene, dancing and endlessly rehearsing, giving lessons because each of them needed the money."

"All right, I'll take it. Good night, Steve."

"Thanks. Good night."

She went out the side door and took the shortcut, along a path through a great hedge of Australian pines, and then to the hotel itself. The wind tugged at her coat. The hedge as she neared it seemed to have taken on angry life. Then she came out onto a wide square of lawn and swimming pool, surrounded on three sides by the looming white outlines of the hotel. There were lights springing up in the hotel, as guests, taking the main path around toward the front entrance of the hotel, returned to their rooms. There were lights in the broad archway that ran like a tunnel through the midsection of the building to the entrance.

A man, sitting in a chair at the edge of the swimming pool, rose, tossed away a cigarette, and walked rapidly toward the black emptiness that just then made the fourth side of the grassy square and was, in fact, another hedge, the pier, the beach, and, stretching outward into an infinity of night, the sea.

He was a small man, wearing a raincoat that flapped in the wind and a cap pulled down rather low. Perhaps the haste in his departure caught Fran's attention; perhaps there was a definite unfamiliarity about him, for she thought briefly that he was some stranger, someone strolling on the beach, idly curious and taking advantage of the emptiness of the hotel grounds to rest, smoke, survey the hotel—and since he was not a hotel guest, making a quick departure when he found himself observed.

There were lights in Miss Halsey's corner suite on the second floor of the north wing. By the time Fran skirted the swimming pool, the man in the raincoat had disappeared completely in the dense, opaque darkness toward the sea.

One of the luxuries of a superluxurious hotel, as the Montego House undoubtedly was, lay in its architectural plan. It was not only gracious and attractive, with its two long wings, its green-shuttered windows, its lawns and shrubbery; it was also exceedingly comfortable. Each suite had its own small veranda and its own entrance, and on the second floor had its own stairway. There was a light above the entrance to the stairway leading to the Halsey suite.

Fran called, "Miss Halsey. . ." and went up the narrow flight of steps. At the top, light streamed out from the open door. She could see into the room, with its light-wood furniture and bright cushions, but neither Miss Halsey nor her nephew Henry Halsey was there. She knocked and waited, and knocked again. "Miss Halsey, I've brought your evening bag."

There was still no answer—only the crash of the sea beyond the open doors to the veranda and the clatter of palm trees against the screens. She'd leave the bag and go. She went into the room. She put the small gold bag down on a table beside a vase of gladioluses, turned, and saw Miss Halsey lying in a huddle near the door that had shielded her from Fran's view—a strange, twisted little huddle.

Fran ran to her and knelt. But, after a long moment, she could not bring herself to touch the crumpled figure in black lace, with its face down against the rug and a deep red stain spreading outward on the ivory-colored rug.

Waves broke and crashed upon the beach. The palm trees outside the veranda clattered and whispered. Fran got up, awkwardly, stumbling in her black chiffon. A telephone stood on the table. Mr. Brenn, the owner-manager, answered it himself. . . .

Mr. Brenn, always kind, sent her to her room; he told her to wait. From her window on the land side of the hotel, she saw the police cars come hurtling from the highway and park in the lighted area.

Mr. Brenn said it was murder. It wasn't true, it couldn't be true, but that was what he'd said. He'd looked for a gun—that was after he'd called the police. He'd searched the room, lifting bright red and yellow cushions from the sofa and chairs, asking her if she'd seen a gun. But nobody would murder gentle, kindly old Miss Halsey.

She couldn't have killed herself without a gun.

*I must change my dress,* Fran thought; *they'll send for me.* Mr. Brenn had said that, too, hadn't he? Something about a statement for the police.

Fran liked Miss Halsey. So did Steve, in spite of the fact that Miss Halsey took so many—too many—dancing lessons. "She's doing it to help me!" he had said once, wryly. And it was true, for Miss Halsey thought she was indebted to him; he had pulled her out of the sea once when she got beyond her depth and the lifeguard was at the other end of the beach. Steve was trying to save money to resume the law course that the war in Korea had interrupted; the G.I. Bill would help, but a little backlog, a few hundred dollars saved, would help, too. That was why Steve had taken a job that, Fran knew, he didn't like; he could save money for four months and there'd be time to study. Miss Halsey knew it too, so she danced resolutely, until her breath and her little feet gave out, and then she'd sit and watch Fran and Steve rehearse, and chatter endlessly.

Fran thought of telephoning Steve. But the switchboard would be busy. The news of murder—murder! she thought— would have gone like wildfire over the whole place. . . .

It was a long time before Finial, the elderly head porter, came for her. She went ahead of him along the corridor leading from her room, and down an outside stairway. Even there, on the land side, the wind tossed the massed hibiscus and bougainvillea wildly, and as they turned through the lighted archway, the sound of the sea swept ominously upon them.

But Mr. Brenn's office, with its desk and filing cabinets and rattan chairs, looked homely and familiar and shut out the roar of the waves. Mr. Brenn was at the desk, and Henry Halsey sat near him as if in a state of collapse, his small face in his hands. There were two uniformed policemen, one of them writing in a tablet, the other apparently asking questions. And they were arguing, all of them, about an envelope on the desk.

"Of course I know what's in it," Mr. Brenn said. He gave Fran a brief nod and went on: "I witnessed it. Two days ago. She told me to put it in my safe until she could send it to her lawyer. So I did. But I don't think it's legal to open it now unless Halsey agrees."

A third policeman opened the door and shouted above the wind, "Can't find him, Captain Scott! Nowhere on the grounds, nowhere in the hotel."

The man he addressed was tall and lanky, with a lined brown face, a bald head, and an air of authority. He snapped, "Send squad cars in both directions along the shore road. Warn the Miami flying field and the Coast Guard—Palm Beach and Jacksonville."

"Yes, sir." The door banged. The captain spoke to Mr. Brenn: "We'll pick him up, all right."

Mr. Brenn said, "I don't think this will has anything to do with it. Somebody tried to rob the hotel, and Miss Halsey came to her suite and caught him. He came up from the beach, got away the same way. Nothing easier."

The words seemed to set off another argument. Captain Scott looked gloomily at Henry. "You say she didn't know any of the people here in the hotel?"

After a second or two Henry said from behind his hands, "Not until we came here, two months ago."

"Was she very friendly with any of the guests? I mean, did she see much of anybody in particular?"

Henry put down his hands. His doll-like face was pale and rather sulky. "She liked everybody. Anybody in the place could have walked in and shot her."

"Well, is there anything in her life that could explain . . . What I mean is, had she any enemy?"

Henry looked at a glass on the desk near him and said, "No!"

Mr. Brenn said, "Really, Scott, my clientele . . ."

"I know, I know—nice people, substantial citizens. But the woman was killed. . . . Look here. How about Finial? He was alone, on duty at the switchboard . . ."

"Don't be an idiot!" Mr. Brenn interrupted with some heat. "Elder of his church. Working for me ever since I built this hotel, eighteen years ago. Fine man, honest to the penny. Wife superintends the maids. You've lived in town all these years. You know him! *Finial!*"

"Well." Captain Scott rubbed his bald head. "Somebody got into that suite."

Mr. Brenn was still angry. "Somebody came up from the beach, some thief, some vagrant, somebody you fellows ought to have picked up before."

Captain Scott appeared to have a brain wave. "See here! Any new guests?"

"Yes," Mr. Brenn said reluctantly. "One. Arrived today. Name is Abernathy. Librarian at Harnell University. Nothing doing there."

Captain Scott was persistent. "Did she know this Abernathy?" he asked Henry.

Henry shrugged. "Not to my knowledge. And I'd know."

Captain Scott brooded a moment. "What about keys? How would anybody get into her suite?"

Mr. Brenn uttered an explosive word. Then he said more calmly, "I tell you, Scott, we've never had even so much as petty thievery. Sometimes guests lock their rooms, usually not. *My* clientele . . ."

"Oh, I know. I know. It's an exclusive joint."

*Joint* was not exactly the word for dignified Montego House, but nobody smiled. Captain Scott added stubbornly, "But the woman was murdered, just the same. I've got to question everybody in the hotel, Brenn. Your whole guest list." He sighed.

Mr. Brenn sighed, too. "In the morning, Captain. Not now, please. Give me time to arrange it, explain to them." Mr. Brenn was a diplomat; a hotel owner must be. "Give me a little break, Scott."

"All right," Captain Scott said, "I'll question these people in the morning, give you time to pave the way, make them feel all right about it, if you'll play ball with me. Open her will."

Henry Halsey rose, staring angrily at Captain Scott. "I insist on things being done properly and legally. This is no time—"

Captain Scott interrupted, "You say you are her only close relative. You admit that she had many times told you that you would inherit everything she had. Have you recently disagreed with her?"

"Never!" Henry said curtly.

*But that was not quite true*, Fran thought suddenly. Miss Halsey, gentle though she was, had kept an obstinate and disapproving eye on him and Nanette. Yet all that had passed when Nanette was diverted to the Senator, handsome, obviously rich, and at forty or thereabouts an extremely eligible bachelor, far more attractive than Henry Halsey.

Mr. Brenn said, "Remember, Scott, Halsey's got an alibi. He was in the bar the whole time. Jim and Mrs. Lee both told you that."

Jim was the bartender and had worked for Mr. Brenn, as Finial had, since Montego House was built. Mrs. Lee managed the clubhouse and nobody, after five minutes' conversation with her, could have doubted her efficiency, her accuracy, or her word. Captain Scott sighed again, acknowledging her unassailable honesty and Jim's, but turned back to Henry: "So you don't know any reason for a new will?"

"Aunt Flora didn't need reasons." Henry Halsey picked up the glass, drank thirstily, and said, "She was like that. Whims. Probably wanted to change something in it."

Mr. Brenn tapped the envelope. "Miss Halsey asked me to witness it. Jane—that is my secretary—typed it up for her. Jane's a notary public; she witnessed it, too. I thought I ought to tell you of its existence. But, as Halsey says, there are proper and . . ."

"I'll have to take the responsibility for that," Captain Scott said, and took the envelope.

Henry clutched at it, missed, cried, "You can't! It's not right!" and stopped. Captain Scott already had the long double sheet out of the envelope.

He read slowly, seemed to go back to read again, and then put it on the desk. "So that's it," he said to Henry.

Henry snatched the will. His round face seemed to shrivel as he read. He dropped the paper, clawed at his neat black tie, and shouted, "She's left everything—everything she had to Steve Greene! That dancing man! Everything she had!" he screamed. "He killed her!" His bright eyes darted around and fastened on Fran, stared at her wildly, and he pointed a shaking finger at her. "She helped him! They did it together!"

Everybody looked at Fran.

But it was preposterous! The paper in the envelope was Miss Halsey's will, a new one, apparently leaving everything she had to Steve. To Steve! And the man they were trying to find, the man they were searching the beach and highway for and warning the flying field and Coast Guard about—was that Steve, too? It was preposterous.

Fran cried, *"That's not true! Steve didn't kill her!"* And there was a reason why Steve couldn't have shot Miss Halsey. "Steve was dancing with me! We were together, dancing, in the spotlight. Everybody saw us. He couldn't have killed her."

"That's so." Mr. Brenn got to his feet. "That's right. Both these two—I mean Miss Allen, here, and Steve Greene, do exhibition dancing from eleven to twelve-fifteen. Miss Allen found Miss Halsey immediately after that. Nobody knows when Miss Halsey left the dining room in the clubhouse, but it was after the exhibition dancing began. And, from then until a quarter after twelve, Steve and Fran were dancing. Together. Under spotlights. The doctor said Miss Halsey must have been dead at least half an hour when she was found."

"Too bad nobody heard the shot," Captain Scott said morosely.

"How could anybody hear it! The waves and the orchestra—" Mr. Brenn said.

Henry broke in. "Steve Greene had a motive. Everybody in the hotel's been laughing at the way my aunt pursued him. He got her to change her will! You hear such things: elderly women, money, taken in by some handsome young scoundrel."

Fran cried, "That's not true! She was grateful because he pulled her out of the undertow. She did take dancing lessons and she insisted on Steve dancing with her, over and over again. But she wasn't like that," Fran said desperately.

Henry Halsey was beside himself, his little eyes glittering, his dimpled small hands clawing at the desk. "Handsome young hero saves her life! Handsome young dancing master! And as soon as she's made a will in his favor—"

"Just a minute, Halsey," Captain Scott said. "You say

you knew nothing about this new will. I believe that. But did you know she intended to make a new will? Did your aunt ever threaten . . . ?''

"Threaten!" A purplish flush came into Henry's cheeks. "I didn't kill her! I've got an alibi!"

"You didn't know she had made a new will. But did you know she intended to? And exactly why did she cut you out of it?"

Henry wavered. "I can make a guess. I've had—bad luck with jobs. My aunt was always after me to—to get some steady sort of work. She got the idea that she had, she called it, indulged me. In fact, as I've told you, I'm her only close relative; there was no reason why she shouldn't share some of her money. I wasn't to blame for sheer bad luck. But she couldn't see it that way and—"

"You mean," Captain Scott said, "she made this new will in order to force you to—"

"To stand on my own feet. That's what she used to say. But"—a complacent smile touched his delicate mouth—"if she'd lived she'd have changed that new will. She was fond of me. You're trying to fasten this murder on me. You're saying that I killed her because of that new will. But she'd have changed it again, later. So I had every reason, if you're trying to fasten a motive on me, for keeping her alive."

Truth has a certain ring and conviction of its own. It was not a nice confession, but it sounded true. "And, besides," Henry added, "I've got an alibi."

And that was true, too. Captain Scott glowered at Henry, admitting that truth. But he said shortly, "Alibis can be broken."

"Not this one," Henry said with a certainty that was almost airy. "It's my good luck. I wasn't out of the clubhouse and you've already proved it."

There were hurrying, hard footsteps outside the door. The door flung open. "Here he is!" a policeman cried. "We caught him two miles up the beach."

Steve, a policeman hanging to each arm, came into the office. Wet sand clung to his heavy oxfords. He gave one quick look around the room. "What's the matter, Brenn? What have *I* done?"

Henry Halsey screamed, "There he is! There's the murderer!"

"Take it easy now, Steve. Take it easy," Mr. Brenn began.

Fran ran to Steve. "Steve, be careful."

The tall policeman's voice rose above the tumult: "I'm Captain Scott of the police. We want to question you. And I guess . . ." He cleared his throat and seemed to fumble for the right words. Clearly, he wasn't accustomed to murder—speeders, maybe, and drunks, but not murder.

"What are you talking about?" Steve demanded.

"About the murder of Miss Flora Halsey," Captain Scott said.

"Miss Halsey—" Steve said, and stopped as if someone had struck him.

Mr. Brenn said quickly, "She's left a will, Steve. She's left everything she had to you."

Steve said, "She couldn't have—not to *me*."

There was an implication that Captain Scott seized upon instantly: "So you knew she made a new will."

Steve turned slowly to meet Captain Scott's eyes. "She talked, you know. I didn't pay much attention."

Mr. Brenn intervened again: "Did she tell you why she was making a new will, Steve?"

"No—that is, yes, in a way. She said she was worried about . . ." His eyes went to Henry. "About him. She said she didn't know what to do. She said she'd indulged him too much—that sort of thing. She said she had told him she was going to change her will and it might make him go to work and . . . See here," Steve said. "This is *her* business. She talked, but—"

"Oh, she talked," Henry said nastily. "Very confidential, wasn't it? And she also told you that she was going to put you in her will instead of me."

"No! That's impossible! I don't believe it!" The faces around the desk seemed to convince him. He said slowly, "If she did that, she meant it only as a threat to Henry.

She'd have changed it later, back to him. He was her whole interest in life."

"But you saw to it she didn't have a chance to change it!" Henry flashed.

Captain Scott said, "When did she tell you all this, Greene?"

Steve looked angry, undecided, and stubborn. "A few days ago."

Scott said slowly, "A threat like that couldn't serve its purpose unless young Halsey knew about it. You did know about it, didn't you, Halsey? But you didn't know that this time she had carried out her threat and actually made a different will."

Henry pounded on the desk. "Suppose she did tell me! That lets me out! I'd have known she'd change it. But he knew that, too, so he shot her before she could change it."

Captain Scott pounded on the desk, too. "Sergeant, make a record of all this. Now then . . ." He sat down and turned to Fran: "You claim she was dead when you went to her rooms. Brenn had no business letting you leave. What did you do with the gun?"

Again everybody seemed to speak at once.

Steve said clearly, "Whatever has happened, Fran has nothing to do with it. I asked her to take Miss Halsey's evening bag to her. If she was in the Halsey suite, it was sheer coincidence. She didn't kill her."

Mr. Brenn said, "I've forgotten something." He gave Fran and Steve a worried, half-apologetic look. "There was an intermission while they were dancing. Seven minutes."

And Fran had forgotten something, too. A then trivial-seeming incident that might now have horrible significance. She cried, "There was a man. A man in a raincoat, there at the swimming pool. He wasn't a hotel guest. He hurried away . . ."

Captain Scott heard all three of them, nodded to the sergeant, and began to question. . . .

The sun peered over the distant horizon, seemed to take a look at the beach, strewn with litter the angry waves had brought in, at the quiet hotel with its closed shutters, and then leaped up to take a long look at Fran and Steve. Last night Captain Scott hadn't believed either of them.

Toward the last, the same questions had been pounded at them, over and over again.

"Now then, Greene, why did you take a walk along the beach? Funny time to take a walk, wasn't it? A night like that. You say you changed clothes in the locker room of the clubhouse, went straight to the beach. Anybody see you go? Hard walking, wasn't it, wet sand? Funny time to take a walk, after you'd been dancing all evening.

"Come clean. How about this will? She told you she was going to make a new will; she told you why. And she told you it was in favor of you—didn't she? You were afraid she'd change it again, give her money to her nephew, her own flesh and blood, weren't you? But if she died while this will stood, the money would come to you. . . . Where's the gun? What did you do with the gun?" This to Steve. To Fran: "Where is the gun?"

Forcing his mind back to the present, Steve watched the sunrise, unseeing. "That will!" He pounded the chair with his fist. "How could I have dreamed she'd make a will like that!"

"It was because you pulled her out of the sea. You saved her life."

"I didn't save her life! She could have got out herself if she hadn't got scared. You can't sit twenty feet away and hear a woman scream for help and not go to help her out. I didn't save her life."

"She thought you did."

Steve gave a kind of groan. "A will like that! If she'd told me that, I'd have stopped it; I'd have talked sense to her. I don't think there's anything in her whole past life she didn't tell me. But she never said she'd put me in her will instead of Henry!"

Fran put her hand on Steve's broad, brown one. "Don't think of it. She couldn't have known."

"Who did it? She told me that she didn't know anybody here at all when she and Henry came here for the winter.

She said Henry had suggested their coming here. She even seemed to be pleased when the place proved to be so nice, as if it were a feather in Henry's cap. But nobody murders a stranger.''

"Steve, there *was* a man at the swimming pool! When I came through the hedge and he saw me, he jumped up and threw away his cigarette and hurried toward the beach. They wouldn't believe me.''

"Scott thinks you invented it to protect me. And honestly, Fran, if he was a burglar, if he did kill her, would he have sat down and smoked? Wouldn't he have got away as fast as he could?''

"Maybe not," she said stubbornly. How could anyone know what a murderer might do? Fran said suddenly, "Is it very much money, Steve? Was she very rich?''

Steve turned troubled eyes to meet her own. "How should I know? Probably. People don't spend the winter in a hotel like this on peanuts.''

And people didn't live on peanuts, either. Fran sighed. But then she thought of the lavish meals Mr. Brenn supplied, and the steadily growing little horde of money she was saving, and how thankful she was not only for that, but for the chance to spend the whole winter in the South. It was miraculously different from the winter before, in New York, modeling for a huge wholesale supply house. Fighting the wet, sneezing crowds in the subway, trying to pay rent for her one-room apartment. She wasn't a top-notch model. No, this was better; this was sheer luxury. Or had been, until only a few hours ago, when a nightmare, a thing of horror, had changed reality into a distorted strangeness. She said, "They'll find the gun. You never had a gun.''

"How can I prove anything if they don't find the gun? Whoever did it has got rid of it forever." He nodded toward the sea and the far-reaching miles of beach, the ridges above it choked with hummocky, spiky tropical growth where the gun could have been buried. "And I know about guns. At least, I did know before I turned myself into a dancing man.''

He was angry with himself, hating his job, and Fran was

part of his job. That was the trouble. They rehearsed long hours in the great, bare room in the clubhouse that Mr. Brenn had turned over to them. They danced, working out involved steps to the tune of endless records. They planned lesson schedules. They were never free of each other's company. It was all matter-of-fact. No chance for anything like romance.

Steve said, "She left before our intermission. I'm sure of that, because when I went outside the dressing room and put my hand in my pocket for cigarettes I found her evening bag, and during the next dance I looked for her, intending to give it to her. But I didn't see her leave."

Nobody, so far, had been found who had seen Miss Halsey leave the clubhouse. And the intermission had lasted seven minutes. "Plenty of time," Captain Scott had said. Plenty of time to hurry to the Halsey suite—and return. So Steve had not waited in the dressing room with Fran? Why not? Had he gone to the Halsey suite then?

There was time. Seven minutes. Steve had a motive. And Fran herself—his dancing partner—had found Miss Halsey murdered.

Steve said suddenly, "The police mean business. I've got to do something, and I don't know what. Would you recognize the man in the raincoat if you saw him again?"

"I'm not sure. I might."

"There's always the chance that he saw something. Heard the shot, maybe. If we can find him . . ." Steve sat up. "Who's that?"

She turned to follow the direction of his eyes. An odd figure was coming along the beach, a man with a bald, gleaming head and big, gleaming spectacles; a tall, very thin man, clad in a bright-colored sports shirt and shorts.

"I never saw *him* before. Is that the man?" Steve asked.

One glance was enough. "No," Fran said.

The rather startling figure disappeared below the pier. Then he started up the steps from the beach to the pier; they could hear his clumping feet on the boards. He came gradually into view and clumped toward them. "Thought I'd take a walk—fine morning. My name's Abernathy."

The new guest. Fran said automatically, "I'm Fran Allen. This is Mr. Greene."

His spectacles twinkled from her to Steve and back again. "Ah, Miss Allen! You're the girl who found Miss Halsey. Shocking. Terrible shock. See here; I got a kind of garbled account of the tragedy. They say there were no clues. That can't be right. There must have been something. Where there is murder there is evidence of that murder." He nodded at Steve, like an oversized bird, and babbled on. "So you must have seen that evidence. I understand she took dancing lessons from you, young man. Surely she must have talked. Women do."

Steve never permitted himself to be rude, even in the most trying circumstances; he was this time. "She didn't tell me she was going to be murdered."

Mr. Abernathy blinked. "Well, well—certainly, Mr. Greene. But may I ask . . . ? My interest is purely academic—but it struck me that she might have talked to you more or less confidentially." He coughed. "I mean to say, with all those dancing lessons and her will . . ."

Steve made a sudden, angry move.

Mr. Abernathy said quickly, "Everybody's talking about it, you know. I couldn't help hearing. Did she ever mention the name *Barselius*?"

"The *what*?"

"The *Barselius*. It is—rather, it *was*—a ship. A cruise ship, back in the early thirties. A Miss Halsey was among the passengers. So was I." Mr. Abernathy's spectacles winked in the sun. "I only wondered—idle curiosity—whether it was the same woman."

He flapped along the pier, into the path through the hedge, and disappeared.

A wave washed in slowly upon the beach and slowly out again. Fran said, "*Did* she ever mention . . . ?"

"I don't know. Maybe. She talked about her trips. I didn't listen half the time." He paused, frowning, and then shrugged. "He's only curious. Thought he might have known her. Let's go in."

The hotel looked peaceful in the morning sunlight, its

white wings glistening, its verandas and green shutters cool and orderly. Halfway along the path someone called, "Steve, darling!" and Nanette came running across the grass. "I've been looking for you. . . . Good heavens, Fran, you do look awful!"

Undoubtedly she did, Fran thought crossly. Nanette Boyer, as always, was made up to the last scarlet fingernail, groomed to the last extremely blond hair.

Steve said, "I can't talk now, Nanette. I've been up all night, and so has Fran."

"I know. That's what I wanted to talk to you about. Do they think that Henry did it?"

"No," Steve replied. "He's got an alibi. See you later, Fran." He went across the square toward the clubhouse.

Nanette gave a swift glance around the sunny, grassy square and said, "Fran, do the police know that I—that is—well, that I come from Middletown, too? You know. The Halseys live there."

Fran stared at Nanette. "Did you know them before you came here?"

Nanette moistened her lips. "Well, I . . ." Fear leaped suddenly and openly into her blue eyes. "See here, Fran. You're a good scout. I didn't sleep a wink last night. I . . ." She swallowed hard. "I was engaged to Henry. That's why I came here. He kept putting it off. He didn't have a cent except what his aunt gave him. I got tired of waiting so I—well, I thought I'd have a showdown. I came here, and Miss Halsey made him break it off. But I didn't . . ." She glanced up toward Miss Halsey's suite. "I wouldn't have done that! Besides . . ."

A look of triumph came into her face. She smiled. "Besides, there's the Senator." She paused, eyed Fran, and said frankly, "But if the police get me involved in this, right now—well, that's the end of little Nanette. She'll never be a senator's wife. He's up for election this year. He was appointed, you know, to fill a vacancy; this time he's got to be elected. Miss Bude doesn't much like me, and if the police know—well, you can see it would give her an argument. *Do* the police know about me and Henry?"

"They'll find out. Tell them yourself," Fran said shortly.

Nanette's hands gripped Fran's arm. "If you'll promise me not to tell them, I'll do something for you. I'll not tell them I saw you go up to Miss Halsey's suite about eleven-thirty."

"I didn't! You couldn't have seen me!"

"I was on the pier, right there where the path goes through the hedge. I was waiting for the Senator. We had a date to meet down there at the pier, and I saw you just as you started up the stairs, there under the light. I saw your black dress, but I won't tell the police if you . . . Oh!" Nanette said, in a different, a very polite voice. "Good morning, Miss Bude."

Fran whirled around. Miss Alice Bude, crossing the grass near them quietly, said "Good morning" icily, and went on, her high-bridged nose, the very swish of her yellow linen dress expressing haughty disdain.

Nanette said, "Wait till I'm Mrs. Senator. I'll get rid of her!" Her eyes came back to Fran. "So it's a bargain!"

"It's nothing of the kind. You can't . . ."

Nanette was gone, strolling along the path behind Miss Bude, defiance in every move of her graceful body. Fran started after her, thought wearily, *Oh, what of it!* and went to her room. Nanette had been engaged to Henry. If Nanette had still wished to marry Henry Halsey and had been blocked by Miss Halsey, Nanette had a motive for murder. But now she didn't want Henry. Quite frankly, her goal was Senator Bude. So she had no motive.

Fran went through the archway and turned abruptly at the outside stairway that led to the corridor beside her own room. She wouldn't tell the police about Nanette and Henry; they'd find out for themselves anyway. It was stupid of Nanette to threaten her with her absurd story about the black dress. Miss Halsey had been wearing black lace. If she had seen anybody it was Miss Halsey. Everything came back to Miss Halsey. What had gentle, kind Miss Halsey against Nanette?

Fran fell into bed, but of course she couldn't sleep. It seemed to her that she was still thinking that when she realized that someone was pounding on the door and calling her name. The midafternoon sun was streaming across the room, and the bedside clock said three-thirty.

Finial was at the door. "I've brought your lunch, Miss Allen. And Mr. Brenn wants to see you."

"Come in, Fran," Mr. Brenn said twenty minutes later. He sat at his desk and Captain Scott sat opposite him, and about both men was an air of exhaustion. Jane, the girl at the switchboard, nodded briskly at Fran and plugged in some call. Mr. Brenn ruffled through cards of a tray from a filing cabinet and said, "Well, that's the lot. Guests, waiters, maids, everybody."

"And not a one knows anything. Or admits it," Captain Scott said wearily. "Except the Boyer girl."

Jane, at the switchboard, winked at Fran.

Captain Scott went on. "Came from the same town as the Halseys. Engaged to marry young Henry. He didn't have any money. Admits his aunt opposed his marriage to Nanette. Says she thought he ought to have a job before he married. Admits all that."

"Maybe it's true," Mr. Brenn said. "In any event, Miss Boyer's got an alibi."

Fran's heart gave an odd jump. *Alibi? Nanette was at the pier, she'd said, waiting for the Senator. So she was alone. How long?*

Mr. Brenn answered her unspoken question. "The headwaiter saw her leave the dining room during the intermission. He said she returned in about five minutes and told him to tell the Senator she was waiting for him. Says he was busy, didn't get around to doing it for a few minutes. Says she waited. Says when he did speak to Bude he came to meet her and he heard him tell Miss Boyer he didn't realize what time it was, and then they strolled away together."

"There's five minutes to account for," Captain Scott said gloomily, "if your headwaiter is accurate. But the Senator gives her a sound alibi from then on till Miss Halsey was found."

Had Nanette told them her absurd story of seeing Fran

herself, in her black dress, going to Miss Halsey's suite? Fran's throat tightened.

Mr. Brenn said, "Now, Fran, I want to tell you exactly what the situation is."

They had questioned everyone in the entire hotel. No one had seen any outsider, any prowler on the hotel grounds. No one—here Captain Scott eyed Fran sternly—had seen any stranger lounging near the swimming pool. No one knew anything of a gun.

No one had known the Halseys, aunt or nephew, before their arrival at the hotel—"Except Miss Boyer," Mr. Brenn interpolated hurriedly. There was simply no link that they could discover between any of the guests (aside from Henry Halsey himself, of course, and Nanette) and Miss Halsey. They hadn't even been able to discover exactly when Miss Halsey had left the clubhouse and gone to her suite, except that it was sometime after eleven. "The waiter didn't notice. Mrs. Lee was busy; she didn't notice."

Captain Scott interrupted, "Too busy to keep a close eye on the bar," he said. "Maybe Henry wasn't really there all the time. It wouldn't have taken very long to go to the Halsey rooms, kill her, hurry back to the bar. I don't know whether Henry told the truth about that will or not. Maybe he's not as sure as he pretends to be that she wouldn't have let it stand. There'd be a motive." He said it dubiously.

Mr. Brenn sighed and continued. They had telephoned to the police in the Halsey hometown; they had got a full report not only on the Halseys but about Miss Boyer. Miss Halsey had been much respected by Middletown, had lived there all of her quiet life, except when she was away on trips; she had brought up Henry, her brother's son, orphaned when he was a child. Miss Boyer lived in Middletown, too; she worked at the perfume counter of one of the department stores.

Captain Scott interrupted again. "Where did she get all those fancy clothes?"

"She explained that," Mr. Brenn said. "She spent everything she'd saved for this trip."

Fran felt a little wave of sympathy for Nanette—spending

everything she had on a last hope of winning over Miss Halsey. And, perhaps, Henry. Two years; surely Henry had not been eager for marriage.

Mr. Brenn said, "We questioned young Halsey first, then Miss Boyer. When she heard that Halsey had admitted their engagement and the fact that it was broken off because of his aunt's opposition, she admitted it, but said her heart wasn't broken and neither was Henry's."

Captain Scott said, "Henry claims he didn't quarrel with his aunt over Nanette. Says his aunt said he had to have a job before he married anybody, but it looked to me as if Henry was glad to get rid of Nanette. And it's clear enough that she's after the Senator now." Suddenly he snorted. "The Senator supported her alibi, all right. But she'd do better to stick to Henry. The Honorable William doesn't look like a marrying man to me. Rich, prominent—he's not going to marry a girl like—"

"Might be a good idea," Mr. Brenn said unexpectedly. "Liven things up." He caught himself and looked severely at Captain Scott. "The Senator is highly respected."

Captain Scott grunted. "Now I'll take over. Miss Allen, how long have you known this guy, Steve Greene?"

"Since a few weeks before we were sent here. We were trained at the dancing school."

"Like him, don't you?"

"Certainly. We work together."

"Everybody here seems to think there's quite a romance between you."

That was the effect of the romantic atmosphere that they had studied to suggest in their exhibition dances! Mr. Garden had put it delicately: "People like to feel young, romantic."

"There isn't any romance," Fran said flatly.

"Folks think so. He needs money, doesn't he?"

"Of course, he needs money. That's why he's here. That's why anybody works."

"Why did he send you to the Halsey suite? What did he tell you to do? Let's have your story again."

The same questions; the same answers . . .

When they let her go at last she walked slowly along the path toward the pier, thinking that Steve might be there. He was not; the pier, the long stretch of beach were deserted. Waves washed with a deep murmur upon the beach and out again. Away off the coast a cargo steamer, lighted by the sunset, plowed its way along toward Miami, toward Cuba.

There was a slight consolation in the fact that, obviously, Nanette had not carried out her threat to tell them that she had seen Fran going into the Halsey entrance in her black dress. Why not? That was clear, too. The Senator had come valiantly to Nanette's rescue, and it hadn't been necessary.

There's no link between any of the guests and Miss Halsey, Mr. Brenn had said. Except, of course, Henry. And, through him, Nanette. Steve, because of that extraordinary will. Fran, because she was Steve's dancing partner. Nobody else's.

Suddenly she remembered Abernathy, the new guest, who had arrived in the late afternoon before the murder. And who had lied! They had questioned all the guests, and none of them had admitted having known Miss Halsey previous to their meeting at the hotel. But Abernathy *had* known her and had questioned Fran and Steve—about a cruise ship, twenty years ago. Was there a motive for murder somewhere, somehow, connected with that ship? Twenty years ago? It wasn't likely.

Someone quite near was smoking a cigarette, perhaps had been for some time before she noticed the fragrance of the tobacco. She glanced toward the path and the mass of sea grape behind her that hid the hotel. No one came from the path. Thinking that Steve might be in one of the beach chairs directly below the pier, and thus not visible from where she sat, she went to the railing and looked down. A man was there, smoking.

He was not Steve. He was a rather small man, with a baldish head plastered over with thin dark hair; he wore a sports shirt and rather dingy white slacks. As she watched, he tossed away his cigarette, glanced at the steps that led from the pier to the beach, seemed to sigh, heaved up his dingy slacks, and started northward along the beach.

Fran ran down the wooden steps after him.

His gesture in tossing away his cigarette, something indescribable about his figure and his walk, were all at once familiar. He was, she was certain, the man in the raincoat who had hurried away from the swimming pool at her approach the night before.

"Wait," she cried. "Please wait . . ."

He jerked around to face her. He had a ferret face, pale, pointed, and aggressive, with sly dark eyes, set too close together. "Yes, miss?"

She hurried across the sand. "Please wait; I want to ask you . . ." Ask him what? Had he murdered Miss Halsey? Not a brilliant approach. And if he *had* murdered Miss Halsey, it wasn't a safe approach. She had acted too hastily; yet it had seemed important to stop him, talk to him, find out something about him. Before she could have got back to the hotel, told Mr. Brenn or Steve or the police, he'd have vanished as quickly and as completely as he had done the night before.

He was waiting, watching her warily, as if poised for instant departure.

She said, fumbling for words, "I saw you here last night, at the swimming pool—and . . ."

"No, miss." He turned away.

She cried, "Please wait. I only wanted to ask you if while you were sitting there at the swimming pool you saw anyone . . ." She stopped. The beach was deserted, too deserted. The pier and the hedge shut it off from the hotel. Nobody ever strolled along the beach at just that hour before dinner. Suppose he chose to disappear again, and this time fail to return.

He eyed her slyly. "I expect you've mistaken me for somebody else, miss."

There was a faint accent in his words. Cockney? There was also, very faintly, something just not quite servile in his manner. And he was turning away again.

She plunged desperately. "No, please wait. You see, something—something happened last night."

"Yes, miss?" There was no acknowledgement whatever

in his eyes. Yet the news of the murder must have been in the papers; everybody must have been talking of it. She plunged again. "A woman was murdered, and I saw you there at the swimming pool and I thought you might have seen something."

He cut in: "I don't know nothing about any murder, miss. You've got the wrong man."

"Wait! I'll make it worth your while if you'll come back to the hotel and . . ."

Something flashed in the ferret face. "How much?" His eyes went past her, upward toward the pier, fixed themselves for an instant. Then he said rapidly, "I got nothing to do with murder," and turned and scuttled like a crab along the sand away from her.

A wave washed in and she cried loudly above its murmur, "Tomorrow morning. You needn't come to the hotel. I'll meet you here." She couldn't tell whether or not he heard her.

She started back toward the pier. She'd tell Mr. Brenn; she could describe him now; the police would pick him up. She ran up the steps, and then she saw why he had hurried away, for Senator Bude, his sister, and Henry Halsey were standing on the pier. Even then, although the scurrying figure in dingy slacks was getting rapidly farther away, she gave a kind of gasp of relief. Then she saw that they were looking at her curiously.

Miss Bude said, "What is the matter, Miss Allen? And who was that odd-looking man?"

Probably they had seen, if indeed they hadn't heard, the whole incident. She caught her breath. "Nothing really— somebody strolling along the beach."

The Senator, smiling and handsome, said kindly, "You ought not to speak to people like that, Miss Allen—a pretty girl like you. You really look frightened." He glanced at the elegant watch on his plump wrist. "I think I'll have a drink before dinner. Care to join me, Halsey?"

Henry, still watching Fran with that curious light in his eyes, started a little, said, "Oh, yes, thanks—certainly."

Miss Bude put out her hand. "But William . . ."

"I'll see you at dinner, my dear," the Senator said politely.

The two men disappeared into the path through the hedge, the Senator bulky yet walking lightly as so many big men do, and Henry seeming even smaller and more delicate, following him.

Miss Bude watched them, too, for an instant. She was perhaps ten or twelve years older than the Senator and looked it, with her neat gray hair and severe, lined face. But as the two men disappeared she turned and unexpectedly smiled at Fran and said, "Let's sit down, shall we? I always think the sunset hour is the loveliest, don't you?"

But Fran felt she must hurry to tell Mr. Brenn she had seen the man in the raincoat. "I'm sorry . . ."

"Oh, don't hurry away. You must have had a dreadful day, poor child. All this inquiry and that terrible thing last night."

The sun went down with the swiftness of a stage drop in a theatre. All at once, in a second, the light and glow were gone and, as always in the tropics, a pall came upon the land. The change was so sudden and so marked that it seemed fraught with something ominous and frightening. Suppose the little man with the ferret face came back, scuttling like a crab through the hummocky growth above the beach.

Fran said, "I have to see Mr. Brenn," and started toward the path.

Miss Bude went with her. "It *is* late," she said. "Time to change for dinner."

But Jane, in the office, said Mr. Brenn had gone with the police, she didn't know where. "He told me to tell you and Steve to dance tonight as usual. Carry on, were his words." Jane grinned.

Miss Bude inquired about her mail. The little ferrety man was far away by now. But Fran could at least prove his existence; three persons besides herself had seen him. She went to her room and changed to a dancing dress. . . .

She danced, Steve danced, always with guests; it was their job. She had, for a long time, no chance to tell him of the man in the raincoat. Senator Bude gave her a wide whirl in a waltz and didn't apparently know that he'd landed with one of his shoes planted firmly on the toe of her slipper.

"Wonderful," said Senator Bude, smiling.

She restrained other views. The Honorable William waved at the table where Miss Alice Bude sat with Nanette Boyer, apparently with the greatest amity, awaiting his return. Nanette saluted with a wafted kiss from her fingertips.

"Lovely girl. Charming," Senator Bude said rather flatly. "Thank you, my dear, for the dance." He gave her arm a squeeze and went to join his sister and Nanette.

It was time for the exhibition dances. Fran went into the little dressing room. As she was tightening the straps of her slippers, Steve came in.

"Oh, Steve, I saw him. The man in the raincoat."

"*Where?*"

She told him swiftly, aware that the orchestra was starting the opening bars of their first number.

"So he got away?"

"I think he was frightened. But tomorrow morning—he *might* come back."

At the intermission Captain Scott was waiting in the dressing room. "Just thought I'd time this," he said. He said nothing further and looked at his watch. The orchestra began again.

There was no chance to talk. But during the last waltz, their final number, Steve said suddenly, "I've got a little news, too." He turned her around him, at fingertip distance. She came back to his arms. "Meet me down at the pier." She went into a long dip; then again, with a swirl of skirts, she bent backward across his arm. His cheek touched her own. "It's not much. Don't count on it."

They stood together and bowed and bowed, and their job was done for the night. . . . Captain Scott was still in the dressing room.

Fran left Steve and Captain Scott and hurried to her room. She changed to a white cotton dress, snatched up a sweater, and went to the pier.

It was a dark night again, overcast, so no glimmer of stars

lighted the sea or pier, but it was quiet and warm, with the waves washing gently in upon the beach below. Steve wasn't there yet. Probably Scott had kept him, questioning again.

She sat down in a chair near the path through the hedge. She waited a long five minutes, perhaps ten. There was only the murmur of the waves, no footsteps on the pier, no steps along the path. If there was a rustle among the thick sea grapes behind her she did not consciously hear it. Yet she must have been suddenly aware of some movement, some presence near her, for she jerked around, started to her feet—and then the black night and the sea all rushed together, painfully, and there was nothing. . . .

Nothing except an odd, salty taste in her mouth. Nothing except blackness and cold, a sense of time having passed. Her cheek rasped against sand. There were hands on her back, making her draw long breaths—in, out, in, out. Her hair and her clothes were wet and cold as if she had been swimming! It was Steve working her ribs in and out in a steady rhythm; artificial respiration, that was what they called it. "Darling," he said hoarsely.

*Darling*, she thought. And coughed, choked, and sat up . . .

Mr. Brenn didn't wring his hands but looked as if he wanted to. The doctor gave her an enormous capsule and said she'd be all right now. Captain Scott said nothing in an extremely skeptical way. That was after Steve had half carried her to the hotel, to her room; called the doctor, called Mr. Brenn, Captain Scott—everybody. That was after the doctor had permitted Captain Scott to question her, and she could tell him only that there was someone in the hedge behind her. And that, that evening, she had seen and talked to the man in the raincoat.

Steve had found her. He had come to the pier and gone down to the beach to wait for her and had seen, faintly through the darkness, the gleam of her white face and her white dress, moving close to the beach in the water. Drowning, it was said, was an easy death—especially if anybody had been struck savagely, dragged unconscious down to the beach, towed out only a few feet into the water.

Mr. Brenn said, "It's the man she saw at the swimming pool. He was scared. He came back and watched for her. He's a murderer—a homicidal maniac, killing without reason. . . ."

Captain Scott's look of skepticism deepened. "You had a date to meet her, Greene, there on the pier. Nobody else knew she was going to the pier."

"Steve pulled her out," Mr. Brenn intervened. "Don't forget that."

"Okay. He pulled her out. Murderous attack foiled by hero. Maybe that's why he did it. So as to make him look like a hero—not a murderer."

Steve's fist doubled up. Mr. Brenn caught his arm, and Fran sat up, hot-water bottles and blankets cascading around her. "He didn't. He wouldn't. It must have been the man I saw at the swimming pool and on the beach. I had to stop him. I was afraid he'd get away. I'm telling the truth. Senator Bude and his sister and Henry Halsey saw him, too!"

Her voice was too high and excited. The doctor said firmly, "You can't talk to her any more now." He made them leave, all of them, Steve too.

*Darling*, she thought drowsily, after a long time. *Darling* . . .

She didn't wake until nearly noon—she felt as good as new except for a painful bruise just above her temple. Steve was waiting for her, sitting on the lower step of the little open stairway. Fran drank coffee and told him several times that she had had only a fright and a bruise. "It must have been the man in the raincoat."

Steve gave a kind of groan. "Fran, *why* did you take such a chance! He might have—"

"I *had* to! He'd have got away. And he might have seen something. He'd be a witness. He'd—"

"He might have been the one who murdered her."

"You said you didn't think so. You said he'd never have sat there at the swimming pool. You said he'd have got away as fast as he could."

"I know. But—at any rate, Scott has sent out orders to pick him up. He questioned the Budes and Henry Halsey, and they said they had seen you talking to some man on the beach. He wasn't near enough for any of them to give a very helpful description. But Scott had to believe them. And he's got a couple of men on the lookout, along the beach, in case he does turn up this morning as you told him to. But—"

"But you think he won't come."

"If he tried to murder you last night he won't come. On the other hand, if, as he said, he knows nothing about the murder—and maybe doesn't want to have anything to do with the police—he won't come."

"But, Steve," she said in a small and troubled voice, "if it wasn't that man last night, then who . . . ?"

"Whoever it was obviously felt afraid you had some evidence about Miss Halsey's murder." A streak of sunlight crept up and over Steve's face; he looked white and strained. "Scott says there's no way to check where everybody was when you were—when it happened, and Scott says if he walks up to anybody and asks did you try to drown Fran, naturally they'll say no. Brenn doesn't want a general exodus from the hotel. Scott doesn't want that, either; he wants everybody to stay here."

"What about Mr. Abernathy? He told the police he had never known Miss Halsey. Or at least he didn't mention that cruise and . . ."

"That's what I was going to tell you last night. It may mean nothing, of course, but I kept thinking about it, trying to remember if she'd ever talked of any cruise in particular. And finally I did remember something odd that she'd said once, so I went to Abernathy and . . ."

Someone knocked. Steve said, "Here he is now," and went to open the door.

"Good morning." Mr. Abernathy peered at Fran. "I do hope you've quite recovered, Miss Allen. Greene told me. Terrible thing."

Steve said, "I was telling Fran about the cruise ship."

"Ah, yes." Mr. Abernathy took off his spectacles and

polished them on the flowing tail of his sports shirt. "I'll put it briefly: As I told you, the *Barselius* was a cruise ship. She caught fire, on a cruise, burned and—some people did not escape. I . . ." He replaced his spectacles and cleared his throat. "I was on the ship. My fiancée and I were with a cruise party. I escaped, as you see. Martha, my fiancée, did not."

Fran caught her breath. "Oh—how dreadful!"

"It is in the past, Miss Allen. Some twenty years in the past."

Steve said, "Tell her about the lifeboat."

"Yes. That was most unfortunate. I expect it would be very difficult for you to comprehend the confusion. No lights, you see. Smoke everywhere. Martha and I at last found a lifeboat just as it was about to lower. They said it was already full. They said they couldn't take another passenger. We tried to find our way to another lifeboat. Martha—there was panic, you understand."

He cleared his throat again. "We were separated. I tried to find Martha; I thought she might still be at the lifeboat station. I fought my way back there. This time somebody shouted to get in, and I thought Martha was already there— so I got into the boat. It was lowered at once. We pulled away, the ship burning behind us and the light from the flames . . ." He seemed to steady himself. "To be brief, Martha was not among them. Naturally, they couldn't go back. I crawled out of the boat; I can't swim—somebody pulled me back. In the commotion I was knocked out."

Fran put out her hand toward Mr. Abernathy. He didn't seem to see it.

"When I became conscious we had come to shore. It was not far from here, as a matter of fact. It was still dark. There were some lights and considerable confusion. I was conscious only in waves; I remembered a few faces, not all of them. We were picked up by some people with cars; I was taken to a hospital in Jacksonville and kept there a few days. Naturally, my only thought was Martha. The steamship office was finally able to check its list of passengers. Martha was among those lost. . . . This is a painful story to tell you; I'm sorry. . . . The point is, I searched the entire list of passengers who were saved, many times. Among them were Miss Halsey, Senator Bude, and his sister. I need not point out to you that they are—I should say *were*—all of them guests here at the hotel.''

"A link," Fran thought, crumbling her muffin, not looking at Mr. Abernathy. "A link between the Budes and Miss Halsey. A strange and terrible link between Mr. Abernathy and Miss Halsey."

Steve said, "I was getting to this, Fran. I think that Miss Halsey recognized one of the passengers on that ship. She was talking during a lesson, chattering away, and she said something about wasn't it odd how often you met people you'd known somewhere else, and that she thought she'd recognized someone who had been on a cruise with her at least twenty years ago. I'm not sure she mentioned the *Barselius*. I do remember she said that of course it wouldn't be kind to remind anyone of such a horrible experience. But that's all. She didn't say who it was; I wasn't really listening. I'd never have thought of it again."

"It would have to be one of the Budes," Mr. Abernathy said. "I've looked at the hotel guest list. There's no other name that I recognized. Now, I wonder if the Senator or Miss Bude recognized her and, if so . . ."

"Tell her about the advertisement," Steve said.

"Yes. Well—I was about to say that the presence of the Budes and Miss Halsey here should be coincidence. People who travel, who stay frequently in resort hotels, cross one another's paths. But the advertisement. I saw it in a New York newspaper; I daresay it appeared in various newspapers along the eastern seaboard. It requested passengers on the cruise ship *Barselius* on a certain date to get in touch with the advertiser. Anything concerning the *Barselius* was painful to me. But I could not ignore it. In short, I went to Middletown."

"Middletown!" Fran cried. "That's where the Halseys live!"

"The telephone number was that of Miss Flora Halsey. By then, however, she had gone away for the winter. I discovered her destination. As soon as I could arrange for my vacation I came here, intending to question her. I—you understand—anything concerning that cruise . . . She was murdered that night.''

"But I don't see—" Fran began, bewildered.

Mr. Abernathy sighed. "It's merely the fact of their presence here—Miss Halsey and the Budes—and the advertisement that just might have some bearing on the murder. Plus the fact that Miss Halsey appears to have recognized someone who was associated in a painful way with some cruise; this is not certain. But Miss Halsey was in the lifeboat with me; in fact, she supported me against her knees and tried to do what she could for me while I was unconscious. I remembered her face and that of the woman sitting beside her. Except for two of the crew, I was the only man in the lifeboat.

"I saw Miss Halsey in the clubhouse, only a glimpse of her, the night I arrived. She had changed very little. I did not remember Miss Bude, although the records had it that she was in our lifeboat. The Senator was on the cruise, but I don't remember him at all.''

Mr. Abernathy knotted his knuckly hands together. "As I say, their presence here may be sheer coincidence, but there's the advertisement. Miss Halsey wanted to find someone who was on that cruise. Why?''

Fran asked after a moment, "Was Henry on the ship?''

"No, he was very young then—probably in school. I have not questioned him. I intend to. He may know nothing.''

"Have you talked to the Senator or Miss Bude? Did they recognize Miss Halsey?''

Steve replied, "Brenn says none of the guests admitted having known Miss Halsey before they met her at the hotel.''

Mr. Abernathy chose to explain his own silence: "I preferred to say nothing just then of Miss Halsey and the ship. And, in fact, as you see, there is nothing I could say.''

"All the same," Steve said slowly. "I'm in favor of telling Scott about this.''

Mr. Abernathy sighed again. "It would be better if we

had more to tell him. You are both in a rather dangerous position. The police have to make an arrest soon. It's going to take some very convincing piece of evidence to clear you—in view of that unfortunate will.''

It was grimly true. No one spoke for a moment. Then Steve said, ''But the *Barselius* is the only scrap of evidence that might help.''

''If it *is* evidence,'' Mr. Abernathy said. ''Miss Allen, what about this man you saw on the beach last night? Can you describe him?''

She described him, as she had described him to the police.

Mr. Abernathy stared at his knuckles. ''Cockney accent, you say?''

''I thought so. Very slight.''

Steve said suddenly, ''Mr. Abernathy, has Miss Bude recognized you?''

''Me!'' His eyeglasses winked. ''Oh, no. I've changed, you know. I was younger then, and . . .''

Nanette flung open the door and ran into the room. ''Steve, Fran, I've got news! I'm going to be Mrs. Senator Bude!''

Mr. Abernathy neatly extricated himself. ''I'm sure I hope you'll be very happy. Good morning, Miss Allen. I'll see you later, Greene.'' He disappeared.

Nanette stared after him. ''What's his hurry? Well, Fran, what do you think of it? What's the matter, Steve? Aren't you going to congratulate me? I'm terribly fond of you, darling, but I know you didn't take it seriously; and when a girl has a chance like this . . .''

Steve took her hand and walked her energetically to the door.

Fran ran after them. ''Nanette, wait. You said you saw me in my black dress . . .''

Nanette's eyes turned cold. ''Oh, that! I didn't tell the police and I'm not going to. I'm not going to get involved. Especially now—I mean, becoming Mrs. Senator—well, you can see it wouldn't do.''

''Did you really see anyone?''

"I'm not going to..."

"Was it Miss Halsey herself? She was wearing black. Who was it?"

"I thought it was you. I just thought so. But I'll not tell the police. Forget it!" Nanette slammed the door.

Steve's eyes blazed. "What's all that about?"

Fran told him quickly, and after a moment he said thoughtfully that her first explanation might be the right one. "Nanette was scared. Miss Halsey opposed Henry's marriage so firmly that Henry, obviously, was the one who broke it off. So Nanette, panicky for fear the police would suspect her, asked you if they knew, then realized that she'd given herself away to you and made up her story to try to keep you quiet, threaten you. But then, when the police got the whole story out of her but didn't make a case against her, because she had a firm alibi, she had no reason to carry out her threat to you. Sounds like her—scared, not very bright, but shrewd, too, when it comes to protecting herself. And now that she's going to be"—suddenly Steve grinned—"Mrs. Senator, she only wants to stay out of a murder inquiry."

In any event, Fran thought swiftly, he didn't seem to mind Nanette's engagement. Had he really said "darling" the night before? Or had she imagined it?

His face was sober again. "On the other hand, she may have seen Miss Halsey. Or she may have seen another woman in black. Who's got a black dress?"

"Who? Steve, that's hopeless! Probably every woman in the hotel has a black dress."

"Who was wearing black that night? Nanette? Miss Bude?"

"I can't remember, I don't—" But suddenly she did remember something. "Steve, Miss Bude left her table! Sometime near the intermission. The Senator was sitting alone when we came back after the intermission!"

He looked at her thoughtfully for a moment and then shook his head. "I don't think it was a woman, unless Nanette... See here, Nanette's got a black dress. Sort of satiny. Maybe..."

"What, Steve?"

"No, it's no good. I thought that maybe it was Nanette herself. Or maybe she really did see somebody, and whoever it was had put on a black dress purposely—like the one Miss Halsey was wearing or like the one you were wearing. A kind of disguise, I mean. So, if anybody did happen to catch a quick glimpse of her near the Halsey entrance, they'd only see a woman in a black dress, who might be anybody."

"If Nanette really did see somebody and thought it was me, then she *couldn't* have had more than a glimpse! She couldn't have known who it was. But the fact that she saw a woman, that's something." Fran was excited. "Question her, Steve. Make her tell you. Or tell Mr. Brenn. Tell Captain Scott."

"She might stick to it that it was you."

"If it was while we were dancing . . ."

He thought for a moment and then shook his head. "I don't know. The time of the murder is too hazy. Scott . . . No, it's too dangerous, Fran. Besides, that was a man last night. You're a slim young woman, Fran, but you're no featherweight. I carried you up from the beach last night. A woman couldn't have got you down from the pier and out into the sea. At least, most women couldn't. Nanette maybe but . . . No, it was a man." All at once his face was rock-hard. "And I'm going to get that man."

Terror caught at her. She whispered, "Why did he . . . ?"

"That's the point, Fran. There's only one answer: The murderer has reason to believe that you can identify him."

Terror in the night. Terror in the sunny, still morning. Terror in the blue waves and the soft breeze and the clatter of the palms. She said stiffly, her mouth and her throat making speech difficult, "I can't. There isn't anything . . ."

"There's something. Let's go over it all again. Everything. From the time I gave you her evening bag—and I wish to heaven I hadn't."

But there was nothing. Steve at last rose, paced up and down, into the light and out again, thinking. Finally he stopped, with an air of decision. "There's a chance that the police will pick up the man you talked to on the beach last night. I'm going to Jacksonville now."

"Jacksonville!"

"That is, if the police will let me go. I'll borrow Brenn's car. There's an office of the steamship company that owned the *Barselius* there. It may come to nothing. On the other hand, it's one of the motives for murder, I suppose. Revenge and—but it's rather thin."

"*Revenge . . .*"

"She was murdered the night Abernathy got here."

"You mean because Miss Halsey was in the lifeboat, and his girl, Martha . . ."

"I don't know what I mean. Brenn says we can skip dancing tonight. It may be late when I get back. Fran, stick around with other people. All the time. But if anybody tries to question you, don't talk. Promise me."

"All right," she promised. But after he had gone and the big room seemed too quiet she decided to talk to Mr. Brenn. She'd tell him about Nanette's story of the woman in the black dress.

Steve had said it was dangerous, the police might call it evidence against Fran; Steve had also said not to talk to anybody about the murder. But if Nannette's story was a true one . . . Yes, she'd tell Mr. Brenn.

She met him as she crossed the sunny lawn, and she told him quickly, giving herself no time to reconsider.

Mr. Brenn rubbed his forehead wearily. "See here, Fran, if I tell Scott this he's going to make it tough for you."

"Nanette didn't see me. I wasn't there. So if she saw anyone—"

"Maybe she didn't. Or maybe it was Miss Halsey herself."

"I know, but—I wonder how many women in the hotel have black evening dresses and who they are."

Mr. Brenn stared in dismay. "They've all got them! I never see why so many women wear black evening dresses."

"It would be easy to find out."

"Listen, Fran," he said almost pleadingly. "My guests have put up with plenty already. I can't go too far. If the police begin on this angle . . . Wait a minute." He rubbed his head and finally said grudgingly, "I'd rather not tell Scott, not unless there's something in it; but I'll tell you what I'll do. I'll get somebody to take a look—not that I think it'll prove anything."

Fran drifted down to the beach. There were guests in swimming suits, but nobody was swimming. They were gathered in excited, earnestly talking little groups that fell abruptly silent at her approach. The Budes, with Nanette, made a family huddle; Nanette sun bathing, Miss Bude sitting under an umbrella, knitting, Senator William wrapped in a gay beach robe, with a towel draped peasant-fashion over his head, protecting himself against the sun.

A little farther on, Mr. Abernathy sat with a book and dark glasses. He didn't seem to see Fran. And away beyond him another man in swimming trunks, vaguely familiar in spite of dark glasses, proved to be the sergeant of police— watching her. Watching everybody, but mainly, it struck her, watching for a little man in dingy white slacks. So at least, perhaps, Captain Scott had believed that much of her story.

She felt rather cheered as she went back along the beach and up to the clubhouse. But her wave of encouragement didn't last long, for she found a newspaper, read and cast away on a bench.

She read it and put it down because her hands were shaking. Steve Greene, dancing teacher, frequent lessons to Miss Halsey; the remarkable will; the body found by Miss Fran Allen, Greene's dancing partner. Greene questioned after he returned from a long walk, in the night, along the beach. The gun had not been found.

Nothing was said outright, but the implications were all there in black and white. One of the headlines read, POLICE PREDICT EARLY ARREST. Steve—or Fran herself—or both of them. She went back to the square and sat stubbornly beside the swimming pool. Nobody could approach her unseen across that open, sunny lawn. Smoke rose lazily from one of the many chimneys; each suite in the hotel was cannily equipped with a fireplace in the event that the weather let Mr. Brenn down; still, it was odd that anybody should like a fire on a sunny, warm day.

The sunbathers straggled up from the beach. The shadows began to slant across the grass. She couldn't hope for Steve's return before midnight. She went to her room at last, changed for dinner, took the shortcut again to the clubhouse, and when she passed the office door, Jane had a long-distance telephone call for her. She took it there, at Mr. Brenn's desk. Steve?

It was Mr. Garden, head of the Garden School of Dancing. The police had telephoned him to inquire about her and about Steve. He didn't think that either of them had shot the woman. He'd send them money for lawyers if they needed it. But the will, the publicity—in short, they were fired.

Her knees were unsteady; she wanted to run back to her own room, but instead she went to the clubhouse. She sat at a small table alone. Henry was in the bar. The Budes and Nanette sat together, Nanette beautiful and triumphant, her lovely shoulders bare above white taffeta, Miss Bude knitting vigorously between courses. She was wearing pale blue lace. Fran searched the room and nobody, not a woman in the room, wore black. Perhaps there weren't as many black dresses as she had thought.

Perhaps Mr. Brenn's reluctant and quiet inquiry would turn up no evidence at all. Perhaps her first impression of Nanette's story had been the right one, and it was only a story.

The orchestra played resolutely all through dinner, and there was dancing between courses, but nobody, this time, asked her to dance. She pushed food around on her plate.

Mrs. Lee noted her isolation and came to coax her to eat. "It's this dreadful murder. Everybody's on edge, but don't look like that, my dear. It must have been a burglar." Mrs. Lee and the bartender had offered Henry that alibi—Henry, who, otherwise, was the logical suspect.

Fran said rather desperately, "Mrs. Lee, are you sure Henry Halsey was in the bar all that time?"

Mrs. Lee's kind blue eyes grew troubled. "To the best of my belief, yes. That's what I told the police. But I've been worrying about it. I'm so busy all the time. So is Jim. I *could* have gone to the kitchen for a few minutes or arranged somebody's table or . . .'' She shook her head. ''But I can't remember it. And Jim is sure young Halsey didn't leave. . . . There's the chef wanting to speak to me.'' She whisked away.

But Mrs. Lee had some doubt of her own memory. And Henry could have had a motive.

Fran was sipping coffee when Mr. Abernathy, unexpectedly civilized and urbane in dinner clothes, sat down opposite her. There was an odd air of restrained excitement about him, but he hadn't yet talked to Henry.

''Couldn't find him,'' he said. ''Brenn said he was at police headquarters part of the day. But if they suspected him they've let him go. The girl in the office says he's here somewhere.''

''He's in the bar.''

''Oh.'' He summoned a waiter. ''Please ask Mr. Halsey to join us.''

Henry strolled to the table, a pouting, reluctant look on his face. ''You want to see me?''

''Yes,'' Mr. Abernathy said. ''I want to talk to you about the *Barselius*.''

Henry's jaw dropped. ''The—*what*?''

''I was one of the passengers.''

''You . . .'' Henry stared. ''Do you mean to say . . . ? Look here. How'd you get away? In a lifeboat?''

Mr. Abernathy nodded. ''You mean with your aunt? Yes.''

Henry's small face flushed deeply. ''Then you are a witness! You're the man I . . . Look here!'' He cast a quick glance around him and clutched Mr. Abernathy's arm. ''Come with me.''

They went out of the dining room, with Henry still clutching Mr. Abernathy's arm as if he was afraid Mr. Abernathy might get away. Witness! Witness to what?

A waiter came to her. ''Miss Allen, there is a long-distance call for you. Over at the phone booth.''

This time it was Steve. His voice was tense and excited: ''Fran, we're on our way home.''

"Did you find out anything about the *Barselius*?"

"It took time for them to dig back in the records. Miss Halsey was one of the passengers all right, and Abernathy, as he said, and the Budes. There was a volume of correspondence about the whole thing. Nothing that concerned any of those four people particularly. But there's an odd sort of thing. Somebody else was here inquiring about the *Barselius*, and it sounds like your man in the raincoat, and his name is Jenkins."

"Jenkins!"

"That's the name he gave, and he said he was a steward on the *Barselius* and got away in one of the lifeboats. He wanted to see the list of survivors. That was about three months ago."

"What did he want? What was he after?"

"The clerk didn't know. Thought he was only curious because he'd been on the ship. But after he was gone, the clerk got curious too and found—" The excitement left Steve's voice: "Oh, it's only a clerical error of some kind. Their first records didn't check with the final records. I'll tell you when I get there. The important thing is Jenkins, if it's the same man. A policeman came with me. He's phoning Scott now. We'll be there soon."

She went back to her table. Jenkins—a steward on the *Barselius*. The steward in the lifeboat with Miss Halsey and Miss Bude and Abernathy? She remembered his Cockney accent, his air of servility. "Yes, miss." "No, miss." But why had he searched the *Barselius* records?

Henry and Mr. Abernathy did not return. Tables were thinning out; Nanette and the Senator had disappeared—into the bar, apparently, for she had a glimpse of Nanette's blond head in a corner. Miss Bude sat alone at her table.

As the orchestra was playing its final number Mr. Abernathy returned. "I didn't get much out of Henry. He turned cagey. Questioned me to make sure I had been on the *Barselius*. Said he didn't know a thing about the advertisement. But, of course, his telephone number is the same as Miss Halsey's. Either Henry or Miss Halsey placed that advertisement, and from his questions just now I believe it was Henry. I kept talking, trying to get something out of him. He was edgy, nervous—very eager to get away from me. Finally he said he had to see somebody, and ducked into the hedge and I can't find him."

She cried, "Steve phoned!" and told him.

"The steward in the lifeboat!" He nodded, his spectacles winking. "That could be! If it *is* your man, I might be able to identify him. There were two of the crew, eighteen women passengers, one man, myself." He hesitated, that odd, restrained excitement in his eyes. "I think I ought to tell you. This afternoon I recognized another passenger in that boat."

*"Who?"*

He didn't reply. His glittering spectacles were searching the tables. "Where's Nanette? Where's . . . ?"

"In the bar."

He stretched his thin neck and peered for a long moment toward the bar. "Murder," he said, "murder . . ." and looked at her strangely. "Go back to the hotel office and stay there." He was gone, sliding through the clusters of people who were now drifting away.

Fran rose as Miss Bude passed her table on the way to the doors, and followed her, by way of the main path this time, close to Miss Bude's fluttering silk coat.

Suppose Mr. Abernathy hadn't recognized anybody really except Miss Halsey! Suppose Miss Halsey, somehow, had prevented Martha's escape. Suppose, even, it was Abernathy himself who attracted the man Jenkins's dubious surveillance of the hotel. But why? And Mr. Abernathy had searched out Nanette in the bar, and then hurriedly, saying "murder" in a queer, almost absent way, had disappeared.

Another question struck Fran for the first time and was appalling in its simplicity. If Miss Halsey had had some real and solid reason for opposing Nanette's marriage to Henry, nothing to do with Henry's being unable to support a wife, a reason that if Miss Halsey had lived she might have told Alice Bude or the Senator, would Nanette have removed that danger forever? Nanette was shrewd, she was ruthless—and now triumphant.

Cars were thudding along the road as always. She stopped, hoping one of them would turn into the hotel grounds bringing Steve. Miss Bude went on into the lighted archway. Fran waited, close to the shrubbery below the stairway leading to her own room; other guests drifted past her and into the hotel, and still none of the cars along the highway turned in. "Stay with other people," Steve had said. Something rustled in the shrubbery near her.

Her heart lurched. She turned swiftly toward the archway, and before she could take a step a hand came from the shrubbery and clutched at her arm. "Miss—miss . . ." A narrow, ferrety face peered from the heavy mass of shrubbery, a pale face in the lights above the parking oval, a frightened face. "You said you'd give me money. Give it to me now."

'Are you . . .' She was going to say, "Are you Jenkins?" And she was going to jerk away from him, run, scream, anything.

He said, "Quick, miss! I've got to get out of town. I don't hold with murder. You said money, didn't you? Anything will do. What's in that handbag? You must have something there!" He seized her little handbag, dug into it with shaking, clawlike fingers, snatched out a five-dollar bill and a ten, thrust the bag at her, and darted back into the shrubbery.

It was so unexpected and so swift that she stood for an instant, staring at the shadows, listening. Then she thought, *I must tell Mr. Brenn, Captain Scott; I must hurry.* She whirled and touched the balustrade of the little stairway and caught at it to save herself from falling. And then saw, in the shadow of the balustrade, a deeper, darker shadow, flung down on the lower steps—a black, inert object that had a dimly white coat, a dimly white face. It was a small, doll-like face in the gloom, except part of the face simply wasn't there. It was Henry Halsey. . . .

A car raced along the main road and turned toward the hotel. Its lights shot across her, glaring against the white wall, making sharp black tracery of the vines, leaving the thing at her feet in deep shadow. Two men came, running, across the pavement. One was a policeman; he went past the stairway, into the archway. The other was Steve. "Fran, I saw you in the lights. What's happened? . . . *Henry*!"

After a time Steve rose. "He's dead. There's nothing we can do for him. We'll go to your room. Then I'll tell them."

They went past Henry, close to the wall; Steve led the way, snapped on lights. "Did you hear the shot? Do you know anything about it?"

"No . . . No . . . Jenkins was here." Her voice seemed to come from a long way off, yet she must have told him, for Steve's eyes were blazing.

"We'll get him this time. Henry must have been shot before the orchestra stopped; anybody in the hotel or in the office who might have heard it thought it was a backfire. But it wasn't by chance that Henry was shot on that little stairway. They gave him a different room, but it's in the south wing. Whoever did it wanted to implicate you."

Henry murdered on the little stairway leading to the corridor outside her room. And she had found Miss Halsey. The police wouldn't believe it could happen twice merely by chance. But this time it hadn't happened by chance; somebody had meant it to happen like that. And it was easier, wasn't it, after an outright attempt to murder her had failed, simply to arrange evidence against her and let the police do the rest?

Steve said, "Lock the door after me. Don't let anybody in. I'll be back."

He was gone. Lock the door. As she started toward it the telephone rang and she turned back automatically to answer it. Mr. Brenn said, "Fran, Finial's wife found something in one of the rooms. It's a black dress that somebody tried to burn, so you were on the right trail. I've called Scott. Come right down here, will you?" He hung up, quickly.

Steve had told her to do something. Oh, yes, lock the door. She turned from the telephone and, across the room, the door into the corridor was closed. She hadn't remembered that she'd closed the door. Steve must have closed it.

She went to turn the key; it was already locked; she didn't remember doing that, either.

She must tell Mr. Brenn that she couldn't come to the office and see a black dress that somebody had tried to burn and that Finial's wife had found. Smoke rising hazily from some chimney that hot afternoon! From what chimney? Whose dress? Nanette's? Miss Bude's? Or some other woman's dress? A woman whom Mr. Abernathy had recognized that afternoon, another passenger in that lifeboat? Suddenly, very clearly, something Abernathy had said recurred to her; he didn't remember Miss Bude but he remembered two faces—Miss Halsey, who had tried to help him, and the woman who sat beside her. *Who?*

Henry had gone out of the dining room with Abernathy, and Henry had not come back. Suppose Henry knew something that Mr. Abernathy had done or failed to do in that strange and horrible affair of the burning ship. Miss Halsey, always talking, her gentle voice running on like an endless brook, would certainly have told Henry, many times, all that she had known of the doomed *Barselius*.

It was a flash of light through a chink in a dark curtain; she was suddenly convinced that Henry was murdered because he had some dangerous knowledge that he had learned from Miss Halsey. Miss Halsey wouldn't have injured anybody intentionally. It was different with Henry.

But then the chink of light closed. She must tell Mr. Brenn something—anything; he was expecting her. She went to the telephone. Palm trees seemed to rustle and whisper—somewhere very near. But there was no wind that night. And *she* hadn't closed the door! She hadn't locked it, either.

All at once that too was very clear in her mind. Her back had been turned to the door. Someone had come quietly into the room while she was at the telephone, closed the door—so quietly, so stealthily, with only the faintest whisper of—of what? Silk! She whirled around, and the closet door, in the corner at right angles to the door leading to the corridor, swung open.

"Don't touch the telephone!" Miss Alice Bude swung the

closet door wider, her silk coat rustling. A gun was in her hand.

Fran clung to the back of the chair beside her because she had to hang on to something. Miss Bude bent to listen at the door.

"You can't kill me! They'd know it was you! They've found . . ." Another chink of light shot revealingly into the tortuous paths of human motivation. "It was your black dress! You tried to burn it. You saw my black dress and Miss Halsey's. You thought if anyone saw you from the pier or anywhere not too near they might think it was me or Miss Halsey. But you didn't think you'd be seen then, while everybody was at the clubhouse. Nanette saw you and . . ."

Miss Bude was listening at the door. The gun and her voice were steady. "Nanette thinks it was you. I heard her tell you about it. Besides, if you think Nanette would accuse me now, you are quite wrong. She's engaged to my brother."

Engaged to William—Mrs. Senator. So that was why Miss Bude had put her official sisterly stamp upon that engagement!

But there hadn't been an easy way to shut Fran's mouth. One attempt had failed. "It was you last night! You tried to drown me. You were afraid I'd tell the police what Nanette said about the dress."

Miss Bude leaned closer to the door and gave a kind of satisfied nod. "You're quite right, my dear, but perhaps too right for your own good. Now we'll take a short walk."

"No—no . . ."

"There's really nothing else I can think of," Miss Bude said. "I've got to end this. First I want you to write a little note explaining it. You're to say you shot her for this young Greene."

Fran's hand went up over her mouth. "I can't! I won't."

"Suicide, a confession—and that's the end of it. Don't make it harder. You don't suppose I like this, do you? There is simply," she said in a hurried yet reasonable way, "nothing else to do."

Fran sought wildly for a threat—anything: "They'll find Jenkins. He'll tell them about—about the lifeboat!"

It was a mistake. Miss Bude gave her a deep look. "So you did get something out of Jenkins. I was sure of it. You were afraid when I tried to keep you there on the pier. You wouldn't wait, you wouldn't talk to me. I heard you say you'd meet him again the next morning."

"You tried to murder me. You were afraid that Jenkins would talk."

"You know too much. Now we'll go." She forgot the note, the confession. She unlocked the door, carefully. She opened the door, her hand steady with the gun.

"The gun," Fran cried. "They'll find the gun. They'll trace—"

"Yes, I must get rid of it. It's William's gun; I brought it from home so as to be prepared for Henry Halsey if he followed us here, as he did. Naturally, he induced his aunt to come here with him when he discovered where we were."

There was some implication in her words that Fran did not understand, and there was no time to discover its meaning, for Miss Bude remembered then the important confession, which would end it for her, which must be found—later. Fran saw her swift glance at the writing table. If she could be induced to put down the gun, even for a second, there was a chance. Miss Bude was her size but Fran was stronger, younger. But Steve had said no woman could have pulled her down from the pier into the water!

And Alice Bude hadn't killed Henry! She couldn't have, because she hadn't left the dining room until Fran had, herself, seen her leave, had walked close behind her all the way along the path, had seen her pass the stairway, where already Henry lay dead! Yet she had all but admitted it, hadn't she? And her hand on the gun was steady and lethal. She had the will and capacity for murder.

There were running footsteps outside, in the corridor, Miss Bude's head jerked toward the door.

"If you say a word, I'll kill him first." Her silk coat flashed into the closet; the door was almost closed, not quite, when Steve came running into the room.

"Fran, are you all right? Brenn said he phoned to you and

you didn't come down. They've got Jenkins. You'll not believe this! Miss Bude killed Henry.''

*No*, Fran thought. *No!* Yet she didn't dare look at the small black space between the closet door and the wall.

Steve was excited. "They've got most of the story. Everything broke all at once. Brenn had already sent for Scott. They found a dress she got in a panic about and tried to burn.''

Fran must have nodded.

He said, "Oh, yes, you know about that. Well, Scott's men had picked up Jenkins at a bus stop. Abernathy recognized him; he's the steward, all right. Abernathy had been trying to find Henry; he thought Henry was asking for murder, blackmailing the Senator, intending to use Abernathy as a threat, a witness and put the screws on. Abernathy was too late; Henry had already acted and was murdered. We've told them about the *Barselius*. Bude admits the lifeboat affair. Admits his sister knew about Henry's attempts to blackmail him. Admits he had a gun. They can't find the gun, and he admits his sister may have taken it, but— What's the matter?''

"Nothing—nothing. Go on.'' She must keep him talking so he wouldn't look around the room.

"It explains Miss Halsey's murder, you see! Henry's blackmail threat had no teeth without a witness; Miss Halsey was a witness, so Alice Bude got rid of her first. Besides, if Henry was killed and Miss Halsey was still alive she'd have hooked things together. Bude's sister must have believed that Miss Halsey was in the deal with Henry. But tonight, when Henry came up with the threat of another witness, Abernathy, Alice Bude decided to end the thing then and there, and shot Henry.''

Fran's thoughts began to seesaw wildly. Henry, of course, must have known from the beginning that Alice Bude shot Miss Halsey and why, but he kept quiet about it. He wasn't going to kill the goose that might lay a golden egg. Yet Alice hadn't shot Henry.

Steve saw she didn't understand. "The Senator resisted Henry's first attempt to blackmail him. Henry followed

Bude here to the hotel to keep after him. The point is, Miss Halsey was Henry's only witness and he knew his aunt wouldn't touch blackmail, so he advertised, hoping to find another witness.''

Steve stopped; he was looking at her rather oddly. She must get him and herself out of the room!

Steve said, "The crux of the thing is that it would have blown Bude's career sky-high. Henry knew it. Bude knew it. His sister knew it. It's the kind of thing nobody could forget and forgive. He was vulnerable; it would have made headlines.''

Fran wasn't listening, because Steve was looking around the room. He was still talking rapidly—and searching the room. The curtains, the bed, the door to the bathroom. His eyes traveled on toward the closet door.

She cried, "What happened in the lifeboat?"

It didn't stop him. He talked, but his eyes searched. "Oh, that's what Jenkins dug up at the steamship office in Jacksonville. The first records of survivors didn't square with the final records. Jenkins must have suspected it at the time, but the Budes and some other passengers had joined the cruise only during the last two days before the ship burned, so the crew and the original passengers hadn't had time to get the newcomers straightened out as to names and faces. But the records show first that there were nineteen women and one man besides the steward and two of the crewmen in Jenkins's lifeboat. The final, corrected records show eighteen women, two men and two of the crew, including Jenkins. The names were scrambled in the confusion and eventually put together in the final list of all survivors. They put the discrepancy down to error.''

She was listening now—and knew that the woman only a few feet away was listening intently. Then it struck her that Steve had an odd, listening look, too. But he said clearly, "Abernathy recognized Bude this afternoon. Bude was draped in a beach robe and towel. He's twenty years older and a hundred pounds heavier, but Abernathy says he was in that lifeboat, dressed in women's clothing. Trying to make sure he'd get away, you see. Women and children first.''

Steve came to Fran so quietly, so leisurely, that it was like a moving picture turned to slow motion. He said with peculiar distinctness, "Jenkins is spilling everything. The Senator's going to break down and confess his sister did it."

"She couldn't have shot Henry!" Fran cried. "She was in the dining room all the time. I saw her—I'm her alibi."

Steve heard and understood; she knew that. But he flung open the closet door.

Alice Bude's eyes were on Steve, but she pointed the gun at Fran. "Don't move—I mean it."

She moved toward the door, watching Steve, aiming at Fran. One hand groped backward for the doorway; when she touched it she said to Steve, "You are quite right. William will break down. He's always done that. He's like a child, but he's a coward. He always turned to me to save him. As he did that night on the ship. He'll do it again, even though they can't hold him for the Halsey murder." She flashed out the door.

"Phone! Get Scott!" Steve thrust Fran back and ran after Miss Bude.

Brenn answered the telephone; it was already too late. Escape down the little stairway, into the heavy shadows, was too swift and easy.

The police took over the search for Alice Bude. Steve called Scott aside and had a few murmured words with him. Steve nodded. "Okay, thanks." His eyes took in Fran, too. "Come into Brenn's office. Jenkins is talking."

Jenkins was indeed talking; he was frightened and voluble. Much of what he said was part of an already known pattern, but some of it was not.

It was a story that, begun and forgotten twenty years ago, came into evil life again when Jenkins had seen in the newspapers the announcement that William Bude, appointed to fill a vacancy, was now a candidate for election; he had recognized the name. He had remembered a notion he had that one of the passengers in his lifeboat was a young man dressed as a woman.

"So it suggested blackmail," Captain Scott said.

Jenkins squirmed, but he was terrified, too.

He had gone to Jacksonville, made fairly sure of his facts, and approached Senator Bude, who denied it. ("Told me I couldn't prove it," Jenkins muttered.) So Jenkins, even more positive, had sought for proof—somebody else in the lifeboat, somebody to back up his accusation, somebody, in fact, who just might be induced to enter the deal with him. Unluckily, he had chosen Miss Halsey.

"But I didn't talk to her," Jenkins said wildly. "She wasn't there. It was Henry I saw, and he got it out of me. And she'd told him—she didn't know it was Bude—but she'd told him that she thought the woman in the lifeboat who sat beside her was really a man dressed in women's clothes. And Henry remembered it. She'd talked a lot about it. He wouldn't let me see her. He said she'd stop it. But Henry"—Jenkins sighed—"said he'd take over."

"And split with you," Scott said. "So Henry advertised for another witness—hoping, as you did, to get somebody who'd be willing to back you up." He turned to Bude: "You told your sister all about it."

William Bude moistened pale lips. "I never thought she'd kill anybody. She told me not to give in; not to pay him a cent; that was right. But then Henry followed us here, and his aunt . . . Alice recognized her. So she shot her. Poor Alice. Thought people would believe Miss Halsey; knew nobody would believe Henry—or even Jenkins. Not the kind of people anybody believed, you know. Blackmailers." He moistened his lips again.

Fran started to speak, and Steve put his hand down hard on her wrist.

Scott said, "Now then, Jenkins. You say that you saw Miss Bude leave Miss Halsey's suite."

"Oh, yes. Heard the shot, too. It scared me; I was afraid. Well, I didn't want no violence, you see. So I watched from the hedge. Miss Bude didn't see me, but I saw her come out. She had on a black dress and she ran, sort of sly, as if she didn't want anybody to see her, over to the door to the Budes' rooms. I'd made Henry tell me where their rooms were. So then I didn't know what had happened, but I had to find out. Henry didn't turn up. Nobody did till the girl . . ." His eyes went to Fran.

Scott said abruptly, "How do we know you didn't do it?"

Jenkins began to snivel. "I knew you'd blame me! But why would I kill Miss Halsey? She was on our side—Henry's and mine. She'd have had to tell the truth, wouldn't she, about the Senator, even if she got onto what Henry and me was doing. We needed her."

It had weight. Scott said, "You say you were hanging around the hotel to keep your eye on Henry."

Jenkins said simply, "How would I trust him unless I watched him? Made him meet me every so often, too. Until yesterday early, when he phoned to me at the motel I've been living in. Wanted to know why the girl"—he nodded at Fran—"said she'd meet me that morning. Henry said to keep away."

William Bude wiped his glistening face. "My poor sister! How could she have done it! Miss Halsey! And now Henry—"

Jenkins's little eyes glittered angrily. He turned swiftly to Scott: "Did you mean that about state's evidence?"

"If you were an accessory after the fact, I can't do much about that. But it'd be easier than hanging."

"All right," Jenkins said after a moment. "The sister shot Miss Halsey. But she didn't kill Henry."

"Alice did it," the Senator gasped. "Alice . . ."

Jenkins rose, a little contemptuous figure. "Henry was talking to the Senator. I was there beside the stairway. Henry told the Senator that he'd found another witness named Abernathy. And the Senator said, 'Let's go where we can talk. This stairway goes up to Miss Allen's corridor; girl won't be there, still in the clubhouse.' And then he pulled Henry into the stairway, and a car was coming along the highway, loud, and—and the Senator shot him and ran right past me back around the hotel. Left his gun in his room, I guess, and maybe the sister got it. But that's the way it happened, and I'll take my oath . . ."

Steve said, "Miss Bude shot Miss Halsey. The Senator's

got an alibi for that. But she didn't shoot Henry. Fran, tell them . . .''

"Always a coward," Alice Bude had said; "he'll break down."

"It was Alice," the Senator sobbed. "It was all her fault, all of it; I'd never have murdered Miss Halsey. Alice . . .''

Jenkins's little eyes shot scorn. "Blame a woman, would you? You made her do it. You told her she'd got to help you. You hadn't got the nerve to do it yourself. Look at what you did to get away from a burning ship! All right, Captain Scott, take me away. I can't stay in the same room with him. . . .''

They took William away first. Two policemen, hurrying, brought Alice's silk coat. Nanette, sitting back in a corner, saying nothing, stared at the coat.

"The Coast Guard plane will find the body as soon as it's light," Scott said. "Tell them to be on the lookout. Obviously the woman has drowned herself."

Mr. Abernathy went to Nanette. "Come," he said kindly. "It's all over."

Nanette rose. "I guess it was all over for me from the beginning. He didn't really like me. I could tell. He'd have got rid of me as soon as they thought they were safe. It was that black dress; I suppose they didn't want me to talk about it. And then I was his alibi when Miss Halsey . . .'' She stopped and drew herself up, so her blond head shone in the light. "Oh, well," she said hardily, "I'm well out of it. I'd never have got along with both of them, and he'd always have needed her. She was the strong one. But it's funny; it's as if they were one person. I mean, one murderer. Isn't it?'' She looked at them with wide, startled eyes, the eyes of one who stumbles upon a truth.

"I think that's right," Abernathy said gently. "One motive—in a real sense, one murderer . . .''

Steve said, "Can I borrow your car, Brenn?"

Fran went with him into the village, to a little lighted patio, still open, where they had scrambled eggs and talked until the waiter began suggestively to blow out candles upon the other tables.

"He wants us to leave," Steve said then. "Back to dancing lessons tomorrow."

"No. I forgot. We're fired," she told him.

After a moment he took out an envelope and wrote something and passed it to her. It was a telegram to Mr. Garden: "Police have cleared us. Murder case closed. Fran is going to marry me. Regards from both."

"Is that," Steve said, "all right with you? I mean sometime, when I can afford a wife. Oh . . ." His face went blank. "I forgot to tell you. You can't marry me for my money, you know. I'm not having any. I mean the will. Brenn talked to her lawyer. There's a cousin somewhere, and she's going to get everything except . . ." He fumbled in his pocket and brought out a ring, an old-fashioned little ring, gold with two tiny hands clasping each other. "I think Miss Halsey would like you to have it."

After a long moment Fran took the ring in her hand. "But I'm not going to wait. You may as well understand that now."

Steve got up. "We'll argue that out later." He kissed her. He put the little ring on her finger and he kissed her again.

The waiter said rather wistfully, "Please, sir, I do realize— but it's time to close."

Steve linked Fran's arm close in his own and they went together out into the warm, southern night.

were on their feet in the booth, craned to look, and
bent over them, and started quarterbacking along "Yes